VAE VICTIS

BOOK 2

VAE VICTIS

BOOK 2

Ivan Kal

Cover design by Antti Hakosaari

ISBN: 978-1-0394-5548-1

Published in 2024 by Podium Publishing
www.podiumaudio.com

VAE VICTIS

BOOK 2

Alone

I sat on the cold wooden floor, my back against the wall behind me, and my knees bent so I could lean my hands and chin on them. I listened to the sounds around me, to the cries of birds as the sun rose above the cabin. I could feel it crawling across the sky, and the sensation was not pleasant at all. I wondered what the other vampires were doing right now. I wondered if they even knew that the sun would not hurt them now.

The fear of the sun was so ingrained in us that I couldn't imagine anyone just testing it, even if they felt different while the sun was out. If I hadn't woken up with light striking my face a month ago, I would've never let it touch me for fear of burning up from the inside.

I rested for a couple of hours, as Saia told me to. I hadn't had a chance to really rest since before I fought the pack of kiji. Saia's field protected us from any animals that might've been alerted to our presence, though I hadn't noticed anything other than the birds. I assumed that the field was working as it was supposed to on Earth's wildlife. The jungle around the estate had always had animals, with snakes probably being the most dangerous thing that I could encounter. Though a jaguar or a bear were also possibilities.

I knew that I had to be careful, especially after the encounter with the boa. I didn't know how the Source had affected the Earth's wildlife, but all of it was changed.

From what Shadow had said, the year that the Earth spent isolated would also come with an accelerated gain of Investment— boon that the Grand Spell allowed for the newly integrated worlds, allowing them to catch up to the rest of Kirios, somewhat.

Though Shadow had said that it was unlikely that many people would cross the Fourth Investment. Apparently, there was a set amount of the extra potential Investment assigned to the new world. And the higher people reached, the more it would get depleted.

I had an advantage compared to the rest of the world, and I had to make use of it. Not only had I survived the most dangerous place on Kirios, I also knew what was happening. The majority of the world would still have no idea, though the two moons in the sky might give them some clues. That would change soon: the other twenty-nine Exemplars had returned to Earth, just as I had, if they survived their ordeals, at least.

What worried me the most was that my skills were yet to return. The only thing that I knew was that using my skills in conjunction with my Mask put them on a long cooldown. I had no idea how long, though, and it had already been days.

"Saia," I started, as an idea occurred to me. "Can you use that [Mask Reader] engram for me? Maybe it'll give us an idea of how long my skills will be down."

The tiny dragon AI that was bonded to me tilted her head, and then her eyes flashed, and text appeared in my vision. I blinked at the sudden appearance, but then focused and started reading. Immediately, I noticed a change.

"Uh, Saia, my name, did you change that?" I asked.

"Feedback: I did. Was I wrong to?" Saia responded.

I looked at the text where she had changed my name from Marianna Rojas, the name I had gone by for the most of my life, to the one given to me by Shadow. I shook my head.

"No, you weren't," I told her, then read the entire list.

The Star That Dances in Blood Beneath the Light of the Broken Moon

Mask of the Blood Invoker (Weave, Esoteric) — First Investment; Third Carving
Ornament of the Revelator (Weave, Esoteric) — No Investment; Fourth Carving
Ornament of the Student (Physical, Weave, Esoteric) — No Investment; Eighth Carving

Attributes:
Physical: C
Weave: F
Esoteric: C

Skills:
P1-Beast Bonus
[Mist Step]
[Lesser Strength]
[Debilitating Wave]

P2-Beast Bonus
[Sonic Screech]
[Lesser Impale]
[Quick Claw]

[Swap Profile]
[One Truth Verified]
[A Lesson Remembered]
[Practical Learning]

There was nothing in the list indicating how long my skills would remain on cooldown. I sighed, even though I didn't really expect there to be anything. Then I took another look at everything. My Mask had gained three Carvings just from drinking Shadow's blood, which was the same amount that I had gained from the sikiri. Though since at the time I drank Shadow's blood I was on a higher Investment, it meant that his blood was more potent, since the Investment requirements increased with Carvings. Still, I was just a tiny bit disappointed that I hadn't gotten a new skill.

I knew better than to expect it, as Shadow had explained that a single Investment tier granted anywhere from one to a handful of skills, with two being the average. I had already gained three skills in my first tier from my Mask, my three [Empty Slot] skills. And I already gained a skill from my First Investment, the [Swap Profile] skill. I could expect one more at least, if my last tier was anything to go by.

My Ornaments had advanced too, but neither had given me a new skill, nor were their skills able to help me in combat. I could tell that they at least were available to me, and not on a cooldown. I still didn't know how exactly my [One Truth Verified] skill worked. I would need to experiment as soon as I had the chance.

I settled down to wait as the sun moved across the sky. Sometime later, boredom got the better of me and I looked back at Saia.

"What are you doing?" I asked. The tiny dragon was smaller now than she used to be when we first bonded. She hadn't consumed enough matter to create a bigger drone. Right now, she was about the same size as a sparrow. I remembered the body of the boa I had killed. *We should probably go back for that.* I made a mental note to get her some more biomass to consume. Our bond had grown stronger, and I had gotten stronger, which meant that I could sustain a larger drone.

"Feedback: I am reviewing and attempting to rebuild my engrams. So far I have had no success with any of them."

"So Shadow's gift didn't help that much?" I asked.

"Feedback: Not so far, but it has given me an idea of which engrams might be more likely to still work under the rules of this reality."

I grimaced. That was unfortunate, for sure. From what Saia had told me, the engrams that she was capable of using would've come in handy.

Then, something else occurred to me. "Hey, couldn't you just, like, create a weapon that doesn't need Source to be used? Like how you make your drone, or turn into weapons for me?"

"Feedback: There are some number of weapons that the Ke Erzi utilized that weren't reliant on the Source-Weave. And I am capable of recreating them, though not at this time."

"Why not?" I tilted my head.

"Feedback: Because I lack the necessary ingredients to make them usable. I believe that the word you would use is ammunition. The material I am made of, ferosim, the living metal, is incredibly conductive to Source-Weave, which allows me to arrange my inner matrix in different formations to enable engrams. It cannot substitute any other type of resource."

I nodded in understanding. Saia's drone was made of a metallic substance that I wasn't familiar with, but it was obviously strong and versatile. Though, she had sustained injuries in her drone form, which showed that the material wasn't invulnerable. Still, it was definitely tougher than steel.

"So, if we find any of those resources, you could make weapons?" I asked.

"Feedback: I could, with sufficient biomass and materials, yes."

"So, what would you need? What even can you make?"

"Feedback: A variety of light-based weaponry, as well as some defensive items that the Ke Erzi used in conjunction with the Armor form of this Unit. The materials that are necessary are mostly silica-based crystalline minerals. A few would be suitable, but the ones that would be the most effective are: enes, shikha, and brils."

"I don't think that we have anything like that on Earth," I said as I heard the unfamiliar words. The Grand Spell's translation would've translated the words if Earth had the same minerals.

"Statement: It is unlikely that the minerals are present on your world. While the minerals are not inherently very conductive to the Source-Weave, they do possess some qualities linked to it, as all materials on Erzi did. Your world had no Source."

"So these materials might manifest themselves now? Or some of what is already present might change."

"Feedback: Change is almost guaranteed. Whether materials will become something new or something that I am familiar with, I do not know."

"Maybe it would be a good idea for you to start testing materials we come upon. You can detect their properties, right? Maybe we can find replacements?" I asked her.

"Feedback: I have some capabilities in that field, yes."

I nodded, adding one more thing to my mental checklist.

"Hey," I continued as another thing occurred to me. "You do know that you don't need to clarify your sentences every time you say something."

Saia tilted her head. "Query: This Unit doesn't understand."

I opened my mouth to try to explain, and then I paused. What I was hearing was a translation, she wasn't actually speaking in my language. Some words weren't translated, while others had meaning attached in the forms of images or sensations. It was possible that it was just a result of the translation from the syntax of the language Saia was speaking in.

"You are speaking in the Erzi tongue, right?"

"Feedback: Correct."

"Can you learn my language?" I asked, wondering how that would even work. How it worked now even. I had no idea how an AI was hearing translated words.

"Feedback: Of course, this Unit will set aside processing power to learn your language."

I narrowed my eyes at her, noticing something else. The tone of her voice was the same, but I could sense like there was something different. If she was a human, I would've said that her last sentence felt colder. Sometimes Saia would refer to herself as "this Unit" and other times she would simply use "I." There was something more going on with Saia than what I had seen so far. For a moment I nearly asked her about it, but then decided not to push.

I turned my eyes to the window, and looked out through the faint shimmer of Saia's protective field. I turned my mind toward the situation I was in. I had returned to my world, or at least what was now the continent of Earth on Kirios. I came back to the estates that had been my home for most of my life, the place where I had been hanged, and I found it empty. I wondered where everyone had gone. I could only assume that once the Grand Spell arrived, everything went to shit quickly. All forms of communication had probably shut down. Satellites were no longer above us after all, at least I didn't think they were.

I tried to put myself in their shoes, imagine what I would do. Probably head back to civilization, seek out people. And the closest thing we had to that was a village nearby. Or perhaps the small town of San Pedro. Eventually, I would head to Medellín, hoping to find safety in the city.

It would be a long trek on foot. I could move fast, but even a vampire couldn't sustain that pace for long. It would take me days to get down from the mountain.

I shook my head. There wasn't much that I could do about that. I had to look for people. None of my plans mattered until I found survivors.

By the time nighttime drew close, Saia and I were ready to set out. It had been two days since I put on my Mask, and I still didn't have access to my skills, which worried me somewhat. I didn't want to risk entering my soul space, not yet, at least, as I didn't know if I would be able to get out again. I knew that I had to experiment, but I was not in a space that was safe enough to do so.

I stepped out of my sire's home, fully equipped for the trip, or as equipped as I could be. I wore woodland camo pants and a simple black tank top with a short jacket over it. On my shoulders I had a backpack filled with the few items I had managed to scavenge. The H-tech Rhino Model 3 revolver in its case, the photo I found of me and my sire, the gourd filled with blood from Ish Vimza, a line of rope that I found in the shifter camp, a few bottles filled with water, and some food. The food and water might not do much for me, but I wanted to be prepared in case I found survivors.

I also grabbed a face mask and sunglasses to store in my pockets in case I ran into anyone. I didn't want people to immediately know that I was a vampire. On my shoulder I leaned the blade part of the serpent-tongue spear, and I had Shadow's dagger on my hip.

The sky was painted in the orange light of twilight as the sun dipped beneath the horizon and the two moons rose above us. I felt myself growing stronger by the moment, and decided that it was time to head out.

"Saia, can you scout ahead? Report back any signs of life you see, animals or people, or anything of interest in general," I told her.

"Feedback: Acknowledged," Saia said and took to the skies, heading in the direction we had agreed on previously.

I took a deep breath and then started jogging down the road. I figured that staying on the proper path would be the best. The road was paved, something that the cartel had paid for by themselves, since the government had no need to make roads this far into the jungle. Nor did they want to, really. They didn't control these lands.

The road was abandoned and overgrown in places. The asphalt was cracked, and plants grew up through it. Roots of the trees around the road had bulged in places, raising the road up. Everything was changed, even the plants. I could recognize most of them, but all looked like they had evolved. Larger leaves, thicker trunks—it was as if someone had given every plant some kind of a growth serum. And perhaps that was close to the truth. Source might as well be a super serum.

As the sun fully set and the world was thrown into darkness, I became wholly alive. The two moons above shone brightly enough that I could see everything. The forest around me was silent, save for a few bird calls in the distance that sounded like nightjars and owls to me.

It was about an hour of jogging later that Saia returned.

"Report: I discovered something of interest up ahead."

"Of interest how?" I asked.

"Feedback: I believe that you should see it for yourself," Saia responded.

I frowned but nodded, and had her lead the way.

A few minutes later, we reached it. It was hard to miss. The road ended in a sharp line, and a forest continued onward. Except that it wasn't anything like the forest I knew should be there. The trees were different. These were not the Cedro trees that were behind me, but something else.

The trees were thinner and taller, the color of their leaves brighter green. I didn't recognize them, though perhaps I did know them. With the arrival of the Source, it could be a tree I was familiar with, but that had changed.

But that wasn't all there was of interest here. I walked over to the edge, where the road stopped, and knelt down. The soil that started from the edge of the road was different from what was behind me too. It was brown, tinted with orange.

"This shouldn't be here," I said out loud.

"Statement: The entire valley ahead is the same, though I can see that the terrain changes back again in the distance."

It was as if someone had picked up a piece of land and just wedged it where it didn't belong.

What Shadow told me now made more sense. He had said that the Grand Spell would take our world apart and then put it back together into a single landmass. That it would change our topography.

I realized that what I knew of Earth might no longer be true. Landmarks, rivers, and directions could all be different now. I had to make some changes in my plans. Pieces could be missing, taken like how Saia's home had been, a piece just floating out there for the Grand Spell to use.

I grimaced, then stood up, trying to decide if I wanted to risk going through the unfamiliar area or try to go around it. For all I knew, the places I wanted to check were no longer where they were supposed to be.

Before I could make a decision, it was made for me. In the distance I heard a scream, and I immediately straightened. Someone was in trouble. I glanced at Saia and offered my arm. "Bracelet," I said, and she shifted to rest on my wrist. I pulled out my glasses and mask, and put them on. Then I started running as fast as I could in the direction of the scream, gripping my weapon with both hands.

I found them quickly, and took in the situation at a glance.

The source of the scream was a kid, a boy that was probably not older than ten. He was small and scrawny, obviously malnourished. I could smell his fear, the sweat on his skin, and accumulated dirt from days of not washing. He wore jeans and a simple shirt, and had a backpack on his shoulders. In one hand he was holding a long stick with a sharpened tip. He was running, and an animal was pursuing him.

I recognized the animal too, even with the obvious changes. It was a Spectacled bear, I recognized it because of the familiar pattern on its snout. The rest of it was . . . different. Its muscles were bulging, and its fur a lot shorter. The claws on its paws were curved and red in color. It roared and jumped on the kid, and I pounced.

I felt the ground give beneath me as I pushed off, and in less than a heartbeat I was in front of the bear. I swiped my weapon below, bringing it up across the animal's throat, cutting through it cleanly and decapitating the bear before it even had a chance to notice that I was there.

The head hit the ground first, followed quickly by the rest of its body in a loud thump.

The kid took a few more steps, then glanced back and saw that the animal was dead on the ground. He missed a step and tumbled to the ground. I didn't move from my place above the bear, as I just realized that I had to be careful. I made sure to make a show of breathing heavily, as if I had just run a marathon. I couldn't sweat, but the kid would probably not notice, not now at least.

"Oh," the kid said. "Thank God." He closed his eyes and made a cross with one hand before opening his eyes and looking up at me with awe in his eyes.

"Are you an angel?" he asked, and I blinked.

"No," I said.

"Well," the kid whispered, his eyes growing unfocused. "You look like one."

Then he promptly passed out.

I sighed, then glanced down at the blood still pouring out of the bear.

End Times

found a small clearing in the middle of the forest and made camp quickly. Saia sheltered us with her field, and we agreed on a few things to keep her presence a secret. The kid had a lighter in his bag, and there was plenty of wood around for a fire, so I had little issues getting one going.

I did go through his bag, looking for any clues as to why he was out there all alone, but I didn't find much. He had some junk food snacks as well as two small bottles of water and one of Coke. He had a change of clothes, a small bag filled with markers, and a big map of Colombia that was scribbled all over.

I didn't look at it for long, despite being very interested. I had invaded the kid's privacy, but I didn't want to step too far. I put everything back together and placed it next to the sleeping kid. The poor guy was obviously exhausted, and malnourished, from the looks of it.

From the way he breathed, I knew that he would be waking up soon, so I pulled out a can of beans and a wooden spoon from my pack and opened it. I pulled the mask off my mouth and put it around my neck as I ate a single scoop, just enough so that it looked like I had been eating.

His breathing changed, and I heard him shuffling, then he went still. I didn't react. Instead I kept my eyes on the can in my hands, swirling the spoon as I looked at the fire.

I heard the kid turn his head, looking around, and his heart beating faster. He was frightened, as well he should be. His hand crawled across the ground, searching, and finding his improvised spear. I had left it next to him. It wasn't like he would be much of a threat to me, even with it, and I figured that it would provide him some comfort.

"Good morning," I said, making sure to keep my face turned away from him so that he couldn't see my mouth. He twitched, then froze again. "Or is it good evening?"

He didn't respond, and I pulled the mask back over my face as I turned around to look at him.

His eyes were wide and fearful, so I offered the canned food to him. "Hungry?" I asked.

That made him blink, and got him out of his shock. I heard his stomach growl, and I leaned over, placing the can next to him before turning back to look at the fire.

I heard him grab the can, and after a brief pause, start eating. I spread my hands in front of me like I was warming them on the fire. The night was cold, more so than what I remembered, but low temperatures didn't bother vampires that much.

I let him eat in peace, wondering when the last real meal he had was. By the sounds I was hearing, it was probably a long time ago. Once he was finished, I glanced in his direction.

"Good?" I asked.

He raised his head to look at me, then quickly nodded. "Yes, yes, thank you," he answered hurriedly.

"*De nada*," I said.

"I remember you," he said slowly. "The bear, it was . . . you're the angel that saved me."

The side of my mouth raised behind the mask. "I'm not an angel," I said. "But yes, I saved you. What's your name?"

The kid looked at me with uncertainty for a moment. "I'm Felix," he said, then after a pause he continued. "I thought that bear was going to eat me, if you hadn't been there . . . thank you." He stood up.

I just waved my hand, slowly, trying to appear human.

"What were you doing in the woods alone? If I may ask?"

He gave me a guarded look, then raised his chin and answered. "I was out hunting."

I tilted my head at him, then glanced at the improvised weapon next to him. I didn't think that the wooden spear was good for much, and I knew that he didn't have any other weapon on him. Hunting with that would be difficult for even a grown man, let alone a child. I didn't say that, of course.

He kept his eyes on me, a touch of defiance in them. Then he noticed something behind me. I saw him look at the faint blue sheen of the field around us, and his mouth opened up in awe.

"What is that?" he asked.

"A skill," I said.

His eyes lit up, and he looked back at me. "You have a skill!" he exclaimed.

My gambit had paid off. The kid knew about skills, which meant that he had encountered someone who had gained one before. Everyone on Earth should have their Masks by now, but actually gaining Investment in them was another story.

I turned to look at him from behind my glasses, then nodded.

"You leveled your Class?" he said excitedly, and I tilted my head.

"Class?" I asked, then continued before he could answer. "You mean my Mask."

"Same thing," he said, his face turning eager now. "That's so cool! How'd you do it?"

It made sense that people would have made connections and used terms that were closely related to Earth culture. I knew more than they did, so I could see how people would be trying to use any knowledge they had to make sense of things.

"Do you have a Mask?" I asked instead of answering his question.

He frowned. "Of course. Everyone does."

That was good. From what Shadow had said, that was supposed to happen. But I couldn't be sure until I saw it by myself.

"And what's your Mask called?" I asked.

The kid rubbed the forearm of his right hand with his left and fidgeted in place. I knew that I was taking advantage of his naïveté, but I needed information.

"It's a Student Mask," the kid said, almost as if he was ashamed. "I haven't been able to level at all."

He was studying me, waiting for a response. I didn't say anything. A Student Mask or an Ornament were very good. I had gotten to choose because I was an Exemplar. People on Earth would get their first Mask based on what fit them the most. It made sense that a kid would get it, as most kids were required by law to attend school. I realized that Felix had turned his eyes to the ground, and from his body language I could tell that he didn't like his Mask.

I cleared my throat. "That is a good Mask," I said.

He raised his eyes, and stared at me in anger. "You don't need to lie to make me feel better! It's the worst!"

I raised an eyebrow. "Why do you say that?" I asked.

"Because! I haven't been able to level it at all! All the others have gotten at least one level in theirs. And I've gone on two hunts already!"

There was a lot there to unpack, but I had to be careful. I didn't want him to know that I was prying for information. It was better if I pretended like I knew a lot more than I did. True, in some ways I did know a lot about Masks and the Grand Spell, but I didn't know how Earth viewed these things. They'd had a month to come up with a lot of their own theories.

"Okay, Felix, how about we start at the beginning?" I said slowly. "You said that there were others? Were you separated from your group? Did you get lost?"

The kid shook his head, again looking defiant. "No, I know these woods!"

The kid obviously didn't like being looked down upon. He probably thought that he was grown up already. And perhaps in this world he would have to be.

"So you went out alone?" I asked.

That made him wince, and he started drawing a circle in the dirt with his leg. "Yeah," he whispered almost too low to hear, but not for me.

I almost told him how stupid that was, but I managed to stop myself. "And you did it in order to hunt? Try and get a Carving, level?"

He nodded, then raised his eyes looking me over, obviously looking for any signs of judgment. I was wearing a mask and glasses, so there wasn't much for a human child to see. He narrowed his eyes, almost as if he saw me for real for the first time. He looked me over, then his eyes landed on the weapon next to me.

"Is that what you used to kill the bear?" he asked, and took a step in my direction. "It's not rusted," he said, then paused. His eyes rose to look at me with something approaching fear. "Are you a raider?"

I tilted my head. "I don't know what that is," I said.

He narrowed his eyes. "Where did you get it?"

I did not like the kid turning this around and interrogating me. I was the one that was in control of this conversation. But I also didn't want to spook him. "It's mine," I said simply.

He looked at me for a long time. "Where did you come from?" He took a step back, then glanced around, looking for a way out.

I spread my arms. "I'm not going to hurt you," I said slowly. "I wouldn't have saved you if I did, now wouldn't I?"

That made him pause, and I continued.

"I don't know what a raider is, really. You could say that I've come from far away. And . . . I haven't talked to another human since all of this started." I told the truth, technically. I hadn't talked to another human before him. Shadow and Saia didn't count.

He blinked. "Really?"

I nodded. "I was in the mountains when the light came." The estate was in the mountains, surrounded by the forest, so again I said the truth, just not the whole of it.

"Oh," Felix said, now looking ashamed.

"How old are you, Felix?" I asked, trying to get him to relax a bit.

"What does that matter?" he asked, immediately back to being defensive. I cursed myself, I should've remembered what I was like as a kid. Being dismissed because of age was one of those things that rubbed me the wrong way a lot back then.

"Well, we are getting to know each other," I told him.

He narrowed his eyes. "I'm thirteen! And you haven't even told me your name." He raised his chin at me.

I suppressed the desire to chuckle. The kid had spunk. "Of course. I apologize for my rudeness," I said, trying to keep my voice level. "My name is . . . Estrella." *Star.* It might not be a common name, but it was a real one. And it was also the truth: it was the first part of my new name.

It wasn't that I wanted to lie to the kid, but I didn't know if anyone from my old life was still alive. There was some cause to be careful.

"Now," I started, this time allowing some hardness to slip into my tone. "Why don't you tell me what you were really doing running around the wilderness all alone?"

I had to assert at least some sort of authority here. The kid had gone through a lot, but I could already tell that he was used to not listening to others.

For a moment, Felix seemed like he was going to refuse, but then he glanced back down at my weapon, studying the blade for a few seconds. I haven't wiped off the bear's blood yet. I could see him remembering and realizing that he really was in a tough spot. I could sympathize. He was like how I was back when I first met Shadow. Unsure if I could trust him, but having little choice. It was a strange feeling, knowing that I was now playing the role on the other side.

Felix swallowed, then raised his eyes back to my face. "I was looking for something." He shuffled his feet.

I glared at him, though the effect was probably diminished with my eyes being behind the glasses. Still, my lack of a response seemed to get to him after almost a minute of silence, and he spoke again.

"I was looking for a dungeon," he said.

I blinked, then tilted my head. "A dungeon?" I asked. But already I had a suspicion from the ways he had talked about things before. He had called the Mask a Class, and Carvings, levels. It wasn't that hard to make the connection. "That wouldn't be a light suspended in the air, like a rift in space?"

Felix nodded, and I grimaced behind my mask. So, those places were here too. Shadow hadn't known if they would be. Rifts were something new even for Kirios. I could only assume that they were like the one on Ish Vimza, and that they dropped loot. I could see how that could be useful, especially if a lot of the stuff that Earth had was now useless. His interest in my weapon was now even more intriguing.

"And why were you looking for something like that?" I asked him.

Felix's lip quivered for a moment, and then he launched into a fast-talking outburst. "Because I need to level! All the others already have, and I'm stuck. The boss already said that he won't take me on any more hunts because . . . because I didn't level the last time. And I heard them say that my Class was useless, and that they were just wasting food on me . . . and, and, I almost died, and they'll leave me behind if I don't level . . . So I'll die anyway . . . I need to . . . I . . ."

Oh God, he's crying. I froze, not really knowing what to do as tears streamed down the kid's cheeks. I stood up, too fast for a human. *Shit.* I forgot about keeping appearances in the moment, but the kid didn't seem to have noticed as he had a hand on his face, trying to wipe away the tears.

"Hey, hey," I said softly. "It's okay."

I knelt next to him, and realized that I was still taller than him.

How did I not notice how small he is? The kid said that he was thirteen, but I couldn't see it, not now. He was thin. He barely had any meat on him. I took in more details now, saw how his clothes were dirty and haggard, how his hair was unwashed. I had noticed all of these things before, but I didn't really think about what they all meant.

This kid had been in survival mode for a long time. And I saw as everything spilled out of him. He jumped forward, startling me as he put his hands around me, crying on my shoulder.

For a moment, I froze, I didn't know what to do with such expressions of emotion. And I didn't have many examples in my life to take inspiration from. My thoughts moved to the only people who had ever shown me any kindness. My sire had always been stoic, and held himself back. But before everything happened, he had always been . . . a reassuring presence. Even though in the end, when I had looked in his eyes, I saw none of that, it had helped me in the past. But that wouldn't work now. Next was Khalil, my old friend. He was a man of faith. He would've offered words of God as comfort. I had never believed as deeply as Khalil had, so I didn't think that that would work.

The last was Shadow. And in a short time, he had been a teacher and a mentor to me. He had helped me survive, as now I had to help this young kid survive. This was what I came back for, to help my people get through this hell.

Slowly, I put my hands around his shoulders, somewhat awkwardly, as I didn't know how to provide such comfort myself. Felix didn't seem to mind. He just cried, and I held him, trying not to think of all the horrors that he had to have lived through in order to survive this long.

A while later, I sat next to the fire. Felix had fallen asleep, exhausted, and perhaps a little bit embarrassed at his outburst.

At least he would get a good night's sleep, with no threats able to get to him.

I had pieced together a few things from some of what he had said while crying. Enough that I knew that his life had been hard of late. I was pretty sure that he was part of a group that managed to survive the initial arrival of the Grand Spell, and were now based in a church in a village nearby. Most of the others were kids, like him, if I understood right. They had been taken in by a priest and a few hunters that had also survived.

He had mentioned his parents, and though he didn't say much I knew that they were dead. Most of the other kids were orphans too. They were barely surviving, and they were trying to "level" in order to get the tools that would let them survive. That's what the hunts he mentioned were most probably all about. Hunting animals in order to gain Investment. They didn't know how Masks worked yet, which was why they had no idea how Felix's Mask gained Carvings.

I thought that most kids would get the Student Mask, but it seemed like that wasn't the case. Felix was the only one in his group that had. Perhaps he was just a better student, or others had different things that interested them more. It didn't matter in the end.

They thought that killing things was how you gained Carvings, which was why Felix's never improved. Shadow had explained how the Student Mask worked to me—you had to have a teacher, and intent mattered. Even if Felix was learning something new on those hunts, if there was no real intent by others to teach him anything, it would net him a lot less Investment. Thankfully, I had been in the right place at the right time, and I had the power to help him.

It had hurt my heart to hear his story, but I knew that I would hear many similar ones in the future.

I settled in to wait and rest as I felt the dawn coming. There was a lot that I had to do, and I would need all the strength that I had to see it through.

Teaching

I watched Felix as he ate from the can, and wondered where he managed to put it all. He looked barely able to fit half of what he had eaten in the last day. Still, I was glad that he felt comfortable enough to eat in my presence. I had always found the simple act of eating a meal to be somehow . . . vulnerable.

The sun had risen above the horizon, and with it went most of my strength. In a perfect world, I would've waited until nightfall to go and explore again, but with Felix here I would have to adapt. Still, even during the day I was stronger than most humans, and while I wasn't at my full strength, I was still a vampire. Even weakened, my senses were superior to those of a human.

"So," Felix started as he finished his meal. "Why are you wearing a mask and glasses?"

I had expected that question, though if I was honest, I had thought that he would've asked that before now. Still, I did have an answer, somewhat at least.

"You could say that I am a very private person," I said. "But, it is also practical."

He tilted his head. "What does that mean?"

"It means that there are skills that can flash bright lights and there are those that can spread disease through the air. One has to be smart, and protected." I tapped the mask and the glasses.

The kid's eyes widened. "Should I wear one too?" he asked.

I almost laughed that he didn't even question it. But then again, he was still a naïve kid.

"Well," I started slowly. "Probably not, I'm just paranoid."

It was the truth; I was not going to get myself caught off guard again. Or at least I didn't plan to.

The kid looked like he wanted to argue, but I stood up. "Now, why don't you tell me where your home is. I plan on getting you back by nightfall."

The kid really shouldn't be out here in the wild. If the bear that nearly killed him was anything to go by, he was completely unprepared for the dangers that lurked around.

Felix didn't answer. Instead he got . . . fidgety. "I can't." He shook his head. "I can't go back, not like this. They'll throw me out."

"Why do you say that?"

"There . . . isn't enough for all of us. I need to be useful, or . . ." He trailed off, then bowed his head to the ground.

I remembered some of what he said to me yesterday, about overhearing others say that he was a drain on their resources. I could see how desperate people could think that. A Student Mask didn't have much to offer to a community that was fighting for survival. Though it had potential, the issue was that they had no idea about anything concerning Masks. They would have no idea about how Masks evolved with each Investment tier.

"I need to find the dungeon," Felix murmured, just barely audible enough for me to hear.

"Felix," I started. "You are in no way equipped to do that."

The kid had gotten what I thought was a big wake-up call last night, though it seemed like it hadn't really sunk in. "If I wasn't there last night, you would've been dead."

He winced, but I knew that harsh words now might keep him alive tomorrow.

The kid clenched his fists, and then raised his eyes up to glare at me with determination set in his face.

"I'm not going back! I'm going to the dungeon."

I tilted my head. I could see that he was resolved, even though it was stupid and he was going to get himself killed. I thought about how to respond, letting him sit there in silence for a bit. I could just tell him that he didn't have a choice, that there wasn't much that he could do besides refusing to tell me where he came from. But I wasn't that concerned. I doubted that he could've gone far from his home. The mountains had been dangerous even before the Grand Spell arrived. I would find it eventually.

"Why are you so set on going there?" I asked, curious. "You must know how dangerous it is."

Felix shook his head. "I need to find it before the others get there, I've overheard them planning a trip. They want to get to it before it breaks open."

"What do you mean 'breaks open'?" I asked.

"You know, when monsters start to spill out of it?" Felix said, then immediately continued. "We can't let that happen so near the church, and the raiders aren't going to be back this way for at least two weeks. So the hunters are going to go and try to beat it."

Monsters spilling out? I wondered if perhaps the rift here was different from what I had encountered on Ish Vimza.

"And you think that you can fight monsters, all on your own?" I asked.

Felix scoffed. "I'm not stupid," he answered. "The hunters came this way just last week, and they didn't see the dungeon. That means that it's a new one, so it's probably not that difficult. Or I could get lucky and get a puzzle one."

I narrowed my eyes at the new information, drawing some conclusions. "You're telling me that the rifts break open?"

He nodded. "Dungeons, and yes, the longer the dungeon exists the stronger the monsters inside get, until eventually the dungeon breaks open and they spill out and start attacking everything."

"Rifts," I stressed. I had to at least try to make people move away from the terminology I heard from Felix. Not because it particularly mattered what something was called, but because using the terms he had been using, mainly ones from games, was dangerous. It might make them think that things were less dangerous than they really were. "Have you seen any rift break before?"

Felix nodded. "I've seen it once, yes," he answered, his tone subdued.

"And these 'monsters,' did they have red lines covering their bodies?" I asked.

Felix shook his head. "No."

I sighed in relief. "Then they were beasts, just animals, not monsters."

Felix frowned. "They weren't animals anyone recognized. They looked like monsters, giant wolf-like monsters with wicked teeth. Like hounds from hell."

I waved my hand. "Just because something looks scary doesn't make it a monster. Not that they are any less dangerous," I said slowly. "Any beast is dangerous, but if you ever see one with red markings on its body, like it is diseased, then you run no matter what," I told him.

I didn't know if there even were any monsters on Earth. Shadow had said that they were rare on other continents, and that only Ish Vimza seemed to be a place where they were more common.

"Did you encounter something like that in a dun—rift?" Felix asked, his eyes falling to look down at my weapon.

"Something like that," I answered. Then I pulled the topic back on track. "So, you want to find this rift and beat it. You still haven't told me exactly why you want to find it before the others?"

"For the loot, of course," Felix answered. "And to level!"

I opened my mouth to press him further, but I paused as I realized that the kid's motivation probably didn't extend far beyond exactly what he had said.

Felix seemingly took my silence as a silent question, so he continued. "If I could get a weapon like yours, or just one level, I know that I can get a skill and be useful."

The poor kid had no idea; a Student Mask was powerful, but . . . he was a child, he saw others getting skills that were flashy and he wished to have them too. But his Mask was unlikely to grant him anything that would be useful now. It was an investment in the future, its power came from the better Mask evolution down the road, and at his age I didn't think that he would be able to understand that. Still, I knew that feeling, wanting to be useful. Feeling like you could be discarded at any point just because you were a drain on the already strained resources. Hell, I was discarded just like how he feared he would be. My parents sold me to the cartel in order to put food on the table.

I took a deep breath, then released it slowly.

"Do you know how to make a fire?" I asked.

Felix frowned. "What does that have to do with my Class?"

I tapped my fingers against my knee and glared from behind my glasses. He sensed my attention and coughed, then corrected himself.

"My Mask, sorry," he said, and I detected just a tiny amount of pouting in his tone. Progress.

"Every Mask gains Investment in a different manner. What your Mask requires depends on what type it is. You said that you were taken on hunts?"

"Yes, I got to stab a deer with a knife, after the hunters took it down, make the killing blow. I didn't get any le—uh, Carvings."

I nodded. "That is because you gained no Investment that matched what your Mask required, or you gained very little of it."

He blinked. "So what do I need?"

"You have the Mask of the Student, which means that you gain Investment when you learn new things."

Felix frowned. "Learn?"

"Yes," I responded. "You gain more if you are taught by someone too. Now, do you know how to make a fire?"

"With matches or a lighter, yes," the little smartass said.

I gave him a look, that was probably lost on him because of my face being covered up. "Without that," I said, and he shook his head eagerly.

I gestured for him to get closer. I pulled out my knife, the one that I got from Shadow, and a piece of flint I recovered at the estate.

I collected some branches and started explaining how to properly arrange them to get the best possible start. I showed him once, then had him repeat the work, putting the thin sticks in a loose pyramid shape with a hole in the middle. I pulled out some paper and a small piece of char cloth.

I explained how to strike the knife against the flint properly, and how to get the fire going. Then I let him try it, only offering instruction.

It took him a while to get a consistent spark, and a while more until he finally managed to ignite the cloth.

"I did it!" he exclaimed, and I pointed.

"Quick, the paper and the pile."

He scrambled to set the paper on fire, then push it into the hole beneath the pyramid pile. Thankfully, he managed it in time. As soon as the pile started catching fire, he froze, and I saw his eyes go wide. After a second, he turned to gape at me, then his face transformed into a wide grin.

"I got it! I got a level and a skill!"

"Carving," I corrected. I was glad, but the fact that he got it immediately probably meant that he had already been very close to the Investment threshold. I doubted that a single lesson would've been enough for even a single Carving. "What is the skill?" I asked.

He blinked. "[Fire Learning]?"

That sounded interesting, and it fit what Shadow had told me about how Mask skills worked. What skills one gained was directly linked with what a person did to earn Investment.

"You'll need to go to your soul space and check what the skill actually is," I said.

"My what?" Felix asked, his eyes confused.

I paused. The people on Earth got their Masks based on what fit them the best. They didn't have a chance to choose. *Was it possible that they didn't know?* "A soul space, the place where your Mask is." I tapped my chest. "In here."

Felix blinked, his eyes still filled with incomprehension.

"Okay," I started, then put my hand over my chest again. "Have you ever felt something here, like a sense of pressure?"

Felix tilted his head, and then hesitantly nodded. "I think so? Back when the light came, when I heard the words in my head."

"Good," I said. "I want you to focus on your chest, on that exact spot, and think about getting pulled into it. But, once you go there, don't do anything, don't choose anything if you are offered it without talking with me first."

It was pretty intuitive to figure out, as Shadow had said and I had experienced. I doubted that the Grand Spell wanted it to be difficult for people to figure out.

Felix nodded and did as I asked. Quickly I saw his eyes go unfocused, and I watched in fascination as he entered his soul's space. He looked . . . kind of goofy, just staring into nothing with his mouth open.

"Do I look like that too?" I asked.

"Feedback: Yes," Saia's voice vibrated out of my bracelet.

I grimaced, then shook my head. "What do you think?"

"Feedback: There is a lot of information in the few things that the child has revealed. But their ignorance is apparent."

I realized that I would have to start sharing, telling people what was really going on. Perhaps, that was the purpose of Exemplars in the first place. I just had to do it in the right way, find people and teach them what I knew.

Felix stirred and started blinking his eyes. "Wow," he said. "That was awesome! It was a big schoolroom, with blackboards all around . . ." He continued describing his soul space, and I only half listened. Then he switched topics. "And I got the option for something called an Ornament?"

I nodded. "Yes, Ornaments are additions for your Mask, that can eventually merge into your Mask, making it stronger."

He immediately got interested, his eyes flashing. "Like subclasses?"

I glared at him, and even from behind the glasses he seemed to get it.

"Ornaments, right," Felix said slowly. "I got the options for a Hunter, Cook, Woodcutter, and . . . Survivor."

I blinked at the last one, but didn't comment. I knew that life experiences shaped what Masks and Ornaments one got access to, and I could imagine what happened to him when the Grand Spell arrived from the few details that he had shared.

"You can pick one, but you should wait for your second one. Try to get a better option," I told him.

"What should I pick?" Felix asked.

"It is your choice." I shrugged, but then continued. "I would recommend something that you can advance quickly. The Hunter Ornament would mean hunting, obviously, Cook, cooking, and so on. Survivor might be interesting too. You should think about what kind of skills each of those options will give you too. Speaking of, what is your new skill?"

"It said that learning all fire related knowledge is accelerated. What does that mean?" Felix asked, a hint of disappointment entering his tone.

I could see how he would be disappointed, of course. He had probably expected something that he could use to fight. But that wasn't how the Student Mask worked. Still, it could be a good skill.

"I have a Student Ornament," I told him, and saw his eyes widen.

"Really?"

I nodded. "I have a skill called [Practical Learning]. It means that I learn faster through practical means. Just because your skill doesn't give you a direct tool doesn't mean that it isn't useful. You will need to find a way to make it useful on your own. It is your Mask. But, you should also know that your Mask will change after you reach ten Carvings and gain your first Investment tier, or at least you will have a choice to change it. What you do now will all be taken in account."

He blinked, then started thinking about it. "Wait, can I get something like a Mage Class? Throw fireballs around?" He made throwing gestures.

I opened my mouth, almost laughing, but then I paused. "I . . . perhaps." I didn't know the specifics, but there were Mage Masks. Of course, some type of knowledge was required for it, but . . . Source existed all around us now. Perhaps just wanting it bad enough would be enough.

I saw Felix's eye brighten at the idea, and I could tell that he was already enamored by it. I wondered if I should try to curb his excitement a bit, but then decided against it.

He entered his soul space again, and picked his Ornament, deciding to go with the Survivor, which surprised me.

"Why did you choose that?" I asked after he came back out.

"I . . . I don't know," he mumbled.

I recognized a difficult topic, so I let it go and changed the topic.

"Now, tell me, where's the rift?"

He raised his head and looked at me. "Are you going to take me with you?" he asked.

I wanted to tell him no, to take him back home first before exploring it. I had to admit that I really wanted to check out the differences between a rift here and one that I was in before. I didn't think that I would be in much danger, though having to protect the kid might make things difficult. On the other hand, him going with me might be a good way to get some Investment. I wanted people on Earth to grow, and starting with one young kid might be the best.

"We'll see," I said slowly. "First, I need to learn just how dangerous it is, then I'll decide. Tell me what you know."

Felix looked like he wanted to argue, but then he sagged in defeat. A moment later he started telling me what he knew about the rifts his people had encountered.

The Dungeon

Walking through the forest with a kid in tow was cumbersome. I had forgotten just how slow humans were, especially children. It was also quite strange walking around without Saia. I had grown used to having her drone around, scouting ahead for me. But at least I could feel her weight on my wrist, a reminder that she was always there. That, and the fact that she was literally attached to my nervous system.

I still wasn't sure about taking the kid to the rift with me, but I knew that I was playing against the clock. We had six months before portals opened up and allowed people from Kirios to arrive and explore Earth, another six after that before we joined the new world fully. I had to start putting pieces into place.

I had fought to survive, and I had earned power for myself. In that regard, I was lucky. Now, I had a responsibility. I had made a choice to help those who had been trapped by the circumstances of their life, like I was long ago.

Felix kept glancing my way, probably noticing things that I didn't want him to know yet. I couldn't let him think more deeply about why I wore a mask and glasses. It was daytime, so I didn't worry that he would see anything strange in the way I moved. It was easier to pretend during the day, even though I was still stronger than a human. Still, I had to distract him.

"How many of you are there, at the church?" I asked.

Felix startled, then looked away. "There are a lot of us," he said slowly.

I then realized that he might still not trust me too much. It was smart, and I had managed to get him to say things that he probably wouldn't have otherwise, but he had some time to think and calm down now. I was a stranger, and obviously dangerous in his eyes. Hiding my face probably didn't help at all.

"You don't need to tell me," I said. "I'm just interested in how you survived. You are actually the first person I've met since all of this started. I was in the woods the whole time. I don't know anything about what happened since the light came."

"Really?" Felix asked.

"Really." I nodded.

"Well, you know how everything got moved around when the light came, right?"

I inclined my head. I had seen it back on the road, where it was suddenly cut off and a strange forest that didn't belong was in its place. Shadow had said that our entire world would be turned into a single continent, that places would be shuffled around. I hadn't really thought about what that would really mean.

He seemed hesitant to speak. "You don't need to say anything that you don't want to," I told him.

He looked up at me for a moment, then away. He took a deep breath. "It was really scary," Felix started slowly. "Before the light came I was on a trip with my mom and dad." He bowed his head, his tone sad and shaky. "We were in Medellín to visit my aunty. I don't remember much, only that Dad woke us up early, before dawn because he wanted an early start on our trip back home to Cartagena. We were almost out of the city when the light came. It was so bright that I had to close my eyes, and it made it hard to think for some reason. Then I heard the voice in my head and I got my Cl—my Mask." He glanced in my direction, but quickly turned to look back in front of him.

"I remember stopping, and people yelling all around us. The lights stayed on for a few minutes, I think. Then we started hearing animals—dogs and cats howling. And then the rats started pouring out of everywhere. They started attacking people in big swarms." He shuddered.

I remembered the frenzy that made the animals on Ish Vimza attack us. It would make sense that something similar happened on Earth when the Grand Spell first arrived.

"We got in the car and started driving away with all the others. I heard gunshots," he whispered. "The cars still worked back then, though our phones didn't. We had no signal. We headed north in a big group, with some other people who headed the same way, until we found one of the moved places—the road just cut off, and a big building was there, like just in the middle of nowhere. It was an animal factory, Dad said. Cattle farm or something like that. The animals had broken free, and as soon they saw all the cars . . . There was a lot of them. Cows, they . . . We didn't see them in time. They hit the cars, and flipped them around. We tried to get out, I remember crawling out of a window with my mom. But then . . . I don't know, the cows were attacking everything in their way, stomping on people. Mom was pulling me by my hand, but it slipped and . . . I don't remember." He shook his head quickly. And I reached out to him, more on instinct than any real thought.

"I'm sorry that happened to you," I whispered, patting his shoulder awkwardly.

He didn't look at me. He just shrugged his shoulder away from me, then spoke again after a few seconds. "I couldn't find Mom and Dad. I haven't seen them since. I ran into the forest, I . . . I don't even remember for how long, days probably. Mr. Martin found me. He is a hunter who was in the woods when everything happened. He took me back to the church, where the others were. There were other kids there. They were all from an orphanage, on a trip with a nun, old Tita. Mr. Martin found them too and brought them to the church. It was one of those places that was moved around, just the church and the town square, with a couple buildings that were part of San Pedro before. Now it was just there in the middle of the woods. The hunters, the father, and Tita were the only adults there. They took us in and kept us safe."

"They must be good people," I commented.

Felix shrugged. "They're okay, I guess. But we don't have much to survive on, not with what the raiders take."

I tilted my head. "What the raiders take?" I repeated.

"They come every few days, and they take whatever they want. There are a lot of them, so there isn't much that we can do," he said.

I narrowed my eyes. That I didn't like, not at all. "Who are they?"

"Survivors, like us I guess," Felix answered. "They have lev—Carvings and weapons. They raid the rifts to get them. There isn't much that we can do other than do what they say."

I didn't say anything. I knew that there would be people like that. The world wasn't a good place even before all of this happened. But when Felix told me about the group that took him in, I thought that perhaps the threat would have made us look out more for one another.

"This place of yours is safe though, yes?" I asked.

"As much as it can be," Felix answered. "We sleep in the church at night to keep safe."

"So what kind of dangers are around here, aside from bears?" I smiled, trying to change topics slightly.

"Well, jaguars are the most dangerous thing around, Mr. Martin mentioned that he spotted one a few weeks ago. Snakes, owls, bears, all animals have gotten a lot more aggressive. And the closer you get to the big cities, the worse it is, at least that is what Mr. Martin says."

"Really? Wouldn't it be safer there, where there are more people?"

Felix shook his head. "They're all dead," he said.

"How?" I asked.

"Mr. Martin says that people turned on each other, and then the beasts got stronger and killed the rest. He says that he saw rat swarms where each rat was the size of a dog." He shivered. "From what the raiders have said, the big cities are death for anyone stupid enough to get close. There are a lot more rifts there, and many of them broke open, filling the cities with all kinds of monsters."

That was worrying. If rifts were like the ones on Ish Vimza, and had animals from other worlds . . . that could be a real mess.

We settled into a silence as we walked. I didn't want to press him for more, I could tell that he didn't like thinking about it all, which I understood. Having your parents ripped away from you at such a young age and in such a way would be hard for anyone. Or at least that was what I thought. I didn't really have that much personal experience. My family gave me away willingly.

It didn't take us long to find a rift. I saw light coming from in between the trees. I glanced at Felix to see if he noticed it yet, and saw him still looking around. Human eyesight was worse than mine, so I didn't say anything as we got closer.

"There!" Felix exclaimed a little while later. "There it is!"

He rushed forward, and I quickened my step to follow. We came to a stop in front of the rift's opening. It looked the same as the last one did. Like a coin-sized orb casting a light all around it. The only difference was the color of the light that it gave off. The one that I encountered had been white, and this one was green. I didn't know if there was a significance to that.

I caught Felix as he took a step closer. "Careful, it will draw you in," I said, already sensing the strange buzzing that I felt the last time pulling me forward.

Felix shook his head, looking terrified, then stepped back next to me.

"What do we do now?" he asked, his voice hushed and filled with worry. He sounded like the scared kid that he actually was, not the someone older filled with bravado that he liked to pretend he was.

"Do you know why it's green?" I asked.

Felix shook his head. "I only know that it would be bigger if it was closer to breaking."

That was good to know. "So," I started slowly as I faced him and forced him to look at my face. "Here are the rules: You stay behind me, I say jump, you jump, I say stay, you stay. If you disobey me . . ." I trailed off, and he swallowed nervously.

"Understand?" I asked.

He nodded quickly. I took a long look at him, and then before I could change my mind I grabbed hold of the knife at my belt and offered it to him. It was Shadow's blade, so it was not affected by whatever it was that impacted Earth blades. The Source, the magic that had been brought to Earth, was like another law of physics, a new one. It had effects that impacted everything, some of Earth's metals would have their properties altered. Some in subtle ways, others more extreme. From what I had seen so far, most of the ones we used in everyday life were being affected by something very close to extreme oxidation, rendering them useless for the purposes they were intended. Perhaps we would eventually figure out a way to change that, but it would take a while.

Felix looked at it with wide eyes, and shakily took it out of my hand. He pulled the blade out of its sheath and looked at the silver metal.

"Really?" he whispered.

"Do you know how to use that?" I asked.

He looked a bit uncertain, so I took a step to stand next to him. "Here." I carefully took his hand in mine, minding my strength as I had him grip the knife properly with both hands. It was too big for him, so I figured that gripping it with both hands would be better. "You point this end away from you. If anything comes close, you swipe at it, keeping it away. If it still keeps going, you stab, like this." I showed him how to do it properly. Or as well as I could under the circumstances. If anything got through me, I doubted that he would be able to survive on his own.

"Now." I turned to look at the rift and took a deep breath. Bringing a kid with me was stupid, I knew that, but this was a new world. People had to grow, and grow fast. "Let's go."

I stepped forward, holding a hand on Felix's shoulder. I could feel him shaking beneath my palm. I gripped my spear tightly and reached for the rift.

It pulsed, and an echo sounded out of my chest. I heard Felix grunt, and then the light exploded around us. It pulled us in, and I heard Felix screaming. The world shifted, but I was far more centered now than I had been the last time. A moment later, there was solid ground beneath my feet again, and I landed gently, catching Felix as his scream got louder.

Then I lost my grip on him, and he fell to the ground as I felt a surge pierce through me. I sighed loudly as I felt my strength return to me, the sun no longer stifling me.

I opened my eyes and saw a familiar sky stretching all around us. Stars and nebulas painted everything, awash in colors of red, blue, and yellow, with no sun in the sky. Well, the stars were suns, but were too far away to have any effect on me.

Sand was beneath my feet, and Felix was on his knees, looking around with the knife tightly gripped in his hands. This place was smaller than the last one, a lot smaller. We were on an island floating in space that was barely the size of a basketball court.

It was covered in sand in all directions, with no signs of life.

"This is amazing," Felix said as he got up to his feet.

I shook my head and put a finger over my mouth. Immediately, he closed his mouth, and I turned my attention to our surroundings. I didn't hear anything moving, but that didn't mean that there wasn't anything around.

I turned around and found that the rift entrance was there, just behind us. I frowned. That wasn't right.

"What is it?" Felix asked as he saw me studying the green light.

I gave him a look, that he probably missed because he couldn't see my eyes. Then I decided to risk it.

"I'm trying to figure out why this is here," I told him in a whisper.

"What? The exit?"

"Yes."

"Where else would it be?"

I turned to look at him. "The last rift I was in had an exit in another location. I could only leave after I finished the rift."

He blinked. "The hunters never mentioned anything like that. They could always leave the rift whenever they wanted."

It seemed like there was a lot that I didn't know about the rifts, not that I ever had any illusions that I knew much before.

Well, at least being able to leave at any time was good.

I turned my attention back to what was in front of us. Quickly, I spotted something in the center of the island that looked like it was stone. I headed that way, gesturing for Felix to follow. It was indeed stone. Brown stone surrounded a hole with stairs that led into the darkness below.

I gripped my weapon and pointed it in front of me, then took a step forward.

"Follow behind me, but keep a distance," I said and started descending.

Felix nodded, and I turned my attention back in front of us. I could see the bottom at the end of about two dozen stairs, and quickly made my way down. At the bottom, I saw a long, straight corridor stretching in front of us, with a light source coming from the end. The corridor ended around twenty meters ahead, with a chest along the back wall.

"Oh," Felix said, his voice filled with relief. "It's a trap dungeon."

I glanced in his direction. "A trap dungeon?"

Felix nodded. "Mr. Martin encountered one once. It didn't have monsters. It was just a room with a chest surrounded by traps. He said that an arrow coming out of a wall nearly took his head, so he didn't try to reach the chest. He gave the location to the raiders, and apparently they managed it," He gave me a side glance. "Though I overheard them talking when they came around that they lost three people in it."

"So," I said. "Dangerous."

He nodded nervously. Well, I could understand the sentiment. The ground in front of us gave way to a giant hole that stretched all the way to the end of the corridor, and it was filled with wickedly sharp metal spikes. It was pretty deep also. I didn't see any way across that was obvious, but I took a step closer and then knelt next to the edge, studying everything.

He had called it a trap dungeon, or rift. That didn't mean that it was actually that. We didn't have nearly enough information to make that assumption, and just calling it something did not make it that thing. The last rift could've had traps, but it could've been that the Grand Spell had just taken a trapped area and made it a rift at random.

My rift had been a piece of the Ke Erzi world, a lot larger than this place, but it was also in an area on Kirios that was considered the most dangerous place on the planet.

We were on Earth, a newly integrated area. Perhaps the difficulty and size of the rift correlated to the danger of the area it was in? I couldn't know for sure, but I knew that I had to be cautious.

I raised my head and looked at the walls, noticing small holes placed at three different heights. They looked too small to be handholds, and instead looked more like murder holes, which I was very familiar with. We utilized them often in our trap houses and bases of operations in the barrios.

"How do we get across?" Felix asked.

I tsked to myself. If I were being honest, I could probably jump across with little issue. Well, the ceiling was a little low, but I didn't think that I needed that much of an arch. I was confident that I was strong enough to make it. There were two issues, the murder holes which I had no way of knowing if they would fire, or what would trigger them. And the fact that me jumping over would most certainly reveal to Felix that I wasn't exactly human.

I paused as I thought that, and then frowned. *Perhaps it wouldn't, I could always just say that it was my Carvings or a skill. I have a perfect way to hide my vampire nature. Everyone in this world has them now, and they have no idea all that skills can do.*

"What do you think?" I asked, wondering if he had any ideas.

"Well." He looked over, squinting to see. "Are those holes in the wall?"

"They are," I answered.

"Maybe we could use them to climb over the wall?" he said hesitantly.

It wasn't a bad idea first idea. I'd had it too. "What if those are traps too?"

He blinked, then frowned. "Yeah, they probably are, aren't they."

I nodded.

"So what do we do?" he asked.

There was no real good option. Not unless we left and came with more tools. Which, as I thought about it, was probably the point of this rift. Too bad for it that I could cheat.

I stood up and walked back to the stairs.

"What are you doing?" Felix asked as I leaned my weapon on the wall.

"You wait here, I'm going across."

"What?"

I didn't answer as I started running. If I had my skills, the [Mist Step] would've probably prevented anything dangerous from hitting me, but I hoped that with enough speed I could avoid it anyway.

I reached the ledge and jumped. I heard and felt the crack of stone beneath my feet, and then I was soaring through the air. Immediately, I heard the snapping of strings, and impacts behind me, but I was moving too fast for anything to hit me.

I landed on the other side and took a few steps to bleed my momentum and then came to a stop.

I glanced back and saw Felix looking at me with his mouth open wide. I saw bolts embedded in the walls on both sides, and walked over to one that was close to the edge. I pulled it one out of the wall and looked it over.

It was short, like a dart, with a narrow and sharp point that was encased in metal while the rest of it was made out of wood. It was relatively heavy for the size, so I decided to gather as many as I could. I could use them as throwing weapons.

Once I was done, I turned my attention to the chest. I didn't open it immediately, as I was worried that it might be trapped. I walked around, taking a closer look, then I sniffed around it looking for anything out of place.

Once I saw nothing amiss, I raised the top open.

The chest held four items, the same as the last time I opened one. The first things that caught my eyes were the two cloth pouches, identical to the ones in my backpack. I already suspected what they held, so I pulled them out and looked in them. The first was filled with coins, silver again, which made me grimace. There were less coins than there had been in the last rift as well. The second pouch held two gemstones, both of them brown in color, earth stones it seemed like.

The two other items were far more interesting. They were two boxes of ammo. The text on them was written in a language that I wasn't completely familiar with, but it looked German to me. One of them was rifle ammo, a .22 LR box, and the other was in English, with the words Sellier & Bellot 460 S&W written on it.

I opened one of the boxes. Immediately I was surprised to see that the ammo wasn't decayed, and looked to be in pristine condition. I took a sniff and then licked one of the bullets. It tasted the same as the weapons I got from Shadow. I could tell that they weren't made of any alloys from Earth. It confused me, I didn't know why this would be here. I remembered the glaive that I found. It too hadn't gotten decayed, even though it wasn't anywhere near the quality of Shadow's weapons.

I stored the things in my backpack, and then took a running leap back.

The traps fired again, but again I was too fast for them. Absently I wondered how they detected me, but that wasn't a priority.

I landed, and Felix rushed over.

"How did you do that?" he asked.

"Masks give us many different skills," I said, avoiding the truth.

Felix gaped at me with wonder in his eyes. I turned my eyes, uncomfortable with what I saw there, and pulled my backpack and grabbed the two ammo boxes.

"This is what we got," I said.

"Oh, that's great. We always need more ammo," he said as he took the .22 box.

"You have guns?" I asked. "They aren't rusted?"

Felix waved his hand. "The old ones are, but Mr. Martin found a hunting rifle in one of the rifts. It is what has helped us survive."

So, guns still worked, or at least the ones that the Grand Spell gave out did.

"They are rare though," Felix said. "Like really rare, and we have to hide ours when raiders come, otherwise they would take it."

The more I heard about these raiders, the more I was worried about them.

"So, this is good?" I asked.

"Yeah," Felix answered excitedly. "If I come back with this, the father and Mr. Martin will be very happy. And I even have a skill! They won't be able to say that I'm a burden anymore."

"Why do you think that I'll just give you this? I was the one that got it."

The expression on his face made me immediately regret my little joke. "Don't worry. You can have that one." I pointed at the box in his hand.

The look of relief on his face was too much for me. I put the other box in my backpack then straightened.

I turned toward the exit. "C'mon, let's go."

The Scarlet

We climbed back up the stairs and stepped onto the sandy surface. Felix clutched the ammo box tightly in his hand, his eyes looking up at the sky.

"Where do you think we are?" Felix asked, his voice filled with wonder.

I turned my eyes to the sky as well, looking at the beautiful display of colors all around us. I didn't detect any signs of a threat, so I figured that we could indulge in a moment of respite in this place. "Somewhere in space, far away from our world," I answered.

The sky above Kirios didn't match what we'd seen here. Saia had confirmed it for Shadow and me. This was a place that the Grand Spell could reach, but not a place that was anywhere near the planet. For all the people of Earth knew, what their eyes were seeing in these rifts was all fake, made by magic.

"Really?" Felix asked.

"It's what I think, at least," I answered.

Felix nodded. "What do you think the light was? Why did it come here and do all of this?"

"What do you think?" I asked, instead of answering his question.

Felix's brow furrowed in thought, and then he spoke. "Father says that it is a test from God, to see if we are worthy of Heaven. He says that we must've disappointed him with all the sin we did. That we must cleanse ourselves of it, and that at the end, rapture will come to those who have true faith."

I wasn't a true believer, but I could see how those who were would think something along those lines. Especially since what happened was so far beyond anyone's ability to explain.

"That's what he thinks, not what you think," I prompted gently.

Felix turned to look at me, then turned his eyes away. "I don't know what I think."

I didn't say anything for a little while. We both stood on the sand and watched the beautiful sky. My purpose on Earth had always been clear to me, to do good. To help Earth survive the integration. It was a hard thing to plan, harder even to start. So, I took a deep breath.

"It is a spell," I said finally. "A Grand Spell with the power of a god. It might even be what we'd call a god, for all we know. It has found our world and taken it, joined it with its own world."

Felix turned to look at me with a shocked expression, and I decided to tell him everything that I knew. Well, mostly everything.

I started the story at the beginning, when the light came and took me away to another world. I skimmed over many of the details, but I told him about Kirios, and the fact that we were now part of another world filled with numerous other races, and that in time they would be coming here. That we weren't ready for them.

It was . . . like a test for me, to see how people would react to what I knew.

Felix was young, and his reaction was not what I had expected it to be.

"That's so cool!" he said excitedly. "So you are one of these Exemplars? Is that how you are that strong? Why you could jump that far? How many skills do you have? How many Carvings? Can you teach me to be like you?"

His questions were the exact opposite of the existential panic that I had thought learning about different races and our world being broken down by a magical spell and put back together would bring. But I guess that I shouldn't have expected anything different from a kid like him.

"Perhaps I'll answer you, one day," I said. "Now, we need to get you back home. I need to speak with the people there. There is much that I need to learn about what happened on Earth while I was gone, and just as much that I have to tell them."

Felix looked like he was about to pout, but ultimately ended up nodding. Cute kid. "Well, we should hurry then! I want to show everyone what I got." He raised the box of ammo like it was some great prize, and perhaps it was.

We headed back toward the rift entrance, with Felix rushing ahead, excitedly.

"Wait up," I said, but he didn't slow. He jumped at the exit of the rift, and the light swallowed him whole. I sighed and shook my head. I paused and looked around me one more time, making sure that there wasn't anything that I missed. There was nothing that stood out to me, but I did wonder what was going to happen to the rift once I left. Would it just be destroyed? Or would it be filled with new treasure and available to be entered once more?

"Did you see anything strange, Saia?" I asked, taking advantage of being alone with her.

"Feedback: Nothing out of the ordinary. The stone walls did not match what we encountered in the Ish Vimza ruins, nor did they match anything from Ke Erzi."

I nodded. The little dungeon was simple. The stone blocks had been crudely cut. It could've even been from Earth for all I knew.

I hefted my spear on my shoulder and shook my head. "What do you think about the kid's story?"

"Feedback: It matches what Shadow told us would happen. The collapse of your technology is what interests me more."

"Yeah, we still believe that it is because of the Source?"

"Feedback: Nothing that we've experienced suggests otherwise."

I thought about the box of ammo in my backpack and wondered about it. "Felix gave me the impression that rounds gained from these rifts can be fired, but the propellent in the bullets we found at the estate had decayed."

"Statement: The propellent could be different, or it could be protected from the effects by the casing around it."

I grimaced. It was another thing that I would have to try to figure out.

I hurried after Felix, reaching the rift entrance and letting it pull me out. The world twisted, and light flashed before my face before I felt the solid ground beneath my feet and heard a whooshing sound behind me.

The weakness hit me immediately, making me feel disoriented. That's when I heard the yelling.

"Drop the weapon, put your hands up!"

I felt my heart start to beat faster, pumping my thick blood through my body faster and faster. Slowly, I opened my eyes and saw the scene in front of me. Three men stood in front of me, wearing mismatched clothes and holding weapons in their hands. One had a big staff carved out of wood. Another had a short sword, clearly medieval European in make, but with no signs of decay. The last one was standing behind them, and was holding Felix by the neck of his shirt, pulling him up as the kid looked wide-eyed and terrified back at me. The man had a short knife in his hand, clearly threatening the kid.

I narrowed my eyes, but didn't move at all otherwise. My weapon was on my shoulder, but the weakness of the daylight was making me feel almost nauseous.

"Didn't you hear, puta? Drop the weapon, now!" one of the men said.

"Estrella, they are—" Before Felix could finish the sentence, the man holding him hit him in the head then threw him on the ground.

"Shut up, trash," he said.

My eye twitched, and I felt anger rearing up inside of me. I could imagine what he was going to say. These people were most likely the raiders he was talking about.

"You don't want to do this," I said, as calmly as I possibly could.

"This is our turf. You stole that rift from us. You are going to surrender everything that you got from it. Drop the weapon, and your backpack, or we'll take them," one of the men said.

"I didn't get this weapon here," I said, trying to buy time to figure out a plan. I was weakened, but I was still stronger than a human. Though, fighting more than one opponent was always tricky. All my instructors had always said that in situations like this, the best course of action would be to run away. I agreed with that, unless of course I got gripped by rage and just reacted. I knew just how lucky I had gotten the last time I fought against a group. I had taken them by surprise, and I was stronger than they had expected.

"Well, we can't know that for sure, now can we?" the man on the right, the one with a staff, said.

"Are you deaf, puta?" the one in the back, next to prone Felix, said. "We won't ask you again, drop your shit on the ground or we'll take it off your corpse."

I narrowed my eyes behind my glasses. The silence stretched after his words, I looked to Felix holding his face on the ground, tears streaming down his face. These people were everything that I was worried about what would happen on Earth. People who would take advantage of everything and everyone in their way.

"Fuck this bitch," the one with the sword on my left said, and before I could really react, he jumped forward with a raised sword. As he swung, I felt the imprint in the world around me.

It surprised me and made me pause for just a moment. It wasn't anything like what I had felt on Ish Vimza, from the beasts or Shadow. This was far . . . less, in every way. And it was loud. It felt to me like someone telegraphing a punch in a fight. Even still, I reacted too slowly.

[Double Strike]

For a moment, his sword split in two, one coming after the other. I jerked back, evading the first sword, but the second caught me across my face, from my temple over my cheek and down the side of my jaw. I jumped back, getting some distance. I felt the warm blood slowly oozing out of my wound. A vampire's blood is thicker. It didn't flow in the same manner as a human's does. He cut the side of my glasses and mask, and they slipped from my face. I turned my head slowly and looked at the man with the sword. Rage filled me, and I felt it burning up inside of me. He had just tried to kill me, with barely any discussion, with no good reason.

"What the—" He was looking at my cheek, and then his eyes slid to mine. I saw his face lose all color, and he took a step back. "Adult vampire!" he yelled to his people.

"Impossible, it's daylight!" one of them said, but at this point I was too far gone. Life was cheap, and trying to kill me was crossing the line.

I let anger fill me to the brim. I pushed my weight to my front leg and took the first Kata of the **Veiled Mist Assault**: *From the Mist, Strike.*

Emotion is the fuel that grants me Purpose.

And today, my purpose was to kill the fools in front of me. I felt my lips twitching in a snarl that bared my fangs. I lowered the spear from my right shoulder and pulled it back. Then in an instant I attacked, taking a step forward at the swordsman. I brought the weapon up in a wide arc and then slammed it down on top of his head.

He put his sword up to block, but that was the wrong move. I might have been weaker during the day, but muscle was muscle, and mine was greater than his. My serpent-tongue spear hit an overhead block and pushed it down like it wasn't even there. My weapon hit his head and cleaved it down to his chest before it got stuck.

The man on the right yelled and raised his staff. The one behind him jumped with his knife, moving to grab Felix. I whispered, "Saia, get Felix," and she melted from my wrist and turned into her dragon form, flying straight for the third man. The staff wielder was surprised, but then I felt a skill, this one far more controlled. I didn't hear the skill in my head, but I saw his staff blur in my direction. I tried to pull the spear out of the corpse of his friend, but it was stuck, and I was starting to feel lethargic. I couldn't pull it out, so I dropped it, and jumped to the side.

The staff missed me and hit the ground, and I pounced on the man. I grabbed his wrist and squeezed, feeling the bones grind against one another. If it were night I would've broken them. With my other arm I grabbed his hair. The scent of blood had filled my nostrils, awaking the **thirst** from its deep slumber, and I pulled the man to me and bit his neck. I drank deeply, and as the blood touched my tongue, all else faded away. The taste of human blood felt like something completely new. It had been a long time since I last tasted it. It wasn't as powerful as what I tasted on Ish Vimza, but the taste of it was . . . It was everything.

I felt the surge come barreling through my mind in a burst: flashes of images and the man's most recent memories.

"A new rift!" a voice said to my right. "If we return to the boss with good enough loot, we might get pushed up the ladder. Get to join a real raiding team!"

"Don't jump ahead of yourself, Louis," I said, gripping my staff tightly. "You know the rules. We don't enter rifts, we only report on their location. It's too risky. We aren't equipped to fight them."

"C'mon, Mateo," Louis started. "You can't be content with scraps. We'll never advance unless we take risks. And besides, it is only a green one. There is like one in three chances that it doesn't even have any monster inside. You tell him, Cristo."

I shook my head and opened my mouth to reprimand him, when Cristobal joined in. "Wait, what is that? It's opening!"

I turned to the rift quickly, and saw it flash with light and grow suddenly. Worried that it was breaking, I raised my staff above my head, and then a shape tumbled out of the rift, a kid.

"What the fuck?" Louis said, his sword pointed straight at the kid. "Who are you, and what are you doing here?"

The kid looked at us with wide eyes.

"Hey, I know him," Cristo said, his eyes narrowing. "He's one of the orphans from the church."

I looked at the kid and recognized him. "Why are you here, kid? The boss told your people that all rifts in these woods are ours to claim," I said, my anger rising. I knew that this was going to be an issue. The boss wasn't going to like it at all.

"Come 'ere kid," Cristo said as he caught him and pulled him up by his shirt. "You are going to talk, or we are going to make you regret it. How many more are inside, a full five?"

I turned my eyes to the rift, waiting for anyone else to come out, Louis did the same. And then, before the kid had a chance to answer, the rift flashed, and another person exited. A woman, with a mask and glasses . . .

The memories ended in a series of rapid flashes as they approached his death, and I pulled my teeth out of his neck and threw him on the ground. The wound on my cheek didn't close, though I felt the blood stop oozing out. The sun prevented the **thirst** from granting me all of its benefits.

I looked around and found the third one, Cristobal, lying on the ground dead with his throat cut open. Saia hovered above him, her claws covered in blood.

I looked around and found Felix leaned against the tree nearby. His eye was covered in a bruise, and his lip was open and bleeding. I took a step closer, and he winced, which made me freeze. I closed my eyes, letting my anger go. It had served its purpose. Then, with a calm mind I looked at him again.

I felt the still warm blood flowing down my chin, soaking my shirt. I could hear the silence of the forest, and smell the scent of death around us.

I could taste Felix's terror in the air. I looked up at the sky, and the sun up above us through the trees. Then, I took a deep breath and looked at the kid again.

"Don't worry, I won't hurt you."

"H-how are you standing in the s-sun?" he asked.

I smiled. I didn't expect that to be his first question, but it was good. It was better that he questioned instead of screaming and running away.

I pointed at the sun above us. "That's not our sun anymore," I told him.

He followed my hand, and looked up at the sun. "Oh," he just said.

"I'm really not going to hurt you," I said as I knelt in front of him, a few steps away. I didn't want to come too close and scare him more. I also had the urge to reach up and wipe the blood off my face, but I resisted it. That was the human part of me, the one that had died a long time ago. This was who I was, and I wasn't going to hide or be ashamed of it.

"Yeah." Felix nodded. He seemed to be forcing himself to stand up and walk closer to me. And then, he spoke again. "Thank you, for helping me, I mean."

I exhaled and nodded. "No problem," I said.

Felix swallowed, then pointed behind me and spoke. "And what is that?"

I blinked, then glanced behind me. "Ah," I said. "Felix, this is Saia. Saia, introduce yourself."

"Statement: Greetings, you may call this Unit Saia."

I shook my head at her introduction, and then looked back at Felix, who stared at her openmouthed. "Uh, you have a dragon," he said, his fear of me seemingly forgotten.

As he looked at Saia, I turned my attention to the dead bodies. I had a lot of cleaning up to do.

The Soul Space

W ait here," I said to Felix as I gathered the bodies and started to drag them away. I couldn't leave the kid alone for long, but I really didn't want him to see what I was about to do.

"Are you going to eat them?" he asked slowly, his eyes following the bodies.

I rolled my eyes. "Vampires don't eat people," I answered, then after a beat I added, "We drink them."

His hand raised to his neck, his eyes wide, and I grimaced. "Sorry, that was a bad joke."

He gave me a shaky smile, and I turned away, pulling the bodies behind a large tree, where he wouldn't be able to see. Then, I took a few sips from the other two corpses, taking their essence and Investment for myself. I didn't get a Carving, but I didn't expect it. These people probably had only a handful of Carvings at best, nothing compared to the Investment levels of blood that I drank on Ish Vimza.

I wondered how getting their skills would go, but that was a question for another time. I wished that I could drain their blood, but I already had enough in my backpack, and I didn't want to traumatize the kid any more than he probably already was. Draining blood from human bodies could get messy.

I looked down on the corpses, and realized just what a waste their deaths had been. I reacted without thinking, again. Emotions were tools, but I was the one that was supposed to guide them down the path of my own choosing. Using the anger part of the Heart of Azure and Scarlet, I had few issues with. It was my own personal failing that was my problem. When things happened to me, I was rarely able to stop myself from reacting based on my upbringing. Growing up in the cartel, where hesitation meant death or worse, I had learned to strike back ten times stronger after any slight or insult.

I didn't need to kill them. That was the old Marianna, not someone who had her eyes set on saving the world. I was strong enough that I could've disabled them, gotten more information from them. Instead, all I got were snippets of memories. I didn't have issues with killing. I never had. I knew what I was, and I accepted it. A vampire couldn't survive without blood, and that fact killed any squeamish human part of me that had survived the transition. But the greatest vampires were not the butchers that humanity fears. The impalers, the conquerors, the ones whose names were drenched in blood. No, the greatest of our kind were those whose names were never known, those who pulled the strings from the shadows. They were the ones that I had to emulate.

I looked back at the three dead men. They weren't good people, that much I was certain of. They were threatening a kid, and they tried to kill me, but . . . perhaps it didn't need to end this way.

"You want to consume them, Saia?" I asked after a while. "I'd really like not to leave much evidence of this . . . incident."

Saia tilted her head. "Feedback: Affirmative, more biomass will aid me in engram production and experiments."

I knelt and rummaged through their pockets, taking everything I thought was valuable.

"Well, they are all yours," I said, and the dragon landed on one of the bodies and turned into goo, starting the process.

A while later, I returned to where Felix was nervously waiting, with a bundle of gear under my arm. Saia had consumed all of their biomass, leaving things that I could use.

"You said that you don't eat people." Felix looked at the stuff in my hands with his eyes open wide.

"I don't," I said, then pointed at Saia. "But she does."

He looked up at the tiny dragon with an expression of absolute horror and broken dreams.

"Clarification: This Unit does not *eat* people; rather this Unit can consume biomass."

Felix opened his mouth to say something, then closed it, seemingly at a loss for words.

I rummaged through the gear that I found, taking a closer look at the most interesting items. The first was a compass, that seemingly worked. There was a plastic lighter with half the butane still in it. The serrated steel wheel was slightly corroded, but it wasn't as bad as other metal items I had seen. With a few spins, I confirmed that it still worked. I could only assume that the type of alloy, or rather the percentages of certain metals in it, was what impacted the alloy the most. One of the ingredients had to be extremely vulnerable to the Source. The last item was a bundle of rope. I gathered it all and stored it in my backpack, then turned my attention to the weapons.

I wrapped up the sword in a shirt, then pushed it in between my back and the pack on my shoulders, sliding it in through the straps to more easily carry it.

I would've taken the staff too, but I already had to carry my spear. So I just pressed it into the ground, then slowly pushed it straight down, as if I was planting a beam. It took a bit effort, as it was still daylight, but the staff quickly dropped all the way down, and I covered the top with dirt.

Felix looked at me with an awed expression on his face that I ignored. I recovered Shadow's knife from where he had dropped it, and offered him the one that the raiders had.

There were still signs of a struggle around me, such as the blood in the dirt, but at least it would be harder for anyone to tell what happened now, with no bodies to be found.

The sun was slowly setting, and I decided that the best course of action was to make camp again before heading for the church.

We walked back to our original camp in silence. Felix kept throwing glances at me and Saia when he thought that we couldn't see. I expected it—it was why I had tried to conceal my eyes and mouth. Humans had a variety of reactions to vampires, from outright fear, to disgust, or indifference. Where and how you were raised usually decided on what you would feel. People living in first world countries, in the big cities where everything moved so fast, often didn't care that much. Vampires didn't change their day-to-day life. They lived amongst the civilized, and vampires adapted to fit in. You would see vampires on the covers of magazines, giving interviews, leading companies.

We were very good at fitting in and making ourselves look as harmless as possible.

Then there were those who were more religious in their beliefs, who believed that all of us should be burned at the stake. Thankfully, those voices had died out in the last few decades. The years following the Great War had done a lot to change the image of the vampires in the people's eyes.

But then there were those who lived in backwater areas forgotten by society. In the mountain villages where someone disappearing in the night was just a fact of life. Places where vampires could take control just with the power of who they were. Like how the Master of the Cartel had. Those people knew the danger a vampire represented well.

We found our old campsite just before the sun moved beyond the horizon.

"Saia, field please," I said, and the faint shimmer of a protective field appeared around us.

"You said that it was your skill," Felix said, looking at Saia.

"I said that it was a skill," I told him. "Never said that it was mine."

Felix opened his mouth, then thought better of it. I smiled inwardly and then set him to make us a fire again.

"Can I have the lighter?" he asked.

"You need to practice. The more you become familiar with fire, the more likely you are to get a Mask evolution related to that. If that is what you want, of course," I said.

That made him throw himself at the task, while I sat down and leaned my back against a tree. I felt tired. The fight had been short, but it was intense. I had expended a lot of my energy, especially since it was still daylight. The blood I drank was replenishing my energy reserves, I could feel it, but it was a lot slower than it would've been at night. I sat in silence as Felix gathered twigs for his pile, and the sun moved beyond the horizon. I closed my eyes as my full faculties returned and the wound on my cheek started to close. I cracked my neck and stretched my arms, feeling my full power returning. Then, I sighed and turned my attention back to Felix. I watched as he was struggling with his knife and flint, then I felt something lance through my chest and stood up suddenly.

Felix yelped and knocked over his pile of twigs, looking at me with fear in his eyes.

I remained standing, my back straight and head tilted to the side.

When I didn't move for a few seconds, Felix spoke.

"What is it?" he asked.

I barely heard him—my attention was all on what was inside. I felt my skills return, the cooldown run out. It was a strange sensation, a magnified version of what I felt when any one skill came back from its cooldown. Except that this was several skills all at once.

I shook my head, dismissing the sensation, and looked down at Felix.

"It's nothing. I thought that I heard something," I said. "And I don't see a fire."

Felix scrambled back next to his pile and started working on it again.

I sat back down again, and Saia landed on my knee.

"Statement: The long cooldown appears to be three days," she said in a low tone that a human wouldn't be able to hear.

I nodded, glancing up at the dark sky. It was around this time that I finished my fight against the kiji pack. Three days. That was a long time to be without skills, but less than I had feared.

Night had fallen, and I could tell that the kid was exhausted. He barely managed to start a fire, flint slipping from his fingers on every second strike of the knife. Once he was done, he bundled up next to it, his head on his pack.

I could tell that he was trying to stay awake, and that he was keeping his attention on me, even though he was trying not to appear like he was.

"You should sleep," I told him, and he startled. "I'm not going to hurt you. I wouldn't have saved you otherwise."

He didn't move, but I could hear his breath hitching in his throat. After a few seconds, he finally spoke.

"Really?"

"You have my promise," I said.

He shuffled around and looked at me, and I tried to convey my sincerity. He held my gaze for what felt like a few minutes, and then nodded. He turned back around and closed his eyes. I had no way of knowing if he did trust me, but a few minutes after, he was asleep, so perhaps I had managed to convince him.

Once I was sure that he had entered a deep sleep, I turned my attention to Saia.

"Can you keep watch? I want to check my soul space."

Saia inclined her head, and I focused on my chest, pulling myself in.

The transition was immediate, and I found myself in the familiar yet different room. There were changes, a lot of changes.

"Well, that's interesting," I said.

"Statement: Your advancement to the First Investment tier has obviously initiated these changes," Saia said. It still felt weird knowing that she could send a piece of her to this place with me, but I was getting used to it.

I turned my attention back to the room around me. The ceiling above me had risen, and a second floor had appeared with a ladder to the side leading to it. The walls and everything else seemed to be improved, and the pedestals had turned from simple stone, to one that was somehow clearer. They were now a deep gray color of a thundercloud, compared to the dirty appearance they held before. The wooden planks that were on the walls were likewise improved. They looked like they were made of richer, higher quality wood now. I turned and climbed up the brown ladder, to the second floor. It was just a narrow walkway that hugged the wall in the ring, or rather square around the room. It was just wide enough for me to walk around.

The walls had shelves, like those below, though these ones were obviously empty.

With nothing more to see, I climbed down and looked around. My Mask stood in its usual place, the centerpiece of the room. The two smaller pedestals that signified my Ornaments were now merged with the middle pedestal holding my Mask, but were still lower than the center. The Mask was as intimidating as ever, with only a few tiny changes. There were faint lines etched in the horns, and the jade had spread slightly around the sides of the eyes. Otherwise it remained the same old, mostly obsidian and savage looking, Mask. The plaque beneath it remained the same.

Mask of the Blood Invoker (Physical, Weave, Esoteric) — First Investment; Third Carving
Ornament of the Revelator (Weave, Esoteric) — No Investment; Fourth Carving

Ornament of the Student (Physical, Weave, Esoteric) — No Investment;
Eighth Carving

The plaque beneath that one, that had my trait, hadn't changed either.

|Potential Augmentation| trait

Wearing the Mask of the Blood Invoker grants a significant increase to all attributes. All cooldowns are greatly reduced, after the Mask is removed, all used skills are put on a long cooldown.
Slotting skills of the same type grants bonuses.
Current bonuses available:

Beast: Slotting in skills that all contain <beast> type increases their effectiveness and reduces cooldowns. All physical senses are heightened.

Movement: Slotting in skills that all contain <movement> type increases their effectiveness and reduces cooldowns. Air resistance of your body is reduced.

Currently, I had mostly <beast> type skills, so I only had that bonus, but I realized that I was looking forward to experimenting with the other one as well.

The back wall still held three main pedestals with my skills on them. Each pedestal had two bowls with skills, with one set of three being gray and inactive. I glanced at my slotted skills, making sure that everything was all right.

P1-Beast Bonus
[Mist Step]
[Lesser Strength]
[Debilitating Wave]

P2-Beast Bonus
[Sonic Screech]
[Lesser Impale]
[Quick Claw]

To the side were my other skills, the [Swap Profile], [One Truth Verified], [A Lesson Remembered], and [Practical Learning]. There were no real changes, other than the visual improvements, like everything else in the room.

I moved into the corridor that held my doors. The doors themselves were still the same, but like with everything else, the corridor had been improved. I walked by the old doors, until I reached the new ones.

There were a lot of new additions. The bird that I hunted with Shadow in order to feed after the sikiri fight, the snake I killed on the estate, the new additions, the raiders, Louis, Mateo, and Cristobal. And of course, the one that belonged to Shadow.

His door was the most elaborate one yet. Made of dark wood, with an elaborate image etched into its surface. The bottom was filled with swirls, that I somehow knew represented mist. Above it was a mountain with a giant tree towering over it, and on top of the door was a crown with nine prongs.

I reached for the door, and then paused. I wasn't anywhere near strong enough to fight with Shadow. I didn't even know how he would look. Animals that I had drank from seemed simpler than the originals that I had encountered in the real world. Would he be able to talk? Or would he just be a mindless automaton with his power? I didn't know if I could handle seeing him like that.

I turned away and looked at the other doors. Several were beyond my skill level at the moment: the mature ferrorn's door, the reaper's, and sikiri's. The ferrorn was the least of them, and I knew that I couldn't attempt it now. Shadow was far beyond that.

I glanced at the three newest doors, the raiders, and decided that I wanted to know what was beyond them. I glanced at Saia, who had been following along in silence, and gestured to her.

"What do you think I'll find inside?" I asked.

"Feedback: Impossible to know."

"Thanks." I rolled my eyes.

I took a deep breath and looked at one of the doors. It was simple, and the most familiar to me. It looked like any general door that one could find in the barrio, white wood with an ordinary brass lever handle. I hesitated for just a moment, and then pushed the door open.

Inside was a copy of the forest where I fought the three raiders, and the man stood in the center, his sword drawn and pointed at the entrance. I recognized him from the memories. Louis, the one that had cut my face.

There was no sign of recognition in his eyes, nothing but empty eyes reflecting a hollow mind. My weapon, the serpent-tongue spear, rose from the floor next to me as soon as I thought about fighting him, and I picked it up before entering. The moment I stepped in, the man charged, his sword raised high.

I dodged his attacks, studying him closely, trying to see if there was anything sign of the man that he used to be. I had worried that my Mask was actually trapping souls, but I saw no sign that the man was anything other than a pale copy of the real thing.

"Are you in there?" I asked after I dodged a few of his attacks, but there was no answer. Seeing that I wouldn't get anything more than a mindless attacking puppet, I ended things.

I dodged his attack, then in a burst of speed brought my spear down over his head.

The man fell apart into mist, and left behind an orb with his skill. I picked it up and carried it back to the shelves, placing it into an empty bowl.

[Double Strike]

Execute two strikes at the same time.
<physical><esoteric><martial><offense>

It was a good skill, one that I had experienced personally. The only issue I had with slotting it was that it didn't have the <beast> tag, which meant that I wouldn't get the bonus for the profile I placed it in.

I put it aside for now, letting it rest next to the other skills that I had on the shelves like [Lesser Leap], [Peck], and [Sharp Eye].

"So," I said as Saia and I headed back in the corridor, "they aren't real people."

"Statement: It would seem not."

"Can't you just, like, agree with me for once?"

"Feedback: When the data supports your statements, of course."

"And data doesn't support my statement now?" I looked at her with narrowed eyes.

"Feedback: Insufficient data."

"Right, right. You wouldn't be just playing with me, now would you?"

"Feedback: This Unit was not designed to 'play.'"

I chuckled and turned my attention to the doors. I wanted to get the skills from the other two raiders. As I came near the end of the corridor, I paused, then frowned.

"Saia," I said slowly. "You didn't try to open that door, did you?"

"Feedback: I did not."

My eyes were glued to the elaborate door that belonged to Shadow. It was just a tiny bit ajar. I took a step closer, then reached my hand to touch the door.

"Well," a voice said behind me, and I rounded on it, my spear ready, then I froze.

"This was not what I had expected, not at all."

Shadow stood there, the same as he had been the last time I saw him. He was looking at his own hand, studying it as if he was seeing it for the first time.

"Uh," I started, unable to even form words.

Shadow blinked, then raised his eyes to meet mine. "Hello, Little Star."

Teacher

For a long few seconds, I didn't move. I stood in the corridor, inside of my soul's space, the hall of my Mask, looking at the man standing in front of me. He was about as tall as I was, dressed in the same elaborate robe of dark blue with a red undershirt that he wore the first time I met him. Though, the elaborately woven threads looked like they were cleaner. The clothes I saw him in last had been dirty, covered in dirt, blood, and grime from his trip across Ish Vimza, cut up and ripped by the fights he encountered on the way. This one was brand new.

His skin was pale blue-gray, his nose more elongated and pointed than that of any human I had ever seen. His hair was as black as night and shoulder length. On top of his head there were two foxlike ears that twitched as if he was curious. Nine tails fanned behind his back, swaying gently as if they were in the wind. He looked at me with a grin on his face, with eyes that were like those of a fox, sharp and filled intensity sprinkled with a hint of amusement.

He was an alien being, in a literal sense of the word. He was a being that was not from Earth, a denizen of Kirios, the world that ours was now a part of. He was a Tsu-gi, a hybrid between two races of the YoKai-ni of Kirios.

I had left him back on Ish Vimza, a world away. Yet here he was, standing in front of me. For a moment I was frozen in shock, then in confusion, and then I recovered enough to take a step back and raise my hands up in a defensive stance.

"Statement: This is unexpected," Saia said.

I narrowed my eyes. "Shadow?" I asked, my eyes never moving from him, looking for any sign of movement. I didn't know what kind of a trick this was, but I knew how my rooms worked, how I had to fight in order to gain a skill.

Shadow didn't react immediately. He tilted his head, his eyes scanning his surroundings, looking at the wooden walls, then the elaborate and unique doors that lined the corridor. His eyes then glanced at Saia who stood on the ground next to me, and then finally rose to meet my own.

"It is so strange," he said, his eyes moving away to look back at the palms of his hands.

He didn't look like he was about to attack me. In fact, he didn't look at all like the other denizens of the rooms inside my soul. True, those were animals, and he was most certainly not. I didn't know how he had left the room in the first place. None of the others had ever shown the ability to do that. Though, he was also the first person whose blood I'd drank since I got my Mask. And there were other differences as well. The blood I'd drank before had been from my own kills, or already dead animals. He was the only one who had freely given his blood. I didn't know how or if that changed things. I kept realizing just how little I knew about my Mask in the first place.

"Is it really you?" I asked, trying to keep the hope out of my voice. I had returned to my home, and yet these last few days had left me feeling somewhat lost. I knew what I had to do, but I was yet to truly take a step toward my goals. I missed his advice. This felt almost too good to be true.

One of the ears on top of his head twitched, and as he tilted his head in the other direction, his eyes rose to meet my own.

"Am I?" he asked, his eyes twinkling with light. "I feel like myself, but I know that I am not. I believe?"

I groaned. "Yeah, it's you."

His lips curled into a grin. "Not the real me, and not all of me, but enough, I think."

"What do you mean by that?" I asked.

He closed his eyes, then responded. "The last thing I remember before this place was reaching for the knife to draw my blood and then . . . I was here. I wondered what was going to happen, you know, based on what you said this place was like. You take the essence of a living being, and you turn it into a copy that can grant you power. I am that copy, but I had wondered how my strength would be translated . . . I am a copy, I know it instinctively. I also know things that my original does not."

This time it was me who tilted my head. "Like what?"

"I . . ." He gaped and slowly closed his mouth. "Huh, I cannot say."

He looked confused.

"You can't say what?" I asked.

Shadow didn't answer immediately. Instead, he closed his eyes, and his face turned pensive. Finally he shook his head and spoke. "It seems like I am not much different from other essences you've gathered. I am here to serve a purpose, and I cannot stray from it." Then he smiled again. "Not much at least."

There were so many questions that filled my head that I didn't even know where to start. Though, some things were obvious. The Shadow in front of me wasn't the real him, just a copy from his blood, or essence rather, just like all the other denizens of the rooms inside my soul. It was also obvious that he had the memories of his real self, or at least most of them up to the point of when he drew his blood.

"Can't you try and not be all mysterious for once?" I asked him with a smile. Even if it wasn't the real him, I felt . . . relieved.

His eyes glimmered in the dim light of the corridor. "If only I could."

I grimaced but didn't press, partly because I was still pretty shocked to have him standing in front of me and actually talking with him.

"The others are mindless copies," I said, gesturing at the door I had entered before.

"The others?" he asked, and I realized that he didn't know. His last memory was giving me his blood. I explained what had happened since his gift, and his eyebrows rose as his smile grew.

"You have returned home, I am glad."

I sighed. "Yeah, if only I didn't have to kill my own people the first thing back."

"Did you?"

I blinked. "Did I what?"

"Did you need to kill them?" he clarified.

I opened my mouth to respond, and then I paused. I looked away as I answered. "No, no I didn't need to."

I could see him nod with my peripheral vision, and it just made me feel worse. I knew that I had lost control. They had hurt the kid, and they had threatened me, they attacked me. I wasn't sorry for their deaths, but I knew that I could've overcome them without killing.

I changed the topic. "How did you leave the room?" I asked instead, hoping to find something that he could talk about.

He looked to the side, where the door that led to his room was slightly ajar.

"I feel it pulling me back in, your Mask, your power. You are just not strong enough to keep me from leaving."

I blinked, then glanced at the other doors, namely the ones from the more powerful animals, like the sikiri or the reaper.

Shadow spoke, interrupting my thoughts.

"I don't think that you have to worry about them leaving their rooms," he said, and I turned to look at him.

"How do you know that?" I asked.

"Based on the things we discussed before, regarding the manner in which you gain blood. I believe that the only reason why I am so . . . whole, is because my blood was freely given. It matches the rules of other Masks that rely on the essence of the soul or similar things for Investment. Actions, circumstance, and intent are important to the Grand Spell. I believe that those who you have killed or drank their blood after they had died, are only remnants of an already depart-ing and unwilling essence. You steal a part of them that was tied to their skill, and the Grand Spell creates a copy that is sufficient to pose a challenge. I, or rather, my real self, gave you his blood willingly. Thus, the Grand Spell has copied his memories more fully."

I tilted my head, thinking. That made sense to me. I had been able to tell that there was a difference between the skills I gained depending on the manner in which I obtained the blood. And Shadow and I had talked about what I could expect to gain from him.

"There is more," Shadow said, apparently able to talk about this freely. "We should go inside." He moved toward his door, and I paused.

"Are you sure? I don't think that I can fight you." I worried that he would change if he entered the room. That he would have no choice but to fight me once inside. There was a lot that I didn't know about the Grand Spell and my Mask. Not even Shadow's insights could be trusted, as he didn't know much about my Mask type.

He glanced back at me and grinned mischievously. "You needn't worry about that. You were never going to be fighting me."

I frowned, unsure what he meant. He disappeared through the door, leaving it open just enough that I could see light coming from the inside. I hesitated before entering.

"You think that this is a good idea?" I glanced down at Saia.

"Feedback: Unable to determine with the data currently available."

I narrowed my eyes at her. "Can't you give me a guess, like just this once?"

Saia's blue glowing eyes flashed for a moment, and then she spoke. "State-ment: I think that the danger is low. If he wished, he would've been able to kill us outside of the room. If he has broken the rules of your Mask, I do not think that anything we can do could stop him from killing us if he wanted to, or could actually do it."

"Yeah, somehow I think so too," I said.

I took a deep breath and pushed open the door, entering.

I was met by an unexpected sight. Usually, the inside of a room in this place was the location where I got the essence, where I tasted it. Instead of the camp where he had offered his blood as a gift to me, we were someplace completely different.

I stepped onto a narrow ledge, with the ground cutting off in front of me just two steps away, and the world stretching into the distance.

The afternoon sun, low in the sky, shone in front of me, and below it was a sea of white and gray mist. This was someplace high up, above the clouds. Shad-ows danced below the surface of the mist as if there were things moving under it, and others were just those cast by the few clouds that skimmed the surface of the mists. Mountain peaks rose through the mist in a few places, some barely poking through, others rising like pillars. Some had trees growing from their sides, with purple leaves and strange orange bark, while others were just barren brown stone.

The sight was breathtaking, and the most beautiful thing I had seen in my life.

"Come along," I heard Shadow say, and turned to see him walking along the narrow path to my right, climbing the stairs carved into the side of the cliff.

I took a moment to glance back at the view in front of me, then I followed after. As soon as I rounded a corner, I stepped onto a large plateau where Shadow waited, his back turned toward me, looking ahead at a large white stone arch.

"What is this? Why is this even here? All the places inside my rooms are places that I've been before, where I've taken blood."

Shadow turned his head slightly so that he could look at me from the corner of his eye. "What we discussed before appears to be correct. The manner in which you obtain the blood has meaning. You do not need to fight me in order to gain a skill from me."

I raised my head at that. "Really? Can you just give it to me?"

He chuckled. "No, no." He shook his head. "Your Mask requires you to pass a test. It is strange, but I can see why it is like that. From what I know of Invokers they require a lot more steps before obtaining a skill. If all you had to do was drink blood and gain a skill . . . it would create a very powerful Mask. Imagine a young scion of a wealthy family gaining your Mask. They would have advantages, would be able to obtain a high Investment blood with no effort on their part. No, a test is still required. And I am here to be a judge of it. I presume that is why I have been made in this form, with memories of my real self."

I blinked. "What kind of a test?" I asked.

Shadow gestured at the arch, beyond which I could see another set of stairs leading up to another plateau.

"The stairs will lead you to the Weave Among the Mists trial ground, it is all that remains of an ancient temple of my father's people, the Tengu-gi. It is sacred, and no outsiders are ever allowed on this mountain top, not even those like me who share half of their blood."

His voice turned sad, and his eyes got a faraway look to them. He was supposed to be a copy, and yet here I saw real emotion, memories that still hurt. What reason would the Grand Spell have to create something like him, I wondered.

He shook his head. "I defied their wishes when I first came here, broke with their traditions. I was a different person then. I did not understand the value in such things. I regret doing it, but this place is what has put me on my true path. The trial of the Weave Among the Mists is where people come to master the **Way of the Mind**. Completing the trial grants a skill, and any who completes it is considered a master among the Tengu-gi, and is allowed to come down from the mountains into the world below the mists."

"So, I need to complete the trial to get the skill?" I asked.

He grinned. "Yes," he answered.

"What kind of a trial is it?"

"I have broken many customs of my father's people, but this I will not. No one speaks of the trial. It is for the tester to experience on their own."

I frowned. "This isn't really that place, though," I said. "This is a memory, I guess. This is all inside of my Mask. Do you really need to keep it a secret?"

Shadow blinked, as if surprised. "Yes, you are right, this . . . I . . . None of this is real. And yet . . . I do feel I have knowledge." He chuckled. "It is comforting to know that even when I am a copy of the real thing, I can still hold to the same beliefs."

I grimaced. "It's kinda unfair though. You are part of my Mask. You should be helping me."

Shadow turned to look at me then, and a side of his mouth rose in a half grin. "Oh, but I am helping. You are not going to be attempting the trial, not for a while at least."

My brow furrowed and I put my hands on my hips. "I'm not."

He shook his head. "You are not. As you are now, you wouldn't survive it. Well"—he glanced at me, as if measuring me—"you might survive the first step. The other two would kill you, for certain."

I glanced at the arch, wondering what kind of a test it was. "It is that dangerous?" I asked.

He nodded. "It is. The Tengu-gi do not let anyone below Third Investment attempt it at all. Your physical strength might give you a slight advantage, but it will not be enough."

I sighed. I hadn't really expected that I could get his skill anytime soon, but . . . well, it was no loss.

"Can you tell me what skill I'll get?" I asked.

He opened his mouth, then closed it. "It would appear that I cannot say its name, strange. Let us see, the trial gave a variety of skills depending on the performance. But you will not get any skill other than the one that I had gained. It is not my strongest skill, but it is the one that has greatly shaped me. The one that I am proud of the most."

I tried to find any rules for what he could reveal, but it was hard. It seemed like he could talk about almost everything, with just a few exceptions.

"But, this is better in a way, I think," Shadow started. "I can remain here to teach you, to guide you on your journey. If you will have me of course." His eyes glowed, reflecting the afternoon sun.

Somehow, I was glad. I hadn't expected this, but it made me feel good. I had Shadow back, even if it was just in this place. I had my mentor, my family. It made me feel like things would be all right, after all.

First Steps

I opened my eyes in the real world. Meeting Shadow again had left me somewhat drained, exhausted, but in a good way. I had worried so much about the weight of everything that I had to do, and even though it had been just a few days, I had felt lonely. Shadow's presence, or at least a part of him, was most welcome.

I had his guidance once more, even if there were things that he couldn't talk about, that he couldn't share. I wondered just what the purpose of his presence was, but Shadow had said that all Masks had a variety of features to them, aspects that served different purposes. I didn't know if that was the Grand Spell speaking through this version of him, or if it was the real Shadow. In truth, for all I knew this Shadow was just a shell made out of the real person's memories for the Grand Spell to use as a mouthpiece, as a test. I didn't think that I would ever know the truth of it.

Still, I was glad. This also opened up a lot of different things regarding my Mask. If I could get freely given blood from other people, would I be able to get their copies too? I discussed it for a short while with Shadow, and there were some very interesting questions. But those were matters best left to the future. Now, I had more important matters to think about.

I had taken the other two new skills from the raiders, which were [Quick Strike] and [Quick Step]. They were interesting skills, and I wanted to test them out, so I swapped out my second profile skills for the three new ones I gained, replacing the [Sonic Screech], [Lesser Impale], and [Quick Claw] with [Double Strike] and the other two. When I swapped them, I also felt like the process was different from when I changed the skills of my primary profile. When I did that, there was cooldown until the skills became active, and this felt somehow different.

So, I rolled my shoulders and stood up. I glanced at Felix's sleeping form and then focused inward, triggering my [Swap Profile]. I felt my skills swap around, and the new ones come awake. I tilted my head, then whispered.

"It worked."

Saia flew up and landed on my shoulder, then responded in a low voice just next to my ear. "Statement: I will add it to the data collection about your Mask."

I nodded. She had taken it upon herself to keep track of all the things we learned about my Mask. This meant that I could activate new skills faster, though it cost me the cooldown of my [Swap Profile] skill, which I knew was around an hour. It wasn't that bad, though this new profile didn't have any bonus as none of the new skills had a <beast> tag, and only one of them had a <movement> tag. Though, with the [Quick Step] skill, I did now have three movement skills which meant that I could make a profile that would give me the Movement Bonus.

But I really didn't like having a skill profile that lacked any offense. I would have to think about it, but that was for later. I focused on one of the skills and activated it with a thought. I raised my foot, and [Quick Step] made me skip ahead. I frowned. The movement was strange: I didn't feel like I was moving faster, but my leg had skipped ahead in a blur, faster than what I was capable of. It was a short skill, but I could see how it could be useful. I waited for it to come off cooldown without moving, wanting to see if it had a requirement like [Mist Step]. After a minute of waiting, I felt like it wasn't going to come back without me moving. It didn't feel like a skill that should have a long cooldown. I started taking steps, counting as I walked around the camp. On the tenth step, the skill came back. It was longer than [Mist Step], but then that one had been a higher Investment Skill, at least from what Shadow had said.

With one skill down, I tested out the other two. [Quick Strike] did the same thing that the step did, only it accelerated a movement that was intended to be offensive. From what Shadow had said, there were ways to trick skills and use them in ways that they weren't fully intended to. I tested it out a few times, finding out that it too had a requirement-based cooldown, which was a dozen offensive movements. It also seemed to work on any action that could be called a strike, regardless of which body part I used it for.

The last skill, [Double Strike], was time restricted, with the cooldown being around five minutes. That was a long time in a fight, but the skill was also a lot stronger than the others. If one didn't know that it was coming, it was incredibly dangerous, as I knew firsthand. If someone stronger had used it on me, I could've lost my head. The only reason I wasn't badly injured was because of my superior speed.

I finished my tests and returned to my place in camp.

I looked over at the kid again, wondering how he had even managed to fall asleep after everything that had happened the day before. He had clearly been unsettled by learning that I was a vampire. And seeing three men die in front of him had to have left a mark. Or . . . maybe not. His story about what happened to him had been filled with death already.

Still, his knowing that I was a vampire changed things. I had planned on keeping my nature a secret from most people I met. The reasons for it were many, but primarily because it would give me an advantage when dealing with people. People mostly accepted that vampires were a reality that had to be dealt with, but coming face to face with one was difficult. The vampire population wasn't high enough that average people dealt with them in their everyday life. They saw us on TV, read about us in the news, they saw us from a distance. Very few humans ever interacted with a vampire. Hell, shifters were more commonly seen in public.

Vampires cultivated a certain kind of image. Both in the civilized world, and in the shadier places. The Lágrima Sangrienta Cartel was one of the very few criminal organizations that was led by a vampire and had many other vampires and shifters in its ranks, in this part of the world at least.

And that was the issue. I didn't know where exactly I was. I had returned to the estate, my home, but I also knew that the Earth had been taken apart and put back together into a single landmass by the Grand Spell. I had already seen signs of it: this forest didn't fit what used to be near my home. The trees were different. The bears that attacked Felix were not native. I heard birds that sounded nothing like what I knew.

It was possible that the area around my home had been stitched together with some other part of the planet. For all I knew I was now in the middle of what used to be Europe.

I shook my head. It wasn't that bad. According to Felix, I knew that Medellín was still in this area. We were still in a territory that was predominantly what used to be Colombia, from what I could see, at least.

I just had to meet more people, explore more, and find some way of figuring where exactly I was in the grand scheme of things. Though that wasn't as important just yet.

Getting to people was. And that also meant deciding how I was going to approach them. I still had my glasses and mask, fixing them was a simple matter, but the question I had now was whether I wanted to in the first place.

Felix already knew, and though I could try to trust him not to spill, there was something to be said about just presenting as I was. I would still have to trust him to not say anything about me being able to walk in sunlight. That is what I wanted to keep a secret the most. It was a secret that I didn't think even many vampires knew yet. The fear of the sun was ingrained in the vampires, I didn't think that any of them would ever test it out without being forced to. That meant that I had an advantage over even my own kind, and I intended on keeping it for as long as I could.

Now, I had to decide how I was going to approach the people at Felix's church. It was going to be interesting no matter what.

* * *

We set out from camp in the morning, after breakfast. I pretended that I didn't
see Felix's furtive looks, pointed both at me and Saia, as I let him eat in peace.
Once he was finished, I cleaned up the camp, and we headed in the direction he
said the church was.

From what he said, it wouldn't take us more than a few hours of walking.
He obviously couldn't have gotten that far away from it when he ran away, since
he had still been just on foot. He didn't know the exact way back, but he knew
enough to identify a direction and landmarks, and a mountain that was nearby.

We walked in an uncomfortable silence for a bit, as I was unsure how to even
start a conversation. What did you say to a kid that had just seen you murder
three people in front of them? That had just found out you were a bloodsucking
monster?

I wished that I could just stay quiet, deliver the kid to his people and safety.
But there were more things that I had to know.

"Tell me more about your church and these raiders. You said that they come
around every once in a while?" I asked, breaking the silence.

Felix winced, as if startled by my voice. He glanced in my direction, then
looked away.

I sighed. It was obvious that he didn't know how to act in front of me anymore. I could tell that he was afraid. I knew the signs.

The issue was that I didn't know how to make him not afraid of me. The only
people I had ever interacted with as a vampire were those in the areas that were
controlled by my group. They had been accustomed to vampires and shifters
before I was even turned.

"Felix," I said slowly. "It is still me, you know."

He glanced at me. "I-I know," he said, then sighed. "It's just that I've never
seen a . . ."

"You've never seen a vampire before."

He shook his head. "Only on TV."

I nodded. "So what do you know about us?"

Felix swallowed and tried to meet my eyes. "Well, you drink blood."

"That is true," I said. "But we don't need to kill people in order to do that,
and we can survive without human blood for a while."

"Really?"

"Of course. What do you think I did while I was away for the last month? I
was in an alien jungle with no humans around. I had to drink animal blood to
survive," I tried to say as gently as I could. "You don't need to be afraid of me,
Felix."

Felix raised his head. "Yeah," he said slowly. "I know, it's just . . . the way you,
uh, killed those people was . . ."

"They were attacking us," I said slowly.

Felix looked away. "Yeah, Mr. Martin says that surviving is what's most important now. That we should be careful around anyone new that we run into, with everything that's been happening. That . . . that they might be desperate."

He didn't seem to believe his words.

"You understand why I did it, don't you?"

"Because you are a vampire?"

I sighed. "I'm sorry that you had to see that. I . . . I lost my temper. I saw that they'd hurt you, and once they attacked me, well . . ." I shrugged. "Actions have consequences, and they decided to act in a way that brought them in direct opposition to our survival."

He nodded. "I'm sorry for acting this way. It's just . . . I couldn't do anything when they grabbed me."

I blinked. I thought that he was being standoffish because he was afraid. And he probably was, but now I saw that there was more to it.

"There is nothing to be embarrassed about," I told him. "They were older and stronger than you, and they had skills. There was nothing that you could do."

"Yeah." He turned his head down. "I just have a useless skill and Mask."

"It will change once you reach your First Investment," I told him.

"But will I get stronger?" He turned to look at me. "You told me that Masks change based on what we do, what kind of experience—Investment we get, right? Well, if I'm always rescued, if I'm always weak, what kind of skills will I get?"

"You will get stronger," I said firmly. "I know it."

He narrowed his eyes. "I need to do better, to learn more. That is what my Mask needs right?"

I nodded. "Yes."

He met my eyes, and in them I saw a kind of resolve that reminded me of a look I would see in a mirror when I was a kid and wanted to prove myself to those around me.

"Can you teach me how to fight?" he asked.

I blinked, not expecting it. "I don't know if that is a good idea," I said. I had a lot to do. I didn't need the added responsibility of being someone's teacher, especially when I was still a student myself. Nor did I even know how to teach. I barely knew enough to keep myself alive.

"Please," he said with eyes that bored into me. "You saw what happened. I need to learn how to protect myself."

"You'll be safe once we get you back to the church."

"No I won't." He turned away. "There is no such thing as safe anymore."

I opened my mouth, then closed it. He was right, of course. Even more than he probably realized. I sighed. "I'll think about it."

"Really?" He turned back with a smile on his face.

"After we get you back to the church, and I talk with the adults there."

"You promise?"

"I promise to think about it, nothing more," I said, already knowing that it was a bad idea. "Now, raiders, tell me about them." I switched topics before his puppy eyes made me make promises that I couldn't keep.

He shrugged. "They come and take milk from our cows every once in a while, and then they talk with the father and Mr. Martin."

I tilted my head. "What do they talk about?"

"I don't know. But I overheard Mr. Gomez say that they are bastards once. So, they are probably doing some bad things," he said, with a nod to himself. "Tita doesn't let us go near them when they come, and every time we ask why they are there, she says that kids shouldn't be so nosey." His face scrunched up into a grimace. "I'm not a kid, I'm thirteen! Ana and Diego even go on hunts, and they are the same age!"

I tried not to laugh at his outburst. "What else do you know about them? You said that they hunt for the rifts?"

He nodded while avoiding looking at me. "Yeah, I overheard Mr. Martin say that they had to report rift locations to them once, before Tita dragged me away." He reached up to scratch at his ear. "I don't know much more. Just that they have weapons and stuff."

I chuckled. "Well, I guess that I'll have to wait and see."

As the sun started to make its descent, Saia returned from scouting ahead and landed on my shoulder.

"What's the word?"

"Feedback: This Unit located the compound that corresponds to what Felix described. It is less than an hour from here at your current pace."

"Is everyone safe?" Felix stepped closer, looking up at the dragon.

"Feedback: This Unit cannot say for certain, as it observed from a great height in order to remain undiscovered. But, there were signs of people present."

I narrowed my eyes. I'd noticed her switching between referring to herself as "this Unit" and "I" again. I had some idea why she did that, but I would need to test it out once I had the time.

I glanced at the sky. The sun was coming down but wouldn't set before we reached our destination. Which was . . . a problem. I turned to look at Felix then knelt next to him.

"We should talk about what we're going to say to your people."

Felix blinked. "What do you mean?"

I grimaced, trying to figure out how exactly I wanted to go about this. Hiding that I was a vampire was going to be . . . too hard. I had already seen how easy it was for my face coverings to be removed, and my excuse for it was honestly not that great. Which left the only real option: not hiding what I was. Which was fine, I was not ashamed of what I was, and seeing how the three raiders reacted to it did open my eyes somewhat to what I could expect. It would give me some advantages. My eyes singled me out as an Adult vampire, and most people would associate that with someone at least a hundred years old. Humans valued age and experience, which should make any interactions between us much easier than if they thought I was young. In truth, I was not even thirty, but they didn't need to know that.

What I really wanted to keep a secret was the fact that I could walk in sunlight.

"I'd like for us to wait for nightfall," I told him slowly. "Me being able to survive in direct sunlight is something new that most people won't have any idea about. I'd like to keep it a secret."

Felix blinked. "I can do that."

"You promise?" I smiled at him.

The kid nodded furiously. "I won't tell no one."

"Good." I stood and looked around. "Then we'll wait for nightfall, and then head to the church."

Interlude
Concrete Jungle

Angelo Serrano tried very hard not to move as he peered through his binoculars at the overgrowth that covered the railing of the old watch post overlooking the city.

Sometimes he wondered if he was trapped in a nightmare. Then he remembered that the world had gone mad. But still, he wondered how even in a mad world he got to this place here, sneaking above the city that was crawling with what could only be described as monsters.

In the world before, he was a nobody, just a garbage man that liked to play little games with himself while he worked. He would look at trash bags, and based on their shape and weight, sometimes smell, he would try to guess what was inside. His coworkers would play with him, sometimes even make bets, though not often as he would usually win. He spent his days mostly looking through trash for anything valuable, searching for things that others threw away that he could still use.

There was a reason why the saying "one man's trash is another's treasure" was still heard often. It was true.

Every now and then he would find something interesting: a TV that still worked, an old and weathered bed frame. Sometimes, even valuables that had clearly been thrown out by mistake, jewelry, even once a wallet filled with cash—though, Angelo had returned that. But he had spent his days looking for new things among the trash of millions.

Some looked down on him for his profession, and his scavenging ways, but he didn't mind their words and looks. A person had to survive somehow, and he had never had any one of them offer him a helping hand.

Then the Light came, and the nightmare began, for most people at least. Angelo remembered the chaos of the start, the deaths, the struggle. Yet, in the deepest parts of his heart, he couldn't help but be thankful. Because as the world changed, for the first time in his life, he had been offered a helping hand.

A text had blazed inside of his mind, offering a gift. As the Light burned the world away, he had been given something that made all his struggle before somehow worth it.

The Light came, and he was transformed into a **Seeker**. He didn't quite understand what that had meant at first. He had of course heard whispers from others, mostly the younger generations, talking about Classes, Levels, Skills, and Experience, but he didn't really understand. He had never played games. His family had barely made ends meet when he was a kid. He played on an old Game Boy a few times, borrowed from a kid in the neighborhood. Hell, he didn't even own a good phone. He made do with an older model.

But he didn't need to understand what they were talking about to grasp the changes.

He had done as he always had—he sought anything of value everywhere he looked. Only now it was far more important, because what was valuable had changed, and finding something of value was essential for survival.

And his Mask, or Class as most people called them, had given him the tools to do just that. In just a month, he had managed to get more Carvings, or levels, than most people.

At first, he was part of the scavenging group sent out to search for food, or anything else of interest. He always had a knack for finding hidden things, and he was quickly rewarded with a skill, [Detect Value]. It had completely changed everything for him. He had caught the eye of the big guys in charge of their group, and with that came more work. He didn't mind it at first. What he did was important. People knew his name, they smiled at him when they saw him walk by. He was given a better room, better clothes, and women had even started to talk to him more.

But then came the dungeons, where his talent became even more invaluable. Knowing when a dangerous dungeon was worth the risk was a matter of life and death. It also let him see hidden treasures.

He had leveled fast as they cleared them, sometimes losing new friends, other times celebrating their success. He reached level seven, or the Seventh Carving, and became one of only seven people among the barely a thousand survivors at that level who had gained a second skill: [Detect Danger]. The skill that made him even more important than before. He was an asset now, and helping the scouts had become a priority.

The world had gone mad. The survivors of a literal apocalypse were relying on the talents of a garbage man. Sometimes Angelo found humor in that thought.

His skills worked in very specific ways. For [Detect Value] had to have a certain state of mind. He had to think on what he thought was valuable, which was a fluid concept, and he had to hold it firm inside of his mind. If he thought the food was valuable, he had to hold the concept of it in his mind. And he had to be very specific with it. It was too broad otherwise. Once it had just illuminated the entire forest around him in his sight, because obviously something considered the plants all around them "food." If they were looking for animals to hunt, he had to keep the image of what they were looking for in his mind. And it was hard to keep up. It drained him quickly. More so when he had just gotten the skill than now. He had gotten better at it.

[Detect Danger] was very different. It turned his vision into a world filled with gradients. It showed him areas that were more dangerous than others, though it was usually hard to discern what that danger meant. It didn't seem to take the concepts he held in his mind into account. For example, if he used it on the base, it turned the entire world around him into a light shade of red, indicating moderate danger. That much was obvious—the base was filled with survivors, strong people, they had weapons all around the place, guards, and so on. There was little crime, surprisingly. The big guys had stomped on that pretty hard at the start. But that meant that he couldn't really detect what *kind* of a danger was there, only that an area was in fact dangerous in some manner. Sometimes, that only meant that there was a poisonous plant around, but, again, the big guys had seen the value in it.

Angelo's skill told them something, and after the first time someone ate a fruit that had been perfectly safe in the previous world, but had now turned to be poisonous, Angelo was being called to use his skill more often. They had developed a system for the colors that he saw, that indicated the level of danger, and they had tested things out. Sometimes, just because something was dangerous, didn't mean that it wasn't usable at all.

Which brought him here, to the worst place on Earth imaginable, as far as he was concerned. He wished that he could turn around and run away as far as he could. But he was needed. He was one of the only people who knew Medellín as well as the back of their hand. He had spent years working on the city streets, and besides, his skills were essential.

"What do you see, Angelo?" Gabriela whispered to him from just next to him.

They were both on the ground in the middle of the lookout in their ghillie suits, just above the city. Too close for Angelo's comfort.

"Nothing good," Angelo responded, looking through the binoculars and focusing on his skill. He couldn't use it for long, or it drained him too much.

They were just above the San Antonio neighborhood, in the Villa Hermos district on the eastern side of the city. It was midday, and the sun was shining above them. The sounds that came from the city were enough to bring night-mares all on their own, but it was worse at night, Angelo knew. They had sent scouts at night before, and few had managed to return alive. Gabriela being one of the lucky few. She was one of the best scouts in the group, had a Class for it. He didn't know what she did before to earn it. She rarely talked about her past, but she was very good.

That at least made Angelo feel like he wasn't sent on a suicide mission. The big guys wouldn't risk Gabriela like that. And even though he was terrified out of his mind, he knew that this was necessary. They had to know.

"Doce de Octubre and Castilla are bright red," Angelo said as he studied the city through the binoculars and the lens of his skill. The two districts stood out to his sight.

He heard Gabriela's pen move over the paper in her hands, making notes on the crude map she had drawn.

"Robledo and Aranjuez are a shade lighter," he whispered. "The rest . . . it is all mixing too much, but it is all various shades of mid-red," Angelo said, then quickly turned his skill off. He already felt out of breath. The levels of danger in the city were higher than anything he had seen in the forest. It was ironic, and also very sad, in a way.

He looked at the big buildings, at the roads, the valley, a stretch of land covered by the human hand. A carved piece of nature that they had mastered, turned into their home. And now, just a month after the arrival of the Light, nature had retaken the city. It didn't seem possible, but he saw more green than concrete and brick now. Vines crawled up the buildings, grass covered the streets, trees grew taller than they ever should be. The Light had changed many things, and he had seen firsthand how it had caused some things to mutate, to grow in spurts that seemed insane. He had personally seen a farm plot on the base grow fully developed plants overnight.

And it wasn't just that. The animals were affected too. The city below him was the proof of that. The city of millions of people was no longer ruled by humans. He wondered how many managed to escape it. He had been lucky. He lived on the outskirts, in the poorer area, and had managed to get out easily enough. The rest . . . He heard stories from some of the survivors who had taken a day or two to get out of the city. They were harrowing tales.

Now, the city was ruled by roving packs of dogs, some of which had mutated, and grown to be the size of horses. Not all animals were affected, but for some reason a certain percentage of them had changed, and not all in the same way. The changes seemed unique, as unique as the Classes that humans got. Perhaps the animals got something similar, Angelo didn't know, but then again, he wasn't part of the group that thought about such things.

One never really realized just how many animals lived in a city just alongside humans. Pets, strays, and just wild animals that were part of the city ecosystem. And whatever had made some animals and plants mutate, also made some have other kind of spurts. Some of the base dogs had their gestation periods lowered significantly, with their offspring growing unnaturally fast, and turning out . . . different. Angelo knew of at least two dogs that were barely a year old and had grown to the size of a pony. The big guys kept them separate, testing to see what exactly had happened and if they were dangerous. He had heard a rumor that one of the dogs now had scales instead of fur.

The animals had gone into a frenzy in the days following the Light, but most had calmed down in the weeks after. Some dogs and cats had found the base weeks ago, and were now part of the survivors, along with everybody else. Angelo, for one, was glad for it. The number of times a dog had alerted them of danger coming was worth risking of them going into a frenzy again. Although, there were no signs of it, not that they knew what to look for or what had caused it in the first place.

But the city was a different story. It had turned wild and was far more dangerous than the forest and the mountains where the mutated animal population was much smaller. Dog packs were bad enough, but then there were birds that seemingly fought with other animals for territory, and that could mimic human speech so perfectly that they had lured more than one scouting group into danger. Back when they sent people into the city, before they learned how treacherous it truly was. When they had hoped to find survivors and learned that nothing human still lived in the city.

The day was dangerous enough, but the real nightmare came out at night. Rats, what seemed like millions of them, some as big as dogs, swarming over everything. They'd had issues with some lost hordes of them leaving the city and attacking the base, barely a few hundred of them, but they lost people.

The rats were, in Angelo's opinion, the worst of the lot. The rats ruled Medellín.

A moment later, Gabriela spoke, after she finished noting what he had relayed.

"Okay. Whenever you are ready," she said.

Angelo grimaced, then closed his eyes for a second, focusing on the image of what he considered the most valuable at the moment. They had come here for information, something far more important than what their teams had looked for before. Once, they had come for food, for supplies, weapons. The price they paid trying to get all that stuff wasn't worth it, but it had helped them survive. Now . . . now they knew of a greater danger, and they had to know.

He fixed the thought of dungeons inside his head. He wanted to detect them, to see their value. He opened his eyes, and his vision was filled with bonfires blazing in his sight. He scanned the city with his binoculars as he felt the energy leave his body from the strain of the skill.

"Shit," Angelo said.

"What is it? How many do you see?" Gabriela asked.

"Hundreds, there are hundreds," Angelo whispered, almost not able to believe what his eyes were seeing. "And there are many that shine bright," he added.

"How bright?"

"Too bright," Angelo said.

"Shit," she responded.

"Most are up north," Angelo started. "Doce de Octubre and Castilla."

It made sense that those were the most dangerous areas then. Dungeons could break open, spilling alien monsters into the world. They'd seen them break before, and they'd had to fight monsters. That's why they looked for them, why they tried to complete them quickly, before they could spill open. They knew that the longer a dungeon stayed without being completed, the more powerful it became. They didn't know yet what made them break open—some weak dungeons broke earlier, while some much stronger didn't seem to show any sign of getting close to breaking. There seemed to be different limits for different dungeons, and they were still figuring out how to classify them properly.

But this . . . hundreds of dungeons in the city was beyond insane. They barely found a few dozen out in the wild around the base.

And this was only what he could see from his vantage point. He couldn't see the ones in the buildings, below the ground . . . They were screwed if all those dungeons broke open, if monsters spilled out and crashed with the animals in the city . . . That fighting would drive danger out of the city, and straight to the base. This was what the big guys had been worried about, what Angelo and Gabriela were sent here to confirm.

"We need to head back," Gabriela interjected, pulling him out of his thoughts. "We can't get caught out by nightfall."

Angelo nodded, and then pulled back, turning his skill off and standing up to a crouch.

Slowly, they made their way up the mountain, then headed back to the base they called home, carrying bad news.

The world really had gone mad.

Ramiro Alvarez pulled his jacket closer, trying to keep the cold away. If there was one thing that he hated since the big Light in the sky came, it was that the weather had gone insane. They could have days where the climate was what he knew and expected, and then, suddenly it was as hot as if they were in a desert.

The nights were the worst, and far colder than what he was used to. But he had to keep watch. He sat in the church tower, looking out at the dark forest surrounding their little . . . He didn't even know what to call it.

His home was gone. The town of San Pedro had disappeared and was replaced by a deep forest that didn't belong to any place he knew. The only thing that remained was the church, the square that was in front of it, a piece of the street and three buildings that had been on the other side of it. That was all.

Ramiro had gone through the stages of grief already. He had heard too many stories from other survivors to still have any hope. His wife, his daughters, they were gone. Lost to him forever. He only hoped that God would welcome them, and shelter them from the horror that the world had turned into.

If it wasn't a sin, he probably would've already made sure to follow after them. But he wanted to meet them in heaven, and so he had to struggle. Father Rodriguez at least promised that he would see them again. Ramiro held tight to that promise.

As he sat next to the big church bell, trying to keep the cold at bay, something caught his eye. A light source in the distance. His hand was on the rope attached below the bell immediately, ready to sound the alarm. The only thing that held him back was that for a moment he thought he saw people.

He waited a beat, and then as the light came closer, he saw that it was indeed people. Two of them, one much shorter than the other. It didn't take long for him to realize that one of them was a child. The other one carried a torch, and moved with a sure and confident gait that made Ramiro's hair raise on his skin.

He let go of the rope and grabbed the hunting rifle next to him, then hefted it and aimed over the wall as they approached the church steps.

"Stop right there!" he yelled, aiming his rifle at the big one. He couldn't see well in the dim light of their torch, but the taller one had long hair, and appeared to be a woman.

"Mr. Alvarez? Is that you?" the child yelled back, and Ramiro froze. That voice, it was familiar to him.

"Felix?" he said, hope starting to worm its way into his heart. They had lost too much already, when they had woken up and found the boy gone . . . It hadn't been an easy time.

"It's me! Can you open the door?"

Ramiro hesitated. He had seen too many horrors to trust immediately. Monsters that mimicked human voices had killed one of his friends before. But . . . he hadn't seen ones that could take human form. That didn't mean they didn't exist.

"Wait there, don't move!" he yelled and grabbed the ladder, making his way down.

By the time he reached the bottom, Martin stood near the double doors that they had barricaded for the night, a candle already lit in his hand. He slept near it every night, too paranoid to trust just the lookout in the bell tower.

Martin had to have heard him yelling. The others were all probably still asleep in the back part of the church, where the old stone walls were pretty thick. He doubted that they had heard anything.

"What is it?" Martin asked.

"Felix, and a woman," he said.

Martin gave him a look that Ramiro recognized immediately.

"I know," Ramiro answered the unspoken question. He hefted the rifle in his hands. "That's why I have this thing."

Martin looked at him, then sighed. "You think it's really him?"

"I hope it is," Ramiro answered.

Martin took a long breath, then muttered a prayer while holding the crucifix around his neck. With a nod, he walked over to the door and started moving the barricade out of the way.

A few minutes later they exchanged another look with each other, and Ramiro raised his rifle, pointing it at the door. Martin picked up the axe that he kept next to his sleeping bag, and then put a hand on the doorknob.

He pulled the door open, and they looked outside.

It was a woman, and now up close he saw that she was very tall. Taller than any one of them in the church. She wore dark clothing and had long dark hair. He could barely see her features in the dim light, but she looked attractive, her face angular, with sharp lines. Her eyes sparkled with a light that seemed to be breaking against the surface of them.

She had her hands on Felix's shoulders.

"Hello." She dipped her head in greeting. "I'm Estrella. I think that you lost this one, I'm bringing him back home."

She smiled at them, and Ramiro couldn't suppress the shiver that ran down his spine.

Revelations

I stood silently in the big open nave of the church, which was lit by the dancing flames of candles. The dark space was broad enough for ten people to stand side by side without touching their arms, creating a heavenly scene shrouded in shadows. After we'd arrived at the church and were allowed inside, the two men, who I recognized from Felix's descriptions, had quickly exchanged a few whispered words that hid nothing from me, and then one of them exited out a hidden back door, leaving me and Felix with one of them, who now held the hunting rifle in his hand and was attempting to make it look like he wasn't paying attention to me—though he couldn't quite hide the glances he sent to my eyes and mouth. I stood as still as a statue, not wanting to appear in any way threatening.

I didn't make any attempt to hide what I was. I had planned on doing so at first, but ultimately this world had become a den filled with monsters, and we all had to rise up together if we were to have any hope of survival. It was the decision I had made. Vampires were no longer the worst thing out there.

We would all have to band together if we were to survive.

Felix stood next to the man, who was now looking him over and scolding him in a low tone of voice for running away. I didn't intrude. Instead I looked around.

The church had seen better days, clearly. It was old, but the stone floor didn't look like it hadn't been cared for. Though, there were issues that appeared to be more recent: there were cracks in the walls, and the benches that had been pushed to the side against the walls had seen better days. Anything that had metal was corroded, rusted, and broken up. Several chains were hanging from the ceiling, all looking as if they were barely being kept together. Whatever had hung off them was no longer there. There was a pile of tall candlesticks that had likewise been affected by whatever it was that had been impacting the metals on Earth. There was a big table in the center, with backless benches flanking it and chairs at each end. It was large enough that it could comfortably seat at least a dozen people.

The wood of the church was musty, but I could also detect a few smells moving through it all, clinging to the walls. The candle did a lot to make the smell of the room more bearable, though to my nose the whiff of dust in the rafters was almost enough to make me sneeze. I couldn't imagine what a shifter would be going through right about now.

There was more, of course, all of it telling a story. The scents of incense mixed in with the faint smell of blood and iron were clinging to the wood. The blood had dried on the stone behind me, at the entrance, washed only with water. In the air, I could detect the smell of dirt and mold, and something a lot more familiar coming from beyond the door across from me, hidden deeper in the building. The acrid smell of sweat, urine, and waste. I tilted my head, and my nostrils widened for a moment. They had cattle in the building, cows, it seemed like.

Felix had mentioned something about that. It made sense that they would bring them in for the night. Who knew what danger lurked outside.

There was a draft in the building, making a strange eerie sound as it passed through. It came from the boarded-up windows high in the walls. I could see where the wood from the benches went. They had nailed them over the windows, but the wind still moved through. Deeper in the building, I heard the hurried footsteps of the other man as he approached the sleeping heartbeats in the distance.

I turned my head as I noticed someone's attention on me. The man had seemingly finished scolding Felix and was now studying me intently.

His eyes moved on from mine, though by the rhythm of his heart I was certain that he knew what I was. My eyes would be glowing. They were, in many ways, like those of a cat. Vampire eyes had a special layer similar to tapetum lucidum of the cat species, which acted like a mirror, bouncing back incoming light through the retina and giving them better night vision. He was afraid, I could tell, and I knew based on what he said to the other person, Ramiro Alvarez according to Felix. There were hushed whispers in the distance that even I could barely hear, then the shuffling of clothes and feet.

I decided to at least try to be friendly.

"You are Mr. Martin, I presume," I said with a small smile. "Felix has told me a lot about you."

He called the man Boss, and he was one of the three hunters that had ended up with the group.

The man glanced at Felix, his eyes narrowing slightly. "He did?"

"Only good things, I promise. We weren't properly introduced before," I added as I took a step forward, taking care to do it at a slower, more human, speed. I offered my hand and waited.

The man looked down at my hand, then after almost an uncomfortably long pause he raised his own hand. I felt him shiver as he grasped my hand. My hand was cold, though I didn't think that was why he shivered.

"Martin," he said.

"You can call me Estrella," I added.

"Thank you for bringing Felix back. We were worried about him."

Felix looked away sheepishly, trying to hide the guilt.

"Of course. It was the least I could do for a fellow survivor," I added. "That, and I couldn't just let him die."

Martin glanced at Felix, his eyes darkening. "How did you find him?"

"He was about to be eaten by a bear before I stumbled on him."

"Boy, you . . ." the man started, then stopped himself as more people came in from the back door. The first one through was a short and plump woman, dressed in a black habit, a nun's dress. Her steps were fast and determined as she rushed over to Felix, engulfing him in a tight embrace while he protested loudly. After a few seconds, she pulled back and stared at him, her brown eyes glinting with anger. Raising her hand, she smacked him on top of his head with resounding force.

"Fool child! You took ten years of my life, and I barely have any left!" she chided him, then grabbed his ear and pulled up.

Felix winced and yelped. "Ow, ow, I'm sorry! Ow!"

"You do something that dumb and irresponsible again, and I'll hang you by your thumbs from a window, you foolish little scamp," the woman said.

"I'm sorry, I won't do it again. I promise, Tita!" he said in between wincing.

Tita looked down at him sternly before finally releasing him. "You're a mess," she said softly. "Come, let's get you washed up."

Before Felix could do or say anything, the woman ushered him out and through the door to the back of the building, leaving me alone with four men. The three newcomers stood next to Martin, each with a weapon on them, though they weren't holding them in any threatening way. It was understandable, given the situation they found themselves in. One of them I recognized from earlier as Alvarez, the man that had been on guard duty in the church tower. A middle-aged man with brown hair cut short. Next to him was a burly man with dark eyes and black hair pulled back in a ponytail. He was dressed in a similar way to Martin and Alvarez. From Felix's descriptions I knew that he had to be Mr. Gomez, which meant that the last one was the priest, though I could have deduced that from his clothing.

Martin cleared his throat as the silence stretched. He gestured at the people next to him and introduced them in turn.

"That there is Alvarez, with Gomez next to him." He waved at the two other hunters. Then he turned to the priest. "And this is Father Rodriguez."

The priest stepped forward and offered me his hand. His eyes were gentle, with a sincere warmth that seemed to spread from him in waves. He spoke with a gruff but kind voice. "Hello there, I'm Sergio."

Almost instinctually, I took the older man's hands into mine and smiled gently at him. "I'm Estrella. It is a pleasure to meet you, Father."

He nodded. "I hear that we have you to thank for the return of our wayward lamb?"

I inclined my head. "I found him in the woods. I couldn't just leave him all alone."

He sighed and shook his head. "You would be surprised. God is testing us all, and we're living in a time where the man's darkest impulses are far easier to indulge. That one of your . . . condition, had done what is right, speaks volumes of your character. Come." He gestured at the table in the center of the room. "Sit with us. I'm sure that we have lot to talk about."

It was a far better reception than I had hoped for, though I could tell that he, too, was nervous in my presence. The four men were obviously suspicious of me, as well they should be. Alvarez and Gomez eyed me as we all moved to the table together, their hands almost twitching near their weapons—simple maces with stone heads wrapped around their tips.

I took a seat, while trying to appear as calm as possible. Once we were all seated, the priest walked over to a small cabinet in the corner and opened a drawer. He returned to the table with a candle and lit it with the one that Martin had placed on the table already. Then he walked out behind the wooden wall of the crossing and returned a few seconds after with a pitcher and glasses.

"I've been told that your kind can still drink and eat as we humans do. Is this true?" the priest asked.

I nodded. "It is," I said, not mentioning that it didn't really do anything for us, but there was no need to frighten them.

He poured all of us a glass, his hands calloused from a lifetime of labor, but his grip firm. Then he took a seat. Father Sergio leaned back in his chair, studying me intently. He had a kind face, but he was old, his skin weathered and filled with lines. His hair was mostly gone, leaving only the slightest bit of white around his ears. He was short and thin, with a narrow face, but his eyes were striking, filled with clarity and depth that I had rarely seen. The scent of incense hung around him, undercut by the smell of aged leather that I so often noticed from old people. It was a scent that I associated with those close to death. He had to be in his eighties. Then, he spoke. "Felix was very fortunate that you happened to be near enough to help. May I ask where you came from? We haven't had much contact with other survivors."

I tilted my head; I had already decided on what I was going to say. These people were a good test case for my story. I wanted to see how people would react to the knowledge of Kirios and everything that was going to follow. But first, we had to get the pleasantries out of the way.

"I came from an estate up near Cedeño," I said slowly. It didn't take them long to realize. They had probably heard about the area on the news. Lágrima Sangrienta Cartel was, if not notorious, at least very well known. And while Cedeño wasn't where the cartel's headquarters resided, it was the area where its leader lived.

I saw them piece it together. Alone, it might mean nothing, but coupled with me being a vampire . . . it was a much easier leap to a conclusion. Vampires, in Colombia at least, were either very public figures mixed up in politics, or they worked for the big cartels. There were very few independent covens around.

"Ah," Father Sergio said slowly. "I've visited the Parroquia San José de Cedeño before."

I was surprised. The San José parish was known to be closely related to the cartel. The master might be a vampire, but he still liked to think of himself as a man of faith. He supported the parish with significant donations. I knew that there was more to it, but I had never been involved in the operations that went on there.

"Well," the priest started again, "San Pedro is close enough to Medellín that we have quite the history with . . . your type of work."

That did make some sense. Drug trade had impacted this area, the whole of Antioquia really. He would've been a young man back when the drug trade first started.

"San Pedro," I repeated. "I assume that is the town where this church used to be?" I waved my hand around.

The priest nodded gravely. "After the Light came, the town was gone, leaving only what you've seen outside. The church, part of the square, and a few other buildings. I was alone here once it happened, surrounded by a nightmare straight out of hell."

He looked around, his expression pained. "I was praying at the altar, in the middle of the night, when the Light came. I thought that God had reached down to answer my prayers." He shook his head. "Then . . . this. We have sinned, and judgment has come."

I grimaced, then glanced at the other three men. I tried to determine if they believed the same thing as the priest, but it was hard to say. "Were you from San Pedro too?" I asked them.

The men nodded, and Martin spoke. "We were out preparing for a hunt when the Light came. It took us two days to find our way back—we kept getting lost. We didn't realize what had happened back then, how the world had shifted around. Once we came back, only the church remained. There was no sign of the rest of the town, no sign of our families."

Alvarez leaned in, putting both hands on the table. "Did you encounter a town perhaps? Even if you just saw it from a distance?"

I could see the hope in his eyes, but I had to shake my head and dash it quickly.

Father Sergio put his hand on Alvarez's shoulder. "We can only pray that they have been moved somewhere safer." Then he turned to look at me. "Is your group nearby? We are in need of help. This area is too dangerous for the small numbers that we have. We could use help moving out of here."

"I'm sorry, there isn't any group. I've been on my own for a while. You are the first people I've encountered since the Light came, in fact. Well, aside from Felix." *And Shadow and Saia*, I added silently.

That made them blink, and exchange looks. The priest tilted his head and spoke. "The people from your . . . estate, they didn't make it?" he said in a questioning tone.

Now was the time for me to tell them more, explain things more in depth. "There is a lot that I have to tell you. There is more to this Light than you and everyone else in the world realize. And I need to spread the word as fast and as far as possible. More danger is coming, and we need to be ready."

The men at the table looked at me intently, and I took a deep breath. "The Light is a spell, magic, in a way. Something so grand and beyond our ability to understand, that it might as well be a god."

I saw the priest frown at that, but I didn't stop. His faith had to already have been shaken, and I was about to change his entire understanding of the world. If he believed me that was. "It has come from another world, another universe entirely as far as I know. It has reached and taken our world apart and put back together in a single landmass. That's why some pieces of our land have been moved around."

Their expressions were . . . exactly what I had expected. Disbelief, skepticism, even a touch of anger in some of them. I understood, and I knew that this was a hurdle I would always face.

"That is some tale." Martin was the first one to speak. "We've heard a lot of different ideas. The kids have been telling us about things that they find similar to their games. Other survivors have told us about things that they have encountered. I haven't heard any theory that sounds quite so unbelievable. How do you know this?"

"As I told you, I lived on an estate. There were around a hundred people there when the Light came, but when the Light went away, I wasn't there. I was chosen as one of thirty people from our world to be sent to the origin of the Grand Spell, its home planet called Kirios. I spent the last thirty days there, on a continent filled with monsters that were much greater than anything on Earth. There, I met a native of that world, a member of another race that had already gone through this process before. We weren't the first. The Grand Spell had done this multiple times in the past. It had taken other worlds and added them to Kirios, creating a giant planet with several different races living there. I know that it sounds insane, but it's the truth. I wasn't the only one from Earth that was sent there in advance. Twenty-nine others were as well. Kirios is dangerous, and we're not prepared. Some of those twenty-nine might've died, but some, like me, will have returned with all that they have learned."

I grew silent, giving them time to take in all that I had said. It was a lot, I knew that. But I had to make them believe it.

"Aliens?" Alvarez whispered.

"In a way," I said. "Well, yes actually, exactly that. Though not in the way you imagine."

"The stars are different," Gomez added, while the others remained silent.

Of course, they would've noticed that. Hopefully that made my story more likely.

Father Sergio was the first one to break the quiet that followed. "I don't see what reason you would have to lie to us, even though your tale sounds unbelievable. We have all been seeking answers as to what the Light was."

"I have some proof," I added. "I have knowledge about Masks, how they work, and what they can do. Did any of you manifest your Masks yet? Or enter your soul space?"

"Manifest our Masks?" Martin asked.

I nodded. "Your Masks are physical objects, and they reside within you. You can enter that place and see information about them. You can also pull your Masks out. Once you reach your First Investment, which happens after you gain your tenth Carving, you will gain a trait which will grant you great increase to your power while you are wearing your Mask."

I saw them get interested at that, and so I started to guide them through the process. It would take a while, but it was one of the ways I had to convince them that I was telling the truth. My senses told me that it was the middle of the night. We still had some time before morning came and I had to leave. I might be willing to spill secrets, but some I wanted to keep to myself. I only hoped that I could convince them, because if I couldn't convince these four men, what chance did I have of convincing anybody else?

This had to work, for all our sakes.

Trust

It took around an hour for the first person at the table to figure out how to manifest their Mask. The rest followed a few minutes after. Their Masks were unimpressive, to say the least. Most of them seemed to be made out of wood, with very little or no adornments or engravings on them. That made sense. I doubted that any of them had reached even the Fifth Carving. The sole exception was the priest, whose Mask was white marble with a single golden line splitting it down the middle.

Each of them had also managed to enter their inner realms. They hadn't commented much on what they found inside, aside from the few whispers of excitement. The one called Martin cut them off. Obviously, he didn't want to talk in my presence, which was fine.

"Did you have an option to pick your Ornaments?" I asked as they were examining their Masks.

The priest glanced in my direction. "I was about to ask. What is that?"

"It is an addition to your Mask. It improves in a similar manner. Once you gain enough Carvings in it, and if it is synergistic with your Mask, it might consolidate in order to improve your Mask. So you should be very careful about which Ornaments you pick. Every Mask or Ornament needs specific things in order to gain more Carvings. What kind of actions grant you Investment is decided based on what type of a Mask it is. A Mask of the Hunter for example"— I glanced at the three hunters—"would obviously improve by performing actions related to hunting. It doesn't need to be just hunting animals, of course. It could be preparing for a hunt, or crafting tools or traps. It will all give you Investment."

"Ah," Father Sergio said. "I understand. It's not as the children had explained to us."

I smiled. "I assume that they used terms from their games, such as experience? That you would get it by hunting monsters and finishing rifts—dungeons as they called them? Yes?"

Everyone around the table nodded at that.

"There are some parallels, but this is not a game. A Mask is in a way a life profession. It grows and makes you stronger as you walk down the path of your profession, as you learn more and become more skilled."

"Oh." Gomez blinked. "That makes a lot more sense than all that Class bullshit the kids talked about."

"Language," Father Sergio said offhandedly, as his eyes were glued to the marble Mask in the palm of his hand.

"Sorry, Father." Gomez scratched at the back of his head.

"You said that all of this"—Father Sergio waved a hand around them—"the changes, the monsters in the woods, that all of it's a result of a magical spell?"

I took a deep breath. "In the simplest terms, yes. Though to call it a magical spell doesn't do justice to what it really is. As I've said before, with all due respect, Father, you should consider it a god in all but name. The Grand Spell was created tens of thousands years ago, by a being that was unmatched in power. He created it as a tool to prevent something horrible, a malevolent force that was expanding toward his world. And it has grown since its creation, becoming something that is able to reach out across the stars, perhaps even across time and space, and take entire worlds and incorporate it into its own, as it has done with Earth. We are now just a single continent on Kirios, one out of seven." I paused, remembering what happened just before I was sent back. There were two sources of light that heralded the arrival of a new world. Shadow believed that it meant that two worlds had been added at once this time. "Eight, perhaps. Each one the home-world of another race."

I saw Father Sergio's eyes bore into mine, and then he asked a question.

"I assume that you met these other races, during your time there. That what you know comes from them?"

I nodded. "Yes, I met one," I said. Technically it was two, but Saia wasn't from Kirios.

"Just one?" Martin asked.

I nodded. "When the light arrived, myself, and I assume other Exemplars, were given location options to pick. The place I picked was a jungle that wasn't settled."

"You said that each continent was the homeworld of one race," Martin commented.

I nodded. "The Ish Vimza, the name of the continent I landed on, is what remains of the original world of Kirios. The only thing that lives there now are monsters, corrupted animals that each have more strength than an Adult vampire."

That revelation made them pull back slightly. They exchanged looks with each other, but most glanced in the direction of Father Sergio, who nodded. I forced myself not to react, something about the gesture made bells ring in my head, but I kept it to myself for now.

"It seems that you've been telling the truth," Martin said with narrowed eyes. "Some of it, at least."

I tilted my head. "Do you need more proof to see that we are no longer part of Earth? Are the two moons in the sky above us not proof enough?"

One of them, the brown-haired Ramiro Alvarez, chuckled, and then the burly man next to him, Gomez, elbowed him and gave him a look with his dark eyes. Alvarez gave me a sheepish look, before he schooled his expression.

"It is proof that something has changed," Martin answered. "But there could be a hundred more explanations for it. Not that I'm accusing you of lying, of course," he added as my expression narrowed on him. "I'm sure that you believe it."

Gomez elbowed him again, this time more forcibly. "Can you please try not to offend the vampire?" he whispered in his ear. Martin's expression changed immediately. Perhaps he forgot, or he just got comfortable over the couple of hours that we spoke.

I smiled. "I'm not offended," I said out loud, and Gomez blanched, probably realizing that I could hear his whispers from the other side of the table. "It is a lot to take in, I understand."

The priest cleared his throat and exchanged a look with Martin, something passing between them that I didn't quite catch.

"I apologize for their behavior. It has been a stressful month, for all of us, I believe," Father Sergio said.

I nodded. "That it has." I could tell that they were all tired. It was the middle of the night for them, and I didn't want to keep them awake too long. There was danger outside of their church, and they had to be rested in order to survive. I stood up. "I think that you need some time to talk amongst yourselves, to digest what I've told you. With your permission, I will return tomorrow night. There is much that I'd like to know about the situation in the area."

"You're leaving?" Martin asked, almost surprised.

Father Sergio stood up as well. "We have rooms in the basement with no windows. It isn't much, but you could stay down there."

The others didn't look too enamored by the suggestion, but I just smiled. "Thank you for the offer, Father. But we don't know each other well enough for either one of us to trust the other that much."

I had to keep up some appearances at least. An Adult vampire would never sleep anywhere that wasn't surrounded by their human servants. Perhaps only in the most dire circumstances, which these did somewhat fit. But still, there were things that I wanted to do, secrets that I wasn't ready to reveal.

Father Sergio nodded, then approached me. He took my hands in his and bowed his head. "Thank you, again, for bringing our young Felix home. We've all lost too much. It gladdens my heart to see that there is still humanity left in us all. We'll expect you tomorrow night then."

His use of the word *humanity* was poignant, but I understood what he meant. I bowed in return.

"Until tomorrow night."

Ornament of the Revelator — No Investment; Fifth Carving

I left the church, and I made my way into the forest at top speed, gaining distance easily. I'd gained a single Carving for my revelations to the people in the church. I had expected it. By now I knew what gave me the Investment. I didn't get any new skills, but that I didn't expect. Shadow had made it clear that two skills per Investment tier is the most common occurrence, though there were exceptions, as my Mask was the proof for. But according to Shadow, that depended on the quality of Investment one gained.

Once I was far enough away, I stopped and found a place to take a seat on a nearby root. "So?" I asked as I pulled the backpack from my shoulder and pulled out my bottle filled with blood.

I took a sip, trying not to grimace at the poor taste of it, as Saia shifted from my wrist into her drone form. The tiny dragon rested on my knee and looked up at me with her glowing eyes.

"Feedback: I have done as you asked, here are their lists."

My vision flickered, and two windows appeared, showing me the Masks of the two people whose hands I shook. I wished that I had managed to touch the others too, but I didn't want to appear too suspicious. I had instructed Saia to use her [Inspect] engram if she got the chance, and she had done as I've asked.

I turned my attention to the windows.

Martin Perez

Hunter (Physical, Esoteric):
No Investment; Third Carving

Attributes:
Physical: F
Weave: F
Esoteric: E

Skills:
[Track]

Sergio Rodriguez

Speaker (Esoteric):
No Investment; Fourth Carving

Attributes:
Physical: F
Weave: F
Esoteric: E

Skills:
[Hear Truth]

Well, that made some sense at least. I had noticed them looking at the priest. They probably knew that he had a skill that let him verify the truth of things. I didn't know how the skill worked, but he had seemed the most accepting of my words. That was good, actually, as it gave my words more credence. I tried to remember whether I had outright lied at any point, but it had been a long few hours. I hoped that I hadn't said anything that would've actually made me suspect in their eyes.

Still, there were more interesting things, surprising things. Their attributes for one. From what Shadow had told me, each race had its own advantages, and some had greater advantages than others. The Oni-yi for example, tended to have a high D rating of strength even before they gained their Masks, while Elves usually had high E's or D's for both the Weave and Esoteric attributes as they had an affinity. Compared to the Harpiem that started out with an F rating across the board, they had a clear advantage.

The attributes revealed things about the our race. My Physical and Esoteric had both been rated as a C a result of my vampire nature, while my Weave was F. I had zero aptitude for the magical parts of the Source. Both of them had an E rating for the Esoteric, which was . . . impressive, if I understood things properly.

"Thank you, Saia," I said as I put the bottle back into my backpack. I had a few hours of the night still. I had planned on hunting for more blood and Investment, but I also wanted to update Shadow about everything that had happened. "Can you keep watch?"

Saia tilted her head and then flew above me onto a branch. I closed my eyes and focused, pulling myself inside my soul space.

Shadow wasn't in the main room, but somehow I realized that I could sense where he was. I glanced down at Saia, the other part of her, or the main part. It was starting to be somewhat confusing, the fact that the real her was actually inside of me and not the drone that I interacted most often with.

I turned and headed into the Hallway of Doors, as I decided on calling it. I found Shadow's door and entered. I walked up the stairs carved into the narrow ledge of the mountain, the afternoon sun shining in the distance, and climbed up to the plateau above.

I found him sitting above, his back turned toward me. He was looking out at the clouds and mountain peaks stretching before us. I walked over and sat down next to him with my legs over the cliff.

"You came back so soon." Shadow turned to look at me, the side of his mouth quirked up into a half-smile. "Missed me?"

I returned his smile. "Yes," I said honestly. He was important to me, and I had never really had any friends. When I had to say goodbye to him, I didn't realize just how much I would miss him. To have him back, even if it was just a copy, a shadow of him, it meant the world to me. He was, as we had both agreed to, my family. "How are things in here? When I am not around?"

"Quiet," Shadow answered. "It is a strange state, I must admit. Almost like a slumber of kind. It is pleasant in a way. I get to rest." He grinned.

I was glad. I had hoped that it would be something like that. Having him run around inside my soul while I was outside was . . . well . . .

"I've returned Felix to his people," I said, then filled him in on what I learned.

Once I was done, he got a contemplative look on his face. "The chance that two people in the same area both had a rating of E for Esoteric is very small. Though, it could be that their race had more affinity with the Esoteric."

The same as I did, apparently. Perhaps my high rating with the Esoteric wasn't just because of my vampire nature. I was a human before, after all. The Esoteric was the *perfection in all things*. It was the knowledge and purpose given to a discipline. And humanity had gotten good at that. People devoted their lives to many things. There were masters on Earth who lived and breathed for their purpose. Perhaps the reason we all tended to always search for a purpose was the same reason we had such high ratings for Esoteric.

"Well, I'll try to [Inspect] more people, get more data," I added. Saia's drone nodded next to me. She did enjoy gathering data.

Shadow nodded. "What are you going to do now? You have found people, but you did not stay with them?"

I grimaced. "I didn't want to scare them too much. Vampires are not really accepted fully by humanity. Many see us as monsters hiding in the dark."

One of Shadow's ears twitched on top of his head. "Is that truly it? You know that you have precious little time before portals open and the people of Kirios arrive. You need to build a kingdom, a bulwark to stand against them. You have no time to waste."

"I . . ." I paused. I knew what it was. Of course I did, even though I tried to pretend like I was in control of everything. I was scared of trusting other people.

It had taken a lot for me to open up to Shadow even, perhaps not in time, but a lot had happened. Through life or death situations, trust was built between us. These people were strangers to me, and yet I needed them. I needed to learn more about the situation in the world, and they were my only leads.

"Well," Shadow said after I didn't answer. "If you need time, you need time. Though I would urge you to take them under your wing. You will need as many people as you can gather."

"I don't even know where to start really. I know that I said that I would do this, but now that I am here, it seems like such a daunting task."

"Strength is usually a good start," Shadow said.

I gave him a look.

"What?" he asked, his tails waving behind him. "It is. You must accept this. You follow the Heart of Azure and Scarlet now. You must carve your way forward regardless of what stands in your way. That is what it means to be part of our family, we who live Beneath the Light of the Broken Moon."

I swallowed, unable to get the words past my lips. I turned and looked out at the clouds. I took a deep breath and steeled myself, I had to do this. Even if it meant doing things that people would curse me for. I wanted to save people, save us from what was coming. Give us a chance to grow and keep what was ours, as much as it was possible, at least. *Vae Victis*, I reminded myself.

"Speaking of," Shadow interjected. "Did you give any thought to your vow to the Way? The sacrifice?"

I blinked. "I have, actually. It was partly why I came," I said. "It occurred to me while I was in the church."

He raised an eyebrow and looked at me expectantly.

"How complicated can these vows be? Does it matter even?"

Shadow tilted his head. "As complicated or as simple as you want them to be. What matters the most is the intensity of your sacrifice. If you give up something important, your connection to the Way will grow faster and will be stronger; if you give up little, you will gain little."

I nodded. "What if I made a vow to never drink blood from a sapient being, from other humans or the races of Kirios, unless it was freely given? And if I made a vow to always give something in return for it, a deal, where I do for them a task or give them something that they would value and agree to, in return for the blood?"

"You said that you need blood to survive?" Shadow said.

I nodded. "Yes, I can live off animal blood for a long while, but eventually I would need human blood. And I suspect the blood of any other sapient. Your blood did the same thing that human blood does for me. I don't know what it is, but something in the blood of higher thinking beings is more nourishing for us."

Shadow frowned. "You also gain skills from blood. Making that sacrifice will rob you of the skills you could gain from your enemies. Unless you somehow got them to agree to give you blood. Though, you should be careful not to overstep and break the spirit of your vow. Torturing someone to get an agreement would break the spirit of the oath."

I took a deep breath. "That's what makes it a big sacrifice, right? I can still get skills from animals, but . . . I think that those will never be the same as skills granted to people."

Shadow scratched at the side of his cheek, thinking. "That could be a good starting vow, a strong one. And you can always add to the vow in the future. You would be sacrificing a source of power. The Way might see it and reward you with what you lost, if you can prove to it that you can follow that path."

I thought about it for a little while. "I think that I can, yes."

Shadow studied me for a moment, and then nodded. "Now, if you intend to focus on your connection with the Way, perhaps we should refresh your memory and train the Heart of Azure and Scarlet, for the little while at least."

I blinked, then glanced down at Saia. "Everything clear outside?"

Saia nodded her head. "Feedback: All clear."

I turned to my friend, my family, my teacher. "Yes, let's."

Awkward

The forest loomed around me, a dark and foreboding presence. I moved silently, the muscles in my legs burning with each step. A vampire really wasn't made for prolonged physical exertion. I decided that a break was in order. I sat down on the ground, leaned against a tree, and slipped the pack from my back to pull out my blood bottle. My eyes scanned the shadows for any sign of rifts or dangerous wildlife as I drank. It was the middle of the day, and already I felt exhausted. Less from the physical tiredness than from the mental.

Shadow had made me practice the two techniques of the Heart of Azure and Scarlet that he had taught me, the ***Veiled Mist Assault*** of the Scarlet Moon Style, and the ***Stalwart Mist*** of the Azure Moon Style. We hadn't talked much about anything other than training. I couldn't bring up the topic of the oncoming disaster that awaited humanity. I had made my decision, yet it felt like too difficult a task. What was it that made me think that I, a lonely little vampire girl, could save humanity?

In some moments, the doubt rose to the levels that made me feel so small. And then I remembered Shadow, his trust, the look in his eyes when he accepted me into his family. It made me feel like I was worth more than what my life had made me be.

Kirios was an opportunity for change, and I had decided to grab my life and be the one behind the wheel for once. But I knew what it was that held me back. Why I had run away from the church as soon as I saw an opportunity, why I didn't ask the burning questions that I wanted to. Because I was afraid to know the answers. Afraid to meet those who I served before. The people at the church might've known something about the cartel, and I should've asked. Even if the thought of standing in front of my sire and old master terrified me.

What would my sire even say if he saw me now? My eyes had changed, I was no longer a Fledgling but an Adult vampire. Would he still consider me a disappointment? Would he answer the questions that I wanted the answers to?

I took a deep breath and let all my emotions course through me. I suppressed nothing. Instead I stood up and entered the first Kata of the **Veiled Mist Assault**: *From the Mist, Strike*. I moved in quick bursts, letting the emotions guide my steps. It was so easy to surrender to it. It was as if the Kata knew what I needed from it. My mind quieted, my fears and desires whispered, and I listened.

I didn't know for how long I let the dance take me, but at the end I collapsed to one knee, breathing deeply, my sluggish blood struggling to provide my body with what it needed under the harsh light of the sun.

Saia returned and landed on the ground next to me.

"Query: Status report, Marianna?"

I chuckled, then glanced at her. "I'm fine, Saia," I said as I pushed myself up. I felt completely drained, so I moved to my pack to get more blood. I collapsed on the ground, and Saia made her way over to me and jumped on my knee.

"I know what I need to do," I said, feeling more resolved. I didn't need to hesitate. I made my choice back on Kirios. Arriving on Earth had thrown me for a loop. Seeing other people, humans, reminded me of my place in this world. But that Marianna, who served the cartel, that girl was gone. I stood in her place. A woman who had survived the jungles of Ish Vimza, who had fought monsters unlike anything Earth could imagine. A woman who knew secrets of this new world that not even its inhabitants did. A woman who had power.

There was no need for me to hesitate. I wasn't that weak little girl; I was strong.

I turned my attention to Saia. "What did you find?"

"Report: Several dozen different animal species, most of them avian. None appear to be a threat, but a lack of information makes that statement unreliable. I observed a medium-sized quadruped, a hunter, take down an avian animal from an ambush. That is the only animal in the area that I would offer caution of. Its fur was covered in dark spots."

"How large was it?"

Saia tilted her tiny head. "Feedback: Half the size of the final boss we encountered in the rift."

"A grown jaguar perhaps," I said. "They're the only animal that has such spots and could be found in this place. Though, with the way that Earth was shuffled around, it could be something else. Or the Source has mutated something to make it resemble a jaguar. Regardless, you're right. We should be cautious."

Shadow had warned me that every life on Earth would change, and not all in the same way, some in ways that he couldn't predict. Earth had no Source before. He couldn't anticipate what would happen once it settled.

I could already tell that the changes were . . . significant. The trees around me, for one, were a lot tougher than they used to be.

"Any sign of rifts in the area?" I asked.

Saia shook her head. "Feedback: Negative."

I grimaced. I wanted to find as many as I could and clear them. They were a resource that would give me more power, and one that I was sure would soon become very contested. They already were, if I went by what Felix told me about the raiders.

The sun in the sky started its descent, and I decided to take a few hours to rest before heading back to the church. It was time for me to take charge of my own fate.

I approached the church with a lit torch raised high above my head, with my serpent-tongue spear leaned on my other shoulder. I made no attempt at keeping my arrival a secret. There was no need for it. I noticed the man in the tower about the same time he noticed me. He kept his rifle ready, though he didn't point it in my direction. Quickly, though, he realized who I was. I'd told them to expect me, but I understood them being on alert. Saia was back on my wrist, masquerading as a strange silver band. I hoped that Felix hadn't spilled all my secrets. I had been forced to reveal things about myself that I hadn't expected to, but I still preferred to keep some cards close to my chest. I didn't know the rest of the people in the church, and even if they were trustworthy, I couldn't trust that they could keep my secrets from others, from enemies. And I was certain that I would be making enemies soon enough.

The man on watch in the tower, Gomez, if my eyes saw true, grabbed the ladder next to him, and I heard him make his way down.

I took the time to study the church's surroundings. It was obviously a piece of what had once been a town. There was an asphalt street just next to it and three single story buildings across from it, looking like small street stores, with signs and everything. One was a coffee shop, judging by the sign, while the one next to it was a convenience store, while the last one was a pharmacy. All three had metal roll-down shutters pulled over the entrances, all of which had signs of decay. The park in front of the church had a primitive fence surrounding a section of it, probably where they let their cattle out during the day.

As Gomez made his way down, I heard more movement. Someone else was in the nave of the church, though I couldn't recognize the whispering voices through the stone. Then, before the doors opened, a voice joined the others, this one much louder and recognizable.

"It's her, isn't it! Open the doors!" Felix's unmistakable voice yelled out.

I grinned as I heard the others chide him for his outburst, and more sounds waking up inside the church.

It didn't take long for the sounds of barricades being moved to fill the air, and soon after, the church doors opened.

I didn't take more than two steps inside before a flying missile hit me in the stomach. I had, of course, seen Felix coming. He managed to slip the old woman who tried to stop him, and now looked at him and me with terror in her eyes.

I smiled, being careful not to show my teeth, and patted Felix on top of his head.

"You came back!" he said.

"Of course I did," I told him.

The people in the church were looking at us with a wide variety of expressions. I knew that our talk the night before had done a lot to alleviate some of their fears. They had allowed me into the church again, after all. But I was still a vampire, and they were still humans. The world might've gotten completely thrown on its head, which was probably why they didn't run for the pitchforks the first time they saw me, but some distrust was to be expected.

I looked around as I gently made Felix let me go. The woman at the end of the room kept her hands spread, hiding three more kids behind her. All of them looked at me with wide eyes, with innocence and no fear. I heard them whisper to each other, things along the lines of "she's real." It wasn't hard for me to put things together. The children were wearing their pajamas, Felix included. They had probably snuck out to wait for me. And the woman standing next to them was obviously not happy.

Martin, Gomez, and Alvarez were to the side, pushing the barricades behind me to close the entrance, while Father Rodriguez stood across from me.

I inclined my head and greeted him first. "Father Sergio," I said as I entered the dimly lit church, my boots echoing off the stone walls. He faced me, his eyes filled with things that I couldn't interpret.

"Welcome. I trust that you didn't have much difficulty in the forest?"

I smiled, showing my teeth, reminding him of what I was.

"Not at all," I said, one hand on Felix's back as I led him back.

"See!" Felix yelled. "I told you she was real!"

I raised an eyebrow at him, then looked up.

The woman hissed at him. "Felix, get back here! You were supposed to be asleep."

He looked back at the woman with a rebellious look in his eyes.

"You must be Tita, yes?" I asked the woman, with a small smile.

The woman blinked, looking surprised that I knew her. I turned back to look at the troublemaker next to me.

"You wouldn't be making trouble for her, not after she was kind enough to look after you?" I narrowed my eyes at him.

He had the decency to look at least slightly ashamed. I glanced at the children, and saw their wide eyes transfixed on me, staring in wonderment. I felt my heart swell a little as they looked upon me with such innocence and trust that it made something inside of me ache. It wasn't just wonder that I saw; there was fear as well, though not of me. I recognized it in the way they stood, the way they watched the shadows and were seemingly always on alert. This world had already shown them that there were monsters around, that at any moment something could jump out of the shadows and eat them whole.

I wished that they hadn't been forced to learn that so soon.

"Uh," Tita started, but as soon as I met her gaze, she averted her eyes. "Come children, the grown-ups have a lot to talk about, and you should all be in bed."

She looked at Felix and hesitated. I pushed Felix ahead. "Go, I'm not going anywhere. There'll be time to talk tomorrow."

He narrowed his eyes. "How, when you are only here at night, and she"—he glared back at the old woman—"won't let us stay up. You promised to train me!"

The people around me reacted to that in various ways, from surprise to confusion. I smiled at him. At least he was keeping one of my secrets. "I'm sure that staying up for an hour or two after dusk wouldn't be too much of an inconvenience." I glanced at Father Rodriguez then at Tita. "Though, I do agree with them, proper sleep is important for developing bodies. And the world is a lot more dangerous place than it has ever been. You need to make sure to take advantage of the relative safety you now enjoy."

Felix looked like he wanted to argue for a moment, but then sighed and nodded his head. "Fine, tomorrow then?" he asked hopefully.

"We'll see," I said and nudged him forward.

He walked over and rejoined his friends. Tita gave me one last distrustful look, then walked away, ushering them into the back of the building.

"Forgive her distrust," Father Rodriguez said as he walked over to me. "She is a nun, and her belief doesn't allow for vampires to be part of God's plan."

I nodded. There were two camps in the religious communities. Those who accepted the vampires and shifters as God's children, and those that looked at them as the spawn of the devil. Even though the first camp was the official one, and was the stance of the big churches across the world, something that the vampires had worked very hard to accomplish over the last few decades, some people still hadn't accepted it as truth.

"Your revelations about the nature of the world and this Grand Spell haven't made things easier," he said.

"I understand, it is a lot to take in, for anyone." I looked around at the other three men, seeing the bags under their eyes. They hadn't slept much, which was understandable. I had probably shattered their world view. Though, it did appear as if they trusted my words. Something to do with the priest's skill, no doubt.

"That it is," Martin said as he walked over.

"You've had some time to think, and talk over things on your own?" I asked.

The men exchanged looks, then nodded. "We have, and we were hoping to have a discussion with you about it. There are things that you should probably know."

I raised my eyes at that, and he opened his mouth to respond. Before he could, the priest interrupted whatever it was that Martin was about to say. He gestured at the table. "Let us take a seat. We should be comfortable for this conversation, I think."

The unease around the table lasted for a few minutes, filled with idle chatter. I asked them if they had difficulties during the day, and they responded by asking if I had trouble finding a place to hide. I avoided outright lying to them, not wanting to make Father Rodriguez distrustful of me.

Finally, the priest cleared his throat.

"We've talked with Felix, and he's confirmed much of what you've told us. Though, it was obvious that he is hiding some things on your behalf." His gaze turned intense.

I was glad that Felix had kept my secrets, though I wasn't surprised that they had seen through it; they had the [Hear Truth] skill, after all. "I'm keeping stuff from you, of course, the same as you're keeping things from me." Martin made to argue, but I gave him a look. The priest's truth-seeing skill counted as a secret in my book.

"But we're still getting to know each other, it's not meant as an insult toward you," I said.

Father Rodriguez sighed then nodded, his hand coming up to rub at his chin. "Yes, you're right, of course. Still, I don't know if we'll have the time for that. There is a lot of danger in this new world of ours."

I met his eyes as he grew quiet. I knew that better than any of them. I didn't know what they went through while I was on Ish Vimza, but I knew that it had to be horrible, even if it probably wasn't as dangerous as my journey was.

I decided that someone had to start being more open, more truthful, so I spoke. "I wanted to talk to you about something," I said, and felt their attention land on me like a physical thing. "Felix told me about your encounters with a group of people. Raiders he called them. Felix and I encountered them too."

They all blinked at that, and exchanged looks that I couldn't identify.

"Raiders?" Martin asked. "Oh, wait, you mean the people from the base, the other survivors."

Immediately, I got a bad feeling in my gut. The way that he spoke about them didn't match up at all with how Felix had explained things to me. "I'm going to assume that they haven't been pressuring you for goods?"

"What?" Martin blinked, surprised. "No, well, I mean, sure somewhat. But we are all trying to survive. We trade with them when they come through. Is that what Felix told you?" Martin shook his head. "That foolish kid, I swear, the things that get into that little head of his. Wait." He turned to look at Gomez for a moment then continued.

"Was he there the last time? When that asshole came around asking for more supplies?"

Gomez tilted his head. "You know what, I think that I remember some of the kids being outside for that."

Martin grimaced. "I guess that we did get a bit heated back then. One of the people with them was a real piece of shit." He paused, then glanced at the priest and grimaced. "Sorry, Father."

"No, no, you are right in your description of the man," Father Rodriguez said, then he looked at me. "Why do you ask?"

"Well." This was going to be awkward. "I killed three of their people."

The silence around the table that followed my statement was, indeed, quite awkward.

Offer

The heavy scent of incense wafting through the air mixed with the muted glow of candlelight, casting flickering shadows across the worn stone walls. I sat at the head of the long wooden table, my muscular frame tense, eyes darting between the faces of the priest and the hunters gathered around me even as I tried to keep all emotion from my face. The silence was suffocating.

The hunters shifted uncomfortably in their seats, their gazes seemingly avoiding mine. I could almost taste their fear, though I kept my face calm. The priest was the only one that didn't avoid my gaze, he steepled his fingers together and stared at me intently.

"Killed them, for what reason, if I may ask?" he asked, his voice a gravelly whisper.

"Felix and I were leaving the dungeon—the rift—and he went ahead of me, I followed a short while after. By the time I left the rift they had him. They were roughing him up," I replied, staring right back at him. "They accused us of stealing their rift, and demanded all of our possessions. I refused, and one of them attacked me." I reached up to the side of my face and traced a line from my temple to my jaw. "Cut me across the face. It was an attack intended to kill, that would've killed almost anybody else."

I could feel the eyes of the hunters weighing on me, curiosity and dread mingling in the air like the thick scent of incense. It was to be expected. I was what most people feared, the monster in the night.

I waited patiently in silence for a response.

"Did you have to kill them?" The priest raised a thin eyebrow, his gaze never leaving mine.

I tilted my head, seeing the knowledge in his eyes. I had come to that same conclusion myself, after I'd killed them. I was a vampire, far stronger than they'd been. Killing them wasn't a necessity.

"They made a choice," I said slowly, never breaking the eye contact with the priest. "And I made one as well. I admit, my understanding of who these people were was clouded by what Felix told me. But ultimately, I don't think that it would've mattered if I knew more. They were aggressive, and they attacked me first, despite knowing what I was. You do not attack a jaguar and then expect it not to maul your face back."

A collective shudder ran down the spines of the hunters, and for a moment, I allowed myself the smallest of smirks. They might have been skilled in their own right, but they would never understand the raw power that coursed through my veins. It was why they feared me.

"What did Felix tell you, exactly?" the priest finally asked, his voice betraying a hint of unease.

"That these people have been extorting you, that they have demanded things, claimed all the dungeons in this area," I told him.

Father Rodriguez sighed. "We've been keeping the children away from them, not because they have been doing what Felix had told you, but because we didn't want them to overhear the matters that we discussed. We didn't want to burden them with the weights that we carry. It seems like that has allowed their imagination to run rampant. Perhaps we have erred." He shook his head then met my eyes. "I'm not the one that can grant you forgiveness, or who can even offer any judgment of the righteousness of your actions. That right is God's alone."

I didn't believe as he did, but I was grateful that he didn't see it fit to judge. "I am not regretful for what I did, but perhaps I could've handled it differently. It is done, I hope that it will not make your lives more difficult. That was not my intention."

Father Rodriguez shook his head. "They lose people all the time in the wild. It is an unfortunate reality of our new world."

I nodded. "Who are these people, and what is your relationship with them, if I may ask?" I asked.

The priest turned to Martin, and something seemed to pass between them, and then the hunter spoke.

"They are survivors, like all of us. They are based somewhere to the east, in one of the places that has been shuffled around, a piece of the desert with an abandoned military base on it. We first met one of their scout groups a couple of weeks ago. They are sending people to gather other survivors, to watch for threats, and gather resources. They also have groups that are geared toward completing dungeons. Felix or one of the other kids probably overheard the conversation regarding dungeons." He sighed. "We've agreed to let them know about any that we find."

I tilted my head; it seemed like I had encountered a few bad apples. The memories I experienced from them had told me the truth of it, though I did lack context. The hunter took a breath and continued.

"There's no extortion." Martin shook his head. "But some of the people we've dealt with were hard people, which is understandable. We are all under an immense amount of stress."

"Ah." That made sense. I hadn't considered what the people I met had encountered. For all I knew they had been forced to fight with other survivors. They had looked at me with distrust as soon as they met me, demanded things of me, but the stress and their previous experiences could've colored their world view, though they seemed to feel a little too entitled. I pushed those thoughts away. The matter was done, in the past and buried already.

Martin exchanged a look with Father Rodriguez, and then the priest nodded before turning to look at me. "We've been trying to get them to take us back to their base, but we've been unable to come to an agreement."

"I thought that you said they were looking for survivors?" I asked.

Martin nodded. "They are. They've been bringing them all back to their base. There are supposed to be hundreds of people there, maybe more. The issue with us is the size of our group, the kids, and our location."

I frowned. "What do you mean?"

Martin cleared his throat. "Their base is somewhere to the east, with only two ways to get there that they know of. They've been losing scouting groups when they sent them in any other direction, but both of those routes they know about are difficult. One of them follows the road south that leads next to the city, which is overrun by monsters and is incredibly dangerous. The other leads through a mountain pass that has an unknown monster nesting in it. From what they've told us, the monster stirs if too many people move through it. That's why they've been limiting the groups they send out to two or three people at most. They say that it is too risky to try to take our entire group through the pass, and trying the roads is the same. We've been attempting to negotiate to have us go in small groups, but they are days away on foot, and negotiations are hard when we can only send messages back and forth in person."

Father Rodriguez leaned forward, then spoke. "That's what we wanted to talk with you about. We obviously don't know anything about you except what we can see and what Felix told us. But I have a good feeling about you," he said slowly. "You helped him when you had no reason to, and in these difficult times that is more than most would do."

I tilted my head inquisitively.

"We'd like to ask you to escort us to the base. We don't have much to offer in terms of payment, our rifle perhaps, as such things are rare now. But we are willing to negotiate."

I blinked. I hadn't expected the request. Though, perhaps I should've. They were isolated in the wild, surrounded by beasts and the dangers slipping out of the dungeons that belong on other worlds, and they had kids.

And besides, my plans required me to make contact with more people. A bigger group of survivors would be the perfect place to start. Still, I didn't immediately give them my answer. "I will need to think about it. I will give you a response tomorrow."

The people around the table looked relieved, but also hopeful. They had expected me to reject them, I realized. It only spoke of how desperate they were.

I didn't linger in the church. Instead I walked back into the woods. I wanted to discuss this with both Saia and Shadow. It would put me on the right path, but I also had an idea about my personal oath to the Way.

A little while later I found myself back inside my soul's space, standing on the plateau with Shadow and Saia next to me.

"You want to request blood as payment for escorting them?" Shadow repeated what I had told him.

I nodded. "I think that an oath of never taking blood that is not freely given could perhaps hinder me somewhat. When they asked, I thought that perhaps an Oath of Obligation was more appropriate. Not just for blood, but for everything that I do."

Shadow tilted his head. "Explain."

"Before I do, I'm curious. You said that the Way can somehow measure the weight of what I sacrifice, yes? Does that mean that it is sentient?"

"It—" He opened his mouth then closed it. "I guess that I can't talk about that, hmm . . . Well, let's see." He paused. It seemed like the Grand Spell didn't allow him to speak on the topic, which in itself was an answer of a kind.

"In the time before the Grand Spell, on the YoKai-ni homeworld, there was a thing that we called karma. Some people followed schools of being that were based on the ideas that the universe keeps count of our actions, and that it always seeks to balance things. It was not an easy way to power, but it led many people to devising powerful oaths to themselves and the Way."

It was interesting that he was allowed to say that, but then again it was knowledge from before the Grand Spell found the YoKai-ni. Still, he was trying to guide me, in some way. I was familiar with the concept of karma, though I didn't think that I would want to wrap myself in a life where I always had to keep account of things I did. I would much prefer something else, though some concepts of karma could be useful here.

I took a deep breath and then gave him my thoughts and ideas.

"An Oath of Obligation," I began, pacing around the platform as I formulated my thoughts, "would be a life creed dedicated to always clearing debts, known or unknown, with the parties I interact with. It would mean adhering to the principle of equivalent exchange or at least what I believe someone's debt is worth. For example, getting blood from someone in exchange for a service. They obviously wouldn't know that their blood would grant me use of their skill, so the weight of how much I have to pay for it should reflect that. In essence, for everything that I gain or take, I must offer something of equal value in return."

Saia tilted her head. "Statement: The concept of equivalent exchange was known to the Ke Erzi. It was one of the cornerstones of their civilization."

"It is interesting," Shadow said slowly. "It could be a good sacrifice, a good covenant between you and the Way. It would have the limitation of always having to give and take, living a life in that way would be following a creed. The Way would recognize that. You would never be able to accept a gift, nor would you ever be able to forgive a slight. If people found that out, they could use it to manipulate your actions."

I thought about that. "But I wouldn't need to let anyone know that I operated on those principles. If someone gives me a gift, I could just do something for them without them knowing. It is a covenant between myself and the Way, right?"

Shadow rubbed his chin thoughtfully. "Yes. You said that you did not want to cut yourself from the ability to take blood from your enemies, yes? This oath would make it so that you would be required to give your enemies something if you take their blood."

"Not if they attacked me first or have demonstrated a desire to harm me or those that I consider important. That would incur debt, and taking blood from them would be balancing the scales."

Shadow nodded. "That could work, yes."

"Or," I started, "in the case where I killed or drank from someone unprovoked, I could just repay the debt I incurred to their family or friends."

"And if they have none?" Shadow asked.

I frowned, then thought about it. "It is still a sacrifice that I offer to the Way, right? I don't really need to pay it to them. Would I be able to pay the price to the Way itself?"

Shadow blinked. "I do not know. It certainly seems possible, though I have no knowledge of how someone would do that."

I crossed my arms and narrowed my eyes. I could feel the pieces of my oath to the Way sliding into place within me. I felt like I was on the right track. I didn't need to figure it all out right now. An oath to the Way was something that I could build upon through my life. I didn't need to limit myself fully immediately. Though, the greater the sacrifice, the more power the Way would grant me in return, and the more it would empower the Heart of Azure and Scarlet.

And power was what I needed the most right now. I was in a race against the world itself, and if I wanted to save as much of the Earth as I could, I had to pick up the pace.

* * *

As the dawn approached, I walked through the woods, searching for rifts, or animals to hunt. I didn't have much, or rather any, success. The forest had grown quiet, which bothered me. What the church people had told me was interesting as well. The danger was all around, and I could see why they would want to get out of here as soon as possible. I would accept their offer, though I would need more information about it. I looked up, seeing the dark sky brightening slowly. It was too late for me to return without revealing that I could walk in sunlight, and I didn't want to do that yet.

So, I turned, trying to choose a direction to explore. Before I had a chance to make my decision, I heard a loud noise echoing all around me. I froze as I recognized it: a gunshot, coming from the direction of the church.

Without hesitation, I rushed toward it, running ahead of the sun rising behind me.

Tragedy

I ran back toward the church, racing ahead of the rising sun. I could feel it coming from behind me and knew that the moment it rose above the horizon my strength would be diminished. A few more gunshots echoed ahead of me, and my heart dropped. I could hear the noise, fighting and animal sounds, I could feel the ground shaking from something that made me feel a sense of dread. The stench was the next thing that I noticed, a putrid smell of waste and decay, of blood. Then I crested a hill and saw ahead.

The sight chilled me to the bone. The church was under attack, being swarmed by what looked like thousands of rats the size of small dogs. They were black and brown and gray and some even white. A sea of wriggling creatures that seemed to have no end. A horde set on swarming the church. Their fur was mangy, their heads filled with sharp teeth, and their red eyes seemingly wild. Some of them had mutated growths on their heads that looked almost like horns. Some looked as if they had mutated into something that wasn't even the same species.

The Source had changed them, and probably in more ways than I could see at a glance. I knew that the mutations that happened when a world was integrated weren't always uniform. Animals of the same family could evolve in different ways based on their environment. This was the birth of a new animal species. Not all of them would survive, but some would thrive.

The rats were climbing the walls, breaking through the holes in the barred windows. They were climbing the tower, and I watched as the man on top fired another bullet into the horde ineffectively. The rats climbed into the tower, and I watched as one of the hunters, Alvarez, attempted to run away, to climb down the stairs. The rats swarmed him, and his scream of anguish and horror filled the air, followed by the sounds of a body crashing through the tower to hit the ground below.

The entrance to the church was broken, the barricade seemingly not enough to hold against the swarm of rats. They had punched or perhaps eaten a hole at the base of the entrance, tall enough for a child to pass through. More screams came from inside the church, and without thinking or planning, I ran for the entrance. The rats were in my way, and they noticed me immediately. Hundreds of them turned in my direction in a synchronized maneuver that sent a shiver down my spine. I felt something at the back of my mind, something familiar. An imprint in the Way—they were using a skill, though I had no idea what it did. In front of me, red eyes followed my every move. I ignored them as they charged at me, and just as some leapt toward me, I jumped forward as well.

With [Mist Step] the world turned grayscale, and I flowed through the air as mist. The rats smashed through me, each one that passed through my mist like a physical blow, but I persevered. My jump carried me to the entrance, the hole that they made. As mist, I passed through the low opening and then re-formed inside.

The nave of the church was covered in blood, rats, and the stench of death. I saw a body covered by the rats, each of them fighting for a scrap of meat, as they burrowed into its stomach and ate the flesh from the inside, tearing each other apart in their frenzy. The rats all around me froze as I re-formed, and all of them turned in my direction—again I felt a skill at work. I didn't have the time to ponder what it could be as they headed my way.

I could hear fighting deeper inside the building. I had to move fast. I swung my weapon, the serpent-tongue spear whistled as it slashed through the air, cutting the rats on the ground. I didn't pause for even a moment. I whirled, slashing with my weapon close to the ground, killing scores with every step and swing. I let my anger flow through me as the Scarlet Moon Form filled me, and I moved straight to the third Kata, *Advance, Whirling Mist.*

I was a whirlwind of death, rats dying all around me as I made my way through the nave, swinging my weapon low to the ground. I stepped through the door leading deeper into the building and entered a narrow hallway filled with rats already rushing toward me. I swung my weapon to kill a rat that tried to jump at me, and my weapon hit the wall as I failed to stop my momentum fast enough. I grimaced; I didn't have the room to swing my weapon here. Making a quick decision, I threw it ahead like a spear, hitting one of the biggest rats straight through its back and nailing it to the ground.

"Dagger!" I yelled as I pulled out the knife from my waist. Saia flowed from my wrist and into my other hand, taking the form of a long dagger.

A rat jumped for my face, and I stabbed it through the stomach with Saia; with a flick of my wrist I sent the corpse flying behind me as I stomped on another that went for my ankles. I jumped ahead and dropped with my feet straight on top of a handful, crushing them beneath my full weight. My leg slipped from one as blood spilled in all directions as if a balloon had popped. I was forced forward into a roll to avoid falling. I lashed out with both hands, cutting the rats as I passed. The momentum took me over a rat and back to my feet. As soon as I took another step, my [Mist Step] returned. I didn't use it. Instead I ran toward the sounds of fighting ahead.

At the end of the hallway was a door that had been blown from one of its hinges, making it lie sideways on the frame, which allowed the rats to enter through the hole on the bottom. Before I reached it, a rat jumped on my back, and immediately bit into my shoulder. I sidestepped and turned, crashing into the wall and splattering the rat in between, cracking the stone wall with my strength. I felt the bones break and heard a quick squeak of pain before it died, and its blood and gore splattered all over me. The rats on the ground took advantage and pounced on me. One jumped on my leg and bit hard before I stabbed it through the neck and pulled it off. Another bit my ankle, and a third jumped at my face. I growled and moved, jumping at the door with all of my might. I smashed into it, the wood splintered around me, and the door was thrown off the remaining hinge.

I hit the ground with it, crushing the rats that were in front of it with what remained of the door and my weight. I saw that I was in a living room of a kind, with a kitchen attached to the right. Furniture had been pushed to the end of the room, clearly in haste, where another hallway led deeper into the building where screams, yells, and sounds of fighting could be heard. Another dead body lay in that hallway, leaned against the wall, a man who I couldn't recognize on account of his lack of face, and a head that was swaying loosely across the body's chest. It was still connected to the neck only by a thin strip of skin, barely three fingers wide. I could see the severed spine sticking out, flesh that looked like it had been rent apart. The rats had eaten the skin, and I could see a tail of one waving around out of the throat hole in the neck, as a rat tried to burrow into the stomach. A dozen rats that were in the process of eating him turned, their red eyes flashing with eerie intelligence, and then they charged at me.

They jumped at me, and though I managed to cut two of them out of the air, three landed on me, immediately going on an attack, tearing my skin with claws and biting chunks of me in an instant. My blades cut through them with no resistance, but for each one I killed, another was there to take his place. I got to my feet and grabbed a rat that got tangled in my hair, pulling it out along with a piece of my scalp. I stomped, crushing a rat with a sickening crunch of shattering bones and breaking the floorboards in the process. Then as I managed to get a bit of room to breathe, I leaped over the barricade.

More rats poured into the room from behind, following after me, but I continued running forward, stomping on the rats in the hallway, kicking them as I passed. I advanced and saw three doors on the other end, the wood broken into pieces, as if something big had smashed through them and into the rooms. Bodies were on the ground in front of the open door to the right, or mounds that appeared to be bodies—I couldn't quite see, as rats were swarming them. Small bodies, children's bodies. I didn't stop to look. Ahead, inside the room, I could hear sounds of a battle.

I ran forward, heading to the doors at the end of the hallway. A woman's body, the nun—Tita was being torn apart, her nun's clothes ripped and bloody. Her lower half was on the door threshold. Rats had pieces of her in their teeth, pulling and fighting with others of their kind for a pound of flesh. Her upper half was hidden from my sight as it was half inside the room. Before I had the chance to take more in, the rats were swarming me. They rushed, grabbing my legs and biting. I kicked one, blasting its head off in a shower of gore that splattered all over the wall. I whirled and struck out in a sweeping kick, sending a couple more flying. I was cutting with my daggers, my arms lashing out at the rats that tried to jump at me, killing and killing with no end in sight. I stepped to the side and jumped toward the open door.

Inside, I saw a man fighting, the hunter, Martin. He was on his knees, a machete in his hand was slashing up and down as rats tore pieces of him away in a frenzy. His other arm was hanging limply at his side, covered in blood. Rats were climbing all over him, gnawing, biting and scratching. His blood was flowing freely, and its scent made the **thirst** ache inside of my stomach.

I stepped into the room as a dozen rats jumped on my back, and I growled. They tore my clothes, they ripped my skin, scratching at my back, biting my ankles and thighs. They were climbing over me, a horde of animals, and the noise they made filled my ears, drowning out everything. The stench of them made my stomach churn. The pain of their attacks stabbed through me. I reached for my skill and let it out. A [Debilitating Wave] surged out of me. A wave of red energy expanded in all directions, and the rats toppled to the ground, twitching as the energy stunned them.

I stumbled forward as my right leg nearly gave out beneath me; a rat had gnawed on my tendon. I glanced down and saw a mess of flesh that was knitting together slowly. I grimaced and grabbed one of the rats from the ground, then bit into it and drained it of blood as quickly as I could, trying not to think of the horrible stench that came from the wretched vermin. I walked as the foul blood filled my mouth, and reached a dresser that was nestled next to the door and with both arms pushed it over the entrance, blocking it. My skill had spread through the walls and into the hallway, but I could already hear more rats coming. The dresser wouldn't hold them for long, but long enough. I turned and reached Martin, who was sitting on the ground, leaned against the wall and holding his bleeding stomach. He couldn't move much; my skill had affected him too. I could hear his breath hitching in his chest, the slowing of his heartbeat. He was about to die.

Before I could say anything, his hazy eyes focused on me, and he whispered, "Forest." He tried to raise his hand up at the window above him. It was open, the boards removed from it and placed to the side. Not torn away like what I had seen before. "Kids," he added weakly.

I saw a swarm of rats heading toward the trees. I understood his words immediately. I made to jump out of the window, then paused and looked down at Martin. He was going to die. There was nothing that I could do to save him. His injuries were already too severe, and he was bleeding out. It was not the right moment, but I had made a choice, an agreement with myself, a covenant, an oath to the Way—my way of life, my school of being.

I owed these people nothing, I came to help them because . . . I didn't know exactly why. Because I had saved Felix? Because I felt a little bit responsible for them, not on a personal level, but because I wanted to help humanity as a whole.

The death around me didn't bother me. I was used to that. I had seen bodies butchered worse. What bothered me was that it was so sudden, that the world had changed so much that there was no safety at all. That there was no reason but the will of animals in a frenzy.

I knelt next to the man as the rats twitched on the ground, slowly regaining their faculties.

"You are dead," I told him.

His eyes showed me that he knew that already. His stomach was open. Something had ripped it apart, the wound didn't look like it had been made by the rats around us. They were too small for the kind of damage I could see.

"You want me to save them," I continued. I wanted to go after them, to save them. But, I also wanted power. To never feel weak again. It was time for me to fully commit to Shadow's teachings, to embrace this new world and all that came with it. Perhaps it was selfish, but I had a goal—*Vae Victis*.

"In return for me going after them, saving as many as I can, and granting you a quick death, I want your blood," I offered.

His eyes looked at me for a moment, then glanced at the rats. He had to know that his choices were either he got torn apart by the rats or by me. He made his choice.

I leaned forward and bit his neck, I drained his blood with haste, and felt his death come. Memories flashed before my eyes.

Two people arrived at the church, scouts from the military base. They yelled warnings. He rounded the others, and they prepared. Father Rodriguez and Tita went to wake up the kids, and then the rats arrived. Everything turned chaotic, filled with screams and blood and death. He retreated. They tried to get the kids out of the window, but they were overrun. Three shapes entered the room, larger than rats, walking on two legs. Blurs in the dark room. Two jumped out of the window, while one jumped and its claws cut into his abdomen before jumping out of the window as well. Most of the rats followed, and he was left to die alone.

I pulled out of the memories as the rats starting getting up to their feet, my skill wearing off. My wounds healed faster as Martin's blood filled my stomach, stronger than that of the rat I had drank from before. His memories told me that there was something out there that he didn't recognize, that I didn't recognize either. Some animals from Kirios perhaps, or maybe just a more mutated version of the rats. The dresser was shaking, was being pushed forward and rats wiggling through. I jumped out of the window with [Mist Step] and landed a dozen steps away in the clearing behind the church. Immediately after re-forming, I started running, following the rats. The sun rose behind me, and I felt the dawn sap my strength. I tightened my jaw and pushed forward. I had made an agreement, and I was going to do all in my power to keep it.

Reality

The **thirst** within my blood turned lethargic, slow. The power that it pumped through my veins lessened under the sun's touch. The blood I just drank burned inside of my stomach, its power spent to heal me, but now that burn turned to barely an itch inside of me. The **thirst** was now just barely feeding on the blood in my stomach, its benefits barely impacting me.

I was still faster than a human, still stronger. My body was changed with my transition, my muscles denser, my bones heavier. I was not a human anymore. The weakness made me sleepy, as if I were suddenly thrown into water and had to fight to push through it.

My wounds had closed, but the healing had slowed. I could still feel the aches where the rats had bit deep enough. It wasn't an issue. The rats were many, but they were weak. The only danger they posed to me was in their overwhelming numbers.

But I continued running through the forest, avoiding the rats that were trying to jump on me.

I felt it when my steps reset the cooldown on my [Mist Step]. It was shorter now, six instead of seven steps. It had changed when I gained my First Investment.

I leapt as a group of rats stood in my way. I flowed through the air as mist, surging as fast as I was going the moment I used my skill.

I re-formed dozens of meters ahead, then ran forward again. The world blurred around me, and my [Lesser Strength] fueled me, despite the sun making me weaker. My ascension to the ranks of an Adult vampire had changed me further, had improved my baseline.

I trampled rats, my blades cutting as I ran. Six steps, and I leapt again, turning to mist. I covered ground at a speed that the rats couldn't follow, yet there were always more of them ahead, already waiting as I came. They shouldn't have been able to sense or even see me coming, yet they knew, somehow. Again, I could feel an imprint of a skill in the Way around me, the tapestry of the world filled with Source.

I re-formed again and paused. Three mounds covered with rats were ahead of me, their bodies squirming on top of them, covering them completely. I could faintly smell the blood, could see glimpses of clothes through the rats eating the flesh. Three small mounds, tiny really. Children. I forced myself to run, forced myself not to stop, not to think about who those three children could be.

I heard screams coming from ahead, and I jumped as mist again.

I landed in a clearing next to a large boulder, several rocks surrounding it. I took in the situation with a glance. On top of the boulder, I saw Father Rodriguez, pulling up a child as a man dressed in military garb pushed them up from below. A little girl clutched the priest's robes behind him. A large group of rats was rushing toward the boulder, but ahead of them was a redheaded woman also wearing a military garb and holding a long, serrated knife, fighting . . . Something. She swiped her weapon at one of two monstrous rats, mutated and larger than the others. It stood on two legs and had grown to the size of a small child, standing at perhaps half my height, it was hunched and thin, with elongated limbs that ended in sharp claws already covered in blood. It was one of the beasts that I had seen in Martin's memories. The woman was limping, her thigh bleeding.

I froze. The third of the mutated rats was near the boulder, its hand stuck in a child's stomach. Close to the man who had his back turned to them.

My sight darkened as I saw Felix's eyes bulging, filled with fear and confusion, filled with pain. The ratman opened its maw, uneven sharp teeth looming over Felix's face. The kid that I had saved, the kid that I had made a promise to, stood and stared straight at his death.

I ran, pushing as fast as I could, then I jumped, turning to mist. I rushed by the woman and the man in my mist form, saw their surprise through the gray world around me, and then I landed and re-formed just as the ratman was about to close its jaw.

Saia sang from below, cutting with ease through flesh and bone, slicing off the limb that was still embedded in Felix's stomach at the elbow, and my dagger slammed into the side of the rat's neck. I left it there, then grabbed the rat by the head and squeezed. If it had been night, I would've crushed it in an instant. Instead, I heard the bones crack, then splinter as my fingers sunk into the skin without breaking it. I turned and threw the rat back to the horde, then knelt next to Felix.

He wore a simple blue shirt, with a faded Superman symbol on the chest. The yellow surrounding the S was soaked with blood. He smiled at me through the agony, the fear I saw before was gone and hope filled his face.

I reached down, grabbed the remains of the limb, and pulled it out quickly, I already knew that it was too late. I could smell the wound. The rat's claws had pierced his bowels, had severed his spine, and his blood flowed out of the wound in big gushes.

"You came," he whispered, with a look in his eyes that made me wish that I could turn away, run and hide. "I knew that you would."

I opened my mouth, but I had no words to give. There was nothing that I could do to change things. His hope, his trust, it was misplaced; I hadn't gotten there in time.

I should've never left the church. If I had stayed with them, if I had given a little bit of trust—

He coughed, and blood spilled over his lips, trailing long red lines down his chin and neck. Chaos around me faded into the background as I watched his eyes fill with panic.

"I'll be okay, right?" he asked me.

I forced myself to keep my eyes on him. I opened my mouth to speak, but the words just didn't come.

He grew pale, terror filling his face. His heartbeat was slowing, his lungs struggling to rise, as if someone had placed a great weight on them. I heard the air catching in his throat. He wanted to say something more, but he couldn't get it out. His eyes drew dim, faded.

I said nothing. I didn't know what to say, I didn't know how to act. I was frozen, crippled.

He died with a look of horror on his face, with a silent monster looking down on him, offering him no comfort.

My mind went blank. I felt trapped inside my own body, unable to move or even think. I just looked down at his face, his open eyes staring ahead at me with an absence reflected from behind them. An empty look from an empty shell.

Something jumped on me then, climbing on my shoulder. Then pain as it bit into my ear. My muscles burned. I moved my head as the rat on my shoulder clawed at my cheek and neck, as it pulled with its head and tore a piece of my earlobe off.

Then anger and hate, then fury. My heart boomed inside of my chest like a drum, pushing the sludge that was my **thirst**-filled blood through my veins. A memory flashed inside of my head, of an all-consuming eruption of pure scorching hate, a savage anger. A chorus filled with voices singing anarchy to anything and everything, a churning distaste for order. For life and death, for all things that happened that we couldn't prevent.

I closed my eyes, to the memory of the monster, the sikiri, and the effect of the blight that had tried to pierce into my mind. For a moment I thought that I could hear the words, whispering inside of my mind, but I shook the memory off. I kept the anger though.

I reached up and grabbed the rat, crushed it in my hand and threw it to the side as I stood up. I looked around and saw the two strangers standing nearby. The rats were surrounding us, but they didn't advance. The two ratmen stood near the corpse of the one that I had killed and thrown back. The man had a slingshot in his hand raised toward the horde of rats. The woman stood in front of him, her knife held in front of her, waiting for her death.

The two ratmen were looking at me. They squeaked and hissed, their jaws opening and closing as if they couldn't wait to bite into my flesh. I felt the now familiar imprint in the world around me, of a skill being used, and the horde of rats moved as one, gathering around the two ratmen.

I stepped forward.

"Saia," I said. "Chain and blade."

She shifted in my hands as I reached the side of the woman. She looked at me for a moment, with a slight hope on her face. Then I saw her pause as she saw my eyes, really saw them. With realization, fear slipped through, but I spoke before she could truly think about all the ramifications.

"Get up on the boulder," I told her. "Kill anything that gets past me." With the chain, I needed the room. I couldn't worry about someone I knew nothing about interfering.

She hesitated for just a moment, before nodding and running back with the man. I turned my attention to the horde ahead of me. There were hundreds, maybe thousands of rats, and more were coming in from the forest with every second that passed.

The two ratmen were stepping back, moving into the protection of their horde. And then, as if some silent agreement had been made, they hissed, and the horde of rats surged forward.

I raised my left hand, placed it over my chest, and pulled. My Mask manifested in my palm, obsidian and jade, a visage of a vampiric monster, long incisors framed with gold plates. I raised my Mask and placed it over my face.

Power surged into me; strength filled me as my attributes soared. My power eclipsed even what my baseline at night was, but it was nowhere near what it would've been if the sun was not above the horizon. Still, it was intoxicating, a feeling of being able to fight the storm. I felt the **thirst** rouse from its sleep, just a tiny bit, but still the weakness the sun inflicted on it remained. The Mask amplified my physical attributes, but it seemingly couldn't fight the effect the sun had on the **thirst**.

I grabbed the chain from my waist and started spinning. The large ring hanging from the end sang through the air. I wove the chain around, left then right, repeating, protecting the area around me as the horde came at me without a care.

Before they could reach me, I jumped forward into the center of them. I spun the chain, and the ring tore through the rats as if they were just balloons filled with blood. They exploded around me, a shower of carnage and death, bathing everything with red blood.

I landed and leaned forward, my feet in the position of the second Kata of the **Veiled Mist Assault**: *Tempest in the Mist.* I started spinning and walking forward, rapidly swinging my chain in concentric circles around myself. Every rat that attempted to get closer vanished with a splash of blood and gore.

But for each one I took down, five more rushed to take its place. I was forced to pull the chain closer, make my swinging circle smaller and smaller. I raised my eyes and saw the two ratmen looking at me from a distance, directing their horde, keeping away and safe.

The rats surrounded me now, and then came in one big rush. They crawled over each other, creating one big wall that crashed through, careless for their individual lives. My chain got stuck into a mound of rats, and the horde spilled in my direction. I waited until they were just close enough, and then I let my skill out.

[Debilitating Wave] lashed out of me, the red haze hitting all the rats around me. They tumbled to the ground like a tide spilling over, their wretched bodies twitching and squirming.

My eyes met those of the ratmen, and whatever primal intelligence was nested in their heads knew what was coming for them. They turned and ran.

I jumped, turning to mist. My leap took me halfway to them, and I raised my hand and swung my chain.

It caught one of them, wrapping around its torso, and I pulled. The beast was taken off its feet, sent flying toward me, it squirmed, and I felt a skill being used. Then it slipped through my chain, as if its body had shrunk for an instant, just enough to slip the binding.

It fell on the ground and rolled, and I ran at it, my blade already swinging down toward its head. It dodged, suddenly moving faster in a burst of speed. I missed but didn't stop my movement. I pivoted and turned my stab into a slash, catching the ratman across the shoulder.

It screamed in pain, and I followed after it. A skill activated behind me, and the stunned rats on the ground suddenly rose, like puppets on strings, their movements synchronized and smooth, shaking off my [Debilitating Wave] skill. Before I could react, they rushed me again, climbing over each other to reach me.

They grabbed my legs and started climbing as others jumped off their fellows toward my head. I spun the chain in my hand and ripped the tide around my legs to pieces. I kicked, I swiped my blade and cut every rat that tried to jump at me. I ignored the small cuts, letting them fuel my anger.

Yet, there were too many of them. I was being overwhelmed. I forced myself to take a step even as they tore pieces of my leg, my cooldown reset, and I was mist again.

I barely managed to get any momentum. But my mist form carried me through most of the horde. I re-formed just outside of the pile that had nearly swallowed me, where the injured ratman had just recovered. I threw the end of the chain at the beast, and when it dodged out of the way, I turned and with a flick of a wrist pulled it back. The chain caught it around the neck, and when I pulled this time, I also leapt forward. The ratman tried to squirm out, but it wasn't fast enough. I growled as my blade sunk into its chest. With another flick of a wrist, I cut to the side, opening a gash from just below its ribs to just above the kidneys.

The beast screamed, and I pressed my advantage. I wrapped the chain around its neck one more time as its limbs flailed around, then slipped behind it. I pushed it to the ground, placed my knee on its back, and then pulled.

The rats swarmed me, climbing on top of me and biting with their little wicked and weak teeth, their small claws. I ignored them and the superficial wounds they were inflicting. Pulling the chain was all that I cared about. The flesh beneath me parted, and the ratman's head tore off.

The rats paused as something rippled through them. I saw them shaking their heads, their squeals intensifying. I took advantage of the momentary disorientation and leapt, turning to mist, and the rats attacking me dropped to the ground.

I re-formed in front of the last ratman, my chain trailing behind me, my blade raised high. My muscles spasmed, and I stumbled, as exhaustion hit, and I nearly lost my grip on Saia.

My swing went wide, and the ratman dodged. It dashed beneath my arm and lashed out with its claws and opened a gash along my hip. I groaned as I felt claws scrape against my bone, I pulled my chain trying to swing it, but it was too loose; I hadn't had the time to gather it.

My Mask drained me even as it made me strong, and it didn't help me heal. I didn't have much time. I realized my mistake. There were too many rats around, and I was never going to kill them all. The ratman sensed my weakness and pounced, its claw moving in a blur as its speed increased. An echo of a skill touched my senses.

I stepped back, evading, and rats crawled on my feet from behind. They bit and held me down. In that instant, as I saw the ratman advance, trying to capitalize on the skill I had been sensing all this time. The ratman was controlling them somehow, or at least influencing them. They had been too coordinated, and when I killed the others, their reactions had been telling.

The ratman came in close and attacked, I blocked its first strike with the forearm of my chain-holding hand, but its second swipe caught my stomach. Rage pulsed inside of me, and with the last of my strength I used [Swap Profile].

My skills changed, swapping places.

[Quick Step] pushed me forward, ripping me free of the mound of rats at my feet. I stepped into the ratman's attack, letting its claws wrap around me and cut into my back. I ignored the pain and the injury. My blade snapped forward with [Quick Strike], stabbing it through the head sideways. With a roar, I pulled the beast up by my blade, then my mouth opened wide, the Mask dislodging with my jaw.

I bit down on the side of its neck. The fur stuck to my tongue as I ripped a chunk of flesh out, my tongue sending it down my throat. Then blood followed.

Somehow, it was both sweet and wretched, a reflection of the beast I had killed to take it. Exhausted, I fell to my knees with my teeth still stuck in the rat, drinking the blood as I was bleeding from dozens of wounds. Every gulp sent a faint burn out from my stomach. The **thirst** was lethargic, the healing I received barely even there.

Memories took me, overwhelmed me, and I lost myself in the whispers coming from the blood pouring down my throat, the voices of a swarm filled with a thousand minds.

Failure

The horde was hungry, it was always hungry. The city was cold, the danger ever present. Larger beasts stalked the streets at night, and great winged monsters hunted during the day. The home they had in the sewers were gone, flooded, filled with beasts that could swallow a rat whole.

He was one of three who had grown, who had changed. He understood that he was better than his lesser kind. He could hear their voices in his head, could think through their thoughts, could see through their eyes, could hear through their ears, and smell through their nostrils.

The horde listened to them, and their voices held a greater weight among the whole. And he and his brothers knew the truth. They would not survive for long. The great bursts of light were more common, and more and more greater predators were coming out of them, things that no one in the horde had ever encountered before. Alien things.

They knew that they had to leave the city, to try to survive in the wilderness. They knew that many would not survive, that the city offered more food than the wild. But at least some would survive.

Their minds as one, they left the city, and noticed a trail. A trail that they followed to a building surrounded by trees, filled with warmth and the old giants who had escaped the city long ago.

The three were in agreement. They needed the food; the horde had to eat. They swarmed the building and began their feast. The giants were not strong enough to stop them. They found the small ones, their flesh tender and sweet.

Others escaped, and they pursued. They were hungry, so, so, so hungry.

Mask of the Blood Invoker — First Investment; Fourth Carving

I pulled myself out of the memory. The feeling of having so many thoughts inside of my head was nearly too much. I felt disgusted by the echoes of their hunger. It felt too much like what I myself experienced, the bottomless pit in my stomach that only wanted to feed.

I wondered if that was what I could've become if I hadn't learned control after I was turned. Just a thing that cared only about filling its stomach. I shook my head and raised my eyes. The rats were running away. The three evolved ones had been their leaders, their minds controlling the rest. Without them they were lesser. They scattered back into the forest. Without their leaders urging them on, they were unwilling to fight against a clearly superior predator.

I reached up to my face and pulled my Mask off. Immediately, exhaustion hit me. My muscles turned to mush, and I could barely keep myself standing. All the skills that I'd used went on cooldown, and suddenly I felt far more vulnerable.

I was breathing quickly, my heart beating faster, pumping blood through my veins. I could feel the thirst trying to consume the blood that pooled inside of my stomach. The sunlight made the thirst lethargic and inefficient. My wounds were barely healing, and blood was oozing out of them. With the sun rising, it was only going to get worse.

"Saia," I said, my throat feeling rough, my voice coarse. "I need you to scout and make sure that the rats don't come back this way. Or that there isn't another of the big ones around."

She flowed and took the shape of a dragon. "Feedback: I will do so."

"Wait," I said before she had a chance to fly away. "On your way back, you can consume matter," I said, looking over the dead rats all around us.

"Feedback: Acknowledged." With that she flew away.

I turned around and looked at the boulder. The unfamiliar man was up on top with the priest and two children. I saw the kids looking at me, their eyes filled with tears. The priest held them, and I couldn't tell who was clutching who for support. The woman that I didn't know stood below them, looking in my direction like everyone else, her knife held tightly in both hands. It was dripping blood, and dead rats surrounded her too. She was covered in wounds, from her legs that seemed to have been soaked in blood to scratches on the side of her face.

I didn't keep my eyes on her for long. I looked away and walked. She stiffened as I walked past her, her knife moving slightly before she thought better of it and pointed it away from me. I admired her not taking a step back, despite her fear. I could smell it on her, see it on her face, hear it in the heart that was beating inside her chest at an alarming rate. I sensed it all despite being weakened by the sun.

I knelt on the ground and looked at the dead child—Felix. I reached for his face, touched his eyelids, and pulled them down. I couldn't bear to see them, to see that stare. He thought that I would save him, that I would keep him safe. I didn't. I was too weak, too slow, too . . . so many things.

I closed my eyes, trying to think about what I could've done differently. There were so many things, and I blamed myself for all of them. I was supposed to come back to Earth and try to save people, try to give us a fighting chance. And what had I done instead? I wasted days on pointless things. And in the end the cruel reality of this new world had taken its price.

I felt guilty, and I couldn't even take a look at him now. I was ashamed. I cared more about keeping my secrets than . . . If I was there, things would've gone differently. But I couldn't live in the past. I couldn't change things.

I remembered an old lesson from my sire. It was on what it meant to be a vampire, on the nature of our existence. He told me that human life was fleeting, that I shouldn't get attached. That if I survived my Fledgling stage, I would more than likely outlive them all. He said that humans were fragile. I thought that he meant that they would grow old and die, but I knew now what he really meant.

Felix was dead, and I would never hear his voice again. I would never see that little mischievous smile on his young face. I would never get the chance to teach him how to fight, how to improve his Mask and turn it into something that he would love. The world was cruel. I knew that. It had been cruel to me even before Kirios. Now, now it was worse. The people of Earth were not prepared. And I was a fool for thinking that I had time.

A touch on my shoulder brought me out of my thoughts, surprising me. I twisted around to see Father Rodriguez standing over me, a kind look on his face that was marred with tears. I wanted to run away. I didn't deserve that kind of a look. If it was nighttime, he never would've gotten that close to me.

He opened his mouth to speak, but I couldn't handle his words now. I was afraid that it would be an accusation. I shrugged his hand off and turned to the two strangers.

"Who are you?" I asked.

The man withered under my attention, his eyes looking away quickly. His fear only grew while everyone else's lessened. There was something there, but I had no time to investigate why that would be the case.

The woman swallowed, her hand gripping her knife tightly and looking at my eyes. She glanced at the sun above me, then back to my face as if to confirm that I was still there. I could see her thinking, coming to conclusions, all the wrong ones probably.

Father Rodriguez cleared his throat and stepped next to me. "These are the people we spoke with you about, before," he said slowly. "They arrived last night."

They had led the rats straight to the church. A part of me wanted to tear them to pieces. Some of my thoughts must've shown on my face, because the woman took a step back. I didn't do anything though. I knew from the memories of the beasts that it wasn't really their fault. The rats would've found the church either way.

"You are the scouts for the base," I said, remembering what I'd learned from the church folk.

That made the woman startle, but she nodded. "I—yes, we are scouts," she said, then paused before adding, "Thank you for saving us, uh, Master."

Master. That made me pause. That was what they called old vampires, Elder and greater. I was none of those things. My eyes would designate me as an Adult, but perhaps she didn't know that. Though, me standing in sunlight might make her think that I was far older than I was.

"I didn't save enough," I said, my eyes drifting back to Felix's body. How many kids had there been in the church? I felt terrible that I didn't know, that I never bothered to find out. I saw bodies on my way here, but I didn't stop to count.

I turned my head to look at the two kids behind the priest's robes. They were younger than Felix, a girl and a boy. The way they looked at me made me shy away. There was no fear there, I was not a monster in their eyes, even with the shock that they must feel. The kids cast glances at Felix, and I saw sadness on their faces, but there was no wailing, no great tears and tantrums. It broke my heart, because I knew those looks. They had the look of people who had seen death before, who didn't let it faze them anymore. I shouldn't be seeing a look like that on the faces of children.

"Uh," the woman started, forcing my attention back to her. "We can't stay here for long. There will be more monsters like these." She gestured at the dead rats. "The dungeons in the city were breaking open, the new monsters pushing the weaker ones out. The rats were just the first of them."

I took in her words with no comment. I found that I didn't have it in me to react to it. Danger had been such a constant in my life that more of it was nothing new.

"Yes," I said finally, my eyes falling again on Felix. "We should go."

I didn't know what to do about the body. Thankfully, Father Rodriguez took the decision out of my hands before I had to make it.

"I'll say a quick prayer," he whispered. "It is the only thing we can afford."

I nodded curtly, not daring to speak. I stood above him as he knelt next to Felix, as he bowed his head and clasped his hands. The children knelt next to him, and the two strangers watched from afar. I looked at the face of my young friend, burning it into my mind. So that I would never forget.

Before we left the site of battle, I pulled my backpack from my back and offered water and some cloth to the woman to clean her wounds. They didn't have the time to do much more than that, and I did the same, though my wounds had clotted over by the time we set out. I only had to wait for nightfall for them to be gone. Hers would pain her for a lot longer.

We moved briskly through the forest for hours with no respite, until we finally had to stop. The children had long since been riding on the shoulders of adults—the father and the man carried one each. It was the priest who had gotten too tired to continue, forcing us to take a rest. I kept my eyes open, looking for any danger. We came to a stop on top of a hill, and the others sat on the ground, recovering.

I stood aside, looking in the distance. The sun had crossed its zenith, and I was counting the minutes until it would go down. I felt naked, weak, and vulnerable without most of my skills. I hadn't used my [Double Strike], or my non-Invoker skills, but those wouldn't help me in a fight. I kept twitching in the direction of the noise. The fact that I couldn't fully identify what it was that I was hearing was driving me insane.

I tried not to react as someone came to a stop next to me. I easily identified who it was without even looking, by the scent of incense clinging to him. I didn't react in any way to his presence. I didn't know how. My mind was whirling with thoughts that I didn't want to face.

After some time, Father Rodriguez spoke in a whisper.

"It wasn't your fault."

I didn't know if it would've been worse if he had blamed me. By now he had to have realized that I had kept more things from him. I stood here with the sunlight touching my skin, and I wasn't burning. He saw what I had done, how I fought. He knew that he and the others at the church hadn't been any threat to me. I could've stayed, I could've—

"It wasn't your fault." He placed a hand on my shoulder, bringing me out of my thoughts.

I turned my head to look at him. He was a kind-looking man, a man of faith, of God. He and I stood on opposite sides. I was the monster in the dark, the abomination that lived beyond the grace of his God. And he was food for my kind. And yet, here we stood.

"I could've—"

"Don't," he interrupted me. "The world is changed forever. The past is the past. We can only move forward, learn from our mistakes, and make sure they don't happen again. Be comforted in the knowledge that he is with God now, and free from this hell."

I turned away. I was not a believer; it didn't comfort me the same way it did him. But at that moment I wanted to believe so very much. He had the same look in his eyes that Khalil often had, and that comfort, that faith, it made me feel jealous. I took a deep breath and chose to believe, at least this once.

I glanced back at him, then whispered, "We don't have time." I closed a fist. "No time at all."

He tilted his head inquisitively.

"We are at war with the world itself. And I've lost focus, lost track of what I've set out to do." I shook my head, then added in another whisper, "Vae Victis."

Father Rodriguez looked confused, and I didn't elaborate. I walked back to the rest, the priest following behind me.

I looked down at the two strangers. "We need to head toward your base."

They exchanged looks, then the woman met my gaze. "The road down south was already being overrun by the time we left the city. The only other way back that we know is through the pass, and that . . ." She paused. "We have too many people, it is suicide."

"I've heard about that; something is nesting in the pass? It attacks large groups?" I asked.

The woman nodded. "Yes, any group larger than three people was lost with no sign of what happened to them. We don't even know what it is. We've only caught glimpses, strange tracks that make little sense."

I grimaced. "An animal hunting larger groups but not smaller doesn't make much sense. If it can detect four people, it can detect three too."

"I don't know if you've noticed, but a lot about the world doesn't make sense anymore," the woman said.

The man elbowed her, as he glanced at me fearfully.

"Relax," the woman said. "If she wanted to, she could have killed us without breaking a sweat."

That made me smile, and I allowed my lips to part enough to show my fangs. Both of them shivered.

"What are your names?" I asked.

"I'm Gabriela," she said then gestured at the man next to her. "That's Angelo."

I nodded, then glanced to the side where the two kids had been sitting and listening to everything with rapt attention. I raised an eyebrow at them. "And yours?"

The kids spoke almost in the same breath.

"Lea."

"Juan."

The little girl, Lea, immediately continued. "Can you really fly like Felix said?"

That drew a sad smile from me. "No," I said. The little pout she gave me made me add something, not wanting to disappoint her. "But I can turn into mist and jump really high."

Her eyes widened, and she turned to the boy, whispering in his ear. I ignored her *told you sos* to her friend, and turned back to the two adults in front of me.

"I am . . ." I paused. I had given the name Estrella because I wanted to hide, because I didn't know what information I should keep hidden. I didn't know what the situation was like, if any of my old associates were still here. But it was also my real name. Estrella meant Star, and that was the name that Shadow had given me. I wondered if Marianna even existed, and yet . . . this was Earth. This was the home where Marianna was born, and I knew that I needed her if I was going to do everything that I wanted. I had to think of myself as part of this world.

So, I met their eyes and spoke. "I'm Marianna, and I'll take you through that pass."

Planning

I sat on the ground with my backpack in front of me. Father Sergio sat across from me with the two kids, quietly instructing them on what they should do if they encounter any danger, which was mainly to stay near him. The other two, Gabriela and Angelo, sat to the side, casting glances at me when they thought I wasn't looking.

"Your name isn't Estrella?" Father Sergio asked, making me raise my head to look at him.

"It is," I said truthfully. "Marianna is the name I was born with. Estrella is . . . it's complicated, but it is my name too."

He nodded, satisfied with the answer. I hadn't felt it, but I assumed that perhaps he used his truth-seeing skill. I didn't often lie. I found lying pointless in most cases. Though I did use lies of omission on occasion, which I didn't think he could detect, not yet at least.

"How far away is the pass?" I asked, as I returned to rummaging through my pack, pulling out a bottle filled with blood then taking a swig. I was sated from the rats, but my wounds were still in the process of healing.

The man startled, then looked at the plastic bottle filled with blood as his face drained of color. The woman looked away and cleared her throat. "A couple of hours on foot, uh, Master," she said slowly. "But, maybe we could find another way? If we head down south now, maybe we can get to the road ahead of the monsters fleeing the city."

I shook my head. "If you knew that it wasn't overrun already, I would've agreed, but I am not going to risk an unknown," I said as I pulled the bottle down and stored it in my bag. "And you don't need to call me Master. Marianna will suffice."

She looked unsure, but hesitantly nodded. "The pass is an unknown too," she continued. "The road might be a risk, but the pass is certain death. Groups this large don't survive going through there."

I glanced at her and saw her holding my gaze. That surprised me; most would be too afraid to stand up to a vampire. She had a spine, I respected that.

"You've never had someone like me around," I added.

I saw her open her mouth, then close it. "I . . . you are very strong, of course, Mas—Miss Marianna," she responded. "It is still a risk."

More of a risk than she knew. My skills were on a long cooldown, and would remain on it for a bit over two days. I only had access to the few skills that I hadn't used, and I couldn't wear my Mask again with the cooldown was in effect.

"Everything is a risk. Based on what you said, I don't think that the pass has more than a single beast. The road will have beasts in numbers that could overwhelm even me, if what I've heard about the city is true." I raised an eyebrow, making it a question.

The woman grimaced, but the man answered.

"She's right, Gabriela," he said. "You saw the same things I did. Packs of wild dogs, prides of cats, monsters straight out of our nightmares. With the rifts breaking open, the road will be overrun by now."

"Beasts, not monsters," I interjected.

"They looked like monsters to me," the woman said.

I shook my head. "You've not seen a monster yet, trust me on that. They are animals from other worlds, but no more monstrous than animals on Earth are. Monsters, though, they are real, something more dangerous than you can imagine. But that is a conversation for another time." I sighed and rubbed at my forearm. The wound there had closed, an ugly scab covering the bloodstained skin. It was itchy. "We are going to the pass. I'll deal with whatever it is that has made it a home."

Gabriela started speaking. "Maybe we should split up. The two of us can go ahead? Get help from the base, I'm sure—" My glare made the woman stop, and swallow nervously.

She still looked like she wanted to argue, but thought better of it. I wasn't going to trust her that much, nor was there any need. I was confident in my ability to get by anything that might be nesting there.

Father Rodriguez was the one to speak and break the uncomfortable silence.

"You think that you'll be able to deal with whatever is there?" he asked, his voice low.

I glanced at him. "Yes," I said simply. I wasn't even being arrogant. I didn't believe that there was anything on Earth that could threaten me. The animals on Earth might be changed by the Source, but according to what Shadow had told me, it would be a while till they grew in Investment, the same as people. The animals might be enjoying benefits from an accelerated Investment gain, but so did everybody else. And I was not only a vampire. I had already crossed my first Investment tier.

Even if the pass was occupied by something that had escaped a rift, I still didn't think that it could be my match. From what I had experienced, the animals in the rifts would probably be the same as what I had encountered before, those that had just been changed by the Source. It would take time for them to grow stronger.

I turned to look at the other two. "According to what you've said I gather that you do not think that it is more than a single beast?"

"Uh." The man paused. "No. I don't think that it is more than a single beast. My skill would've given me a different result if it was. More of a series of overlapping clouds instead of one."

I tilted my head at him. "What is your skill?"

He blinked, glanced at the woman as if seeking advice. She gave him a look in return that was comically easy for me to read.

"You have secrets, I know and understand that. I have them as well. But we are in a position where we need to trust each other in order to survive. Or rather, you need to trust me. I could leave you and go at it alone," I said, though in truth I would do no such thing. I'd made a promise to Martin, an agreement to save as many of his people as I could. And I wouldn't consider my side of the deal finished until they were safe. But they didn't need to know that. "If you want me to help you, I need to know anything that might help me keep you all alive."

He hesitated for a moment, then nodded. "It is [Detect Danger]," he said finally.

I nodded. "And it makes you believe that there is a singular danger in the pass?"

He hesitantly nodded.

"That's good," I said. "It will make things easier."

They gave each other a look, and then the woman turned to me. "We should head out then. We only have a few hours of daylight left."

I smiled and showed her my fangs. "I know, that's what we are waiting for."

Her mouth opened in a small *oh* shape.

"H-how are you . . . uh, alive?" the man, Angelo, asked, his eyes glancing up at the sun.

I glanced at it too. It was beautiful, and despite knowing that it wouldn't hurt me I still had an instinctual fear that told me to look away, to run. I pushed it down and turned back to the man.

"That is not our sun anymore," I told him as I pointed at it. "This isn't our planet anymore. Our landmass and oceans have been added to another world. Kirios."

"How could you possibly know that?" the woman asked.

"The two moons in the sky weren't a clue enough?" I raised an eyebrow.

"I don't mean that," she said. "Obviously, we aren't where we used to be. The stars are different, but you are claiming that we are on another world. How do you know that?"

A glint of silver in the trees caught my eyes as I answered. "It is a long story, one that I won't be telling today. Once we reach your base, I'll speak with your leaders. There is a lot that you should know."

Then I stood up and turned, raising a hand. Saia jumped from the trees, gliding on her wings until she landed on my forearm. She was a bit larger than she used to be, probably because she assimilated the corpses on the way as I asked her to. She was just larger than my palm now.

Her arrival startled the others, who all got the their feet, hands going for their weapons.

"Anything?" I asked Saia, ignoring them.

"Report: The forest animals are fleeing north. The horde of beasts we fought has scattered. I have scouted south close to what appears to be a stone road of some kind. It is overrun with a variety of beasts migrating or fleeing. I encountered no threats in the immediate vicinity on the way back."

I grimaced. It was as I had expected.

"What is that?" Father Sergio asked, one of his hands clutching the crucifix hanging from around his neck while the other held the two children back.

I glanced at the priest and the kids, and saw wonder in their eyes. I smiled at that. "This is my companion, Saia. Introduce yourself, Saia."

The tiny dragon turned her head to the priest and spoke. "Feedback: This Unit's designation is Self-replicating Autonomous Interface Armor unit, Prototype Mark 3, current designation: Saia," she said in her slightly high-pitched voice. Everyone around me looked at the dragon with shock in their eyes.

Saia tilted her head as she looked at the priest. "Query: This Unit is curious. Are you an elderly specimen of your species?"

I narrowed my eyes at her. She had switched back to referring to herself as "this Unit". I had a suspicion why she sometimes did that. From what I had observed it seemed like she would refer to herself in the first person when she actually cared about the topic, and referred to herself as Unit when she didn't particularly care. Which begged the question, why did she ask what she asked?

Father Sergio blinked, his eyes glancing at me before turning back to the dragon. "I . . . I am?"

Saia turned to look at me, and I returned her gaze with narrowed eyes. "Query: This Unit requests the specimen for assimilation."

My jaw dropped. "What? Why would you even ask that?"

"Feedback: Considering the current situation, it is unlikely that the elderly specimen will survive for much longer. The assimilation of a live specimen might give me more information regarding Masks and the state of Source-Weave."

"No, you can't assimilate him, especially not alive," I hissed at her. Sometimes I forgot that she was an AI made for war.

She tilted her head. "Statement: Regretful."

I sighed then shook my head. I had to have a long talk with Saia, teach her how to conduct herself in front of other people. It was obvious that her understanding and probably even the culture—if her creators had bothered to give her anything like that—differed greatly from mine.

"What manner of devil is this? What did it mean by that?" Father Sergio asked.

"Not a devil at all, Father," I said. "I found Saia in a rift. She is a remnant from another world that had suffered a similar fate to ours. She is an artificial intelligence."

There was no point in hiding the truth, not when they had seen what Saia could do.

"What did she mean by assimilate?" Gabriela asked from the side.

I tsked, I had hoped that they would've been too distracted for it to sink in. "She asked to eat him, but don't worry, she can't do it without my permission."

The looks of horror on their faces told me that I shouldn't have put it that bluntly. I cleared my throat. "That sounded worse than it is." I looked back at Father Sergio, who had taken a step back with the kids. "If it helps, she tried to eat me too."

From the looks on their faces, I could tell that it didn't help at all.

A bit later, we all sat down again to plan. I had an idea, something that I had wanted to try for a while now, and that could help cover the weakness that the use of my Mask had inflicted.

I reached into my backpack and pulled out a plastic case, alongside a box of ammunition that I got from the rift.

I opened the case and pulled out the handgun. The H-tech Rhino Model 3 looked like an oversized version of a high-tech revolver. It was made out of ceramics and carbon composites. Some of the most advanced tech around. It used a large .600 caliber bullet, and it was a weapon made with the primary customer base being shifters, seeing as it had a kick that would shatter a hand of anyone who was a human, though vampires had no issues using them.

"Is that the Rhino?" Gabriela leaned forward, her eyes suddenly filled with an inner glint. She had been eyeing Saia ever since the dragon climbed on my shoulder and perched there.

"Model 3, yes," I said.

"Where did you find that? A rift?"

I shook my head. "No, I recovered it from my home," I answered. "The issue is that I have no ammo for it. But, I think that I might have a fix for that."

I grabbed the ammo box and opened it up. Inside were twenty .460 caliber rounds. Their color was slightly different from the brass that I was used to, a bit darker in color, though the casings did feel metallic. It had come from a dungeon, so I assumed that it was a reproduction made by the Grand Spell with materials that weren't affected by the Source in the same way that typical Earth metals were.

I pulled one round out and then flipped open the cylinder. I glanced inside and saw that the pin still wasn't corroded, which was a relief. I didn't know what it was made out of, but it was at least resistant to the effect.

The round in my hand was too small to properly fit, but that was where my idea came in.

I glanced at Saia.

"Hey, we spoke about you shaping smaller pieces of yourself before. Think you could shape something around this round to make it fit this caliber?" I asked.

"Query: May I assimilate the round?"

"I don't need you to recreate it, just sheathe it so that it is large enough. You can't recreate the propellant, in any case."

I had already told her how guns and bullets worked.

"Feedback: Knowing the internal structure will help me devise the best way to construct a case mesh around it. I also need to inspect the weapon as well, the size of the barrel and the cylinder."

"Don't assimilate the gun, please," I told her.

"Feedback: Acknowledged."

I glanced at my hand. I was hesitant to lose a round, as they were a limited resource, but ultimately I agreed. The rounds were useless to me as they were.

Saia jumped from my shoulder to my knee, then flowed over the revolver, her body entering the barrel and the cylinder. Once done, she went back to her dragon form and then took a closer look at the round before reaching forward and swallowing it while I pulled out another one out of the box.

A few seconds later, a piece of Saia separated from the main drone body and flowed over to the round. In less than a second, it encased it and made the round larger.

"Statement: I have made the case hollow, and in two parts, it is attached to the main round body via long and flexible threads. On ignition, the case will separate into two parts, one that will be sent out of the barrel."

On closer inspection, I could notice the faint line where her case was separated into two parts, a copy of the bullet and the casing itself.

"Good, now for the test." I slid the round into the chamber then closed the cylinder and stood up.

The rest of the group had watched me in silence and fascination, and now they all held their breaths as I aimed the oversized weapon at a tree some ten meters away.

I didn't wait for long to pull the trigger. The gun roared in my hand, the kick not nearly as high as it would've been with a proper caliber round, but I still felt it. The roar of the fire echoed around us, and the bullet hit its mark. Wood splintered, and a loud thud was heard as it burrowed itself in the trunk.

I grinned. It worked, and now I had another weapon in my repertoire. I couldn't wait to test it out on something live.

The Pass

As soon as night fell, I left our small camp place, and ran out into the woods. I left Saia with the others, to keep an eye on them and warn them in case of any danger. I had a quick stop to make before we continued to the pass. With the arrival of the night, my being awoke. My strength returned, and the small aches of my wounds vanished completely in minutes.

I ran through the forest like the wind, every step perfectly placed, my passage almost silent. The two moons above me shone with eerie light, illuminating the night in a way that Earth's moon had never done. I returned to the church in a fraction of the time it had taken us to escape it. I've encountered a few rats here and there, but the groups were too small to pose any threat to me, and they knew it. The moment they detected me they would turn and run away.

I observed the church from a distance, and saw no great danger. There were small groups of rats around, but I wasn't worried about them. I could hear them scratching and moving around inside, but what I was hearing wasn't anything close to what a full horde would sound like. I made my way to the back, to the window that I jumped out of. The stench was palpable in the air, the scent of blood, waste, and death. I jumped in through the same window I exited the church from almost a day ago.

The few rats inside scattered, running away through the holes in the dresser that I had dropped at the entrance before. Martin's corpse was on the floor, unrecognizable now, the rats having cleaned the flesh from the bones and torn it apart. I didn't pause to offer a prayer or even a moment of silence. The man was gone, and I had already made him a promise, one that I was planning to keep. I pushed the dresser out of the way, prompting another skittering of feet in the hallway beyond.

I made my way through the church, ignoring the human remains on the ground. A part of me was still angry that I hadn't been here to help, telling myself that perhaps things could've been different. But that feeling had faded, especially with the setting of the sun. Vampires felt deeply, but the emotion flared intensely and inevitably burned out. I had something else to focus on, something that I could still have some impact on.

I made my way through the hallway, entering one of the bedrooms, and approached a wardrobe in the back. I opened it and pulled out the clothes to reveal a small safe at the bottom. I pulled it out and grabbed hold of the top, then ripped it open. It was made out of plastic, and didn't pose any obstacle to my strength.

Inside, I found a small ammo box, already opened with less than half of the bullets left. I put it in my backpack and then recovered the rosary that Father Rodriguez asked me to find. It was wrapped in a black cloth, to keep it from fully falling apart, as it had been made out of metal and had been affected by the Source.

I walked into the kitchen to see if any of their food had survived, but the rats had made a mess and had eaten everything. It had always been unlikely that I would find any food. The next thing I looked for was my serpent-tongue spear, which I found impaled in the floor. It was one of the most important things I owned, and I wasn't about to leave it here. It had been a gift from Shadow. I recovered it then continued on.

With nothing else of worth to be found in the back of the church, I turned and made my way to the nave. Near the ladder that led to the church tower, I found the corpse of the man that had been posted up in it, and the rifle he had used to fire from it. It had come from a rift, so it wasn't affected by the Source. I still wanted to investigate the materials it was made out of more closely once I had the time for it. I picked up the bolt-action hunting rifle from the ground and then with one last glance at the church, left.

I didn't head immediately back. Instead I took off running at an angle, scouting the area near the road. The closer I got, the more I could hear the sounds of animals fighting in the distance. It didn't sound good at all. I debated getting even close enough to see them with my own eyes, but my senses told me that there was a lot of them, and I didn't want to risk being overwhelmed. I didn't fear any animal on Earth, not right now. I fully believed that I was stronger than anything that could've been born on Earth, and even the beasts from Kirios. From what Shadow had explained, the Grand Spell didn't allow individuals or beasts of too high Investment to reach the new world immediately. Even the portals that were going to open would have limits placed on them. The rifts were an issue, but if what I had encountered before was any indication, the beasts in there would be those that hadn't had a chance to evolve through the Source. Things that the Grand Spell had in reserve. I didn't know that for certain, but I had seen enough to be confident in my belief.

I decided against tempting fate and turned away, heading back to camp. At my full speed I arrived back at the small hill in record time.

The people jumped as I appeared out of the dark, startled. Which was good, at least they were paying attention. The priest was sitting next to the two small forms on the ground, the kids, who were sleeping. The other two were sitting nearby, alert and looking at the dark forest surrounding them. Saia swooped from above and landed on my shoulder then flowed and shifted into a bracelet around my wrist.

I took a seat next to them and pulled out a bottle, then started drinking blood. I had to take a short break. Vampires weren't made for long stretches of strenuous activity like the humans were, and I had pushed myself to go as fast as possible.

The others looked in my direction, and then Father Rodriguez spoke.

"When are we leaving?" he asked.

"I need a few minutes rest," I answered. "You should all get ready."

As I drank, the man—Angelo—spoke up.

"Back when you were fighting," he started. "You put your Mask on your face."

I looked at him and raised an eyebrow, waiting for the question. He got the hint quickly enough.

"Uh, why did you do that?"

"You aren't surprised that I could manifest my Mask?" I asked instead of answering.

"No." He shook his head. "We've figured out how to enter that inner world and interact with our Masks. We can learn more about our skills there, and some have managed to pull out their Masks."

I nodded to myself. It did make sense that someone would've figured it out. The Grand Spell didn't offer much guidance, but much of what it granted was instinctual. I was certain that I would've figured it out too if I hadn't met Shadow.

I looked at everyone around, then I unslung the rifle from my shoulder and threw it at Gabriela. She seemed a bit more experienced in combat than Angelo. She grabbed it deftly, pulled the bolt, and checked the chamber and the magazine. The rifle was empty, so I threw her the ammo box from my backpack.

"You a good shot?" I asked.

She glanced at me, then nodded. "Yes," she said, with no hint of humility.

"Your Mask, it is a combat one, right?" I asked, I already suspected it from the way she moved and the fact that she'd been the one that was holding off the rats while the others ran.

She gave me a long look, then nodded. "I have the Mask of the Scout," she said. "I have [Sharp Eye] and [Lesser Precision] skills."

I tilted my head. Two skills meant that she probably had a pretty high Investment, compared with everyone else, at least.

"You are close to your First Investment then," I said.

"First Investment?" Angelo asked.

I nodded. "Once you reach ten Carvings, you will gain your First Investment. Your Mask will evolve into something more powerful. Once you hit your First Investment, your Mask will grant you a boost and a special effect while you are wearing it."

Their eyes widened, and then Angelo blinked.

"Wait," he said as he blinked at me. "That means that you have more than ten levels—uh, Carvings?"

I inclined my head. "How close are you two?" I asked.

They looked at each other then turned back to look at me. "We are both at seven," Gabriela answered. "It's the highest anyone's gotten."

I grimaced. That wasn't nearly enough. The Grand Spell had granted Earth a period of accelerated Investment gain. We had to take advantage of it.

"Do you know how you advance your Mask?" I asked them.

"We have some suspicions," Angelo said. "Killing monsters—pardon, beasts—seems to help. Clearing rifts too."

I shook my head. "No, each Mask advances by gaining Investment. And each Mask is unique." I glanced at Gabriela. "Your Mask is that of the **Scout**, which means that you will get more Investment when you do things that are directly linked to its nature. Killing beasts and exploring rifts might overlap with that in certain situations, but it isn't required. What matters is the core spirit behind your Mask, and doing things that are related to it."

They looked like they wanted to ask more questions, but I cut them off before they could even ask. I stood and leaned on my serpent-tongue spear. "But that is for later," I said. I had rested enough. "It's time for us to head out."

Father Rodriguez woke up the kids from their nap, and they all readied themselves for the journey. I wished that I had the time to enter my soul space and get more skills from the rats and ratmen, but I didn't want to delay any more than I already had. We were losing the night, and I wanted to reach the pass long before the dawn.

"Let's go," I said, and led them down the hill, toward the pass.

We approached the mountain at a brisk pace. With my night vision we easily avoided the hazards of the terrain, and that helped greatly. Gabriela's [Sharp Eye] and Angelo's [Detect Danger] were of use as well, allowing them to avoid dangerous areas. His skill couldn't tell what the danger was, only that it was present. I assumed that it was just a predator's territory, which I didn't think was too much of a threat to myself. But avoiding any encounters only served to save us time.

Finally, we reached the base of the mountain, and started heading up. The pass itself was a narrow natural corridor with solid rock on both sides, and cliffs above it. Their assumption was that whatever was nesting in the pass was somewhere in the cliffs above the pass. It seemed like a sound assumption to make.

I debated sending Saia ahead to scout, but I didn't want to alert whatever it was that lived there. Leaving the group behind and going ahead to face the beast alone was out too. I didn't know where it was, or how to draw it out. Gabriela had told me that they had tried drawing it out before, and had little success. Only when large groups entered the pass did the beast's presence become known. They didn't really have much to go on.

"Keep close to me," I said to everyone. "On the first sign of trouble, you run straight ahead and out of the pass while I deal with whatever it is, understood?"

They all nodded, and I took a deep breath. The **thirst** sang through my veins in anticipation of feeding again. We moved into the pass, and I kept my attention focused. My ears could hear only the howl of the wind as it caressed the stone of the cliffs, and my nose could smell too much to easily discern. The scent of the earth, of clean air, of rodents, and yes, of blood. Though that meant little—the scent of blood was often present everywhere in the wild. I kept my eyes on cliffs above us, looking for any signs of movement, and found none.

Our group was double what Gabriela and Angelo usually sent, but perhaps it wasn't too large. As we reached the halfway point, I almost started to believe that we were in the clear. I knew that I shouldn't have allowed myself to relax, let alone think thoughts like that, because a moment later, I saw it.

Something moved in the cliffs above us, and the sound of claws grinding on stone and something long dragging along filled my ears. The sound of a low breath, a hiss really, barely perceivable, followed the scent of stale blood and something very familiar. It glanced down from far above, and I saw one eye meet my own, in that moment a memory of an all-consuming terror that made even the **thirst** hesitate filled my mind. Fear rose, and for a moment I froze.

For an eternity, we remained there, a red eye looking into my emerald ones. Then it twitched, and I reacted.

"Run!" I yelled at the others, startling them. They hesitated for just a moment too long.

Something large and long leapt from the cliffs, and spread its limbs, two membranes stretched between them. It looked the size of a grown crocodile, and had a similar look. It resembled a reptile with wings attached to its front limbs, with a long sinuous tail stretched behind it and a snout filled with sharp teeth. None of that was what made me pause. It was the faint red lines I saw on its body, the signs of blight. I didn't know how it was here. Shadow had assured me that blight was rare outside of Ish Vimza, yet here it was. It explained so much, why it was acting in the way it did. It might not be a full monster, but the blight would be driving it slowly insane. That was why it had illogical rules, why it attacked larger groups when smaller ones would've made more sense.

I jumped as it swooped down on us, kicking off the side of the cliff and heading straight for it. The beast beat its wings as I swung, my long weapon whistling just near enough to graze its side, but not close enough to do anything else.

A gunshot echoed below me, and I glanced down to see Gabriela aiming at the blighted beast. The others were thankfully running away, rushing ahead. She fired her second shot and missed that too. I landed on top of a cliff as the beast made a circle above us and came back, this time targeting Gabriela on the ground. The woman, to her credit, didn't flinch. She pointed her rifle, took the time to aim, then fired.

She hit the beast in the shoulder, making it screech and veer away. It landed somewhere on the cliff above out of view. I jumped, my free hand grabbing the rocks as I vaulted up the cliff.

"Go!" I yelled down, but didn't look to see if she had listened.

I pulled myself on top of the cliff where the beast had landed and found it at the other side of the plateau. It was shaking its head, probably from the impact of its fall, though I noticed that the bullet hadn't pierced its skin. I didn't let it get its bearings and recover. Instead I charged. I crossed the distance in a blink of an eye, my blade raised high above me and coming down as I triggered [Double Strike].

My attack shimmered as an echo of the first one following just behind. The beast saw the attack, and it jumped out of the way, moving faster than I expected. It wasn't fast enough though. My attack carved a line through its left wing and grazed its side, drawing blood. My second strike missed, but I had done enough damage to prevent it from flying.

It hissed at me, but I wasn't afraid. It was a strong beast. I could see how it could be dangerous for humans, especially if a bullet couldn't pierce its skin, though it was a smaller caliber. But it couldn't resist a vampire's strength. I didn't even need to use my gun. The red lines across its skin started to spread, and I spurred myself into motion, remembering what had happened last time.

Its eye turned completely red, and a mist of the same color started to rise from its body. My blade struck it in the center of mass, pinning it to the stone just as I smashed down with my leg and broke its spine.

"KHANUM . . ." the monster hissed, its eye focusing on me. The word resonated within me, and a fire rose, an echo of what I felt before. And then before it could rise high enough, before it could reach the heights that I had felt with the sikiri, it vanished, gone as the monster beneath me died.

I was breathing in ragged, quick breaths—just the memory of what I had experienced before made me fearful. This wasn't supposed to happen. The blight wasn't supposed to be here, not yet. I pulled my weapon out and looked down at the beast-turned-monster. The blight was gone, leaving the dead body alone. But my memory remained, and with it came a lot of questions.

Questions that I feared I would have no time to seek the answers to. I raised my head, looking in the distance where I could just barely see the others running down the mountain. Before I could even take a single step to catch up to them, something made me freeze up. I shivered, and then an earsplitting roar filled the air. I glanced above me and saw a shadow blot out the light of the moons.

Yeah, that's about right, it can never be that easy.

Superiority

The shadow above me was cast by a beast that was of the same species as the one that I had killed in the same way that a bobcat and a tiger were both cats. It was at least four times the size. Its body was more muscular, its wings grander, and the claws on its limbs were long. Its tail ended in a wicked looking spike. It looked somewhat familiar to me, reminding me of the depictions of a wyvern in Earth stories. Less dragon-like, elongated, with a thinner body, but there were parallels, without a doubt. It had similarities with the smaller one that I had killed, only this one was covered in scales and not just thick hide. An adult? Or just a larger specimen, a different gender or a related species? It didn't matter.

It did not frighten me, the same way that I wouldn't be frightened of fighting an elephant. I knew that I was the deadliest predator around. That knowledge was ingrained in my very blood. Ish Vimza had taught me that I should temper that feeling of superiority, that there were threats that were greater than me, at least on Kirios. I had felt fear there. But this was still Earth, not yet fully integrated with the rest of this giant world, and here, I was on top of the food chain. Not even a beast from another world could be my equal. I knew it deep down in my bones. I knew the way the Grand Spell worked, at least somewhat. It wouldn't have sent a beast that had any Investment here. The beasts, even those in rifts, would start on the same playing field as the rest of Earth, from zero. It might have some Carvings now. It had to have been here for a while, since people had issues getting through the pass, but I doubted that it could have as many as I had.

The beast beat its wings and a deep and reverberating sound echoed out of its throat. It rose and fell, like a call of some strange bird, like a rapid-fire owl hoot, except it was so deep that it sounded distorted. It banked and landed on a cliff across the pass, releasing the call again. It was looking around, waiting for something. Then it noticed me and what was behind me.

The hoot turned into a proper roar, a sorrowful cry. The beast's eyes were focused on me as it keened.

"Input: This appears to be a female weirzi." Saia's voice stabbed through my battle focus like a knife. I pushed my surprise back as what she said sunk in. "The one you slew was an infant."

"You recognize it?" I asked as the beast across from me, the weirzi apparently, continued its sorrowful cry.

"Feedback: Yes, it is a distant cousin species to the Ke Erzi. Incredibly intelligent, not to the level of Ke Erzi, obviously. Dangerous, apex predators of Erzi."

So, something like what the other primates were to humans, if I was understanding correctly.

"More dangerous than me?" I asked.

"Feedback: I . . . I don't know."

Classic. I evaluated my chances. I was confident in my own strength, especially at night. The beast was unlikely to have as much Investment as I did, so even if it was naturally stronger than me, I should have some advantages. Though, the reverse was true as well. It could fly.

"Anything I should know?"

"Feedback: Weirzi grow for as long as they live, their scales getting tougher the older they get. This one is barely out of its juvenile stage, just entered adulthood. Young. It is incredibly strong."

"As strong as me?"

"Feedback: On par, at least."

I looked at the wyvern—the weirzi—that was the size of a bus. That looked like an adult to me, especially considering the one that was dead behind me. But, if this wasn't fully grown, then it seemed that fortune was on my side for once. I wouldn't want to stand in front a fully grown one.

One thing did surprise me. The weirzi didn't look like it was blighted. Only its young was, which was . . . strange. I knew that the blight spread in weird ways, and the infant hadn't fully turned into a monster until its last breath, so perhaps that slowed down the spread. I didn't even know how the blight was even here on Earth; it shouldn't be possible yet. Unless something changed.

The only way that this beast could be here was if it had escaped a rift, especially since it was from the Ke Erzi homeworld.

The weirzi seemed to end its mourning. Its keening stopped, and its eyes focused on me. A low rumbling tone rose from its chest, through closed jaws, making the skin flaps over its teeth shake. A growl filled with anger and hate. I had killed its young. I could imagine what it planned on doing to me.

I looked around, trying to decide if this was a good place for a battle. The cliffs surrounded the pass, making it a narrow field for the big beast to maneuver in. But I could also run down the mountain and enter the forest, it was unlikely for it to be able to get to me through the trees. Assuming that I could reach the tree line before it caught me. I didn't know how fast it was, or how strong. There were a lot of things that I didn't know.

I didn't wait for it to make a move. I quickly switched the hand with which I held my serpent-tongue spear and with my right pulled out the gun from the improvised holster at the bottom of my backpack, which was nothing but a hole I cut into the back lower side of my pack. I aimed it at the weirzi and I fired immediately, pulling the trigger five times in a span of a second.

The revolver was made for use by the shifters, made for their strength and reflexes. It kicked in my hand, and the larger caliber rounds blasted out. I targeted the beast's head, and three of my rounds did hit on the mark. The first round ricocheted away from the scales on top of its skull, in between its eyes. The second hit near the same spot, and the scale fractured. The third round slammed through, breaking the scales completely, and I saw the glint of blood, but it wasn't anything other than a surface wound. The hide beneath the scales was even thicker than that of the infant I killed. The rounds had enough power to break the scales, but not enough to punch through the hide beneath at the same time. The last two rounds went wide as I lost control of the recoil and the beast reared back. It beat its wings and jumped off the cliff.

I had four rounds left in the cylinder and no additional Saia-augmented rounds ready to reload. I didn't anticipate coming upon anything that wouldn't die to just a single bullet—an oversight on my part, I could admit. The beast roared, and dove at me, it giant maw open, with wicked teeth the size of my forearm ready to tear me apart. I dashed to the side. The weirzi beat its wings and banked away. I swung with my left hand, holding my weapon by the pommel on the end, extending my reach as far as I could. I hit it on the lower back leg as it moved past me and saw sparks fly, but I didn't do any damage.

That's when its tail slammed into me and sent me flying off the cliff. I soared, then hit the side of a rock and bounced off, falling and hitting a branch sticking out of the side of the mountain and losing the grip on my spear before I dropped into the pass below. I hit the ground hard and groaned, but I recovered quickly.

I wasn't really hurt, well, not too much. I rolled and got to my knees. Quickly I took my backpack off and threw it aside. There were important things in there that I didn't want to get damaged. The weirzi had turned, and I could see it coming, diving straight for me. I raised both hands and gripped the gun tightly.

Time slowed as the thirst reared its head, the hunger within me rising. My heartbeat pounded in my chest, once, sending blood surging through my veins. The weirzi's shadow grew larger as it moved in front of the two moons above, and its eyes were glowing like hot coals in the darkening sky. Its maw gaped open, revealing rows of serrated teeth meant to shred flesh from bone. With practiced calm, I steadied myself. I took no breath since I didn't need it. The thrill of the fight for survival, a life and death battle, consumed me. The Heart of Azure and Scarlet echoed within me and aimed for the beast's eye, one of the few places not protected with scales. My finger tensed on the trigger—steady, ready.

A crack split the air; the bullet whistled, followed quickly by four more, hungry for contact. But fate was cruel and the weirzi smart. It raised its head, tilted its wings, and the shots hit against the scales on its neck and torso. One bounced off, but the other two cracked the scales, yet it wasn't enough. It roared as it brought another weapon to bear. Two limbs came at me, ending in wicked claws. A low growl rumbled from its throat—of anger or amusement, I couldn't tell.

I jumped forward before it could get low enough and ducked underneath its attack. Its claws closed on empty air as it caught wind and was sent into an ascent. Then, I dodged to the side as its tail lashed out—I learned my lessons well. It beat its wings as I rolled back up to my feet, climbing higher and higher.

I threw my gun in the general direction of where I threw my pack, then I jumped onto the side of the cliff, my hands gripping the uneven rocks and climbing up as fast as I possibly could. Above me, the light of the broken moonlight fractured on the stone, painting a chaotic tapestry in shades of gray and silver—a ghostly backdrop for my deadly dance. I scaled the cliff with relentless urgency, my fingers finding holds in the cold rock as if guided by some primal instinct. I reached the cliff where I had left the body of the infant, and for a moment it caught my eye. Something within me stirred, in the deepest reaches of my mind. I had made an agreement with the Way, obligation, debts, and exchange. The infant weirzi had attacked me and the group that was under my protection. It had incurred debt and had paid it with its life. And yet, I was stronger than it. I didn't need to kill it to keep the others safe. I could've subdued it without killing—it was blighted. I didn't know how the blight entered into my oath, but somehow I knew that what I did incurred no debt from my side. The Way, the Weave, the Grand Spell, it was actively opposing the blight. Killing the infant weirzi was the right choice, the only choice. But its mother . . . it had come to find its young dead. It didn't understand what the blight meant. It had probably been protecting its young as it was slowly going insane. It was the cause of the deaths in the pass, I was certain. Every time the young lost it and attacked a larger group, its mother would come to the rescue. It was just too slow this time.

The weirzi was circling in the distance, preparing for another dive. I was suddenly frozen by the weight of my obligation to the Way. Did this weirzi deserve death at my hands? I could run away and leave it alone. It had attacked me, but it had cause. It didn't incur a debt for that action. Yet, it had killed people before while protecting its young. It wasn't intelligent enough to understand the blight and what it did, the people using the pass were unlikely to have incurred any debts to it. And I . . . I wanted to save as many of Earth's people as I possibly could, and the weirzi had taken those lives. If it had been protecting a young that wasn't blighted, I would've understood. But the blight was . . . it was the closest thing to evil I had ever encountered. I followed a school of being that was focused on passion, power, and pursuit of overwhelming victory in all things—the Heart of Azure and Scarlet—and I was building for myself an oath based on debts. No, I owed the weirzi nothing. The blight had to be removed. If it was smarter, if I could argue with it, perhaps I could avoid fighting. But now, we were locked in a battle for life or death. The scales were balanced.

I had some pity for the beast, but I'd be damned if I let it end my story here. I owed a debt to Shadow. I had promised him that I would survive and that we would meet again. I turned my eyes back to the beast as it turned in my direction.

Despite its size, the weirzi was agile, powerful. Its leathery wings beat against the night air with a force that could stir gales. But I was made of tougher stuff: scar around my neck, memories of a deep jungle and monsters, a testament to survival.

"Saia, chain and blade," I whispered, and she transformed. I gripped her tightly and got ready.

I reached a ledge just as the weirzi circled back around, its eyes glowing like smoldering coals. It was a predatory dance between the hunter and hunted, orchestrated by the night's haunting melody. And the weirzi thought that it was the hunter. It seemed to glide through the darkness itself, a nightmare in the sky, a beast straight out of stories. But then again, so was I.

Gripping the chain tighter, I swung it overhead, spinning—the metal links whistling through the air—and as it came with its jaws open, I dashed to the side. In one seamless motion born out of endless practice, movements taught to me by my sire and Shadow, married together in a perfect set that was my version of the Heart of Azure and Scarlet, my feet glided across the stone, moving faster than I had ever moved before. As the beast made its swooping pass I hurled the chain at it. The chain uncoiled like a serpent and found its mark around the creature's neck. The weirzi let out a sound—a cross between a scream and a growl—as it reared back violently. I was pulled off my feet and into the sky. It thrashed wildly, trying to dislodge its new restraints, but I held firm. Its legs lashed out, trying to bisect me, but I was faster. I kicked its leg, and more pushed myself away than I did anything to it, but it was enough. I pulled with all of my strength on the chain, climbing until I was close enough that I managed to grab the joint of its shoulder and climb on its back. The beast's writhing beneath me nearly unseated me immediately. But I had survived too much to be thrown off now. With one hand gripping the chain at its throat, I stabbed with my other one. My first strike glanced off, a combination of a weird angle and the weirzi jerking to the side which made my strike hit with less power.

I grimaced, then made another attempt. I stabbed at its back, the scales once more rebuffing my attack. I kept at it, and I heard and felt my next strike crack a scale. I continued stabbing, as fast and with as much strength as I could muster. Scales broke, and my blade pierced the thick hide beneath, but I didn't yet manage to fully penetrate. Then, finally, I felt Saia sink into its flesh, and the weirzi roared in pain—but it wasn't enough. The blade was barely long enough to pierce the hide, and couldn't do much damage.

I pulled myself forward by the chain, getting closer to its head. I kept stabbing, breaking scales and piercing flesh, letting blood flow. I jerked around as the weirzi slammed into the side of a cliff, attempting to throw me off. Claws scraped stone, and its shoulder slammed against it. Debris, rocks, and dirt rained down on me, pounding my back as the weirzi kicked off and continued flying. The chain wrapped around my left arm bit through my skin from the force, and I felt it cut through all the way to the bone of my palm. Then I felt it start to dive, and I took advantage of the moment. As I was lifted off its back, I got my legs under me and kicked off, leaping forward and grabbing hold of its neck near the head.

I stabbed at its nape, activating [Double Strike] as I did so. My blade sank into the flesh with a sickening squelch. Hot blood sprayed across my face, metallic and thick. The weirzi's roars filled the night as it thrashed wildly in pain and rage. But even in its agony, it fought cleverly, trying to roll and send me flying. Using every ounce of strength left in my battered body, I plunged the blade deeper and twisted, this time hitting something vital.

With a final defiant scream that echoed across the desolate landscape, the weirzi began to plummet. I saw the ground spinning, coming up at me as if to embrace me and never let me go again. We fell together—both predators, a blood-soaked warrior and a ruler of the sky—but there was no fear in me. Only resolve.

As the ground rushed up to claim us both, my mind raced with calculations, plotting an escape from death's cold grip one more time. But my hand was wrapped around the chain, and I had no way of unwrapping it quickly enough.

There was no more time for thought or plans. We reached the ground, and the weirzi smashed into it headfirst, with me on its back.

Interlude
Desert Camp

W e should go back for her," a voice from behind her said.

Gabriela Isa turned and gave the priest a long look. The two kids walking next to him looked as if they were ready to collapse, and that was partly her fault. She had pushed them at a grueling pace that the kids couldn't handle, even with them being carried every few hours. The heat probably had something to do with it, which was also why she wasn't calling for a break. They were getting closer.

"If she hadn't caught up to us by now, she's most likely dead," Gabriela said. "There is no point in us wasting her sacrifice."

The vampire had stayed behind in the pass to fight the big flying monster. And it had been almost a full day since they ran away. If she was alive, she would've caught up to them by now. Gabriela was grateful for what she had done, even though the woman terrified her. A vampire that could walk in sunlight was a nightmare for many. The fact that every vampire on Earth would now be able to do the same . . . She had to get back, report what they had learned, not just about the vampires but what happened in the city too. They were going to have to prepare for the hordes spilling out of rifts to make their way to them.

"She could still be alive," the priest said.

Gabriela didn't respond. She had seen that flying lizard take a bullet without going down, and from the roars that she heard as they were running away, it sounded like there were more than one. She doubted that even a vampire could survive. That pass was a deathtrap, but at least they were through now.

She kept her eyes on their surroundings, looking for any threats, gripping the rifle in her hands tightly. They were so close, she could smell it in the air. They'd been lucky so far. They hadn't encountered any animals in the forest, and she prayed that their luck would hold.

"He's right, you know," Angelo whispered as he walked up and kept her pace. "We shouldn't have just ran—"

"Did you want to stay and fight a fucking dragon?" she hissed at him. "We didn't get to survive for this long by making dumb decisions. She was a vampire. If she couldn't kill it, then we wouldn't have done anything to help."

Angelo grimaced, and Gabriela could see that he was struggling. He always had too much of a bleeding heart. "Her kind eats ours."

Angelo gave her a long look. "She saved our lives," he told her.

Gabriela sighed. He was right. She didn't really mean any of what she had said. The vampire, no, Marianna, had saved them, and she had done what she had said she would—get them through the pass. Gabriela was just . . . stressed and tired, she hadn't had a good night's sleep in weeks. And she was scared for the future. So many things had changed in such a short time, yet it felt like they had been struggling for months, and not just weeks. She shuddered to imagine what awaited them in the future, especially with what they had been learning with every passing day. The old world was dead, murdered by the coming of a force that had taken everything from them. They had to adapt or die like so many others had.

"We must look to take care of those that we can," Gabriela whispered back after a moment.

Angelo didn't respond, and instead they settled into an uncomfortable silence. It lasted until they finally reached the edge of the forest and looked out on the desert ahead. A piece of Earth displaced from its original location. She could see that the boundary between the forest and the desert had shifted again. The climate here wasn't a desert one, so the forest was slowly creeping through the desert, changing it, faster than anyone had expected. They didn't know how or why it was happening that quickly, but it was just one more mystery among too many. They didn't have the time to think about it. Looking out in the distance, she could just barely see a tiny dark spot on the horizon.

Finally, she thought to herself. They were close to home.

They reached the base less than an hour later. The HESCO barrier surrounded it, filled with dirt, and rocks placed on the outside of the fabric. She could see that they had finished fortifying the barrier, since the wire mesh eroded a while ago. Sandbags were on top of them, and concrete walls on the inside. She could see the two wooden towers at the corners of the base—built just days ago to replace the metal ones that had collapsed. Guards had seen them coming a while ago, and the gates were ready to let them in.

The entrance was two big wooden doors, made out of improvised planks. They had to replace a lot of little things with wood, and they were still working on things.

"Gabriela! Angelo! You're back," one of the guards waiting for them in front of the open gates called out to them with a wave. He wore a sword tied to his belt, of all things, a reward gained in one of the rifts. Weapons were few and worth more than all the other resources they had. They needed them to survive.

"Marco," she greeted him then grasped his hand as they walked over. "We're back, yes," she said, finally allowing herself to relax as they walked through the entrance and the gate closed behind them. There were a lot of people inside of the base. Open tents were on one side, with people working beneath them in the shade. Large pots were cooking over fires, and women peeled vegetables to the side, preparing lunch. On the other side of the base were closed tents, serving as the residential area. A long strip of paved road led forward to the middle of the base, where a large tent took the center. There were a few other areas behind it, dedicated to different things, though the collapsed hangars were still being cleared out. But most people were here, near the entrance. Tables were set up in front of the residential tents with people sitting and talking, living. Kids ran around under adults' watchful gazes. It was a lot. They had almost a thousand people all in all. Survivors all.

The atmosphere was relaxed, for the most part, except the people sitting in the four towers at the corners of the base. It used to be a military base, before . . . well, just before. None of them were military. They had a few police officers that had escaped the various towns in the area or had come from Medellín before things really turned bad. At the start, they were just a group of around a hundred people, running away from the end of the world. They found the base abandoned about a week after the Light came. Whoever was stationed there had abandoned it completely, and had taken most of their stuff with them and destroyed what they couldn't take. They didn't even know which nation the base belonged to, though it hardly mattered. It was theirs now. Over the weeks, more groups found them and joined. They were joining them still, though the flow had slowed significantly.

"And you've brought friends?" Marco asked and gave the priest a smile.

Father took a step forward, ushering the kids next to him forward. "Good day, I'm Father Sergio Rodriguez. These two scoundrels are Lea and Juan."

"Good day to you too, Father." Marco bowed his head. "Lea, Juan, welcome to Refuge, I'm sure that you'll like it here." He gave the kids a big smile. Then he glanced at Gabriela and gave her a look with an eyebrow raised. It was just a hint of his real thoughts seeping through.

Gabriela and Angelo weren't supposed to bring back others, she knew. Her mission wasn't a rescue, it was a scouting mission. And the realities of the pass had made any attempt of a relocation of the church people unlikely. They had talked about it.

"A lot happened," Angelo interjected.

"I can imagine," Marco said. "Diego and Catalina are waiting for you in the *big tent.*"

Gabriela nodded. She had expected it. They had seen them coming, had enough time to prepare. "Can you escort the children somewhere so that they could get some rest? We've pushed hard the last few days," Gabriela asked him in a whisper.

Marco smiled and nodded, then knelt and started talking to the kids.

"You want to come meet some new friends? My kid's almost the same age as you guys."

She tuned him out as she gestured for the priest to follow her. "I wish that we could get some rest, but it would probably be best if we talk to the higher-ups. They need to know what happened back there," she told him.

He nodded. "I understand," the priest answered. "There is a lot that I should probably tell them, things that Marianna spoke about."

Gabriela was glad that he understood. They were all in this together now.

It took three days for Gabriela to feel like things were back to what was normal for the world they were now living in. The debrief with Diego and Catalina, their leaders, or at least the people that they all listened to, was long and . . . hard. First there was her own report, the fact that dungeons in Medellín had started to break open and the city was being overrun. That spelled disaster for them and their base, but it was the priest's words that had actually frightened everyone that was part of the meeting. Gabriela didn't know if any of it was the truth, but it was so unbelievable. Other races? Different worlds all smashed together into one big planet? They had some people who knew the science, and all agreed that it shouldn't be possible. That the gravity would've changed, that so much else would've gotten out of control. And yet . . . there were two moons above their heads, the stars were different. They had pieces of the Earth moved around, entire landscapes, while the climate remained mostly the same. They had magic, Masks that gave them power.

It was no less believable than what they already knew, like rifts in space that led to other places.

She spent the three days getting debriefed, and now as the sun was slowly setting on the third day, she was finally free, or almost free. She had just one more thing to do. Gabriela walked through the camp, heading to a scout operations tent in the western quadrant of the base. It was in the area that used to hold hangars, which had eroded and most had been cleaned up. They had four quadrants. The southern area, which was their residential quadrant, and also doubled as the place for all of their food related stuff. The eastern hunters' area where the people that could fight usually met to talk about how to deal with threats and planned out hunts that supplied them with food, though mostly they concerned themselves with the camp security—they were the only reason why they'd survived so long. And then there were the northern *training grounds*, which was basically just the junkyard where they dumped all the unusable shit they recovered from the base. It used to be the base's shooting range, but they had limited guns and even more limited ammo, so they rarely used it for that purpose. The most important area was the middle that joined all four quadrants, what they called the *big tent*. That's where they did all of their logistics.

The tent was a long half-oval, one of the tents that had their inner frame collapse. They'd jury-rigged a new frame from wood and other materials that were still whole, but it wasn't as stable as it used to be. Thankfully, the climate here was not what it had probably been in the area this small piece of the desert came from.

Tarps were set up all around the tent, with people working mostly outside. Tables were covered with papers, one of the few things that they had found on the base, along with office supplies. She walked over to one of them, where a single elderly man sat drawing on a sketched map. This was the place where scouts gathered to talk about what next steps they should take and plan routes to get to rifts or other important resources.

"Hey, old man, I'm back," Gabriela said as she took a seat across from him. The candle next to him wasn't yet lit, but the daylight was slowly fading as the sun set. He would need it if he wanted to continue working into the night.

The old man raised his head from his work and showed her his crooked grin. "I heard, I heard, welcome back. I'm glad you got home safely, girl."

"It was rough. We almost didn't get back." She crossed her arms and scratched at her elbow.

The old man's expression darkened. "You need to stop taking such risks, Ela."

She grimaced and put her hands on the table. "It's my job, Sebastian, and besides we can't afford to take things slow."

Sebastian sighed. "You're right, of course. So," he changed the subject. "You have something for me?"

Gabriela nodded. "We went through the pass, and we explored a bit down south next to the road."

"You went through the pass?" he asked, his voice low.

"It's a long story, but yes."

"What was it?" Sebastian asked.

"A big flying lizard monster." Gabriela shivered. "It was terrifying."

"I'm glad you got out," he said, then pulled out a small box of matchsticks and lit the candle next to him. After that he pulled a new piece of paper from a stack next to him and tapped it with his pen. "So, tell me what you saw."

Gabriela focused and started describing. First were the different monsters they'd encountered, including the ratmen that attacked the church. Once he'd sketched all of them, she switched to describing the new areas they scouted out, letting him fill in the gaps in the map of the area. They had mapped a lot of their surroundings. In most cases, it was the same as it had been before. It was the small areas, the pieces shuffled around from other parts of the globe that were the issue.

"So, something like this?" Sebastian asked as he turned the map and the sketches around.

Gabriela looked at it, then nodded. "You're really talented."

He chuckled, then tapped the side of his head with his pen. "Nah, I am mediocre, always was. Except that now I have this thing in my head that makes it easier to imagine things and translate it to the page."

She knew that he was referring to his skill, [Visualize Art], which let him imagine things with greater clarity, especially when someone else was describing it. He used to be a construction worker. He had no work experience drawing maps, but his Mask had nothing to do with it. Instead, he had gotten the Mask of the Dauber. He had always loved painting, and had done it as a hobby when he had the time. He never got to be any good at it, yet he had gotten the Mask related to it. They suspected that the Masks they gained were related to the things that they enjoyed doing the most. The same way how Gabriela was a photographer, but had gotten the Mask of the Scout. She used to travel the wilderness, looking for the hidden gems, best places to take photos. But it was never really about the photos, it was about discovering incredible vistas. Places that were hidden from everyone. Her [Sharp Eye] skill had made her a good scout for their group, so she just fit in that role.

"Well," she said finally. "Your maps are a lifesaver."

He smiled then opened his mouth to say something else when they were interrupted. "Gabriela, there you are," a breathless man said as he ran over.

Immediately, she was on guard. "What is it, Marco?" She stood up quickly.

"We need you at the southern gate, quick," Marco said in a single breath. He pulled her arm, and she hurried after him. Sebastian stood and followed as well.

"What is it?" she repeated.

Marco glanced back at her. "We got something coming."

Gabriela frowned, but didn't ask any other questions. She noticed that something was spreading around the people. A lot of them were running for the gate, while others were gathering up the kids and ushering them away from it. She noticed Diego and Catalina on top of the improvised platform next to the gate, that would let them see over the concrete wall.

She could see people with rifles in the two towers, one in each, and another two armed guards up on the platform with a handgun and another rifle, the one that she had brought with her.

Marco led her to the platform, and she climbed the wooden ladder to stand next to Diego.

"Gabriela, good," Diego said in relief. "Can you look with your eyes, tell us what you see?"

She glanced in the direction he was pointing, and saw a black dot on the horizon. "You didn't send anyone out?"

Diego shook his head, then gestured at Angelo standing next to Catalina. "He sees danger, deathly danger."

Gabriela swallowed, then turned her eyes on the distant dot and used her skill. Immediately, she stumbled back in surprise.

"Impossible," she whispered.

"What is it?" Catalina asked.

Gabriela turned her head to look at the woman. Her black hair streaked with gray was billowing in the wind, but Gabriela could see the fear in her eyes.

She took a moment to compose herself, then she told them.

They gathered to wait in front of the gates—too many people, though nobody was thinking about that now. Gabriela stood with Diego, Catalina, a few of the guards, and Father Rodriguez, who had also come out. He looked ahead with awe in his eyes, where everyone else was terrified.

Gabriela had to hold her hands clasped behind her back to keep them from shaking. The vampire had survived, and she was coming. The night had fallen fully by the time she reached the gates, which was more than an hour after she was spotted. They probably should've sent a group out, but if she was being honest, it didn't occur to any of them. Torches were the only things that were giving them light. So the only thing that Gabriela could see was the vampire, Marianna, walking at a slow steady pace, each foot digging deep into the sand before pushing forward.

"I knew that she was still alive," the priest whispered next to Gabriela.

She turned her head and glanced at him; his eyes were glued to the vampire. His face showed no signs of fear. Instead something else lurked in his eyes. Awe? Gabriela was unsure what it was that she was seeing. She turned back, looking at the shape moving in the darkness, slowly stepping into the light.

What most people were looking at wasn't the vampire, actually, but what was behind her. A massive black shape that they had trouble seeing in the dark, a shape that she was dragging by rope and a silver chain. It was hard to say just how big it was, especially in the dark, but it looked much larger than the creature that attacked them in the pass.

Finally, the woman reached them, dropped the chain and the rope, then looked straight at Gabriela.

"Sorry for the wait, that thing is heavy." She smiled.

Her eyes were different—the emerald flowing into her eyes was more pronounced, deeper. Her eyes reflected the light from the torches like a sea reflecting moonlight, sending shivers down Gabriela's spine.

Introductions

I looked at the group assembled in front of me. They were a dirty and ragged bunch. I could smell the sweat on their skin, soaked in their clothes that hadn't been washed in weeks by the look of the dirt on them. There were many scents coming in from beyond the walls too, and I doubted that they realized just how far away I could smell them from. Most predators might've avoided them before, but who knew how the Source would mutate them now. Some might get more aggressive.

The first person to respond to my presence was Father Sergio. He walked up and reached for my hands—it took me by surprise enough that I didn't react. He grasped both my hands in his, then brought them close and bowed over them before touching his forehead with them.

"Thank you, my child, for saving our lives," he whispered, low enough that the others probably hadn't heard.

"I'm glad you got here safe," I said, though of course, I already knew they had. I had sent Saia to scout ahead and make sure that there was no danger on their path to the base. I wasn't about to abandon them. I had made a deal. But seeing as Saia saw no danger, I decided to stay behind and recover from my fight and my many broken bones.

After the weirzi had slammed into the ground with me on top of it, I shattered just about every bone in my body on impact. Thankfully, I was close enough to the bountiful source of blood that I could heal. The blood I drank from the two beasts had also granted me two Carvings. I was now on my First Investment; Sixth Carving, alongside one new skill. I hadn't yet had the chance to go into my soul space to learn the details, but I could feel the skill and knew how to use it instinctively.

After healing, I took one more day to recover fully and rest. I did some scouting of the mountain pass the day after that, to make sure that there weren't any more of the weirzi around. Saia had mentioned that weirzi usually lived in pairs, but there was no sign of the male. If they had escaped a rift, then it was possible that there were no more of them. I found the weirzi nest in a cave, filled with bones and chewed up clothes and equipment, and no sign of any other danger.

With Saia's scouting ahead of the others, I had enough time to figure out what to do with the body of the weirzi. It occurred to me that it could be useful. The scales were incredibly tough, and we were in a world where materials were scarcer than they once were. Our metals had different properties—the erosion seemed to be some kind of extreme and accelerated version of oxidation, and though there were probably ways that we could protect them from that, it would require research that we didn't have the resources or time for.

Earth had to start from scratch, rediscovering fire under the new rules.

"We are only here because you stayed behind to fight that—" Father Sergio glanced at the large carcass behind me and nodded in its direction. "It is a lot larger than it appeared to be."

I grinned, showing my fangs. "Oh no, that was the young, this was the mother."

"Ah," the priest said with a strange look in his eyes. "God has sent you to us, I see."

"I sent myself," I told him with a lighter tone, but his eyes didn't waver.

Before he could say anything else, someone from the bigger group approached.

"Good evening, Master," a man said. He was dressed in a military garb, like a lot of the people around him were, though I could tell that they weren't military. From what I heard before these people had just found this base, and probably recovered equipment inside. His hair was pulled back into a ponytail and completely gray. His face was wrinkled and damaged by sun exposure, a clear sign that he used to spend most of his time in the open. He seemed fit, and his heart beat with a sure rhythm, though slightly elevated, indicative of someone who was afraid. His eyes kept sliding over my shoulder, looking at the weirzi carcass.

"Ah." Father Sergio turned to stand next to me. "This is Mr. Diego Murillo, and next to him is Ms. Catalina Flor. They are . . . well, something like the leaders of this group."

I eyed the woman that stepped forward after the father named her. She looked to be about the same age as the man next to her, probably in her fifties. She wore a long brown skirt and a green blouse. Her hair was brown, with gray streaks near her scalp. The smell of food clung to her—too many different flavors to count. She had been spending time preparing it, and a lot of it. But there was also something else. I detected a familiar scent that reminded me of hospitals— alcohol and other sanitizing agents. The tips of her fingers were slightly darker, stained with iodine.

She stood straight, and her eyes met mine with no hesitation—too bad that her pulse betrayed her too. It'd been a long time since I'd had to meet new people, new humans. I had grown up in a place surrounded by other vampires, shifters, and the humans who were part of the organization. The barrios I patrolled and visited were places that were under the organization's protection. There was fear, but they knew me. They were our humans. This was actually the first time I was meeting someone who probably never saw a vampire in their life. Despite us being *out*, most people would have only seen and heard about us on the television.

"A pleasure," I said slowly. I didn't move to offer my hand; humans were fragile and easily frightened, and I didn't want to spook them. Especially not with around two dozen people staring at me, a couple of them even with guns. Not that I was worried that they could actually hurt me.

"I'm Marianna Rojas, and just Marianna is fine," I said after a beat, then turned to look at the group behind them. "Gabriela, Angelo, I'm glad to see that you got home safely."

Gabriela swallowed, then nodded. "I—yes, we . . . thank you for your help."

"*De nada*," I told her, then looked at the two that stood in front of me.

I could see that they were struggling to find the words, so I offered them a mercy. "I brought you a gift." I pointed over my shoulder. "I'm sure that food is one of the main issues a large group like yours is having."

Everyone looked at the weirzi, and whispers started spreading among them. I let it go on for a moment before turning to Father Sergio. "I trust that the children are safe?"

He nodded. "As safe as they can be."

I sighed, then glanced at the silver chain and rope around my hand. "Saia, drone please," I said, and the silver chain shifted, flowing until it turned into a dragon. She was almost the size of a football now. I had her consume the young weirzi, which was made out of biological matter she was more familiar with, allowing her to gain more mass from it. Everyone around me was startled at her. I turned back to the two in front of me and spoke.

"So, are we going to stand out here and talk, or are you going to invite us in?"

It didn't take long for everyone to scatter after the two leaders agreed to at least a conversation. There was a lot that I needed to do, but first I had to talk with the ones in charge. I dragged the carcass inside, and some women directed me to drop it beneath a tarp near the entrance. It seemed like they'd set up a large cooking area there, and I could see other animal meat being treated on wooden tables.

Then, they led me through the base and toward a big tent in the center of it. From what I could see and hear around me, the camp was struggling, which wasn't surprising at all. It seemed like I was being watched by everyone in the camp as we walked down the road, and I tried to ignore the looks as best as I could.

We entered the dimly lit tent, and I was escorted to the center, along with Saia, who sat on my shoulder. I wasn't above using her as a tool to keep people off-balance. Once inside, I found myself standing across a table from five people.

The two leaders, Diego and Catalina, were in the center, flanked by Gabriela on one side and two people that I didn't recognize. One was a gruff looking fellow who looked to be in his thirties. He wore a dark green uniform that I recognized as a police uniform with a rank visible—he was a *teniente,* a lieutenant, if the uniform was his. On his hip he had a scabbard with a sword holstered in it. The last person was a young man, very young. He barely looked old enough to drink. He had a wild blond hair, and wore a simple blue shirt and cargo pants. He also stood out among the others, as he was clearly not from around here. He alone wasn't apprehensive. In fact, he had a grin on his face.

Diego cleared his throat, then indicated the two. "This is Lieutenant Carlos Cabrera, and next to him is Maximilian Dawson."

"Max, please," the kid said with a chipper tone.

Diego then gestured to his other side. "And you already know Gabriela."

I inclined my head but didn't speak.

"Carlos is the . . . I guess that he is the head of security for the camp. He organizes our hunters and guards for the camp," Catalina added. "And Max is . . ."

She paused, and Max chipped in with an answer.

"I'm in charge of figuring out all the magic shit! The Masks, and how they level. I have so many questions for you—"

Diego coughed, again, interrupting him. "I'm sure that there will be time for all that, later."

"I assume that Father Sergio told you about the things I revealed to him and the others?" I tilted my head.

"Yes, he did," Catalina said slowly. "We are, obviously, unsure what to think about that."

I nodded. "That's understandable, it is a lot to take in."

"Excuse me, Mas—uh, Ms. Marianna," Diego started slowly. "We are grateful for your help with our people. Gabriela had told us everything that you did. But . . ." He trailed off.

"But you want to know my intentions?" I could read it on their faces. They were terrified of me. "The world has changed," I started. "In more ways than you even realize. We, the people of Earth, don't have the time to get our bearings. To understand what has happened and to accept this new reality. The danger has only just begun. And if we want to not only survive, but have a chance to thrive, then we all need to work together. That's why I'm here. Because you are the first survivors I've come across since I returned. Because you have people, and I've made a decision to save as many as I can from what is coming. I'm here to help. My intention is to aid you in survival, to prepare you for what is coming, to seek out other survivors."

They exchanged glances with each other. I could still see doubt in their eyes. That was fine. I'd expected it, if I was being honest. And now I had to add more doubt.

"We can discuss this and other things tomorrow, for tonight I have only one thing that I have to say to you." I looked them in the eyes, and they looked back expectantly.

"You sent out a group of three people to search for rifts, scouts. Their names were Mateo, Louis, and Cristo, yes?"

They blinked. Obviously that wasn't what they had expected me to say.

It was the uniformed man, Carlos, who answered. "How do you know that? They're missing, they missed their return date."

I nodded. "And they won't be returning. They are dead."

He grimaced, and the others closed their eyes. "We've assumed as much," Diego added with a shake of his head. "We shouldn't have sent them that far. We've been losing too many of our groups beyond the pass. But they insisted. They wanted a chance to level their Masks . . . I assume that you found them? Was it a rift or a monster?"

He didn't yet make the connection, but I could see that Catalina, Max, and Carlos had. They'd noticed that I knew their names.

I shook my head. "No, I killed them."

They froze at that, and the fear that had been slowly ebbing away returned in most of them. I didn't let it sit for long, instead continuing.

"They ambushed myself and a child in my care as we were leaving a rift. I exited last, and by the time I did, the three of them had the kid in their hands. They were being rough with him and they threatened us. They demanded what I had gained in the rift, claiming that it was on their *turf* and that I had stolen it. Once I refused, they attacked. I defended myself."

Carlos closed his eyes, and I heard him whisper to himself. "Idiots."

No one said anything, so I continued. "I was defending myself, yes, but I didn't need to kill them. They didn't realize that I was a vampire when they threatened and attacked me. And I was strong enough that I could've just subdued them. But the truth is that they angered me, and I had a . . . different picture of who they were. I believed them to be something akin to bandits, and their demeanor did nothing to convince me otherwise. I tell you this because I didn't want to start this relationship with a secret like that."

"We all know," Carlos started, "that every time we leave this base, we might never come back. But, these men were ours, they survived with us. They were our friends, family."

I nodded. "I understand. You can consider the carcass I brought as blood price for their lives. Not an apology, because I only reacted to their actions." I held his eyes for a long moment, and finally, hesitantly, he nodded.

"This is what I came to tell you tonight. You know my intentions," I said. "I'll leave you all to discuss, tomorrow I'll return and tell you the rest of the story, the things that you don't yet know and what awaits our world. Then you can decide if you want me around or not."

I left the base and made my way out of the desert, heading north. The desert surrounding the base was perhaps thirty square kilometers at most. I reached the forest quickly enough, with Saia flying above me and scouting. I found a good spot and sat down to wait. I didn't have to sit for long. Saia returned and landed next to me.

"Report: There are no visible threats in the area, nor have I detected any recent tracks or other signs of beast presence."

"Good," I said. "And the rift?"

"Feedback: No change."

I nodded. "You'll keep watch then?" I asked.

"Feedback: Of course, Mari."

With that I closed my eyes and pulled myself into my soul space. Saia's manifestation within this place followed a moment later. I was too busy to come here before, and I was worried that the mountain pass had more dangers than just the weirzi, so I delayed. Then I decided to take the carcass with me, and I barely had the time. Dragging something that heavy was exhausting even for me. Not because it was that much of a strain on my muscles, especially once [Lesser Strength] returned from cooldown, but because I was a vampire and we weren't as good at prolonged exertion. I had to take breaks, and daylight interfered as well.

The first thing I did was walk over to the three pedestals in the center and take a look.

Mask of the Blood Invoker (Physical, Weave, Esoteric) — First Investment; Sixth Carving
Ornament of the Revelator (Weave, Esoteric) — No Investment; Sixth Carving
Ornament of the Student (Physical, Weave, Esoteric) — No Investment; Eighth Carving

My Ornament of the Revelator had increased after my talk with the people at the base. I guessed that sharing about their dead people counted as revealing the truth. It only solidified my decision to tell them. I had done it for a few reasons.

What I said to them was part of it—I didn't want to start a relationship that depended on trust with a lie. But perhaps more importantly, it was because of my oath to the Way. Obligation and debts. I killed them without needing to, because I believed a child's words and made mistaken conclusions. I owed a debt for that, even though I was justified. I had made a decision to abide by my own rules, and they didn't need to know why I had done as I had. I believed the weirzi was more than enough to pay for their deaths. Ultimately, they had attacked me first.

I turned my eyes away and looked around at the shelves that held my unused skills; the change was noticeable. The simple shelves had changed into dark red wood, framed by jade stone in between every bowl, which had changed as well. Instead of the drab stone, the bowls now had lines of jade as well.

It was the effect of his new skill. In the corner, next to one of the walls, a single pedestal stood with the exact same bowl as the ones on the shelves. I approached it and took a look, very interested to see what the skill actually was—I only knew its name.

[Overburn Skill]

You may use this skill to utilize any of the skills on your shelves at a boosted effectiveness, burning it out in the process. The used skill is lost alongside the door it was obtained through until another source of it is found and the skill regained.

I had a suspicion that it had something to do with my shelved skills. Every time I focused on the skill, I had a vague sense of the skills I had on the shelves. Right now I had six skills on my shelf: [Lesser Leap], [Peck], [Sharp Eye], [Sonic Screech], [Lesser Impale], and [Quick Claw]. All skills that I didn't think had a place in my main profiles.

[Overburn Skill] felt powerful, like it was a more meaningful skill somehow. It felt like what Shadow had described to me as a capstone skill. A skill that defined an Investment tier. I couldn't wait to experiment. But before that I decided that I probably should go and gather more skills.

"What do you think? Cool skill, huh?" I grinned at Saia.

"Feedback: It is very intriguing. Though I wish that these descriptions showed numerical values of effects. What does *boosted effectiveness* mean in practice?"

"We'll just have to experiment and find out," I told her.

Saia turned her head away almost as if she was sulking. I smiled then headed out into my corridor of doors. I passed by all my old doors and decided that it would probably be best if I cleared them all now while I had the time. I walked past Shadow's door, deciding to visit with him after I was done with the skills.

The first of the new doors I reached belonged to the rats, a rundown wooden door with holes and tiny claw marks all over it. I opened it and saw only one rat in the forest, and I frowned at it. I closed it and looked next to it, there were three identical doors, that looked only slightly better than the first one. I opened them, and in each I saw a ratman.

Immediately, I realized why I had only one door for the rats despite drinking from dozens of them. I was already aware that my doors were not related to individual races, but sources of blood. What this now confirmed to me was that it was also skill related. The rats that I had killed were probably all low Investment, with only a single skill available to them. It was probably why I only had a single door for the deep dwellers, the monkeys I killed in Saia's rift.

This probably meant that I couldn't have multiple doors containing the same skill. That dashed the dream that barely had the chance to be born, of me stacking on a powerful skill to use with my [Overburn Skill]. I would need to go out and find a new source of the skill every time I used it. But that still left me with a lot of options.

I entered the rooms and started killing, obtaining skills in the process.

Going Forward

Once again, I fought the adult weirzi in the mountain pass. It was bleeding, struggling to get away from me on the ground. I had already ripped holes in its wings. I had time to think about my first fight with it, and had realized just how much my inexperienced fighting had cost me. I relied too much on my physical strength, when I could've been much more strategic about it. The weirzi's scales were incredibly tough, but its wings weren't as protected. This time I attacked them with my chain and blade, ripping strips through it and forcing the weirzi to the ground. After that, it was easy for me to dance around it and tire it out, attacking the weak points. Especially since I had my handgun in here as well. The soul space manifested everything available to me in the real world.

Once the weirzi died, I approached the floating orb that represented the dropped skill and carried it over to my shelves. I placed it in the empty bowl on the shelf and took a look at it.

[Lesser Constitution]

Gain a passive increase in constitution.
<beast><physical>

It was an answer as to why its scales were so tough, at least one of them. And it was actually a very strong skill. The [Lesser Strength] had served me well, and I had no doubt that this one would too. Especially since these type of skills scaled of my physical attributes. I was almost certainly going to put it in my active skill profile.

Then, I glanced to the other shelves where I had gathered the skills from the other doors in my corridor.

The weirzi infant granted me [Bite], a physical skill that did exactly what it suggested: it increased the power of my bite. It wasn't a bad skill for a vampire, especially if I wanted to bite something that had tougher skin. The three ratmen each gave me a different skill: [Slash], [Dodge], and [Lesser Command—ratkin].

The two physical skills were solid, though I didn't know if they had a spot in my profiles just yet. I had to think about what I wanted the profiles to be; the cooldown on my [Swap Profile] was too long for me to use it more than once in a single combat, unless I used my Mask, but that wasn't something that I should plan my profiles around.

The rat had granted me the [Hive Mind—ratkin] skill, which I didn't even know if I could use. Though it was obvious that the combination of it and [Lesser Command—ratkin] was what allowed the ratmen to control the rats as I had seen. Still, I would have to experiment if I got the chance.

The last skill I gained was from the snake I killed at the estate, which granted me the [Lesser Camouflage] skill. That could prove useful if I ever needed to make a scouting or a more stealthy profile.

With all of those skills gathered, I had one more door left. I walked back into the corridor, Saia following behind me, and stopped in front a very basic kind of a door of the type that you could find in any house: simple brown wood with a lever handle. The door belonged to Martin Perez, the hunter whose blood I had taken at the church. I wondered what I would find inside. Shadow was a copy of himself, a fully conscious one. The other three humans I killed were just mindless puppets that I had to defeat again to gain the skill.

With Shadow, it was different. His blood, like Martin's, was freely given. I would have to overcome a test of a kind in order to gain his skill.

I left him as last on purpose because I didn't know how to explain it to him if he was fully conscious. Shadow's copy had understood his fate on his own, but then again, he was old and powerful.

I shook my head then pushed the door open and entered. I walked into a forest, and I saw Martin immediately. He was crouching on the ground, dressed in an outfit suitable for hunting. In one hand he held his hunting rifle, and the other was on the ground.

"Martin," I said slowly.

He turned his head to look in my direction and brought his finger to his mouth. "Shh," he shushed me, then in a low whisper he continued. "You're finally here, girl, come." He motioned for me to get closer.

I frowned, but did as he asked. I knelt next to him, and he pointed at the ground.

"What do you see?" he asked.

I frowned but glanced down. "The ground?" I whispered back.

"No, no, look here." He pointed. "The position of the leaves, the slight dent in the earth, the broken twig. Something passed through here, and recently."

I looked him in the eyes, and quickly realized the truth. "You don't remember anything, do you?" I asked, but mostly for myself.

It was his turn to frown. "I remember you begging to learn my skill, girl. Now focus and listen. The basis of tracking lies in the observation of your surroundings."

It seemed like he wasn't like Shadow after all. Shadow was unique, one of the most powerful Masked in the world. His power had likely allowed his copy to retain much of who his real self was. I was lucky in a way. I still had my teacher, my family with me. It would've been harder if he was like Martin.

I focused my mind and leaned down, listening to what Martin was saying.

"To properly track, you need to know your quarry. An herbivore would need more cover, so look for vegetation that could serve that purpose. Look for travel routes. An animal would likely take the easiest route it could take. Trails that are often used can be spotted with greater ease, and they indicate the presence of different game. Look for polished places on the landscape where animals would rub, hair and feathers, gnaws and chews, scratches. All of these are clues that most would overlook."

The more he spoke, the more I realized that there was actually a lot all around me that I hadn't noticed before. I listened and I learned, time passing slowly, until Martin finally turned to me and asked for me to track the animal.

I'd always relied more on my senses, but now I saw just how much better I could've been doing if I had also learned. I used what he taught me, and quickly we found our quarry.

"There it is," Martin said with a smile on his face. "Good job."

Then his body slowly faded away leaving only a skill orb on the ground. I picked it up and walked out then closed the door behind me. As soon as I closed it, the door broke down and vanished. I froze. It seemed that how I obtained blood had more rules than I had already discovered. The doors of those whose blood I had taken remained even after I took a skill, but this . . . It seemed that freely given blood had another rule.

I walked back into my main room and placed the [Track] skill on a shelf. I had only four doors left from which I didn't gain a skill: the mature ferrorn, the reaper, the sikiri, and Shadow. None of those doors were anything that I could take down right now.

I looked back to my shelves and all of my skills, trying to figure out new profiles based on what I felt I needed the most. My physical attributes were my greatest advantage, and I had to lean into that. So on my first profile I swapped out [Debilitating Wave] for [Lesser Constitution]. I felt like [Mist Step] was one of my most powerful skills, and that added mobility married with my physical abilities would allow me to utilize my strengths better. But I considered putting it in my second profile along with my other two movement skills: [Dodge] and [Quick Step]. It would activate my Movement trait bonus, but I decided against it and left it in my first profile. I planned on my first profile being my main one, and the loss of [Mist Step] in it would be too much. It really was my best skill.

And besides, all three of the skills in my main profile had the <beast> tag, meaning my Beast |Potential Augmentation| trait bonus was active, increasing all of my physical senses and reducing my skill cooldowns—which just meant [Mist Step], since others were passive, but even a single step reduced in the cooldown requirement was more than enough.

For my second profile, I removed [Double Strike] and [Quick Strike]. They were good skills, but as a vampire, they weren't as crucial to me as they would be for a human. I had more than enough strength to kill anything in my way, at least for now. I looked over my shelves and then settled on a more offensive build. For when I had to fight. I put in [Debilitating Wave] and [Sonic Screech], both skills which were capable of stunning my foes. The [Sonic Screech] scaled of the power of my lungs and throat, and since I was a vampire, it was very powerful. For the last skill I was torn in between [Double Strike] and [Dodge]. The offensive one had proven to be very strong, but having at least one defensive skill did appeal to me.

I mostly fought with my serpent-tongue spear or Saia's chain and blade form. Both of them had reach, which did afford me some room. But I had gotten pressed into close quarters enough times to know that being able to escape was paramount. I decided on [Dodge]. It was never wrong to have more defensive options.

The skill allowed me to double my dodging speed for a single moment, which with my attributes was a significant increase.

With my two profiles done, I moved on, heading back into the corridor and toward Shadow's door.

I found him on the plateau, sitting on the ledge and gazing out at the afternoon sun. I walked over and sat next to him, staying silent. Saia jumped in my lap, and together the three of us we watched the sunset for a little while. It had been a while since I had a moment to myself. This might all be just in my Mask, but it was still a breathtaking vista. I felt like I hadn't had a moment's rest in months, and yet it had only been days.

Finally, I decided to break the silence.

"A lot happened," I said slowly.

"Tell me about it," Shadow simply said. So I did. I told him everything that had happened since the last time we spoke. It came out in a rush, my voice filled with emotion. I didn't realize just how much all of it had affected me. But it felt good to speak about it with someone. Once I was done, I could feel the tension leaving my body.

"I am sorry that happened, Little Star," he said softly. "Life is fleeting, and that of children more than most."

"I made him a promise, and I failed him."

"You could not have known what would happen," Shadow added.

"I shouldn't have left the church, if I was there—"

"Do not dwell on what could have been. That is the path to madness. Regrets are poison. They are a burden that only serves to weigh us down. I know it well. Learn from mistakes I have lived through. Remember, but do not hold the blame."

I didn't know if I could do what he asked, but I nodded. I would try. "I slowed down," I said after a while.

Shadow tilted his head. "Slowed down?"

"You told me that the Grand Spell gives the new continent an accelerated Investment gain, to help the survivors catch up to the other continents. The weirzi and the rats that I killed gave me almost as much Investment as the higher Investment beasts on Ish Vimza had, despite having much lower Investment. I should've taken advantage, hunted beasts every day. Looked for rifts, done more."

Shadow nodded. "Yes, you should have. But that too is in the past. Let it go. You can do more from now on. You didn't lose much time."

I knew that he was right. It had been barely a week since I returned. I had a bit less than five months before the portals opened and expeditions from other continents arrived. I had to accelerate all of my plans.

"What are you going to do with the group?" Shadow asked.

I grimaced. "Help them survive, get stronger. Prepare them."

Shadow sighed. "You know that isn't going to work, Little Star."

I turned away. We'd had this discussion before. "Vae Victis, huh?"

"Yes," Shadow said. "Why are you hesitating now?"

"Because I don't know how to do it," I said, frustrated. Words were easy. When I made my decision, I was in a death-filled jungle, surrounded by monsters. I had to have something to push me forward, a desire that would help me survive. It was different now, when I saw their faces.

"How do your people choose leaders?" Shadow asked.

"Humans usually choose them by majority vote. Vampires leaders are the oldest ones, though what really makes them leaders is strength. It just so happens that we grow stronger with age. Shifters are the same, they fight for leadership positions."

"You are a vampire. Why not act as is your nature?" Shadow asked.

"It isn't that easy. They don't know how old I really am—"

"Age does not matter. You said that it is about strength. You are stronger than them. And you have the knowledge and experience that they lack. You have survived Ish Vimza, you know what is coming. You were chosen as an Exemplar. It is a heavy burden, but it is one that you must bear."

I sighed, then glanced at Saia.

"What do you think?" I asked her.

"Feedback: Mastery, knowledge, and strength in the Source-Weave related matters was one of the prime qualities of Ke Erzi leadership. Ke Erzi believed that power is one of the main components that a capable leader must have. No matter how that power is embodied."

"Most people are the same," Shadow continued. "They gravitate toward the powerful, because they can protect them, and because they can bring them riches and help them get powerful too. Show the people your strength, show them your power, and they will follow."

I took a deep breath then nodded. I could do that. I planned on helping them survive, on helping them clear rifts and getting them supplies. Helping them gain Investment and advancing.

"Help them, I can do that," I said slowly.

"Help them," he repeated. "But do not tie yourself to them, Little Star," he said.

I frowned. "Why not?"

"A thousand survivors are nothing. You need to spread, to gather more. To find other settlements and bring them all together. You need to build a small kingdom that can hold off the expeditions and other groups that will be working with them. You need to build up something that can survive, and you don't have much time to do it."

I closed my eyes. *Yeah, that seems about right.* I sighed to myself. Sometimes, the weight of it all felt like it would crush me. But then I remembered the message I recovered from the ruins, a being that had cast a bottle in the river of time and had it land on my shores. I remembered the blight and the horrible things I saw in that vision.

There was more at stake here than just whether or not the Earth would be under someone's boot. There were dangers in this world beyond anything I could've imagined before. Shadow was better equipped for it, yet I had taken it on myself to help. And no matter my doubts, no matter how difficult it was, I would do it. It felt like it was my calling, my purpose in this life.

I spent the rest of the night and the next day exploring the surrounding area. I came upon a few of the survivors' scouting groups, but I didn't approach and made sure that they didn't see me. The area was mostly safe. The most dangerous thing I saw was a bear, which I killed and drank its blood. I had to get into the habit of killing beasts more often. My Mask granted me a relatively easy way to gather Investment, and I had to take advantage of it.

I had Saia consume the dead bear, getting more mass. The larger she was, the more I could do with her. She was now large enough that instead of looking like a bracelet on my wrist, she was closer to being an entire bracer.

I noted the few rifts in the area too, and that their light was mostly green, with one rift being blue. I didn't know what the light meant, but I was starting to think that it designated difficulty. Though what point of reference the Grand Spell was using if that was the case, I had no idea.

I observed one of the survivors' groups enter a rift. They were a group of seven, though only five entered, while two remained outside to keep watch. They were equipped with one rifle, and a mix of axes and swords. What was interesting was that they all wore some type of ballistic body armor. It looked like they had recovered more than I thought from the base.

They completed the rift in something around an hour, and all five of them left. I couldn't see what they had gained from it, but they dragged a large sack with them, which was obviously filled with something and took two people to pull. But they seemed satisfied. I waited for them to leave before approaching the rift. It was time for me to start getting stronger.

I took a step and entered the rift.

The Arena

When I entered the rift, the effects of the sun outside vanished, my strength returning as I found myself in a strange place. Sand was beneath my feet, and stone walls surrounded me. It was an arena—like the Colosseum—straight out of some history book. The night sky above was filled with so many stars that to my eyes it shone almost as if it was daylight. The stands were empty, and the arena floor had six pillars set in the circle near the edges of the floor, close to the walls.

"You recognize this place?" I asked.

Saia answered from my wrist. "Feedback: The architecture is not Ke Erzi, at least none that I am familiar with."

I looked behind and saw no sign of the rift exit.

"Well, I'm sure that we'll find out what it is soon enough."

I heard a click in the distance and turned my head swiftly. Ahead, on the wall across from me there was a board with five metallic cylinders. Each of them was blank, but the first one was turning, and it was the source of the clicking sound.

I watched it warily from across the arena and prepared. I took down my backpack and dropped it behind me, then raised my serpent-tongue spear with both hands and leaned forward, entering the first stance of **Veiled Mist Assault**: *From the Mist, Strike.*

Once the turning was finished, a strange symbol was now displayed on the surface of the board. The moment it stopped, a grinding sound echoed all around me. The floor of the arena opened, and from beneath it rose my opponent. I could hear them as the elevators brought them to the surface. The chittering and hollers were getting louder.

"Yeah." I grinned. "That seems about right."

The eight beasts entered the arena, standing upright and surrounding me, then immediately rushed across the sand. They were small, barely half my size. They looked reptilian, with rough looking reddish hide, long thin tails, and elongated snouts with spikes on their heads. They had rags tied around their waists and carried crude weapons, sharpened sticks and stone spears.

I blinked, freezing momentarily. The primitive weapons and clothing made me think that they were an intelligent species, which made me conflicted. I wondered how they arrived to this place, if I could avoid fighting them. I did not shy away from killing, but in this instance, it felt slightly . . . wrong. They looked like people, ones that had done me no wrong. But I knew that there was no choice, the rift exit was gone and probably wouldn't return until I had finished all the fights in the arena. I had to fight. Before I could get a chance to think more about it, they reached me and attacked, taking the decision out of my hands.

From my stance I leapt forward, avoiding the stabs of their weapons. I looked into their eyes, trying to see if there was anything there, but I saw only a desire to see me killed. I had ideas, but I didn't really know how these rifts worked. Were these beings just things that the Grand Spell had created from a template? Or were they real? Captured like everybody else, just serving whatever the Grand Spell's purpose was.

As they stabbed and swiped at me, I realized what they reminded me of—kobolds. They were slightly different, but the resemblance was enough that I began to refer to them that way in my mind. They were no threat to me. I knew it even before they attacked. They were small and weighed barely anything. There was no power behind their attacks.

Seeing as how they seemed set on killing me, and since I figured that fighting in this arena was the point of it all, I decided that there was no other course of action other than to fight.

A kobold attacked, and I slowed, moving just enough out of the way that its attack managed to scrape my right hand. It didn't even break my skin. The creature was weak, true, but it seemed that my [Lesser Constitution] did make my skin tougher. That attack should've at least scratched me.

I bent my knees and switched to the second Kata, *Tempest in the Mist*. I spun and extended my hand, letting my serpent-tongue spear swipe in a wide arc. I cut two of the kobolds in half, then I jumped to the side, pulling the weapon close before stepping forward into an attack twisting just right to let it pass next to my hip while I stabbed forward with both hands sideways. I impaled the creature through the throat and with a twist of my shoulders cut the blade out, half decapitating it.

The others went into a frenzy, attacking widely, and I danced, cutting them down, every step bringing death. I grabbed the last one by the throat then bit deep and drained its blood live. The blood flowed down my throat, and a heat spread through me, the ecstasy of life.

The memories that flashed through my mind were . . . weird. Not at all what I got the last time I drank from a rift animal. It was all jumbled together, flashes of incoherent images that didn't make much sense. I pushed the memories away and focused on drinking.

Once I was done, I moved over to the other corpses, and drank their blood too. No point in leaving Investment behind. The memories were the same with the other bodies.

"Any chance these are from Erzi?" I asked in between draining blood.

"Feedback: No, there is nothing in Ke Erzi records that resembles these creatures."

"Yeah, who knows how many worlds the Grand Spell has harvested and what it has in its shed." I shook my head. "You should consume one of them, get some more mass."

She flowed from my wrist and fell on top a kobold body as a glob.

If what Shadow suspected was true, the Grand Spell had gone through a lot more cycles than what the people of Kirios thought. It could've found worlds with no races on the levels of Earth and the others that it had decided to integrate. But it could've still kept lifeforms and pieces of those worlds for later use.

Just before I reached the last body, my attention was pulled away again. The clicking noise came again, and I saw the next cylinder on the board turning slowly. So, it seemed like there would be five fights, if each cylinder represented one.

I finished draining the last body then threw it aside as the next challengers were raised into the arena.

"Input: Should this Unit assume the defensive form on your person again?" Saia asked.

I narrowed my eyes at her. "You know that I realized what you are doing when you speak like that, don't you?"

"Feedback: This Unit isn't aware of doing anything," she said, almost smugly.

"Riiiight, any time you use the term *Unit* it is about a topic you don't particularly care about. You use *I* when you are actually interested in something."

The tiny dragon tilted her head at me, blue light flashing in her eyes. "Feedback: I was not aware of this discrepancy. I will endeavor to improve my conversation protocols."

I shook my head and snorted, then looked ahead.

"Just keep an eye out, okay?"

"Feedback: Affirmative."

This time, three beasts rose from the same point on the opposite side of the arena from me. They looked like hairless dogs, with wider heads and long thick strands on their bodies sticking out like spines all along their back in a single line. Their tongues lolled out of their mouth, long and thin. They growled in my direction, and their claws dug deep into the sand.

I bent my knees and got ready. I didn't have to wait long. The three beasts launched themselves forward, running at full speed.

I waited until they were about a dozen steps away from me, then I leapt forward with [Mist Step]. I re-formed in between two of them, spinning and lashing out with my weapon, bisecting them with ease.

The last one halted its momentum, its feed skidding across the sand, but I had already pounced on it. I stabbed it through the shoulder, pushing the blade into its stomach and out through the bottom of its body in between its hind legs. It squealed, and I grabbed its snout as I knelt and bit its neck, draining blood and killing it. Again, the memories were disjointed, though I did see a bit of them in a sandy area, hunting before white light came.

The arena wasn't a challenge, at least not to someone like me. I had expected that. If five humans were able to finish it without casualties, it shouldn't have anything that could threaten me.

Again, the board's cylinder started ticking around a minute after I killed the last beast. It was enough time that I drained the other two before the next countdown started.

Turning around, I saw that this time there were five new arrivals. I blinked as I recognized the animals. Five black boars rose from beneath the arena, only slightly mutated, with longer tusks that were tipped with a black substance that glinted in the dim light.

"You want to take one?" I asked as they charged me.

Saia's response was to jump and take flight. I saw her gain altitude quickly then swoop down on one of the boars, her claws digging deep in its back and even picking it up slightly, enough to throw it off balance and make it stumble.

I sidestepped the first boar that reached me and swiped my spear, cutting off its front legs, then spun and danced out of the way of the second one while doing a back kick that cracked bones in its hip and sent it flying across the sand. The third one I vaulted over and cut while upside down, slicing straight through its spine.

The fourth paused as it saw the others fall, and I rushed it with my superior speed and stabbed it through the head before it even realized what was happening. I returned to the first one, and put it out of its misery by draining its blood as I watched Saia fight the last boar. Again, the memories were the same.

There wasn't much that the boar could do against her. She was fast, could fly, was small, and mobile. She wore it down with dozens of wicked slashes all over its body until it collapsed from exhaustion, then she landed on top of it and pushed its claws through its eye into the boar's brain. It was quite a gruesome sight.

"Good job," I said.

"Statement: If I was at one hundred percent operating capacity, these creatures would have been nothing more than afterthoughts."

I grinned at her. "They are afterthoughts now."

Saia tilted her head, but didn't respond.

"How has our synchronization rate been going?"

Saia turned and met my eyes. "Feedback: Increasing with every Carving you obtain. We are approaching 30%. You are also capable of providing more energy to my systems. I am in the process of reworking and retooling my [Manufacturing] engram."

"Your what now?" I asked.

"Feedback: The [Manufacturing] engram allows the one bonded with the Self-replicating Autonomous Interface Armor to manufacture parts and tools necessary for completing the mission, using only the materials on hand. What could easily be found in the field."

I immediately realized what it was. Saia was basically a nanite swarm guided by an AI system. What she was describing meant that she could probably serve as something akin to a 3D printing station, only far more advanced.

"Well, that will be useful," I said.

Saia nodded. "Input: Unfortunately, it was necessary for me to remove the Source-Weave related components from the engram. The change in the natural laws means that I am incapable of reproducing the main elements of a Source-Weave enabled spare part."

"So what will you be able to do?"

"Feedback: Any material, composite, or tool that I have the blueprints for or have consumed and have the materials for, I should be able to recreate, provided they do not have any Source-Weave elements, obviously."

"You know, Saia, I don't know where I would be without you. Thank you for being here with me."

"Statement: Gratitude is unnecessary. Without you I would have perished in the laboratory. This way I have an opportunity to fulfill at least part of my programming and serve my Host."

"I know that we are bonded, but I don't need a servant. It's not how I view you, Saia. You are my companion, my friend. We are on this journey together."

Saia tilted her head. "Statement: Yes, I like that."

The clicking of the next countdown started, and I shook myself. The arena was filled with corpses, and it seemed that more were on their way.

The fourth wave was a group of flying bat-like creatures the size of grown dogs. Saia did most of the work by hunting them down in the air, while I jumped and managed to take down three.

There was now only a single wave left, if I was interpreting the board correctly. The last challenge.

The ground opened up, and the elevator rose depositing a large grizzly bear into the arena. It roared and charged, and I got ready.

I motioned to Saia as it got close, and she swooped from above, aiming for its head and distracting it. It reared up, trying to bite Saia in the air. I stepped forward, turning to mist and re-forming just next to its shoulder. My spear fell from above and cut straight through its head as it jaws closed on nothing.

The beast fell to the sand, dead.

"Well, that was easy," I said. Immediately, the ground shook as another elevator rose behind me. I jumped and turned, ready for anything. But instead of a threat, it was a wooden chest. I sighed and relaxed, as at the same moment the rift exit appeared behind the chest.

"Let's see what we got," I said to Saia, but before I headed toward the chest I bent and drank some of the bear's blood. Once I was finished, I frowned. The memories I gained were . . . it was like someone had jumbled them up on purpose. It almost made me wonder if the Grand Spell had done it, if it had realized that vampires could see into its secrets by drinking blood from the beasts in rifts.

I rolled my shoulders, just a tiny bit disappointed that I didn't get a single Carving from this. But I knew that the requirement increased with every Carving, and somehow I could tell that I was close to the next. I had to push forward, get as much Investment as I could. The accelerated gain would last only for a year, and I had already missed the first month by being sent to Ish Vimza. Though, I was lucky or unfortunate enough that I was sent to the continent filled with much more powerfully Invested beasts.

I walked over to the chest and put my hand on top of the latch, then swung it open.

There were three things inside. The first was a small sheath with a dagger nestled within. It looked and felt like a black leather of some kind. I picked it up and then pulled the dagger out. The blade was slightly curved, and I noticed that the blade had a faint orange tint to its surface. Other than that it didn't look like anything impressive. I offered it to Saia, and she tasted the blade.

"Input: It does not appear to be made out of the same material as the weapons gifted to you by Shadow."

I nodded. There were probably dozens of different metals that the people of Kirios used for their weapons. I slid the dagger back into its sheath and then attached it to the belt on my pants, letting it lie on my hip.

The second item was a stone, a whetstone, I was pretty sure, an item for sharpening blades. I put in my pack then moved on to the last item, a large pouch.

I opened it and was met with about two dozen gemstones. The same as the ones that I had gotten in the first rift I finished, though these were all brown and light green—earth and air. I stored them too, then with one last glance at the arena turned and walked out through the rift exit.

I waited until the night started set in before I walked up to the gates of the base. I arrived and was met with startled guards. They sent people running to announce my arrival the moment they saw me, so by the time I reached the gate they already had an escort waiting for me.

They led me down the same road I walked last time, heading to the big tent. I was led inside and was met with the same group of people.

Diego and Catalina were in the center, wearing clean clothes this time. Next to them was Maximilian—Max, the young man with an easy smile on his face. He seemed almost eager by the look of him.

Lieutenant Cabrera was on the other side, wearing a grim look with his arms crossed over his chest. He was in his uniform, his sword on his hip, with one more addition. I could smell the silver on him. Probably a knife, or maybe an improvised shiv, I doubted they had access to any real weapons made to fight vampires.

Gabriela was there too, standing to the side. She was clearly not part of the leadership, though I surmised that she was important in their hierarchy. The additions were the two other people in the room, obviously muscle, guards. They wore ballistic vests and military fatigues, and carried weapons. They had swords at their hips, and one of them had a gun.

They'd taken precautions, though that wouldn't do them any good if things took a wrong turn—not that I had any intention of killing anyone.

"Where's your . . . companion?" Max asked, and Diego elbowed him and gave him a look.

I smiled at the young man, but didn't answer. Saia's drone was currently masquerading as a silver ball in my backpack. Gabriela had probably mentioned what she had seen during the fight, if she remembered it, so I didn't want her present as a bracer right now.

"Welcome back, Ms. Rojas," Catalina started.

"Marianna is fine," I told them, again. "I hope that you've had a chance to talk amongst yourselves."

She glanced at Diego, then back at me. "We did. There was a lot to talk about."

I nodded. "And now I've come to fulfill my promise and tell you the rest of what I know."

"We will listen," Diego simply said.

So I told them. I told them that Earth had only five months left before portals opened and other continents were allowed to send expeditions. I told them of the previous Great Expansion Intervals and how those races had fared. The loss of life that they had suffered and the expectations for Earth. It would be even worse for us. We had greater cities, more beasts within them. With our pets, flocks of birds, rats, our zoos, our factory farming, and so many other things. The breakdown of our technology, of our supply lines. We weren't like those other worlds, weren't self-sufficient in the same way. Our cities didn't grow their own food, they imported it, and without our supply chains, so many were going to starve.

And on top of it all now we had to deal with the rifts.

"That paints a bleak picture of our future." It was Lt. Cabrera who spoke first, breaking the silence that followed my words.

"It is a bleak world that we are a part of now," I answered him.

"Why?"

I turned to look at Max who asked the question.

"Why what?"

"Why did this Great Spell do this?" he clarified.

I had part of the answer. I knew who created it, and could assume why. But ultimately I didn't know the truth. I didn't want to lie; it felt wrong somehow. Perhaps that was in opposition to my Oath with the Way. If I was to make deals with people, I didn't want them to make them based on false information. But, I also didn't want to be forced to reveal everything. So I spoke the truth, just not all of it.

"No one on Kirios knows the true purpose of the Great Spell," I told them. "Think of it as a god, the absolute ruler of everything. We are now part of its domain. There is no other choice but to accept this reality; to do otherwise is to invite death."

They grimaced, but I could see that they did understand, partly at least. They were survivors, they had seen the death that this new world had brought, and they had emerged with their lives.

"It isn't all as bleak as I paint it. In time, we will join the community of Kirios fully. The only question is how much of our own autonomy will we retain."

It was a hard thing to wrap one's head around, I knew it from experience.

"I was chosen as one of the thirty Exemplars. I've seen what the end of a civilization looks like. I've seen the beasts of high Investment and have met someone from this new world we are part of. I've taken it upon myself to help Earth survive. That is all I am here for. So I have an offer for you. If you refuse, I'll leave and won't bother you again."

"What kind of an offer?" Catalina asked.

"I'll stay with your group. I'll help you get stronger, advance your Masks. Gather more survivors, if there are any. Clear rifts and learn the secrets of Masks. I have only one request, I am a vampire, and that means that my needs are . . . different from yours. If you accept, I ask only that you donate a single liter of blood once a week."

They blinked, Diego took a step back, and I felt the guards stiffen. I smiled at them, showing my teeth. "I need blood in order to survive, and a small donation once a week isn't too much. Only from volunteers, of course." They didn't need to know the true reason why I wanted their blood. The power that it could give me. But it was part of my code, of the oath that I had decided to live my life by. An exchange, the things that I could offer in return for blood.

Even Max seemed taken aback. "I remember reading that vampires can survive on animal blood too," he said slowly, uncertainly.

"We can get by on it, but it isn't the same. A vampire needs human blood every once in a while. I can give you time to think, come back tomorrow—"

"No," Diego interrupted, and I tilted my head. He seemed to be trying to gather himself as he took a deep breath. "We've agreed, we would like to welcome you to our camp. If you want to join that is. As you've said, we are all in this together now. Human or vampire, it doesn't matter. And we . . . we just don't have the strength to keep everybody safe."

"Well then," I said with a nod. "I think that I can do something about that."

New Home

spent the night at camp, in a small tent that was given to me to use. Inside was only a small bedroll, which was more than enough for my purposes.

A vampire generally didn't require rest, because we rested all the time. Our bodies, when we weren't exerting ourselves, slowed down. Our heart beat once every minute in our resting mode, and we moved slower. What appeared as grace and fluidity to humans was actually us conserving energy. It was what allowed us to use short bursts of incredible power.

I was mostly rested now, but I still sat down with my legs crossed on top of my new bedroll, placing my weapons in front of me and my backpack to the side. I closed my eyes and took a deep breath, before releasing it slowly. I cleared my mind, as my sire—Akatsuki Jin—taught me to do.

Then I focused inward, entering a deep meditative state. Or attempting to. It was . . . against what Shadow had taught me. Meditation conflicted with the Heart of Azure and Scarlet. But I wanted to try it anyway. One of the things he had said about my Ornament of the Student was that it could gain Investment through meditation, and I wanted to try it.

My attempts didn't go well. I couldn't completely empty my mind—my emotions kept intruding. So, I switched gears. Instead of trying to push them away, I embraced them. Brought them up to the forefront and studied, dissected what it was that I was actually feeling.

My life had been turned on its head, and a part of me felt angry at that. I traced that feeling back to its origin, to the moment when I was sentenced to death by the Master of the only family I had ever known. Pascual de Andagoya, Master of the Lágrima Sangrienta Cartel, a person who ran an organization that consisted of many smaller criminal enterprises, and some not so criminal.

I was never part of the inner workings of the cartel. I worked for Andagoya's personal organization, the *Cuartango*, named for the place where he was born.

We controlled the production of various substances, and we ruled the area surrounding Medellín. I knew both a lot and very little of Pascual de Andagoya. The history I had learned from other people, mostly what I had overheard from other, older, vampires that had lived back in the days when he crossed the ocean.

I knew that he attempted to conquer the Inca empire, and was thrown back, which forced him to settle in Colombia. He had lived there, well, here, since then. He had served a powerful vampire lord that ruled in Spain, and when he failed to conquer what was now Peru, he was forbidden from returning.

In his exile, he had built up his criminal empire, culminating in the formation of the Lágrima Sangrienta Cartel with the other criminal organizations in the Americas. From what I remembered, he hoped to grow his influence enough that he would be allowed to return home, to Spain.

I knew only rumors and speculations, but Europe was considered the old continent. It was where the oldest and the strongest vampires lived. Once, I couldn't have imagined anyone who could order the Master that I had served my whole life, but now, I knew him to be what the vampires in Europe already knew—worthless.

He sentenced me to death for a single mistake, for killing our adversaries in what might as well have been self-defense, and if not that, at least a provocation of the highest degree. They had executed a child in front of me, a child that had been part of our people. I've always been taught that we were supposed to keep our people safe. Yet I was sentenced for doing exactly what I was trained to do.

It angered me still—the rage at that injustice simmered beneath the surface for all this time. I should've let it go. I knew the world had changed. It didn't matter anymore. I was not who I was then. The Grand Spell's arrival had freed me from the chains that had bound me since I was a child.

I wished that I could stand in front of him now, that I could look him in the eye and stab a knife through his heart and—

I stopped myself as I realized that memories and my anger were slowly taking over. With an effort of will, I switched focus.

Emotion is the fuel that grants me Purpose.

I didn't push the anger away. No, it had brought me here. It had allowed me to survive. In a moment of revelation, I realized why I wanted to do so much, why I wanted to save so many, to do something that was actually worthy.

It was to spite those cerulean eyes, that arrogant face that looked down on me and told me that I had failed when all I did was punish those who had struck against us first. To demonstrate to my sire who had just stood in the background without saying a word, who had looked on as they put a silver rope around my neck and dragged me away. My sire who didn't think to even try and argue with the Master for my life.

I'd accepted that past, but it didn't mean that I didn't carry the emotions that event caused.

I do not suppress my Emotion, I Embrace.

Anger was a powerful emotion, Shadow taught me that. And I wasn't about to let go of it. Coming back to this place, I had imagined meeting those who had hanged me. I imagined fighting, killing, and ended up finding an empty estate. They were long gone by the time I arrived. All that pent up emotion remained.

And it was good, I needed that emotion as fuel.

Ornament of the Student — No Investment; Ninth Carving

Traditional meditation seems unlikely to work for me, but it also seems like there are different ways of meditating. I smiled to myself. *Or did I just gain Investment for learning something about myself?* Did self-discovery count as learning? Perhaps it did.

I let the emotions flow through me, sharpening them in my mind, fanning the fire.

I will show them, I will show them all.

The next morning I left my tent at dawn, once I heard the camp waking up around me. Looking around, I saw a lot of people turning their eyes away from me, though they were all curious. Whispers were spoken where they thought that I couldn't hear. Some were dumbfounded by how I could walk in the sunlight, thinking that I had to be an incredibly old and powerful vampire. Some were worried about my presence, afraid that I would kill them and drink the blood of their children. But there were also the voices of those who were glad of my presence, who said that I could protect them.

I didn't want them to start being completely reliant on me, but at least some could see the benefits of my presence. Last night had ended in me just helping around the camp, introducing myself to different groups. That was going to take a while, since there was a few hundred of them.

I walked around, looking at the camp and familiarizing myself with it. Eyes of the guards in the towers followed me, when they should've been focused on the outside, but I paid them no mind. I understood their reticence. I'd only seen the area near one of the entrances, so I headed out of what I thought as the residential area.

Immediately, I found something very interesting. A large open tent was set up, with a group of people gathered around one of three trucks. They were military trucks of some kind, sand-colored with armored bodies. All of them were broken down, rust and decay covering them completely. They had sunken in and looked like they weren't anything more than scrap.

A group waited nearby, around eight of them, all dressed in military uniforms, with body armor; two of them carried rifles, while others had swords, axes, and one even a bow and arrows.

A single person, a middle-aged bald man, wearing dirty pants and a simple shirt, walked over to the truck. He wiped his hands on a rag then tucked it into his waist. The smell of oil clung to him.

"Do try to bring it back before the deadline, *parcera*, I don't want to have to drag it all over the base again."

"That wasn't my fault," a woman from the military dressed group said. "One of the sand worms attacked us on the way back. We had to stop."

"Next time, just drive over it. You don't need to kill everything in your path, my friend."

"Then how will we level and get stronger? We don't all have the luxury of growing just by sitting in a corner with thumbs up our asses," a man said, and the group laughed.

The bald man rounded on them and pointed. "Boy, you want to go out there on foot?"

The man took a step back and raised his arms. "I was just joking. Sorry, chief!"

The bald man gave him a long look, then turned and put his hand on one of the broken trucks. Immediately I felt the imprint in the Way of a skill activating. I didn't feel it all the time. It had more to do with how a skill was used. Some could keep them silent to my perception, though from what Shadow told me that took exceptional control.

I watched in awe as the skill activated, and the decayed truck slowly rose up and was restored before my eyes. In less than ten seconds, it was whole.

The woman hollered. "Go, go, go, don't waste any time."

Quickly, another group that stood nearby rushed over and poured fuel into the truck while the group of eight loaded into it. In less than a minute they were finished, the truck was started, and they drove it out of the tent, passing by me and heading to the camp exit.

I looked after it, impressed and confused in equal measure.

"First time seeing it, huh?" a voice said from behind me, startling me. I turned and looked at the bald man.

"Yes," I said, towering over him. He was on the short side, but it wasn't like he was unique. I was on the tall side, almost everyone around me was shorter.

He recoiled, took a step back, then stopped himself.

"Uh, fuck me, you're the vampire," he said slowly. "I heard about you."

I smiled as he glanced at the sun rising up in the sky, then back at me.

"You heard good things, I hope?" I asked.

He gave me a shaky half-smile. "Uh, things," he answered. "You saved our scout team."

I grinned. "I'll be staying with you, for a while at least," I said then I turned looked back at the truck as it left the camp. "That was impressive."

"It's an M1224 MaxxPro, a—a damn good vehicle," he said, his voice hitching only a tiny bit.

I turned back. "I meant what you did to it."

"Oh." He blinked. "It's nothing, just a skill. It's temporary."

"It's not just a skill. You restored it from that state." I pointed at the other two trucks. "That's incredible, it's magic."

He looked at the two piles of scrap, then smiled to himself. "Yeah, it's pretty fucking awesome."

"Marianna," I said, extending my hand to him.

He hesitated, but after a moment he extended his hand too.

"Salva," he introduced himself.

"So, Salva, what's that skill, if you don't mind me asking?"

He looked at me for a moment before answering. "[Temporary Repair]. It only works for five hours, and not on everything. Not that there was much aside from those trucks for us to try it on. The damn army took or destroyed almost everything else. Idiots." He snorted. "It probably all broke down for them on the road. The bigger something I repair is, the longer the skill is on cooldown. I won't be able to use it for another week after this."

"I can't imagine how you got such a skill," I said with a raised eyebrow.

He shrugged. "It happened as we were running from the city. Our cars started to break down, and I kept trying to fix them. Then, as the damage started to get worse, we ended up stranded. We were being chased by a pack of feral dogs, and I tried to make the car work. My wife and kid were inside, and I managed to get the car to start, and it just came to me, I got the skill."

It was such a powerful skill, especially since it could repair Earth technology. "That is amazing, Salva. You must have a very powerful Mask. Have you advanced much? Do you know how you gain your Investment?" I asked him, the questions coming out in a rush.

I was excited, I had to admit.

He looked confused. "Investment?"

"It is how our Masks advance and gain Carvings. The Investment you need in order to progress is different based on what kind of a Mask you have."

"Oh." His eyes lit up. "You are talking about leveling. Yeah, Max said something about that. I need to tinker with mechanical things, which is damn near impossible, seeing as everything is broken down and we have barely any resources for me to use. I've had to use wood, make simple things like levers, pulleys, things like that."

That was very interesting. And it seemed like they had figured some things out. It wasn't that hard, especially if you had some knowledge of media at least.

"Max," I said slowly. "I've been meaning to talk to him, can you—"

"Salva!" Someone called his name, making him turn. A woman was waving for him to come over.

"Sorry, I have work to do at the gate," Salva said with narrowed eyes. "Someone decided to drop an elephant-sized carcass on our doorstep."

I tilted my head and showed my teeth, making him take a step back. "No problem. Just point me in the direction where I can find Max, please?"

He raised his hand. "Head to the eastern section. It's where our hunter and raider operations are. He'll be in the big tent, can't miss it."

I thanked him and headed the way he pointed. I reached the area he indicated, and saw groups of people, mostly five or six, sitting around tables with pieces of papers scattered all over, talking softly. From what I overheard of their conversations, they were talking about rifts that they had found all around the camp and how to best clear them.

It seemed like these people were on top of things, from what I could see around camp so far. They didn't seem like they needed much help. Yet I remembered some of the things that I heard in the church, and from the conversations with Gabriela and Angelo. From them I got a slightly different picture.

I found the tent I was looking for easily enough, and I walked over and entered. A group of three people was focused on two tables placed in the middle littered with all kinds of things. I saw a lot of chests to the sides, some filled with weapons like knives or swords, staves even. I was confused for a moment, but before I had the chance to study what they were doing closer a voice called out my name.

"Marianna!"

I turned and saw a young blond man wearing a bright blue shirt, Max, walking toward me from the side. "I was just about to go out and look for you, and here you are! Thanks for saving me the effort."

I tilted my head in a bemused fashion. "And why were you planning on looking for me?"

The other three people in the room had turned to look at me, startled.

"We've got to talk, of course! You visited another world. You know more than we do. We gotta document everything, figure this shit out!"

I liked his enthusiasm. "Well, that's actually why I'm here. I wanted to hear what you knew."

"Come, come." Max ushered me in, next to the central tables where the three people stood. "This is my team—that's Ana, Leto, and Joe." He indicated each of them. Ana was a mousy little girl with brown hair tied in a braid, wearing a black shirt and pants. Leto was a lanky kid with a face full of piercings, and Joe was broad, looking like he was a lumberjack with a thick beard on his face. I inclined my head to them in greeting.

"What are you working on?" I glanced at the papers scattered around. They had a lot of numbers on them, but I couldn't exactly figure out what they meant.

"We're trying to determine how much experience is needed for every level, or at least how much our people gained and how they gain it in the first place."

"Investment, you mean," I said offhandedly as I leaned down. "And what have you figured out?"

"Is that what it's called?" Max said, then leaned over next to me. "Well, we have classified Classes, or Masks, into the fighter, knowledge, exploration, and miscellaneous. That is to say, we have no idea what we are doing." He laughed. "But, it has worked somewhat. We had some people level, or gain Investment as you say. But we seem to be hitting a wall. We have only three people on the seventh level—uh, Carving?"

I picked up a piece of paper. It had a name of a person and their Mask written on it. They had the Mask of the Lawman, and it looked like they were part of the group that both went out hunting for game to feed the camp and went out to clear rifts. The numbers below were nonsense to me, but I could kinda see what they were meant to represent.

The person had a single skill [Lesser Reinforced Skin], and from the description written on the bottom I could see that it made his skin slightly tougher. I could already see what they were doing wrong. But I didn't say anything yet. I just kept reading. Then I found something interesting.

"What is this here?" I pointed at a column with numbers.

Max leaned over and looked at what I was pointing at. "Ah, the exp, or Investment gained from finishing the dungeons."

"I've been calling them rifts. It seemed more apt a name," I added.

Max tilted his head. "You know what, I like that more. I think we are going to change it. Dungeons seems too gamey. Though, they are in a way."

I frowned. "What do you mean by that?"

He tilted his head. "Completing dungeons—rifts—gives you Investment. We've had people with Masks like Cook or Merchant gain a Carving after leaving the rift. We are pretty sure that it is the rift giving the Investment and not anything they did inside. Our fighter types gain Carvings as soon as they finish combat."

I blinked. I couldn't say if it was true or not. It didn't happen to me, but then again I'd only gone through three rifts. Perhaps I'd just never gotten enough Investment from one to push me over to the next Carving.

"You didn't know about the rifts?" Joe asked.

"The rifts are something new to Kirios. The Grand Spell introduced them with this Expansion Interval. No one knows anything about them."

"Huh." Max scratched his head. "I wonder if it got the idea from us."

I frowned. "The Grand Spell?"

"Yeah." Max nodded. "I mean it has similarities to a lot of what we had in our media, you know? Like loot, different types of rifts, the fact that they break and release monsters sometimes. A lot of other little stuff."

That sounded . . . terrifying, in a way. I shook my head, shelving that thought for later.

"You classified this one as a fighter," I said, pointing at the paper and turning us back on topic. "But he isn't; he is a Lawman."

"He gained Carvings when he was fighting monsters, while we were retreating," Ana, the mousy girl said in a timid voice.

I nodded. "When the world changed, yes, I'm sure that he had orders from his superiors to protect the civilians, right? He would've been protecting people, serving in the spirit of his job. Masks gain Investment from things that you are meant to do. Mask of the Lawman is one that would probably have to be related to doing things in service to laws, or rules at the very least. Fighting would probably be part of that, but the type of fighting would differ. I see that he didn't gain any Carvings from fighting beasts in the wild, only one from finishing a rift?"

Ana nodded at my words.

"He would be better suited staying in camp, keeping the peace, protecting people. If the camp has any rules, then have him enforce them."

"So, you know how Masks work?" Leto asked.

"I do," I answered.

"What's your Mask?" Max said, then continued speaking before I could say anything. "Mine is the Mask of the Trainer—I used to be a personal trainer—Ana's is Mask of the Student, as is Leto's, and Joe's is Mask of the Builder."

Leto gave me a peace sign, which made me blink. I turned to look at Joe, the odd one out.

He shrugged. "I worked construction with Diego before."

Well, that made sense. People got Masks related to what they were doing, what they were most proficient with or what they loved doing. Though, if your whole life was just work, it would probably fit the bill.

Max continued again. "We've all taken Researcher Ornaments, though we have options to take one more. We've just waited because we don't know what exactly they do. We've been leveling them like crazy, even more than our Masks, though we didn't get hardly any skills."

I nodded. "Ornaments are like subclasses that can merge with your Mask every time you reach an Investment tier. And they can only ever reach the second Investment. But if they are successfully merged with your Mask, they will improve it, and free your Ornament slot for something else."

Understanding blossomed in their eyes, along with a lot of questions. I spoke before they could say anything else.

"On Kirios, that is the world that we are part of right now, revealing the details, even the name of your Mask, is considered taboo. It can give others an advantage over you. People mostly use just general or starting Mask names when they have to divulge information. But since you've shared yours with me, I'll do the same; my starting Mask was the Mask of the Drainer."

They blinked, exchanging curious looks in between themselves.

"Starting?" Max asked with a glint in his eyes.

The rest of Kirios had the advantage of thousands of years of knowledge, of being established and living with the reality of the Grand Spell for generations. We on Earth would have to work together until we figured things out.

"Yes," I said. "I've reached my First Investment, I have the Mask of the Blood Invoker now."

Their eyes widened, and I could see more questions coming alive in their eyes.

I took a deep breath. It was time for me to start spreading the knowledge I gained from Shadow. At least some of it. I looked them over, then started explaining.

Rift Raiding

That's fascinating," Max said.

I'd spent the better part of an hour explaining all that I knew. They were all ecstatic, of course. They'd been getting Carvings in their Researcher Ornaments, and Ana had gotten two in her Student one. I'd also gotten one in my Revelator Ornament, raising it up to the Seventh Carving.

"We are going to have to change so much," Ana whispered. "We need to shift our groups around, have them start doing things to get ex—uh, Investment."

"And you need to do it quickly," I said with a sigh. "There isn't much time. This accelerated advancement won't last forever."

Max grimaced at that. "I can't even imagine what type of people exist out there on other continents. This is not good."

"No, it isn't," I said with a sigh. The three of them were young, but I could see that they understood the threat. It gladdened me. I was worried that I would need to convince people. Though being a vampire, and people thinking that I was probably hundreds of years old, had to have something to do with why they believed me so easily. Or perhaps they were just pretending. It wasn't like they would dare say anything to my face.

That soured my excitement somewhat. I didn't want to come in here and just take over, but already, just a day in I could see how it could happen. Who was going to try to say anything against me? I was something out of stories to them, and I appeared to be on their side. When the world went mad and monsters attacked you, having a monster of your own had to feel good.

"It's going to be hard," Joe said slowly. "We rely on rifts to get supplies to survive."

That was another thing that I learned over the past hour. I had wondered how they got their supplies. It appeared that they were harvesting these rifts for resources. Some of them had animals that they felt were safe to eat. They hadn't tried to eat anything that they didn't recognize yet, though from what Shadow told me I knew that most of them would fine to eat. But there were rifts filled with Earth animals, like the boars in the arena rift, which was actually one of the things that they got from it—the two sacks I saw them dragging away were two boar carcasses.

I'd also learned that rifts could close completely. Some of them could only be cleared a set number of times before they closed down and were gone. Others seemed to be permanent, but weren't repopulated once cleared. Those, Max and his group had dubbed resource rifts, since they've found some that looked like they used to be mines.

Then there were puzzle rifts, like the one I cleared. Each rift had its own loot table, and they tried to prioritize those that gave them things they needed. There was a lot of stuff around. They'd been doing this for almost three weeks, clearing rifts daily with at least three, sometimes more, teams. It piled up.

Most of the stuff in the tent were weapons that were of poor quality. Some were even obviously things made on Earth, with clear signs that they were made in a factory, such as etched names of companies, screws and bolts. Only, they were altered so that they didn't decay.

But one of the boxes in the corner had something that was familiar to me, and it reminded me of what I wanted to ask. I pulled out a pouch out of my backpack and showed it to them.

"I was going to ask about these," I said. "Have you found any of them?"

"Oh those," Max nodded. "Yeah, we did. We figured some stuff about them. We just don't know what to do with them."

"Really? What did you figure out?" I asked.

Max walked over to a corner and brought a box filled with pouches.

"Here, look," he said as he poured a dozen or so red ones on the table. "If you put ten of them together, like this, and keep them there, this happens." He gathered ten gemstones and put them together in a tight grouping. The started to shake under his palm, and then a flash of light made me blink my eyes.

When I opened them, the ten gemstones were replaced with one, a slightly larger and differently shaped one, but of the same color.

"See?" Max grinned. He pulled another pouch from the box and poured out more gemstones that looked exactly like this new one. "It only happens if there is the exact number of them. And, you can merge these ones too, though it takes double the number of the next tier to get to the one after, it goes from ten to twenty then forty, doubling for the each next level. We figured that they were some kind of a resource, but we haven't been able to work out how to use them. We didn't do anything with them beyond that, since we don't have enough of them yet."

If I understood correctly, then it would take ten of the smallest gemstones to get one of the next one, and twenty new ones for the one after, which would be . . . two hundred of the smallest ones, if I got my math right.

I narrowed my eyes as I looked at the table, and he pulled out more gemstones of various sizes, arranging three different colored gemstones on the table, each larger than the next.

"You know what they are?" Max asked.

"They are skill improvement gems," I answered.

"What? How do you use them then?" Leto asked, leaning in.

"They can't be used on every skill, and you use them like this." I pulled out my Mask, and heard the collective breath hitching all around.

"Whoa." Max and the others reacted to my Mask, but I ignored him as I picked up one of the gems. He had put one of each color gemstones on the table. I picked up the second biggest one since it was light green in color, and I knew that it would work with my skill. I touched it to my Mask, and the gemstone melted into it.

[Mist Step] skill upgraded.

"There," I said after. "It upgraded one of my skills with the air element. You can take it out of the skill, but that destroys the gemstone."

"That's so awesome," Leto said, and the rest of them nodded.

"C'mon, show us what it did! You can't do that and then keep us hanging." Max looked at me with puppy eyes.

I grimaced, I hadn't intended on doing a demonstration, but then I decided to indulge them. I took a step back, turning to mist. The moment I re-formed, a gentle breeze spread out of the place I re-formed in. It traveled outward and scattered all the papers on the table, sending them flying.

"Sorry about that." I grimaced. "That's a lot stronger than last time I did it. I guess that upgrading them like that does make them stronger."

"What was that?" Ana exclaimed, her eyes filled with wonder. Everyone was staring at me.

"A skill. It's called [Mist Step]. It doesn't usually do the wind part."

"That's so unfair," Max lamented.

I smiled. "Well." I shrugged. All my skills were earned in blood, one way or another. "The gemstones are elemental in nature, orange for fire, blue for water, brown for earth, and green for air."

"What about the other ones?" Ana asked.

"Other ones?" I tilted my head in confusion.

Leto opened a few more pouches and poured out more gemstones. There were four additional colors. I blinked. It appeared that there were in fact eight elements, not four as I believed.

"I haven't encountered these ones yet." I reached for them, and with my Mask still in my hand I felt that I could use some of them for my other skills. That was incredible.

"You know of any way to learn what elements they are?" Ana asked.

I kept my face blank. Saia could figure it all out, but I'd kept her hidden. Hidden, but not secret. They knew about Saia, even if not all of them had seen her. I was certain that Gabriela and the others would've reported it. But, I hadn't shown them the process of her taking a different shape. They probably didn't know that she was here now. There was a little voice in the back of my head that kept telling me that I should be cautious, that I shouldn't trust easily. And yet . . .

I remembered doing the same with Shadow. I had kept things from him that might've made things different. Might've given us more time for him to teach me things.

I struggled with myself, trying to decide what to do. The four people in this tent were kids, even though they were closer to my real age than some of the others I'd met in this camp. There was a gulf between us, one of life experience. Yet, I found myself easily falling into a rhythm with them, talking and exploring the rules of this new world.

I pulled my backpack from my shoulder and pulled out a silver orb covered with hexagonal lines.

"Saia, introduce yourself."

She flowed out on the table, startling everyone, and assuming her dragon drone form.

"Statement: Greetings, you may call this Unit Saia."

"Is that a tiny dragon," Ana whispered.

"Feedback: This Unit is not what your kind would consider a dragon. Though the resemblance is present."

Then the questions came, and I settled in, I knew that it was going to be a long time before they ran out of steam.

"Statement: I am 90% certain that this one corresponds to the element of darkness," Saia said.

They had finally moved back to the topic of gemstones. It had been a tiresome thirty minutes. I was glad that I wasn't the one that had to answer all the questions, though Saia had refused to answer some, mostly about her nature and Ke Erzi.

Max leaned forward. "So that makes these four light, darkness, nature, and metal."

"So there are eight elements then," I added.

"Not exactly," Leto said, then reached over to another box.

"Oh right, I forgot about that," Joe added.

I tilted my head and frowned as I watched him rummage through a box and put another twenty-two gemstones on the table, each a different color.

"What are these?" I asked.

"We got them by joining two gemstones together. Like this—if you place two of them close enough this happens." A resonance started, something that I had seen before, as he put two orange gemstones together. Then once he put his hand over them, they flashed, and only one gemstone remained. This one was the same size and shape, but was darker orange with gray around the edges.

"You can also mix and match most of them with others, though some combinations don't work. Ultimately you get twenty different combinations," Ana explained. "Only these eight basic ones can be used with the copies of themselves, and the results can't be used with any other color."

It was an intricate system, and it was something new that Kirios hadn't seen before. The other races were just as much in the dark as we were about this. That emboldened me. It made me want to figure things out.

"The numbers don't add up. You have two extra here," I said.

They nodded, and Max pointed at two similar gemstones, one black with a white dot in the middle, the other white with a black one. "These two can't be merged with any of them. They are the rarest ones. We only have four of them."

I frowned, wondering what they did. I picked one up and immediately realized that it would work on all of my skills. That both intrigued and worried me. Ultimately, I knew that I could always remove the gemstone if it did something I didn't like.

"Can I try one of them?" I asked. "Though if it does something weird, I might pull them out and destroy them."

"Go for it," Max said. "We need to figure out what they do anyway."

I pushed the white one with the black dot against my Mask and guided it toward my [Lesser Strength] skill. It sunk in, and I heard and felt the echo of the change in my head.

[Lesser Strength] is now [Lesser Burst of Strength]

I sagged as I felt my strength leave me, similar to what usually happened with the rise of the sun, though not as bad. The fact that it was daytime outside made it worse. [Lesser Strength] had made the loss of my vampire strength during the day bearable.

"What did it do?" Ana asked, her notepad ready in her hands.

"It changed my skill," I said as I activated the new version. Immediately I felt a burst of power well up inside of me. I felt strength flow through my body. I knew that it wouldn't last, I could feel it ticking inside of me. But the power . . . it felt stronger than just the passive effect, though not by a lot. Still, it was an interesting change.

"It switched it from a passive to an active form," I said. "We need to test all of these out, preferably somewhere in the open. We don't know what they will do."

"We can go to the training yard," Joe suggested. I agreed, and we gathered everything we might need and headed out.

Testing took most of the day, with a short break for lunch, for the humans at least. Saia had consumed the elemental gemstones, and we got some more understanding of what they did by testing them out on my skills. I even had to swap profiles a few times, since not all gemstones could fit in the skills in my main profile, so that we could test some out. I could put a gemstone in any of my skills, even those that weren't active at the moment. I just couldn't use them right then and there.

Eventually, Ana made a sketch of the gemstones, their elements and how they interacted with each other.

I looked it over, trying to wrap my head around all of it. The image lacked the two unique gemstones, one of which altered the skill in some way as it had done with my [Lesser Strength] to [Lesser Burst of Strength], while the other changed it completely. When I used the other gemstone my [Lesser Strength] turned into [Lesser Reflexes], which did exactly what it said and improved my reflexes. Thankfully, my original skill returned once I removed the gemstone. I was worried there for a moment, as I didn't really need faster reflexes than I already had.

Ultimately, the gemstones were weapons in our arsenals. The others retreated back to their tent to write down stuff and make a plan on how to share this with the rest of camp, and Max had a meeting with the other leaders. Meanwhile, I remained at the training yard with Saia.

I had an assortment of five gemstones in front of me that I had chosen. Max had given them to me as thanks for the info and the testing. I had a couple different choices, and two of them were the third tier of gemstones. I was grateful, since I had come to understand how rare and hard to make those were. The basic ones were the only rewards that they had gotten from the rifts, and at most they got two dozen a run, and it took two hundred of them to make a single third tier gemstone. It would take four thousand of the basic ones to make a single fourth tier one, and that was just an insane number. Who even knew how far this all went?

"What do you think? Which ones should I use?" I asked my ever-present companion.

"Feedback: These gemstones offer additional versatility or power to your skills. You should keep in mind what you use them for most often and make your choices accordingly."

That made sense to me. My most versatile and powerful skill was [Mist Step], which I used all the time in combat, and which had saved my life countless times. It was also great at closing the gap between myself and my enemy, confusing them too.

I had two tier-three gemstones, and those were the only choices I had for my [Mist Step], as they would give the strongest effects. One was gray with yellow edges that seemed like they were vibrating. It was the sound gemstone, the result of merging two air gemstones. This one had cost them the most, as they had merged two tier-three air gemstones. The other one was a tier-three fire gemstone.

Both would work with my [Mist Step], though one would probably have the unavoidable consequence of setting things on fire along my path. I had tried a lesser version of it with my skill, and it made my mist orange in color and added heat to it. The more powerful gemstone would probably ignite things as I passed, though I hadn't tried one of those as I didn't want to waste them.

I chose sound. It would release a sonic wave outward once I re-formed, which was a good substitute for not having [Debilitating Wave] or [Sonic Screech] in my main profile. Though, it would also make the skill loud and noticeable. But I could always remove the gemstone even though that would mean destroying it. The gemstones seemed fairly common, so I wasn't that worried about wasting it.

Next, I added a second-tier primal gemstone to my [Lesser Strength], and a second-tier metal gemstone to my [Lesser Constitution]. It felt like those gemstones made those two skills slightly stronger. My skin at least didn't turn to metal, for which I was thankful.

I had two gemstones left, the tier-three fire and a tier-one nature, along with my own tier ones that I brought from Ish Vimza. I didn't want to take everything from the people here, and if I was being honest, I didn't need them. The improvements were visible, but nothing crazy, not yet at least. I debated putting those two gemstones somewhere, but ultimately decided against it and put them in my backpack. I had some options, but I didn't want to waste them. Perhaps I would get a better skill later that could use them.

I took a deep breath and stood up, then decided to stretch my legs a bit and walk through camp. As I walked, I saw a lot of people. Few looked really ragged, but it was clear that they were struggling in places. Tents had lines spread in between them with clothes hung to dry. People sat in front of the tents just talking, not having anything to do really. A lot of them were elderly, with some teens here and there.

As I walked, I noticed the scent of incense, and heard a familiar voice.

I reached a small tent, with a group of people sitting on the ground in front of it listening to the man speaking.

"And so, I leave you with this: Some of you have said that God has abandoned us, that the devil has taken over and that hell now reigns on Earth," Father Sergio said slowly. "I do not have the answers. I will not lie to you: my own faith has been shaken."

"And yet, we are here, we survive. We've been granted great power, faced great danger, but have also been given people who have helped guide and keep us safe. Even the most fallen of God's children has stepped forward into the light, no longer afraid to stand beneath the light's gaze. If you cannot believe in God anymore, believe in his champions, believe in those who stand between you and the horrors of this hell. And in time, we will all stand in his grace once more."

I froze, pretty sure that I interpreted what he said correctly. I was about to turn and run away, when someone noticed me. The whispers started, and they looked back at me.

"That will be all for today. I'll see you all back here tomorrow," Father Sergio said, and the people stood up and started leaving. As they passed me, they bowed and murmured thanks, as if I had saved their lives. As if I was there to be their savior.

I stood silent, frozen in the moment until Father Sergio approached me.

"What was that?" I asked, perhaps a tiny bit too harshly.

The father didn't seem to mind. "We all need things to believe in, Marianna. God has put you in our path. Gratitude is the least we can offer you."

"No god sent me," I said firmly.

The priest smiled at me kindly. "You don't need to believe yourself for others to believe in you. We are surrounded by hopelessness. Your arrival and presence here has given people hope. Will you take it away from them simply because you don't believe?"

Before I could even think of an answer, a man ran up to me, letting me know that the leadership wanted to talk.

It looked like I was in for another meeting, which was a perfect excuse to turn and run away from the priest.

I was no savior, and I had no answers.

The Red Rift

The now familiar group gathered in the central tent, the so-called *big tent.* Diego and Catalina in the front, with Max next to them and Lt. Cabrera on the other side. The four of them basically ran the camp.

From what I had heard over the day spent with Max and his group, Diego used to be a construction foreman, and had the Mask of the Supervisor. Catalina was a nurse, with a Mask of the Caretaker. She was probably the most valuable person in the camp, as she had the [Lessen Pain] skill. It had helped them immensely, especially since they had limited medical supplies. And Lt. Cabrera had the Mask of the Enforcer.

None of them were in the top of the Invested people in the camp, except for Max who was on his Sixth Carving. The rest were all around four or five, with only one skill to their name. It just went to show how much understanding how Investment worked helped with advancement.

The seven highest Masked in the camp were actually all at the Seventh Carving. With Gabriela, Angelo, and Salva being some of them, and the rest being the people that were raiding the rifts.

"Master—pardon, Marianna," Diego started, his eyes sliding over to Saia on my shoulder. "Thank you for coming."

"Of course, I'm here to help," I said.

"That's good to hear, because a few things have come up, that we hoped you could help us with," he continued.

I tilted my head, and he gestured to Max who picked up.

"You are aware of Angelo and Gabriela's mission, yes?"

"You sent them to scout out Medellín," I answered, wondering where this was going.

Max nodded. "That's because the city is filled with dungeons—rifts now, I guess. A lot more than we've found in the wilderness. We have some ideas why that is. One of them is that they appear based on population density, both human and animal, and since they all appeared as soon as the Light came—"

Catalina coughed. "Maximilian, please, try to keep on topic."

"Right, sorry about that." He gave her a sheepish smile, but in his eyes I saw the promise of a future conversation. Something that I was looking forward to. Rifts did interest me greatly.

"Well." Max cleared his throat. "The reason why we sent them on a mission is because of Angelo's skill. It's been a lifesaver, allowing us to manage the danger. Since a little over a week ago, he's been getting a lot of danger signs from the direction of Medellín, so the two of them were sent to evaluate the danger. It turns out that most of the rifts in the city are on the verge of breaking open. That will mean that all the monsters that are inside will be spilling out—"

"Beasts," I interrupted. It was important to me that they understood the distinction. "They are animals from other worlds, or other continents now I guess, animals native to Kirios. Call them animals or beasts, monsters are something else entirely. That is the term that people of Kirios use to refer to an animal or a person that has been infected with the blight."

"You've mentioned that before, blight," Lt. Cabrera started. "Is that some kind of a disease? Should we be worried?"

"Yes and no," I said. "It is an infection of the Source, the Way. Think of it as corrupted magic. Kirios has fought wars against the blight before. But suffice to say, if you ever see a monster, you will know. They have a mental effect on you; they turn your emotions against you. And they are very recognizable by the dark red lines covering their bodies. It literally looks like an infection."

"*Madre de Dios.*" Catalina put a hand over her chest. "What more do we have to worry about?"

I still didn't know how the infant weirzi got infected. So I didn't want to alarm them without a need. For all I knew, the blight somehow got into a rift by mistake.

"You should just let everybody know, if they come upon a blighted animal, they should just run back to camp. Probably let me know, and I'll go and take care of it. Facing one can be . . . difficult. Though I doubt that you will encounter true monsters, only blighted beasts."

"I'll make sure that everyone knows," Lt. Cabrera said. "Continue, Maximilian."

"Right," Max said. "Well, the closer the rift comes to breaking, the brighter it becomes. And Angelo's report says that many of them are on the verge of breaking open. That means that we are about to have hordes of mo—beasts, heading our way. And it's already started. One of our scouts reported increased beast activity down south, near the roads. A large pack of dogs is heading west, but they could just as easily turn and head north, in our direction."

I nodded. That was a big danger. The base had walls, some protection, but it wasn't impenetrable. It wasn't made like a medieval wall to allow people to bunker in.

"Any help you could provide in teaching our people how to survive a siege, how to prepare, would be appreciated," Diego added.

Ah, they still think that I'm much older than I am. I almost told them, but it wasn't really important, nor had they earned enough to know. And besides, I had Shadow and Saia with me. I was certain that I could offer advice.

I nodded.

"And then there is the second thing," Maximilian continued. "One of our expedition groups returned today with the report that they've found a red rift."

I tilted my head. I knew that they could have different colors but I didn't know what it all meant. "And that is?"

"Right." Max nodded. "From what we've gathered, red rifts are rare. We've only discovered four before. They are more difficult, and they disappear once completed. They also drop much higher quality rewards. It's where we got most of our firearms."

Well, that was good to know.

"We were hoping that you would be willing to go and help clear it with a team. We are going to try to assemble a team based on the ideas we discussed about Investment previously. And, if I'm being honest, we would be a lot more at ease with you there. We've lost people in red rifts before. Entire groups entered and never came out."

So, very dangerous.

"Yes, I'll go," I told them.

"Thank you," Diego said. "We'll plan the trip, and have you leave in a day or two. It will take a bit to get there, as the group used the truck, and we won't have it available again for a week. Max and Lt. Cabrera will be deciding on the group members, and I'm sure that they'll welcome your input."

I nodded my head in acknowledgment, and the meeting came to an end.

A while later I found myself back at the training area. The shooting range was surrounded by junk, but there was enough room for a large group of people to train together. It was empty now, since it was the middle of the night. I didn't need any more rest, seeing as I had rested a bit the day before.

So, I decided to practice. I settled into a wide and balanced stance, not one of the Scarlet Moon techniques, but rather the other half of my school of being—the Azure Moon technique.

Shadow had taught me two techniques of his Heart of Azure and Scarlet school. The most basic ones: the **Veiled Mist Assault**, which was a Scarlet Moon technique, and the **Stalwart Mist**, which was an Azure Moon technique.

Where ***Veiled Mist Assault*** was based on constant aggression, on flawless movement and lashing out through utilization of emotions that fueled me, like anger and determination, the ***Stalwart Mist*** was the complete opposite.

It relied on fear and instinct and on retaliation. Its Katas were lower to the ground, more stable, meant to enable the user to take blows and quickly pivot, utilizing some of the force they had received to unleash a more powerful retaliatory strike.

It was not a technique that could be used by most. In Shadow's case, he relied on his illusion and mists to misdirect and obscure his movements. I, on the other hand, was a vampire, I healed. I could afford to take a blow and then lash out.

Of course, taking a full blow wasn't smart, nor was letting a blow hit a critical area. So I pushed my emotions away, letting only my instincts and fears remain on the surface. I could feel the **thirst** within me stir; it was an organism bonded to me, intelligent, and its purpose was my survival. I had learned to listen to its voice.

Training in ***Stalwart Mist*** was hard. Especially when I had no opponent. So I just went through the motions, imagining an attacker. It focused on wide strikes, full body movements to build momentum and power. It was hard for me to get into it. My emotions usually ran hot, and ***Stalwart Mist*** required them to be cold.

Yet, as I went through the Katas, things started to slowly rise to the surface. Fear and instinct, two things that were at the core of what a vampire was. Fear of the sunlight, fear of stakes in the night, fear of starvation. They sharpened my senses, and I became aware of everything around me in a much clearer way than before. Hundreds of heartbeats of potential enemies. Some were close enough that they could fire at me from cover, or try to ambush me. The breaths taken in the distance, the scent of alcohol and cooked meat. The scent of waste bubbling up from beneath the ground. So many dangers, so many sources of fear. My instincts, the parts of me that were the **thirst,** whispered that I should hide, run away, that there was danger here.

I ignored them, of course. That was the point of ***Stalwart Mist***. To be prepared, not to act out like an animal. Control was a shackle, so I didn't control the emotions. But I embraced, I let all the little fears flowing through me whisper of the threats around me. My instincts and my fear would be the first to know when an attack was coming, I only had to have the presence of mind to retaliate.

I finished the set, feeling the exertion and the fatigue set into my muscles. It was a demanding form, and it was made by a member of a race that didn't tire easily. I was unfortunately a sprinter, not a long-distance runner. I stopped and slowly rolled my shoulders before settling into my resting state. My breath and my heartbeat slowed; my muscles relaxed and slackened.

I turned my head to the side, to a concrete barrier in the corner, then I spoke. "Shouldn't you be in bed?" I asked.

Two tiny heads dipped below the barrier, attempting to hide. It was, of course, futile. I heard them the moment the two arrived.

I heard intense whispers and arguing, and I allowed them the time to come to a consensus. It was a courtesy that I allowed it. They were, after all, vile spies.

Finally, they stood up, and their tired eyes looked straight at me. They rushed from their cover and came to stand in front of me.

I raised an eyebrow as I looked down on them.

"That was so cool!" one of them, a little girl, whispered with an awed look on her face. I was pretty sure that she was Lea, one of the two orphans that had survived the church.

The little boy, Juan, nodded in agreement.

"Whether it was cool or not is not the question," I said slowly, trying to look stern. "Why aren't you in bed?" I repeated my question.

"We weren't sleepy!" Lea said, as if that was all the answer I needed. And perhaps it was. It had been a while since I was a human child.

"And you decided that it was a smart idea to walk around the camp at night? You never know when or where danger can appear."

The little girl snorted. "No one would be able to hurt us while you're here! We saw you fighting those monsters at the church. You were all—boom, pow, kapow!"

Both of them mimed fighting moves, punching and kicking the air, badly.

I blinked. Their trust made my heart hurt. It was such a misplaced belief, a child's trust. And I realized that it was the same thing that the rest of the camp, or at the very least their leadership, believed. They'd asked me to accompany their group as if that would guarantee their survival. I couldn't make such promises, the world didn't work that way.

I shook my head, then looked back at the kids. "And why are you here? Watching me?"

They looked at each other, hesitating a little bit. Then they nodded at one another and turned to face me with closed fists and looks of determination on their faces.

"Felix told us that you promised to teach him how to fight," the girl, Lea, said. "We want you to teach us too!"

Their looks pierced me like a bullet. It hurt. I made a promise to Felix; I made him believe that everything was going to be all right, and then I watched him die in my arms.

The two in front of me were younger, not even ten years old. They probably didn't even have Masks. They were so vulnerable to everything in this world. Shadow had told me that the children and the elderly rarely survived the transition, that it took years for the new continent to stabilize enough for children to be able to survive in safety.

These two had such a dark future ahead of them. And here they were, standing in front of a vampire, a nightmare from human stories, asking it to teach them.

Any other vampire would've refused. No, they probably wouldn't even be in this position in the first place. They wouldn't be here, among humans that didn't serve them. That could so easily turn to be enemies.

I narrowed my eyes at the kids, and then I spoke. "Copy the way that I'm standing."

I stood in one of the beginning stances that my sire taught me long ago, just after I was turned. It was a human martial art, much easier for human children to understand.

Their eyes lit up, and I walked around them, correcting their bodies, pushing a knee forward here, lowering an elbow there, until they at least looked good.

I spent a good fifteen minutes instructing them on how to stand properly, and then I saw just how tired they were.

"There," I said with a nod. "That's the first lesson, now off to sleep with you. I need you well and rested for the next lesson, early in the morning."

They nodded their little heads and ran off, while I remained where I was, gazing after them. It was a big responsibility, teaching someone. And it created a bond between us, an obligation. I shouldn't have let it happen, and yet . . . I couldn't refuse someone so innocent.

I shook my head and waved to Saia, who was sitting on a tarp nearby, watching over me. I settled on the ground and meditated, or at least appeared to be meditating. In fact, I entered my soul space and checked up on my doors. There were four new ones, with two being identical and belonging to the kobold-like creatures.

Once I cleared them, it basically confirmed that I got a new door only when the source I drank from had a skill to offer me that I didn't already possess. The two kobold doors gave me different skills, [Swipe] and [Stab]. The hairless dogs had only a single door, and gave me [Lesser Intimidation], which surprised me. I didn't feel them using it. Though, I doubt that they would be anywhere close to being strong enough to intimidate me.

The last door was from the bat-like flying creatures, and gave me a potentially useful skill, [Lesser Sonar]. The ones that were missing were the boars and the grizzly. Which meant that either they didn't have skills, or they had skills that I already possessed.

After I finished with that, I visited Shadow and asked for advice on how to improve the base defenses. I tried not to stay inside for too long, as I still had things to do on the outside. But all in all, it felt like a productive day. I hadn't felt this good in a while. I hoped that it would last.

* * *

The next two days passed in a blur. I spent my time around the camp, training on my own or instructing the humans in how to fortify the camp better by passing along the instructions from Shadow, which boiled down to making sure that they had a parapet behind the concrete walls that they could climb on and shoot over. Also, making slings and collecting small stones to throw, and also collecting big rocks that they could drop on top of the beasts from behind the wall. Apparently, a rock to the head from that height could be just as effective as an arrow or a sword.

Since they had nowhere near the amount of wood available to build platforms everywhere, they started relocating and filling new bags with sand and placing them on the inside along the walls, then putting planks over them. It was not the best option, but it was what they could do at the moment. They'd reinforced the doors, added more bags near them that they could quickly drop over the entrances to block them if needed. But mostly they shuffled the people around based on Masks.

It was too soon to say if it was going to help with advancement. I found the time to teach the kids every morning, and somehow the group grew with every lesson. Still, the time came for more important matters. The group for the rift expedition was assembled and equipped, we were ready to set out.

Journey

I was the first one to arrive at the meeting spot, probably because I had no need to sleep. It was still pre-dawn, but slowly the raiding team gathered. First to arrive were Gabriela and Angelo—the scouting duo. They wouldn't be going into the rift themselves, but would be scouting and securing the surrounding area while the rest of us went inside.

"Good morning," I said, startling the two. I was relatively hidden behind a tent.

They glanced in my direction and hurried to greet me back.

"Uh, good morning," Gabriela said.

"You ready for this?" I asked.

"Of course." She nodded. "It's not the first time we've done it."

I nodded and turned my head to the inner camp. People were starting to wake up all around us, I could hear them. As the sun came up and my strength fled, the rest of the group showed up. Four more people.

I'd met them in the days prior, but we didn't get much chance to get to know each other. With hundreds of people being part of the camp, even the six of them didn't know each other well. From what I heard, Gabriela had gone on a rift expedition with them once, but it was a rift that was near the camp, so it wasn't much time to get to know each other.

The first to arrive was a tall woman. I myself was fairly tall, but this woman towered over even me by at least half a head. She had blond hair and a single lock of it dyed red, which fell down the side of her face. Blue eyes and fair complexion made her stand out amongst the others in camp, who were mostly people native to the region. She was a foreigner, a tourist visiting Medellín when the light arrived. She had the Mask of the Fighter, one of the very few with a more traditional type. She gained it because she practiced mixed martial arts, though she never competed outside of her gym. Still, she was one of the strongest in the camp, and one of the seven people who had reached the Seventh Carving and had two skills.

She fought like a brawler, and had two weapons, brass knuckles. One of them was a carbon fiber version that she had carried with her for protection and which had survived the transition. The second one was a reward from the Grand Spell, a metal brass knuckle with a short straight knife attached at the end. It was a powerful combination, I assumed.

"Hey, Kai," Gabriela greeted her, and the woman nodded her head.

She was dressed in military fatigues, like most of the people that fought in the camp. They had acquired a lot of the clothes after they found the camp, since the army that was stationed here had abandoned a lot of stuff. She also wore a ballistic vest, polyethylene by the smell of it, and she carried a Kevlar helmet in her hands. On her hip she had her brass knuckle weapons holstered in a pouch, and she carried a big backpack on her back.

She walked over to the wall across from me and leaned back. She was a quiet person, from what I gathered.

A few minutes later came the last members of our group. Three men walked up with smiles on their faces.

"I'm so ready for this, brother," one of them, a brown skinned man with a shaved head by the name of Carlito said. He had a long scar across his cheek that had barely healed. He carried two short blades on his hips, more like big knives really. He was the proud owner of the Mask of the Cutter—I didn't know how he earned that kind of a Mask, but the tattoos on the side of his neck were probably some kind of an indication. And like the rest he wore the same military dress, vest, helmet, and equipment.

I wasn't offered any of it, but I didn't hold it against them, not really. I was pretty sure that it just didn't occur to them to offer it. What did an old vampire like me need the protection for?

"We are going to level from this, I can feel it," the second man, Rico, said. He was young-looking and slightly shorter than the rest of them. He had a rifle slung over his shoulder, a simple hunting bolt action one by the look of it, with a knife holstered at his hip. He had the Mask of the Rogue, another type that was more . . . traditional.

"Let's first focus on surviving, okay?" the last member of the group, Hugo, said. He was a burly man in his midthirties, and he carried a large mace on one hip, and had a wooden shield in his left hand. He held the Mask of the Vanguard, and from what I knew he was riot police, though not from Medellín. He had fled this way from Bogotá in the early days, while cars still worked.

"Oh," Hugo said once they got close enough to see the rest of us. "We're all here, I see."

I stepped out and nodded. "We are," I said. "Is there anything we need before heading out?"

I had my serpent-tongue spear with me, carrying it on my back. It had a new sheath that was now slung across my hip and shoulder, courtesy of Max, and I had my backpack over it. On my hips were two daggers, and on my upper thigh was my handgun, in an improvised holster, courtesy of Max and the camp tailor. I had six rounds in it, and another six in a pouch on my hip, with Saia's alterations already done. She was currently masquerading as a bracer on my left hand. I'd also brought the rest of my gear, the rope I had, the bottles filled with blood, and gemstones. You never knew when you would need something.

"No," the man said with a shake of his head. "We gathered everything last night."

"Good, then we should be on our way." I smiled and gestured for him to go ahead. I didn't know the way, after all.

"Right." He nodded and then gathered everyone, and we were off.

I walked behind them all, curious about the scent of silver in two of their packs.

We spent most of the morning walking at a brisk pace. The rift was far away. The other team had found the rift while heading north in a straight line with the truck. They had managed to get pretty far. They were attempting to find other survivors, as most that they knew of had headed north in the early days, planning to head to Panama and then Mexico and the States, thinking that the situation was better over there.

The unlucky ones that remained were the ones whose vehicles were stolen, who couldn't find transportation, or who just had accidents and had to continue on foot.

Finally, a bit after midday we came to a stop for lunch. The humans had to eat, after all. We'd gotten out of the desert area by then, and camped by a small mountain stream. What followed was the most awkward five minutes of my life. Humans sitting in a circle, with me, all of them eating food and casting glances in my direction.

Unwilling to remain in that kind of an atmosphere, I raised my head and spoke, breaking the silence. "So, where are you guys from?" I asked, looking at the big guy who was clearly the leader of the group, Hugo.

For a moment, he looked startled, his eyes glancing at the people around him, but he saw no one willing to jump in and save him. My attention was solely on him.

After a long few seconds, he swallowed whatever food he had left in his mouth and answered.

"Bogotá," he said in a deep voice, the expression on his face trying to tell me that he would really like not to continue the conversation.

Inwardly, I grinned. Messing with humans was slowly becoming my favorite thing to do.

"Oh," I said slowly. "How did you end up here then? If I may ask?" There was no may about it, and he knew it.

He shuffled on the rock he was sitting on, then answered. "Not much to it, honestly. Once everything went to shit, I grabbed my wife and kid and got out of the city. It was . . . hard. I didn't sleep the first few days, almost at all. By the time we managed to get out, well, I fell asleep behind the wheel, hit a tree, and wrecked the car. We were forced to continue on foot. Cabrera found us, saved us really. Brought us to the others, the group, and the rest is, as they say, history."

"It was bad in the cities, wasn't it?" I asked, interested.

Hugo shrugged. "It is bad everywhere. There was just too many people, everyone looking to save themselves. Pets going wild, birds attacking, rats—those were the worst—people killing people for supplies. Near the end, as we were leaving the city, I saw bombs falling on parts of the city. It was a massacre."

I still couldn't quite wrap my head around it all. Shadow had told me, other people had told me, but I hadn't seen it, not until the church. And even that was not the same. I couldn't even imagine what it was like those first few days.

I turned my attention to the man next to him, Rico. "And you?"

"Born in Medellín, never really left before," Rico answered. "Got caught up with a group trying to head north. Some army fuckers ambushed us and took our shit, supplies, our camióna too. Nothing we could do about it, they had machine guns and we barely had three pistolas among us and a couple of knives. The fuckers took those too."

He spat on the ground next to him. "Then we ran into a bear that slaughtered half of us. I hid, and my skill let me survive. Eventually found another group that led me to this bunch. Been with them ever since."

"What about you, chica?"

I blinked for a moment, not realizing that the question was directed at me. I turned and saw the third man, Carlito, looking at me with a grin on his face. The others had frozen, their heartbeats beating faster. *Are they worried that I would be offended?*

I smiled, I liked his style.

"I've been around here for what feels like forever, been with *los Cuartango*s, before, well, everything."

Carlito whistled. "Damn, chica, you one of the real, real hard fuckers huh?"

I smiled.

"I heard stories about you bloodsucking *hijueputas*, some hard shit, that."

I wasn't surprised by his reaction. The cartel did have a reputation after all.

"So, how old are you?" Carlito asked.

"A lady never tells." I showed my fangs. He laughed and shook his head.

"*Cuartango?*" Hugo asked with his brow furrowed. "I know that name, where did I hear that?"

"Ah, what's up, po-po, never heard of the *Lágrima Sangrienta Cartel?*" Carlito asked him with a grin on his face.

Hugo's eyes widened, then looked at me in shock. "You are . . ." He paused, the rest of the words leaving him.

I nodded, holding his gaze. "Yes, but it was in another life. We are living in a different world now. We are all something different."

Everybody else looked at me in shock too. The only one who seemed confused was Kai, but she was a foreigner. I doubted that she knew anything about the cartel. I turned my attention back to Carlito, then tapped my neck as I spoke. "And you?"

The man showed his crooked teeth as he reached up to the tattoo of a dog and scratched at it. "Los Perros del Valle! Represent! Guau-guau!"

He barked and made gang signs that I was unfamiliar with, which made me chuckle. I hadn't heard of his gang, but that was to be expected. A lot of the smaller gangs were irrelevant to the organizations I was part of. But it did explain his Mask of the Cutter, at least.

"Gone now," he said with a sad smile after a while. "Rival gang took advantage after all of this fuckery started, wiped us all out. I was the only one who escaped. On the bright side, the idiots decided to stay in the barrio and try to hold it down. I hope the rats ate all of them balls, *hijueputas.*"

I really liked him.

"Hey," Carlito started. "I heard a rumor that you got a pet dragon, that true?"

I sighed. Keeping Saia a secret was too hard it seemed. Not that I had done a good job of it, like at all. But that was life.

"Saia, introduce yourself."

Saia shifted into her drone form and came to rest on my knee.

"Statement: Greetings, you may call this Unit Saia."

She used her customary greeting, and everyone was stunlocked.

"She isn't technically a dragon," I said, breaking them out of their stupor.

"How?" Rico asked.

"I found her in a rift," I said, then continued before they could ask anything. "And no, before you ask, she wasn't a reward. She was left behind by a people whose world was dismantled by the Grand Spell, just like ours was."

"Shit," Rico said.

"You can go back now," I told Saia, and she flowed back onto my wrist. I didn't want to have to avoid an endless stream of questions about her.

"Damn, chica, you are like the coolest bitch I have ever seen in my life," Carlito whispered.

I tried not to let my mouth curve into a smile.

I turned and glanced at Kai, then raised my eyebrow. "And you, how did you end up here?"

She blinked. Her eyes rose from my wrist, and she cleared her throat. "I'm from Sweden," she said. "Came on vacation with my boyfriend. We were here for two days when the Light happened. Lost him in the chaos, never found him after that."

She didn't show it, but I could detect the sadness in her tone.

"I'm sorry that happened to you," I said. There wasn't much else that I could say. Offering false hope wouldn't do anything.

She seemed to understand, and she nodded, accepting my offering.

I glanced at the last two, Angelo and Gabriela. I knew the most about them.

"So, what kind of a life gives you Masks and skills that you two got?"

Gabriela looked uncomfortable, but answered. "I was a photographer, moved around a lot. I liked to explore and scout out new locations for my work. I guess the light or this Grand Spell you mentioned thought that being a Scout fit."

I turned to look at Angelo.

"I was a, uh, a garbage man in Medellín," he said, shame clear in his words.

I blinked, not expecting that answer.

"Wait, what?" Carlito asked. "Really?"

Angelo looked embarrassed, but nodded. "Yes, the Light, it changed my life. Gave me power."

"Damn dude, you're like the top of the camp right now. From garbage picker to being a top dog, congrats, my man!" Carlito slapped Angelo's back, much to the man's embarrassment.

"It's not like that, I don't do any fighting," Angelo said.

"Pff," Carlito said. "Without you we wouldn't know when we would be walking into danger. You keep our lives safe."

"He's right. You are one of the most important people in the camp," Hugo chimed in.

They started showering him with praises and encouragement. And slowly the atmosphere among the group relaxed.

We reached the rift by nightfall. It was easy to spot, as it was glowing in the middle of what appeared to have been a coffee plantation. It pulsed with red color, rhythmically getting brighter then dimmer.

"Oh shit," Angelo said.

"What is it?" Hugo asked.

"The danger is, uh, extreme. It is also very close to breaking open," Angelo answered.

"Shit," Carlito said, grabbing his knives and pulling them out of their sheaths. "Should we rush the bitch?"

"Wait, wait," Hugo yelled as Carlito leaned forward, ready to start running. "We have a few minutes, don't we?" He was looking at Angelo as he asked.

"I wouldn't dally too long," Angelo answered.

"Shit," Hugo cursed. "Okay, we should go in then. We don't want it to break open and monsters to spill out. Since we don't know anything about what type it is or what to expect, there's no use making any plans. We should wait to make them once we get in."

He looked at me as he said the last part, almost as if he was asking for permission. I inclined my head, and he nodded in relief.

"Let's go then, weapons out!"

I removed my weapon and sheath from my back and pulled it out. Apparently, the movies had lied to me. A weapon as long as mine couldn't be drawn over the shoulder, not even by vampires, it was . . . a disappointment.

The five of us made our way down the hill, as Angelo and Gabriela set up outside to keep a lookout. Most rifts allowed only five people inside at most.

We reached the rift and entered it.

The Red Rift Part 2

The sensation of falling lasted for just a moment, and then I hit solid ground. The others appeared around me as we entered the rift.

"The fuck is this?" Carlito hissed.

I agreed with the sentiment, but probably for a different reason.

We were in the open, a flat desert landscape filled with sand and a few rock outcroppings. The area wasn't particularly large. Like other rifts I had visited, it was an island floating in space, and I could see the other edge in the distance.

Stars and nebulae surrounded us, shining light down and illuminating everything. There was no monster visible, nor was there any kind of buildings or strange formations that might warrant a look.

While the others were confused by it, I was more worried about the fact that the rift entrance had disappeared behind us, and perhaps more importantly about what I could hear and sense through my feet.

"What are we supposed to do here?" Rico asked as he looked around, his rifle held ready.

"Run," I said, grabbing Kai next to me and pushing her forward. "Run to the rocks, now!" I yelled.

It took them a moment to react, but they followed as I headed to the closest one. I raced ahead of them, and reached it far before they had. I climbed on top of the rock formation, which was about two meters above the sand, and the relatively flat circle of about twice that width. I dropped my backpack on the rocks and gripped my weapon tightly.

The team ran toward me, their eyes looking around in confusion, not seeing any threat.

I leaned forward and bent my knees, my eyes following them as they finally reached the edge of the outcropping. Then I leapt over them, my weapon pulled back with both hands to my side.

My movement startled them, but I ignored them. The sand bulged and then a massive two-meter-tall centipede looking thing, albeit one with a lot less legs, burrowed out of it, lashing out at the slowest member of their team, Hugo. Its sharp mandibles opened, and I landed on top of it, piercing the top of its skull and pushing it to the ground with my weight and momentum. The rest of its body flailed, sending sand flying in all directions.

The others froze behind me, and I yelled.

"Go!"

I could hear the rumbling all around me, could see the displaced sand moving as more of the beasts headed our way. Behind me on the rocks, Rico had set up on his knees, aiming with his rifle at the sand. Kai was up, looming over him, her brass knuckles ready on her fists.

Carlito jumped and grabbed the ledge, pulling himself up deftly before drawing one of the knives he had sheathed in order to climb.

Hugo was at the bottom of the outcropping. His feet were on the stone but still too close to the sand for comfort.

A large centipede rose out of the sand, rushing at him on its dozen or so legs, intent on grabbing him. I turned and jumped, clearing the distance all the way to him in an instant. I landed next to him and swung my weapon in a wide arc. The serpent-tongue spear cleaved the beast in half with ease and allowed Hugo time to climb.

A shot rang out from above, and I glanced to the side to see a centipede falling from the side of the rock as a bullet pierced its head.

I heard the sounds of fighting above, and leapt after Hugo, catching the edge of the cliff ahead of him and pulling myself up with ease in one smooth motion. I landed on my feet and saw Kai duck as a somewhat smaller centipede tried to catch her with its mandibles. She sidestepped and lashed out with a one-two hit with her fists, a faint white glow surrounding them, a skill. The power of the strikes cracked its carapace.

Carlito was on the other side, his knives flashing and cutting out three of its legs on one side. As it tumbled to the ground, Kai pounced on its head, bashing it in and pulverizing its brain. They were so focused on it that they missed another centipede climbing on top behind them.

In one smooth motion I reached to my thigh and drew my handgun, then fired a single bullet. Its head exploded in a shower of gore, and the beast tumbled backward from the rock top.

I turned, holstering my gun, eight rounds left in the cylinder, and reached over the edge of the rock. I grabbed Hugo by the fabric at the back of his neck and hauled him up with one hand.

As soon as I deposited him, I turned and took in the situation. I could hear the beasts all around us, beneath the sand, and a few that were still climbing, their feet hitting the rock as they looked for their prey.

Rico fired his rifle again, and Kai kicked down at another centipede as it tried to get up on top. Carlito had moved behind her, and Hugo rushed over to them. I jumped to the side that was most unprotected and swiped with my blade, splitting another beast's head horizontally.

The others seemed to realize the danger and retreated, burrowing back beneath the sand. Suddenly everything quieted, the only noise the breathing of the humans around me.

I tilted my head, listening to see if any of the beasts would try and get at us again, but all I heard was noise moving away from us.

"What the fuck was that," Carlito asked after a beat. "Where is the exit?"

I remembered what I'd heard from others before. Most of the rifts they encountered had the entrance available for them to retreat if needed. This one didn't.

"I've been in a rift before that had the exit in a different place, and it only unlocked once I defeated a boss beast," I told them.

"Shit," Carlito cursed.

The rest of them look uncertain too.

Hugo took a long look around. From our vantage point we could see the entirety of the rift. It wasn't that big, and all of it was sand and small rock outcroppings. "What do we do?"

"I think that's obvious," I said as I walked over to the rest of them. "We defeat all the beasts, and the rift exit will probably appear. There are a lot of them underground, I can hear them."

"Dammit," Hugo said. "How do we kill them if they just go underground?"

"They seem pretty territorial," Rico said. "They attacked us the moment we arrived, when we were on the sand. I'm gonna assume that they will come after us again if we provoke them."

Hugo nodded, then looked around. "So, how do we provoke them??"

Kai cleared her throat and answered. "We should have one of us bait them. One of us should go down and provoke a response while Rico supports from the top. The rest of us should be ready for any monsters that follow the bait back here."

Everyone looked around, but all of the eyes ultimately landed on me. I smiled. It was the most logical choice. I was faster, I was stronger, I was just . . . more.

They'd clearly cleared rifts before. They had experience, and they were strong, trained. They had adapted well to this world. But there were too many centipedes. I was almost certain that without me they would've had a lot more difficult time, though, that was why they had asked me to come, I guess. These red rifts were supposed to be dangerous. Although, I could probably clear it on my own.

Still, they needed Investment. And I could provide them that.

I walked over to one of the beasts that was lying dead half on top of the rock. Its blood was yellowish in color. It smelled almost spoiled, like sulfur almost. The yellow blood put the creatures more on the insect side of the animal kingdom.

I knelt and raised it above my head, leaning in so that the blood that drained through the hole in its head landed in my mouth. I waited until it filled my mouth, then quickly swallowed.

The texture wasn't pleasant, but the **thirst** didn't particularly care about the taste.

Hugo and Rico gaped in open disgust, Kai's face was a blank mask, while Carlito watched me in clear fascination with a grin on his face.

"Okay," I said after I wiped my face with a sleeve. "Get ready."

With that I jumped from the rock and onto the sand below.

I led another group of centipedes back to the rock. Rico fired his rifle, hitting another one in the head as it ran after me. Kai was punching at the side of the last one still on top from the previous batch, while Hugo tried to get his breath from keeping the creatures at bay.

We'd been fighting for an hour, or at least they had. I'd only killed a couple here and there, trying to thin the herd before letting them go after the others.

I jumped back on top, and yelled. "Incoming!"

Carlito groaned to himself. "Fucking crazy ass *puta*," he whispered to himself, too low for anyone to hear, well most anyone. He whirled his blades and jumped on a creature that was trying to get away from Kai. His blades pierced its back, and he kept stabbing as Kai hit it in the face then stabbed the blade of her right brass knuckle into the side of its head.

Hugo roared and charged at the edge just as another centipede started to climb. He slammed his shield forward, using a skill that cracked the creature's face and sent it tumbling back down.

Rico didn't fire his rifle again. He had limited ammo, so he used his skill—which did something to make him less noticeable—and he pulled back, letting a creature climb on top. Once it had picked a target, Rico jumped in from the side and sliced through two of its legs before dashing back out of range and letting someone else deal with it.

Kai's red lock was plastered to her face, soaked in sweat, as she rushed forward and attacked. The centipede was fast—it twisted to the side and then snapped forward, its mandibles grazing her upper arm.

She hissed and moved out of the way just in time for Hugo to hit it with his shield then bring down his mace on top of it, cracking its carapace.

Kai finished it with a stab from above, piercing its head.

The last centipede rushed them, and they were too slow to turn and meet it head-on. I leapt, then brought my serpent-tongue spear down from my shoulder in a casual blow that sliced it in half.

It twitched a bit as it was dying, and I kicked both of its halves over the edge and down onto the sand. The base of the rock was filled with at least three dozen of the creatures, and about half that was out farther away on the sand where I had killed them.

Now that I looked around, I noticed that it looked like a war zone. Yellow blood had soaked into the sand, gore and cracked carapace was scattered everywhere. It was quite an impressive sight.

I turned to the other four and gave them a thumbs-up. "Good job, guys!" I grinned.

They looked at me, their faces covered in yellow blood and sweat, their clothes dirty, bleeding from small wounds, their hands on their knees as they were trying to catch their breaths.

"Crazy. Fucking. Puta." Carlito shook his head and then collapsed on his back.

I guess that it was a bit overboard for them. They had been fighting nonstop, and were exhausted. I, on the other hand, had barely exerted myself.

"What now?" Rico asked as he was kneeling and leaning on his rifle. "There is still no exit."

I hummed to myself and looked around. "I don't hear any more of them beneath the ground," I said.

The words had barely left my mouth when the ground started to shake. Everyone froze, and I looked out to see sand vibrating and moving, a large circle of it. Then it bulged, and a much larger version of the centipedes we had been fighting rose out of the sand. Its carapace was black, compared to the sand color of the others, its mandibles larger and sharper. Its legs had sharper spike-like endings, and it had another set of limbs at the front of its body that ended in even larger spikes, with a kind of claw-like attachments.

"Jump!" I yelled as it charged us, its body almost twice as tall as the rock outcropping. I reached for the closest person to me, Carlito, who was lying on his back, and grabbed him. Then I jumped from the top with him in tow, hoping that the others had listened.

I dropped on the sand just as it smashed into the rock, cracking it and sending debris flying in all directions. Rico and Hugo had jumped and managed to get out of the way, Kai on the other hand was unlucky. A piece of stone hit her in the back as she was midair.

The creature surged over the broken outcropping and then turned as Kai hit the ground, rolled, and came to a stop on her back. I saw her face contort in a grimace of pain, and she didn't move. Rico fired his rifle, but the low caliber bullet bounced off its carapace harmlessly.

"Chain and blade," I said as I started to run, dropping my spear. I started spinning the chain even as Saia still formed the rest of it. As the creature got close to Kai, who was only now starting to get up to her knees, I jumped straight at it, using [Mist Step].

As I re-formed, a low sonic wave left my location in a sphere, and it did nothing to the creature. Immediately, I let my chain fly, wrapping it around the creature's body near its head, then I braced with my feet and pulled.

I was a vampire, which meant that I was a lot heavier than I looked, but the creature was still larger than me. Regardless, I managed to pull it enough off course that its head smashed into the ground instead of Kai.

The creature spun toward me as I ran at it. Then as its underside was facing me it rolled its back end like a coil. The move was so fast that I barely had the time to react. Its back end smashed into me, sending me flying near its front. A limb lashed out and pierced straight through my stomach, impaling me and raising me in the air. The other limb came at me as it brought me closer to its mandibles, and I roared.

[Swap Profile]
[Debilitating Wave]

A sphere of red energy exploded out of me, stunning the beast. I brought my left hand on top of the spike, breaking it, then smashed my blade into it and cut it out, freeing me to fall on the ground.

The creature twitched on the sand, and I jumped even as I pulled myself with the chain still wrapped around it. I hit it just under its head, where its throat was.

[Overburn Skill—Lesser Impale]

My hand blurred forward, faster than I had ever moved, my blade sinking through the bottom of its mouth, straight through the roof and then into whatever it was that passed for its brain.

With my arm buried in its body up to the shoulder, it started to lash out widely. I was close enough to its body that it couldn't reach me, but it tried rolling on its back and taking me with it. I raised my left arm and started punching down open handed, ripping into it with my nails. My hands blurred, and the air crackled at the speed I moved. I tore pieces out of it, pulled my right hand out then stabbed down, alternating my left and right. Eventually, the beast stilled, and died.

I grimaced, and stood up on top of it, its limb still buried in my stomach. I jumped off, landing next to Kai who was on the ground looking at me with wide eyes.

I grinned at her. "Don't worry, I got it."

I heard footsteps behind me, then the sound of something sliding out of place.

[Dodge]

I twisted to the side and turned, catching the hand holding the silver shiv with my left. Hugo's eyes widened, and he swung with his other hand, his shield flying toward my head as I felt a skill being activated.

I punched it head-on with my right hand. The wood splintered, and his arm bent as a bone pierced through the skin of his forearm. He cried out in agony as I squeezed his other hand and crushed his wrist, making him drop the silver shiv.

I heard the sound of a round being loaded into a chamber to my side, the bolt sliding it into place, then a loud thump of metal hitting flesh.

I glanced to the side and saw Carlito standing with his right hand extended. A few steps in front of him Rico tumbled to the ground with Carlito's knife buried in his shoulder, which made him drop his rifle.

"Thanks," I said to the man, then glanced at Rico as he looked at me with wide eyes.

In the distance, the rift exit had appeared, along with five chests. He looked at the exit, then back at me, then he stood and started gunning for it.

"Saia, please stop him," I said, and my companion assumed her drone form and flew after the man. She swooped down, and I realized that I should've probably been clearer.

"Saia! Don't—" Aaannd she ripped the side of his neck open. Great.

I turned my attention away from my murderous little dragon and back to Kai. I raised my eyebrow and gave her an inquisitive look. She'd gotten to her feet and had her fists raised, but she looked more confused than anything.

I dismissed her from suspicion of being a part of the plot and looked back at Hugo on his knees in front of me.

"So, who was it that told you to try that?" I asked with a tilt of my head.

Hugo looked at me with only fear in his eyes. A wet spot spread on the front of his pants and the scent of urine hit my nostrils, making me grimace.

"Tell me, or this will end slowly and painfully for you," I told him.

Hugo shook his head.

"At least tell me why?" I asked.

Then he gritted his teeth, looking terrified but resolute in his silence.

I signed. "Fine."

Still holding his right hand with my left, I put my right hand on his shoulder, gripped tightly, and picked him up. With a tug I ripped his arm clean off his body.

He howled. Blood gushed out of the wound near his shoulder. His eyes rolled up in his head, and I dropped his dismembered arm then slapped him across the face.

He woke, then screamed again, and I grabbed his jaw and leaned in.

"Why and who?" I asked again.

He gritted his teeth. I had to give it to the man. He had the look of someone who wasn't going to talk. It was too bad that everyone talked, one way or another.

I let him fall then kicked his leg at the knee, shattering it backward. His scream died in his lungs as he passed out again. I rolled my eyes.

I forgot just how weak humans could be.

"Whatever," I said, mostly to myself. "Not like I don't know who it was already."

I pulled the man back and sunk my fangs in his throat, draining him in less than a minute, killing him in the process.

"Oh," I said once I dropped the corpse to the ground. "Forgot about that." I reached down and grabbed the piece of a monster limb impaling me. I was lucky that it missed my spine. That would've been a pain to heal. I pulled it out and my slush masquerading as blood slowly started dripping. The **thirst** fed on the blood I drank, and the healing started.

Saia landed next to me in her drone form. "Input: The increased synchronization rate seems to have boosted the [Repair] engram's peak capacity. It will need more fuel in order to function properly."

"Huh," I said, seeing that, yes, my wound seemed to be closing a bit faster than usual. Though I didn't really know how to judge. I didn't get impaled straight through my stomach that often.

"Thankfully, there is more than enough stuff to drink around here."

I saw Kai and Carlito, who had walked over to her, stiffen.

"Relax," I said. "I didn't mean you two."

"That's good, uh, boss lady, I wouldn't want to end up in your stomach," he said, then quickly raised his hands and waved them around. "Not that there is anything wrong with being in your stomach or—"

Kai punched his shoulder, sending him sprawling across the sand.

"He's an idiot," she just said.

I grinned, showing my fangs and bloody mouth. She shivered.

Yeah, we were going to get along just fine.

Challenge

I spent a little while drinking the blood from each of the centipede-like creatures, Rico, and then the big boss one. All told, it pushed me to the Seventh Carving. After that, we gathered the loot, which was a lot of ammo of various calibers, gemstones of various colors, some silver coins that I kept—wasn't going to give them any more tools to attack me with—and a few weapons like knives and swords.

After that was done, we left the rift, which gave me another Carving, bringing me up to Eighth Carving, giving credence to Max's theory that clearing one gave the Investment. I didn't get any new skills, though I had doubted I would. Two skills per Investment tier was the average per Shadow. Anything over that was exceptional. I was very lucky in my previous advancement, though I had also been drinking the blood of highly Invested beasts.

The rift disappeared after we exited, which was good. I doubted that the humans could clear it, and if it were one of the resetting rifts, then without regular clearing, it would probably break open and spill those beasts into the area.

The trip back was, suffice to say, awkward. Gabriela and Angelo were upset, understandably so. Though, there wasn't much that they could do or say.

It was night when we left the rift, and I made the decision that we should head back immediately. With what had happened, I didn't want to spend too much time near the rift. I didn't know if another squad had been dispatched to try to ambush me. And besides, I had perfect night vision.

We walked through the night, and thanks to Saia's scouting and my senses, we avoided all danger and made some good time as we walked without taking breaks. Finally, in the pre-dawn hours, we began approaching the camp.

I was bouncing a bullet in the palm of my hand. Every time it landed on my palm, I felt a sting on my skin, a burn-like sensation.

There was silver on the tip of the bullet. Just a tiny bit. It was actually laughable that someone thought it would be enough. Sure, if that bullet hit me, it would burn like a motherfucker, but the layer of silver was just too small to actually do something before I murdered them both. Though, I had found more bullets in Rico's ammo pouch. If he had put a few of them in me then that might've been troublesome. The shiv was a bit more dangerous though. If it had been stabbed into me and left there . . . well. It wasn't.

Carlito interrupted my thoughts with a question. "You gonna go all *sicaria* on their asses, huh, boss lady?"

"Carlito!" Gabriela hissed. "Don't say stupid things like that."

"What?" Carlito raised his head. "They tried to do a straight up hit on her, knife in the back type of shit. They waited until she was injured, until they thought there was a chance. That's straight up gangster shit there. She's right to get reparation for that shit."

"We don't know if any of them were responsible!" Gabriela insisted. "Everyone in camp knows that she killed three of ours. He could've just wanted payback for that."

I raised my eyebrows. I hadn't realized that they'd shared that, but then again it wasn't like anybody was going to say anything about it to my face.

I frowned. That complicated things. I could be wrong then. It could've been anyone. Someone I hadn't even met. I really wished that Saia hadn't killed Rico. Hugo was surprisingly unwilling to speak, though blind hate and fear of the other could've been what gave him the determination. I was doubting myself now. For all I knew it was just the two of them hating vampires. "Hm." I put the bullet back into the pouch at my waist.

We were approaching the gate, and I was thinking about what to do. The guards at the entrance let us in easily enough—there didn't seem to be any ambush planned for our return. The sun was going to come up soon, and people already started waking up.

"Carlito," I said slowly as we entered. "Could you do me a favor?"

"Sure thing, boss lady," he said.

"Can you go into the camp and find Father Sergio Rodriguez? He should have a small tent in the residential area, next to the wall."

"Oh, I know where that is. He's been holding sermons every day."

I nodded. "Right, bring him to the *big tent*, tell him that I need him there."

He gave me a mock salute and then ran off.

Next, I turned to Kai. "I need your . . . leaders? Whatever they are, gathered at the big tent, can you go find some of them?"

The big woman looked at me for a moment, then nodded and left.

"Uh, we should—" Gabriela started, but I interrupted her.

"You two are coming with me," I told them. "Don't know if I can trust you yet. And I just survived an assassination attempt. Can't have you running around unsupervised."

I showed her my fangs, and she swallowed and shivered. It wasn't much of an assassination attempt, true, but I was interested in the reason it had happened in the first place.

I made my way to the *big tent* with the two scouts in tow, entering and making my way to the table where we I usually met with the others.

I walked over to the other side, where they usually stood, then I waited.

The first to arrive was Max. He entered the tent still drowsy, rubbing his eyes.

"Marianna? What happened? I was told that we had a meeting?" he said, looking from me to the two who stood in the corner.

"We should wait for the rest," I told him and gestured across the desk from me.

He frowned, then walked over and stood where I usually stood when I was meeting with them.

Quickly, the others arrived, all looking confused and giving me the side-eye. I could hear people gathering outside, hear the clank of weapons.

Kai entered after them and walked over to me, then stood behind me with her hands behind her back. Carlito walked in a moment later with Father Sergio.

"Ah, Father," I said with a smile. "I apologize for getting you out of bed so early."

"It's fine, how can I help?" He glanced around the room as Carlito walked over to a chair in the corner and sat down, then drew a knife and started playing with it.

I was honestly surprised that Kai and Carlito seemed so much on my side. Well, I wasn't really surprised about Carlito. He was a gang member; he followed strength. Kai, on the other hand, was a mystery. Though, I had saved her life in the rift, so perhaps that was enough.

"If you could come over here, Father, I'm going to need your . . . advice."

He tilted his head but did as I said.

"What is this about, Ms. Marianna?" Diego asked finally. I could feel all of their nervousness, their fear.

"Hugo and Rico are dead," I said with a sad sigh. I watched them for any signs of guilt. Other than their heartbeats increasing, there wasn't anything that could point me at the culprit.

Lt. Cabrera was the first one to speak. "Dungeons are dangerous, a red one especially. We all knew this."

"Oh no, no," I shook my head. "I killed them."

I wasn't concerned with them knowing the truth. Lying to them would've incurred a debt, toward those that weren't involved at least. And as the things stood, they were the ones that owed me. I had to balance the scales somehow. They froze at my words.

"You killed them?" Catalina asked.

I nodded and didn't say anything else. I was watching them, looking for clues.

"Why did you do that?" Max was the one brave enough to ask.

"Glad you asked," I answered, then I pulled out the silver shiv and stabbed it into the table. "It probably had something to do with Hugo trying to stab this in my back. I mean, I don't know why he thought that would work. Though, I guess it had something to do with me having a spike spearing me through the stomach."

That made them understand what this was really about. Max shook his head. "You don't think that we had anything to do with it?"

"Did you?" I asked.

"Of course not!" Max exclaimed.

Diego and Catalina were staring at the shiv, while Lt. Cabrera had a grim look on his face.

"So, you have no idea how he got that?" I pointed at the shiv.

Max opened his mouth and then closed it. Then Lt. Cabrera spoke up, surprising me.

"I gave it to him," he said.

Everyone turned to look at him in shock.

He raised his head and looked me in the eyes. "It was just meant as a precaution. I didn't order him to try to kill you."

I tilted my head, then turned to Father Sergio.

"Well? Is he telling the truth?" I asked.

The priest blinked, probably surprised that I knew what his skill was. But then he nodded. "Uh, yes, he is speaking the truth. Both of them are."

I looked back at Lt. Cabrera. I could sense that he felt relieved. "And the shiv is the only thing you gave to him?"

He frowned, but nodded.

I reached for the pouch on my waist and poured out six silver tipped bullets. Well, silver painted, if that, even.

They looked at it with wide eyes, and Cabrera approached and picked one up. "I have no idea where these came from."

I was conflicted. I was pretty sure that it was him who had given the orders. This was starting to get really annoying.

I turned to look at the last two, who had remained suspiciously quiet. "So, what do—"

The world vanished.

The tent we were all standing in just a moment ago was gone, replaced by a gray void filled with mist. I could see people all around us. Those who were in the camp, they were here as well. Standing in places where they used to be, only absent of the actual camp.

Sounds of surprise, of panic started to spread, and then it made itself known.

It was like the voice yet not voice that I heard when I advanced. The sound and words that announced the names of my skills when I gained them. But it was also more. It blazed in the air above us, like a window into the mind of a being that was a god.

Denizens of **Terra** and **Suul'dar**, Welcome to the **World of Origin**. A New Challenge approaches!

The top 100 Masked from each continent will be brought to a new arena for the ultimate Grand Challenge!

In three days, each of the top 100 will be given a choice of being taken to the Grand Challenge or staying behind. The first of five Grand Challenges that will take place over the next five months will offer a chance for great rewards, both personal rewards and rewards for your entire continent.

The length of the first Challenge is five real time days, and thirty days personal time.

The list of the top 100 Masked is not yet final! There is still opportunity for you to advance and challenge yourself.

What the actual fuck? I stared at the words both inside my head and above me. Stared at them in disbelief and confusion. The Grand Spell did not talk with the people of Kirios. The only time it made itself known was when it chose new Exemplars. This was something new, on top of everything else that was new. And a Challenge? It was so . . . I had to wonder if Max was right, if the Grand Spell got ideas from us. This all seemed too familiar.

And then there was the list that floated above us too. One hundred names, and mine among them. I read, and I froze as I got to one name, then to another. It was impossible.

Top 100 Masked	
1st Investment; 8th Carving	Marianna Rojas—The Star That Dances in Blood Beneath the Light of the Broken Moon
1st Investment; 5th Carving	Kim Jiyun
1st Investment; 5th Carving	Kim Daehyun
1st Investment; 5th Carving	Guo Li

1st Investment; 4th Carving	Jean Dubois
1st Investment; 3rd Carving	Guo Zhang
1st Investment; 3rd Carving	Akatsuki Jin
1st Investment; 3rd Carving	Richard Smith
1st Investment; 3rd Carving	Khalil Abd al-Nur
1st Investment; 2nd Carving	Aurora Everhart

The list continued, but I didn't look beyond the top ten. Two names were familiar to me, and I couldn't stop staring at them. Could they be the people that I knew? The world was a large place, filled with too many people, at least it was before all of this. There could be people with the same name out there.

Akatsuki Jin, my sire. If that was really him on there, then . . . the Grand Spell wasn't ranking us by strength, by power. This was the ranking of how far we had advanced our Masks. Even with the power I had gained, I wouldn't have been anywhere close to the top. I might've stepped into the domain of the Adult vampires, but any Elder would've been stronger than me. Well, the older ones for certain, not to mention any of the truly Ancient vampires.

The fact that I was on top only gave credence to what Shadow had told me. Exemplars got an advantage, and I had survived Ish Vimza, the most dangerous of the continents offered. Which made me wonder, were the other people on this list Exemplars too? Only thirty of us had been chosen, and as I glanced at the list, I realized that the lowest Masked on the list was on their Ninth Carving.

I returned my eyes to the top, and the second name that caught my eye. Khalil Abd al-Nur, the name of my old friend. The man that I hadn't seen in half a decade, who was . . . I shook my head. I couldn't imagine Khalil as an Exemplar, let alone going out into the wilderness and fighting beasts. It had to be somebody else.

But, the real issue was my name on top, and the fact that the fucking Grand Spell had also shown both of my names. It had shared something that was supposed to be private. How the fuck did it even know? Was it watching me? Of course it was, I was an Exemplar. Shadow had said that it used us as experiments to figure out how to best integrate another world.

And what the hell was it with the time for the Challenge? Real time? Personal time? Did it mean that we would be gone for five days on Kirios but spend thirty days somewhere else?

If that was true, and if we could advance during this Challenge, then that would be a great opportunity for us to gain more strength.

And then there was the mention of Suul'dar, which I assumed was the second continent, the second world that the Grand Spell brought over alongside Earth. Shadow had been shocked by that too. It was the first time that the Grand Spell had done anything like that. It seemed like it was the time for so many new things.

I looked around at the people of the camp, still here, next to me. They were looking up at the list with a range of expressions, though most seemed shocked.

And then after who knew how long, just it had appeared, the gray world vanished, and the real one took its place.

We were back in the tent, staring at each other over the table with silver weapons scattered on top of it. Somehow, that seemed the least of my worries right now.

"Damn, boss lady," Carlito said slowly. "You numero uno."

I narrowed my eyes. Yeah, this was a mess.

The atmosphere in the camp changed with the announcement of the upcoming Challenge. First, there was the general feeling I got from everybody. I hadn't met even close to everyone in the camp before. They watched me from a distance, but not everyone realized that I was the vampire, especially if they saw me during the day. Now they stared; the word spread fast. I wasn't just the vampire now. I was the name that they had seen in that strange place, on top of the list.

There was still fear, more of it, even. I could sense it. They had known that I was a vampire, and they assumed I was an old one. They didn't know. They didn't understand the reality. My name on top of the ranking list didn't mean anything. There were people so monstrously strong on Earth that I wouldn't be able to do anything about them.

I didn't know if I was going to go to the Challenge. I wanted to. It was a chance to speak with people from all over the world. Get a real sense of the situation, talk with them, and perhaps agree on how we would deal with the races from Kirios coming in and trying to take pieces of our new world over.

Another part of me was terrified that the names I saw were real. That I would have to face my sire, and perhaps worse than even that—Khalil. I knew of his feelings about vampires. He had never hidden them from me. But then again, he didn't know my history back then. He didn't know that the cartel sent me to the States.

I was uncertain about everything, the attempt on my life felt so distant that I didn't even press the others on it. The camp was in turmoil already. What they had seen had opened the eyes of those who had still been clinging to some semblance of the old world. Now they knew.

I couldn't stand their stares, so I left the camp and headed into the wild, hunting and going on a feeding spree. Every beast I saw, I caught and drained, taking its essence. I cleared two rifts, and then headed south, where the beast hordes from the city were slowly advancing. The scouts were right. There were a lot of beasts pushing north. It was a ripe feeding ground, packs of dozens of dogs, rats, even cats that had been mutated and grown to be much more formidable. I killed everything, taking their blood and hoping to get stronger before the deadline.

I even visited Shadow, and tried to talk to him about what the Grand Spell was doing. Unfortunately, he wasn't able to comment on anything related to it.

Finally, on the second day, I got another Carving, pushing me to the First Investment; Ninth Carving, and again it came with no skill, which was a disappointment. At least I got some more skills from it. Four to be exact: [Lesser Dash], [Lesser Pounce], [Lesser Diseased Bite], and [Lesser Acid Spit].

Nothing spectacular, but useful nonetheless.

As the dawn of the third day approached, I made my way back to the camp, feeling like I'd worked through a lot of my frustration.

As soon as I arrived, the guards at the gate told me that Max wished to speak with me. Seeing as I didn't have anything better to do, I walked to his tent.

"Oh." Ana was the first to notice me when I entered. "You're here."

I raised an eyebrow and looked around at the others in the room. Leto and Joe stood to the side fiddling with a large military tactical backpack.

"Thank God you returned," Max said as he approached.

"You sure you want me around? Silver in the back gives me another impression."

Max grimaced. "I know that you might not believe me fully, but if there was any kind of plot, I knew nothing about it."

I believed him. I was surprising even myself with my reaction. Perhaps if I hadn't seen the attempt coming, I would've been more angry. But . . . I learned from my mistakes. I've acted rashly before, when I killed the three raiders outside of the rift. I wasn't going to do the same again.

"So, you wanted me?" I said, ignoring the big elephant in the room.

"Uh, right." Max nodded, then gestured at Leto and Joe. They picked up the backpack they had been fiddling with and brought it over to the table. "We've prepared things for the Challenge."

I walked over and looked at the backpack with interest.

"It's equipped with everything that you might need. There's ten meters of 850 Paracord—the highest rated we have—with a wooden grapple, courtesy of Salva," Max started listing. "Two boxes of matchsticks, binoculars, a polyester poncho, a change of clothes, two ferro rods—they still work, though getting the sparks is a bit harder—two boxes of .500 ammo—Gabriela mentioned that you can adapt it for your personal arm, and a first aid kit—I know that you are unlikely to need it, but it's better to have it than not—maybe someone else will need your help."

I looked at him in surprise, I hadn't expected that.

"All that, just for me?" I asked.

"It's not even half of it," Leto murmured, and I tilted my head.

Max nodded. "I know that you feel betrayed, especially if someone from camp planned what happened, but . . . I don't think that you realize just what your presence means here. You are a vampire, and people are afraid, rightfully so perhaps, but they are also glad for your presence. It gives them hope, when all we saw before was despair. And with what happened three days ago, them seeing your name at the top. It made them understand just who you are. You didn't need to stay here. You don't need us to survive. We need you."

All that he said was true, except maybe the betrayal part. I wasn't really that bothered. They were humans, doing human things.

Max took my silence for hesitance. "Please," he started. "I want to make things right. I promise you if anyone in camp was part of the attempt on your life, I'll find them."

I gave him a long look, and then nodded as Shadow's words echoed in my head.

Then finally I asked, "What else do you have?"

Equipped for War

It turned out that he had a lot actually. After I looked through the backpack, he led me to the corner where there were three large crates, one of which was open.

"It's an MSV-S, the Modular Scalable Vest—Shifter edition. We believe that they've been used by the base shifter units. A lot of the stuff was left over, though anything that had metal plates was ruined. This one, though, we've adjusted for you," Ana explained. "We've not fitted the plates yet, as we wanted you to choose."

Leto opened another crate and pulled out four plates. Then pointed and explained each one.

"We have ceramic, Kevlar, polyethylene, and hybrid plates. Ceramic is the strongest, though if it breaks its effectiveness goes down to zero in that area. It can't take consistent shots in the same spot well. It is the heaviest of the options, though I doubt that you will be facing much gunfire. If you are fighting monsters, uh, beasts, it will provide solid protection. Next up is Kevlar, light and flexible, provides solid protection against ballistic, physical, and stabbing and slashing, which I assume is what you'll mostly face. But it won't protect against any high velocity rounds, though again, I doubt that you'll be going against that."

I wasn't sure. There were skills that could make beasts fire attacks with just as much speed and power.

"Then there is polyethylene. It's hard but the lightest that will protect against high calibers, and it won't shatter like ceramics. Last one is the shifter-rated hybrid. From what the manual says it is made out of Kevlar and a new type of bioengineering silk mesh. I could barely wrap my head around it, but suffice to say it should stop anything short of the highest caliber bullets, and even then it might be a toss-up. The main issue is the weight, but then again it was made for shifters, so maybe that's not that much of an issue for you."

"It looks thinner than the others," I said as I looked at it.

"As I said, I have no idea what it is. The manual was half gibberish to me. We only offered it because it seems rated for shifter use, so I figured you might consider it."

They were right. It came with an undershirt that was fire resistant and a shirt that had room on the shoulders for two smaller plates. I had them load them all with plates. The vest had room for both front and back plates, as well as side ones. I changed into what they had prepared for me while Saia looked on from the table in silence.

It was all sand-colored camo: brown boots, pants with knee protection, then the shirt and vest. I was fully decked out in military gear. I turned around and did some experimental moves, trying to see how good I could move with it. I didn't often wear protection like this, but it seemed foolish not to use it when I had the chance. It even had neck protection.

They attached pouches along the belt that would let me store my ammo in an easily accessible place. It restricted my movements a little, but it wasn't anything that I would consider too much. It was made for shifters, who moved very fast. Their usual role in armies was to get in, wreck shit, then get out.

I placed my weapons, my two knives at my hips, then my holster and my gun at my thigh. Then I put on the backpack and slung the sheath of my serpent-tongue spear over my shoulder. The last thing was a helmet, the same one as what I'd seen Kai wear. I tried it on, then fastened it at my waist. It had ear protection, which muffled my hearing, and I relied on that too much to cover it up. But there might be a situation where the helmet would be useful.

I turned to look at Saia and spoke. "So, how do I look?"

"Feedback: Like a target."

I snorted. "Ah, don't be like that. I know that you don't like it, but you just don't have enough mass right now to provide all of this protection on your own."

One of Saia's main purposes was to serve as armor for its host. Sadly, she was just too small for it still, though she had grown quite a bit. With my latest hunting trip, she had grown to be the size of a medium-sized dog.

She didn't respond. Instead, she seemed to be . . . sulking. I offered her my forearms. "See, you can still cover me here."

Saia looked at me for a moment, and then flowed over my arms, making two smaller vambraces, one on each arm.

It was getting close to the time the Grand Spell announced the Challenge, I only assumed that the choice to stay or go would be at the same time. I was as prepared as I could be.

"I have one more thing," Max said. He walked to a corner and picked up a wooden bottle and offered it to me.

I already knew what it was. I'd smelled the fresh blood on him, the wound that he kept hidden beneath the sleeve. Still, I raised an eyebrow.

"We had an agreement," Max said and pushed the bottle forward. "Blood for you staying and helping us."

I took it from him. I already knew that it was his blood, and it was part of what I had asked. I hadn't pressed on the issue before, as I didn't want to appear as a bloodsucking monster, well, more of one.

But actually taking this blood would forge that bond between us. Not myself and the rest of camp, but him personally. It was part of my oath, and by taking it from him I would be required to give him something in return. I had already done much, shared information and knowledge, but blood was something more.

I hesitated only for a moment, and then I opened the bottle and drank in front of him. He paled, slightly, and the others turned away, unable to look at me directly. They knew what I was, but knowing and seeing were two different things.

Once I finished, I offered him the bottle back, and he took it with a shaking hand. I'd just consumed his blood, and even though he didn't know it, a piece of him would always be with me.

Afterward, I walked through the camp. The sun was slowly rising, and with it would come the Grand Spell's Challenge. I figured that I would leave, wait for it in the forest.

"Heya, boss lady." I turned to see Carlito and Kai standing near one of the tents on the way out of camp.

I tilted my head. "What're you doing here?"

Carlito shrugged. "Figured we could see you off, say good luck and all that shit."

I chuckled. "Aw, are you worried about me?"

Kai nodded. "Yes."

I tilted my head, and my smile turned kinder. "Don't be. I've survived much worse."

"Well," Carlito said, shuffling his feet around. "We just want you to come back, is all. Need some strong-ass blood suckers around here."

I shook my head and waved at them. "See you soon."

With that I left the camp.

I was halfway across the desert area when the Grand Spell decided it was time. The world vanished, and I was back in the gray expanse filled with mist.

> **Welcome, Challenger!**
>
> As one of your continent's top 100 Masked you are eligible to join the Challenge of Worth.
>
> The Challenge will last for thirty subjective days. You will be placed in a group of twenty Masked, and you may choose to work together as a team or on your own. During the Challenge your task will be to close rifts and eliminate threats, which will grant you points. Your continent will be in direct competition with your counterpart, and the continent that has accumulated the most points at the end of the Challenge will win great rewards!
>
> There will also be personal awards granted to those Masked that have acquired the most points or who accomplish special tasks.
>
> Do you accept your invitation to the Challenge of Worth?
>
> Yes/No

I hesitated for a moment, remembering the names on the list. I was afraid, I couldn't deny it. Going was the only real choice. This was something new, something that the older races on Kirios never got. It could be the key to giving us the resources to come up on top after we were fully integrated. And yet, facing my past somehow seemed far more terrifying than anything I had faced before.

Before I could convince myself to change my mind, I accepted the invitation.

> **The Challenge will soon begin!**
>
> The 100 Challengers representing Terra will be divided into five groups of twenty and scattered across the arena.
>
> Closing rifts or overcoming trials in the arena world will bring variable rewards based on their difficulty. Eliminating another Challenger will grant you their accumulated points, and in the case that they are from the Suul faction, that score will be added to the Terran score.
>
> May fortune favor the bold.

A moment later I was consumed by white light, and the world around me shifted.

* * *

I landed in a clearing inside a lush forest. Blue leaves filled the trees that had thick, robust trunks. I looked around quickly, seeing that I was alone. Didn't the Grand Spell say that I would be placed with others?

I continued taking in my surroundings. The blue sky stretched directly above me, and something else so far away that for a moment I thought that my eyes were playing tricks with me.

It was daylight, but I didn't feel any weakness. I saw no sun. What I did see was something impossible. It was a—

The white light flashed next to me, and I took a step back, my serpent-tongue spear raised and leveled straight at the newcomer.

A woman stumbled forward, dressed in beautiful eastern style combat robes, a hanbok, it looked like. She had a simple brown rucksack over her back, and on her hip she had a straight sword, sheathed—a mistake. She was being transported into an unknown area. She should've known better. She caught herself, then started looking around. It didn't take her long to notice me. Her head turned, and she froze.

"Ah, hello?" she said slowly, without making any sudden moves.

I could tell that she was a human, in her twenties, twenty-five at the most. I could also tell that she was very clearly trained. The way that she adjusted her body once she noticed me, the way her eyes slid over me in an instant.

"Hello," I said back, but didn't change my position.

Then the white light came again, and another person appeared, a man that looked like a spitting image of the woman, down to the way he was dressed and what he carried. He blinked, his eyes clear, and then he saw me. His hand went for the sword at his hip, and I nearly shot across the distance between us.

The woman stopped me by stepping next to him and grabbing his arm.

"Stop, Daehyun," she said. "We don't want to start any violence, especially not with a"—she glanced in my direction—"with a vampire."

The man blinked then looked in my direction. "It's daylight."

I relaxed and lowered my weapon, stabbing it into the ground and leaning on it. "I don't see any sun up there."

The man tilted his head and glanced up. Then he frowned, and his mouth opened wide. "Is that—"

"Yes," I said. "At least I'm pretty sure it is."

Another flash of light interrupted us, and the next person arrived. A large, burly Chinese man, if his clothing was anything to go by, with a shaved head and a thick beard. Immediately I knew what he was. The earthy scent clung to him. A shifter, I could smell it on him.

He oriented himself quickly, his eyes scanning over us and landing on me. He growled and bent his knees. "Vampire."

"Shifter," I returned. He was one of those, it seemed. Some shifters had an almost irrational hate toward the vampires. There were times in the history of our races where we were at odds, at war even. Some still held a grudge for the vampires outing them all to the world during the Great War. The vampires' decision to step into the light had forced their hand.

"Peace," the woman said, her hands raised with palms empty and spread wide. "We are all on the same side here."

Well, at least someone was trying to keep the peace. The shifter grunted, then with one last look at me took a step back.

Another flash of light announced the next person, a man wearing a strange armor and even stranger weapon. It reminded me of some of the weapons I saw in Shadow's armory.

His armor was black, with dark blue and red stripes hanging from the shoulders and waist. His helmet completely sealed his face in, leaving only a thin strip for his eyes to see. And it had a crest down the middle on top, looking almost like a fin.

His weapon was something like a half spear, made out of metal and carved with ornamental lines. The point had a hook, making it look almost like a harpoon.

I wasn't sure whether I was feeling the man's power or if it was his armor, but something was definitely strange about him.

Next came another shifter, looking like an older version of the first one. He looked around before joining his brother, or perhaps son, I was unsure. Shifters aged slowly. They weren't as long-lived as vampires, but the oldest that I had heard stories about were sill close to a thousand years old.

The white light flashed again, and another person arrived.

I froze. My heart beat a single powerful thud that rocked my body, so loud that I feared everyone would hear. And some did. The shifters glanced in my direction, as did the newcomer.

I looked as the two completely emerald eyes looked at me. Eyes that were older, that were wiser, that were cold. He looked at me for a long moment, our gazes locked in what felt like eternity.

Finally, his eyes changed, his face softened somehow, a faint smile curled up in the corner of his mouth. Then, my sire, Akatsuki Jin, spoke. "Marianna."

The only thing he said was my name, a single word, and yet it was filled with meaning, with emotion. More than I had ever gotten from him before. Before I could say anything, I heard a whisper interrupt our moment.

"Fuck me, that's her?" It was one of the twin siblings that spoke. With his words, everyone in the clearing turned to study me again.

It broke the moment, and I turned my eyes to glare at them. Then another white light came, and their attention shifted away from me again.

A man in full-on black riot gear appeared, a gun holstered on his hip and a large mace on his other, while his left hand held a big wooden shield.

He looked around the clearing then inclined his head. I remembered the order of people on the list. My sire was the seventh, which meant that the next one should . . .

The white light deposited another person in the clearing. He wore a breastplate made out of what looked like scales, similar to the ones I had seen on the weirzi. A black robe beneath it, his forearms were covered in vambraces made out of the same material, as were his shins. It was dark gray in color, it looked impressive, but I could see that it was a rushed make. The scales were attached to what looked like a long gambeson, stretching to cover everything down to his knees. Only his chest was covered in scales, and they appeared to be stitched into the fabric.

He carried a long sword on his hip, and a crucifix was hanging from his neck to rest on his chest—it was silver. His face was as I remembered. A short, neatly trimmed beard framed his angular features. His eyes, piercing and filled with wisdom beyond his age.

He clasped his hands and bowed to us. "Greetings, fellow Challengers."

He held his bow for a moment then raised his head and looked at the people around him. I felt an all-encompassing sense of inevitability take a grip on me. I wanted to run. Even more than seeing my sire again, I feared Khalil's reaction.

It'd been years since we last saw each other, since we last spoke. But he had remained a bright spot in my memories as one of my only real friends. I had cherished the time we spent together, our friendship. And now I was going to watch it all be tainted by what I had become.

His eyes reached mine and he froze, he looked me over, but then returned to gaze at my eyes. My eyes stained by the emerald threads of my bloodline.

"It is you," he just said, his face a mask hiding his true emotions.

"Khalil, I . . ." I trailed off, then the light shone again, and another arrived. A woman this time, with red hair and startling blue eyes.

Her appearance stood out so starkly from the others that I couldn't help but stare, almost in disbelief. She carried no weapons, no pack with supplies, nothing. She wore a dress, a blue summer dress with a floral print.

She stumbled, tripped, and fell. Then she pushed herself up to her knees and looked around, noticing all of us. Her face transformed with her bright smile.

"Hi! I'm Aurora, nice ta meet y'all."

It shocked everyone so much that even after the rest of the twenty arrived, most of us were still just staring at the woman in a dress.

I was glad for her interruption. It allowed me the time to take hold of my emotions and bottle them up. It was against what I was taught by Shadow. But I couldn't deal with my sire and Khalil right now. There were more important things to do.

Disagreements

In short order, twenty people stood in a circle. Most of us were humans, which both surprised me and didn't. The list ranked the Masked, and depending on what kind of a Mask vampires or shifters got, some might've been hard to advance. Or they didn't quite understand how it all worked yet.

If it was a ranking of power, then the list would've been filled with Elder and Ancient vampires, and perhaps a few shifters.

Regardless, the last of them were mostly as equipped and ready as the others were. Some wore simple improvised armor, reminiscent of medieval times, furs or leathers, while others had more modern versions, Kevlar vests, or stuff made out of hard rubber, ceramics, or plastic that was probably looted from somewhere, the same as mine. Only a few of the people in the clearing had firearms, and none had anything larger than a handgun, except a single person who had a hunting rifle.

Most weapons were swords, maces, a few spears, two crossbows, and a single bow. All were probably rewards granted by the Grand Spell.

Among the twenty, there were a few that stood out, in different ways. The woman, Aurora, who had no weapons or gear at all and who still had a big smile on her face. The man that had arrived fifth stood out the most, as he had exotic metal equipment covering him head to toe and the weapon.

Then there were the two Chinese shifters, obviously family, and giving everyone the stink eye. Mostly me and my sire, who had a simple shirt and pants and a bag slung over his shoulders. He had no weapons, but then again, I knew that he didn't need them. He was probably the most powerful among us.

An Elder vampire, perhaps even close to Ancient. I never learned my sire's real age. I only knew that he was older than the Master of the Cartel.

A silence stretched as we all arrived, and it was obvious that everyone was studying and measuring everybody else. It was also obvious to me that most of the humans had distanced themselves from me and my sire, not by a lot, but it was something that both of us would notice.

"So, any idea where we are?" one of the last humans to arrive asked.

"You should look up," one of the twins, Daehyun I thought, answered.

Everyone other than me and his sister looked up.

"Holly shit," a female human said.

Someone else whistled then spoke. "Is that what I think it is?"

"Yes," I answered.

"God, we are on a halo?" Khalil breathed out.

I glanced up at the size, the scale of it. It boggled the mind. It demonstrated, in no certain terms, just how powerful the Grand Spell was. If it could've created something like this—actually, I paused as something occurred to me. It might not have been the one to create it at all. The Grand Spell could've just found it somewhere, in another universe, and took it to use it for its own purposes. I didn't know if that made it more or less impressive.

"Damn," the human dressed in the full riot gear said. "The Grand Spell went all out for this."

"The what now?" A lot of the people seemed confused.

"Well." Daehyun glanced at his sister. "I guess now we know that not everyone is an Exemplar."

He was right. If they didn't know, it was likely that they were not Exemplars. It made sense. Even with the advantage of being on other continents, they wouldn't have had as many opportunities to advance as far as I had on Ish Vimza. Their advantages would be in knowledge. Assuming that they met with friendly people on Kirios or anyone at all.

"Exemplars," Khalil started explaining, "are the thirty people that had been chosen when the light of the Grand Spell first arrived. We've been transported to other continents of Kirios, given opportunity to learn more about this new world we are now part of."

I stared at him in surprise. Khalil was an Exemplar, and he had survived his trip. I was glad for him, impressed even.

"You're telling me that you know what is happening to Earth." One of the humans took a step in a threatening manner toward Khalil, who stood his ground and stared him down.

"We do," I interjected, turning his attention to me. I didn't like him threatening Khalil, or anyone else really. "Not all of us here are Exemplars, so this is a great chance for us to share with you all the truth, to prepare you for what is to come. The worst is yet to arrive."

That got everyone's attention. But before I could continue there was a pressure inside of my head. And then I felt the Grand Spell's intent once more.

Challenge of Worth has now begun!

Rifts have been seeded, beasts released, trials both fixed and time sensitive have been enabled. Each individual score will be added up as a total for your side. The score will be kept in the middle of the ring for all to see.

Clearing a rift will grant you between 500 and 50,000 points, depending on difficulty.

Clearing a trial will grant you between 500 and 100,000 points, depending on difficulty.

Killing a beast will grant you variable points, depending on difference in strength.

Killing a Challenger will grant you the points they had personally acquired.

Achieving any of these tasks in a group will split the reward between those involved.

Strive for greatness, advance your Masks, and claim your rewards!

I raised my head and looked to the sky. My eyes widened as I saw what was up there, for all to see. There was a timer, ticking down from thirty days. And also a list of both the Earth, or rather Terran, Challengers as well as those from Suul'dar. It was a weird effect. It looked almost like the words were written in the sky, as if they were so impossibly far away and yet close at the same time. Even with that distance, I could see them clearly. When I focused it almost looked like it scrolled and showed what I wanted to see.

Each side was at zero, but I knew that would be changing soon.

"That"—I pointed at the sky—"is the Grand Spell, a magical construct of immense power and intelligence, for all intents and purposes a god. It rules the world that Earth is now a part of. Our home has been taken apart and put together into a single continental mass as it has done at least five times before." I pointed at the sky again, at the two boards, Terra and Suul'dar. "We are the fifth and sixth worlds that it has taken, our realities flooded with Source— magic—which gives us our Masks and will mutate our nature and wildlife in unexpected ways. It has already affected elements of our world, turning most of our technology useless. No one knows why the Grand Spell does what it does, but Earth is now just a single continent on the world of Kirios, which is occu- pied by five other races. Elves, dwarves, YoKai-Ni, Naga-shan, and Harpiem.

Right now we are in the survival stage. Our continent is separated from the others. But, even if we survive in the next few months, if we gather survivors, those five races are out there, and in five months they will be granted access to our continent, and they will want to take what we have. New land for them to expand in, new resources."

There was disbelief from some, but quickly the other Exemplars in the group confirmed things.

"We are all a world away, but here in this place we can earn a reward for our entire continent," I said, pointing up at the board above us. "And we can plan, reclaim what the transition has taken from us, and make sure that when the other races come we will be ready to face them. To hold what is ours."

"So typical of vampires." A voice spoke from the side. It was one of the shifters. "You see everything as threats to your rule. The Earth doesn't belong to you."

I turned in his direction and frowned. "This has nothing to do with who or what we are. This concerns all of Earth and those who live in it. Who are going to need all the help they can get in order to survive."

"And we should just believe everything you say?" He turned to look at the others in the circle. "I'm Guo Li, and I've spent my life trying to cleanse the world of the taint her kind has spread across the world. I say, do not trust the vampire. I've met the elven people, and they are a people in tune with nature, as we were supposed to be. And now, Earth is finally healing from the harm we have done to it, the progress"—he spat on the ground as he glared at me—"that the vampires pushed on us all. She would see us turn to war, when we could meet these new races in peace. They have been through this before, and they can help us acclimate better."

I grimaced. Shadow had warned me that others would get to Exemplars, that they would offer things in return for aid when the portals opened.

But if I was being honest, I knew that this would happen the moment I saw that killing another Challenger would grant someone their points. The moment it said that points would be split. People were greedy, I knew that very well.

The shifter, Guo Li, stepped into the circle and spread his arms as he turned to look everyone in the eye. "The old world is gone. It is dead. We have no means of traveling as far or as fast as we could before. We have no ways of communicating with each other. Make no mistake," he said with conviction. "Each one of us here is on their own. Only personal power will help you save what you want to save, if that even is your goal. But you cannot save anyone if you can't survive by yourself."

I looked around and saw that most listened to his words. And why wouldn't they? It was the truth.

"That may be so, but we should still work together for this Challenge, to help our world."

Li met my eyes. "And split the rewards? You are a vampire, they are human." He pointed at the other people in the circle, the non-vampires or shifters. "The Masks give us power, but it will be a long time until it catches them up to your or my kind. You don't need to worry about your survival, vampire, they do. Why would they sacrifice the power that they could earn here to help you when they could ensure that they leave this Challenge capable of more?"

"This is not something that any of us should face alone."

"Who said anything about alone?" Li sneered. "Only without your kind."

I saw distrust pointed my way. I was a vampire in their eyes, and while my people had done much to improve our image in the public eye, we remained the ones who lurk in the darkness.

I turned to study the others, the man wearing the exotic armor. It was obvious that it was not made on Earth, and while he could've found it as a reward, everything he had on him was too much. The power of the armor was a physical thing, I didn't think that the Grand Spell would've left something like that as rewards for low tiered Masked.

He had been granted that by someone on other continents of Kirios. He had sold himself to a faction. Many of the others had to have been the same. I saw it in some of their eyes.

"I've met the Elves as well." Khalil's voice rang out in the clearing. "They are not all peaceful, but I agree we should not treat all other races with hostility. As for working together. Gaining the reward for our entire world should be our goal."

They didn't understand. They had met people who were on their home turfs, their positions of power, who had told them what they wanted to hear. Shadow was . . . he was at my mercy, and even before, I knew that he told me the truth. He had nothing to gain from lying.

"Fuck, look!" someone yelled and pointed up, interrupting whatever the shifter was about to say.

The board had changed, the Suul'dar side had gained the first points. We were falling behind.

"We are wasting time," the shifter, Guo Li, said. "None of these words matter now. We are in this Challenge, that is all that we should focus on. If we win, we win."

"So," the woman, Aurora, spoke up in cheerful tone. "How are we all gonna to do this? Separate in smaller teams and look for rifts or?"

"Do as you wish. My brother and I are leaving on our own," the other shifter said.

The woman blinked. "Wait. We are here for our world, right? We need to work together—"

"Work together?" Guo Li laughed. "With vampires? With polluters?" He nodded at the man dressed in riot gear. "The world is healing, and the disease that had plagued it for thousands of years is finally gone. There is no world anymore. We are all alone in our struggles. What point is there in working together with people we are never going to meet again? The rewards are personal, and I will not share with those I don't know."

"B—but, the reward? The Grand Spell said that our world will be rewarded if we win," she said, looking around the circle with a confused look on her face.

I could already see which way this was going. A few of the people in this group had come together, but not many. Still, we had all survived on Earth, many probably on their own. They got the taste of power that the Mask offered.

"And we should sacrifice personal rewards for some nebulous reward that will impact the entire world?" Li asked, then shook his head. "We have our own problems back home. You do whatever you want. We are not going to be part of it."

With that, the two shifters turned and left the clearing.

"You shouldn't act so hastily," Khalil called after them, but they didn't react.

The man in the exotic armor turned next, and left the clearing without a word. Then, as if a dam broke, others started leaving too.

It didn't surprise me. We were power hungry creatures, vampires, shifters, and humans all. The world had ended, and we were looking out for ourselves.

It made sense. There was no way to communicate across the world. We were as separated as we were before such things were invented. The world had gotten larger, more than even we realized. It was not just Earth now, but seven other continents, six other races.

I turned my eyes to one man that lingered for a moment. My sire looked at me from across the clearing. I wished at that moment that I had more courage, that I was stronger, that I could say something, or walk over to him. But I did none of the things that I wanted to do.

He turned and vanished, moving faster than even my eyes could follow.

I bowed my head and sighed.

"Well, that went well," a voice said and made me raise my head. It was one of the twins, the woman.

"Not really, they all left!" Aurora cried, sounding almost indignant.

"That was sarcasm," the woman responded.

"Oh." Aurora looked crestfallen.

I looked around at them, the only ones who stayed.

The woman looked at me then bowed over her fists. "I'm Kim Jiyun, and this is my brother Daehyun." She indicated the man next to her, who bowed as well.

Khalil cleared his throat, turning his eyes away from me. I had sensed him looking at me, or casting glances, ever since he arrived. Another person that I was terrified of talking with.

"I am Khalil Abd al-Nur," he introduced himself.

The young woman raised her hand, suddenly cheerful again. "Aurora Ever-hart! At your service!"

That was going to get annoying quickly.

I took a deep breath, then introduced myself. "I'm Marianna Rojas."

"Ohhh." Aurora looked at me with wide eyes. "You are at the top of the list! What's up with that other name? The star and the blood and all that? No one else has anything like it?" The words flew out of her mouth at speeds that even a vampire struggled to grasp.

I grimaced. But I could see that everyone was looking at me with interest. "I can't believe that the Grand Spell put that there." I sighed and shook my head. Did it know what that name was, what it meant? How did it know our names at all? Did it put the names that we identified with? If so, that would make some sense; both of those names were mine. "It is . . . a private thing. A second name."

I could see that the young woman wanted to ask more questions, but Jiyun interrupted her.

"Of course, you need say no more." She inclined her head.

Aurora glanced at her, then blinked, for a moment she looked as if she really wanted to ask more, but then thought better of it. "Uh, y—yeah!"

"So, we stayed," Daehyun said.

I looked at him, then nodded. "Why?" I asked. "You're not afraid of me? A vampire."

Daehyun glanced at his sister, and after a moment she nodded. "I wasn't an Exemplar," he said. "My sister was. But if what she said is true, then . . . there are other monsters out there now. A vampire at least isn't an alien."

I glanced at his sister, and Jiyun took a deep breath. "When the Light came, I chose to go to Asha Kai-ni," she said, and I leaned in, interested. That was Shadow's homeland. "And I've seen their power. There are old monsters in their mists that could crack mountains with ease. And . . . their clans love war. The Oni-yi do at least. They are . . . brutal; they don't value life in the same way we do. They don't even think like we do. I've not met any of the Tengu-gi, and I only had a single encounter with a Kitsu-oi—though I wish I hadn't. They will come to conquer. That is not a question. The Oni-yi don't respect anything other than strength. They will take anything that we can't keep. I don't know about this Challenge, but I am looking for what is going to happen in the future, what we will face when they come."

I sighed in relief. At least someone understood, someone believed that we had to do something.

"Thank you for staying, for sharing," I said, then I glanced to the side. "Khalil, I . . ."

"There is a lot that I would like to talk about," he said, his expression unreadable. "A lot that I would like to know. But we don't have the time, and there are more important things to consider. For now, I'm . . . With everything that happened this last month, I thought . . . I thought that you were dead."

He reached for the crucifix around his neck and closed his eyes, taking a deep breath. "I have a duty that comes over everything, to help humanity survive and prosper in the light. But I'm glad that you are still alive."

It was not what I had expected from him. He had grown, I realized, had changed. There was a hardness in his face that I didn't see in him before.

"You two know each other?" Aurora asked.

"We do, from another life," Khalil added. "It is unimportant now."

He looked in the distance, after the ones that had left.

"I wish that they had stayed. We should've all talked, shared what is happening in the world, got more information about everything."

"Yes," Jiyun said. "They are shortsighted."

I nodded. People made their choices, and we made ours. "Then, do you want to continue this Challenge together? There is strength in numbers, and perhaps we can help each other and Earth."

Aurora jumped up and raised her hand. "I'm in! Also, the Grand Spellima-thingy is calling us Terra for some reason though."

I tried not to let my face twitch in annoyance. "I don't think that we should try to discern why the Grand Spell does what it does."

"At least we don't have time for it right now," Khalil said.

"So," Daehyun started. "We pick a direction and go look for rifts or these trials? We can talk on the way."

I sighed, then nodded my head. It was going to be a tough month, I could already tell.

Group

I wish I could say that our trip started in silence, but the moment we headed into the forest Aurora started asking questions.

"So, where are you all from? I mean where were you before you got here?" Aurora smiled brightly at us.

I tried to glare at her, but it was a good question; her bright demeanor was just clashing a bit with my brooding and depressed one.

"I'm in Colombia," I answered as I looked around, searching for any threats. "Well, I can't actually be sure. I'm in a military base that is actually in a desert. A piece of it was swapped around when the Grand Spell arrived. So for all I know I could be in a big piece of Colombia that was swapped around to someplace else."

"Wow, and you're a vampire! Why aren't you burning up? Are you just that old?" she asked.

I saw Khalil narrow his eyes at me. I wished that I knew what he was thinking.

I gave Aurora a long look. "Do you see a sun anywhere?" It wasn't a lie, though it was a fine line.

I felt Khalil's heart skip a beat at that. His mouth opened then closed. He knew that vampires could walk in sunlight. It gladdened me that I could still read his tells. Though I wondered how he found that out. I was pretty sure that even most vampires wouldn't know yet.

"Wow, didn't think about that." Aurora looked around. "But how is it then daylight?"

I shrugged.

Aurora turned and looked at the others. "Well, I'm from the United States! From a small town called Monroeville in Alabama. The town was abandoned. After I returned from my Exemplar trip there wasn't anyone around, so I'm all alone out there." She grinned at us.

I blinked. She survived in the wild by herself? My estimate of her capabilities increased, slightly.

She turned to look at the brother and sister pair and raised an eyebrow.

The twins exchanged looks, then Jiyun spoke. "We are from Korea. Our family has a temple on the outskirts of Seoul. My family managed to keep it safe, so I returned there after my thirty days on Asha Kai-ni. We remain there still, sending out parties looking for survivors, though the situation is worsening quickly. Seoul has fallen, and dungeons—well, rifts as the Grand Spell calls them—are breaking open. Thought half of them were destroyed in the early days, as my brother told me."

Daehyun nodded. "They bombed the rifts, back when technology still worked."

I shuddered. How many had done the same? Did someone nuke a city? I couldn't imagine what was going through people's heads when everything happened. It had to have been chaos.

Jiyun continued. "Beasts are threatening to overwhelm the land. We came here in hopes of getting strong enough to be able to keep them at bay."

"You didn't think about leaving the temple? Finding someplace safer?" I asked.

Jiyun shook her head. "It is our ancestral home," she just said.

Aurora reached over and patted her shoulder. "I understand, I'm still near my home too."

Then, quickly before Jiyun could react Aurora turned to look at Khalil.

He cleared his throat, then answered. "Constantinople."

I blinked. "You went home?" I asked before I could stop myself.

He looked at me, his face flinching for just a moment when he met my eyes. If I wasn't a vampire, I wouldn't have noticed it.

He nodded. "I did, yes."

"You are in a city?" Daehyun asked, surprised. "It was our understanding that all cities are overrun. Too many rifts opened up in them."

Khalil nodded. "Yes, that is true. But"—he glanced in my direction—"the vampire coven of the city joined forces with the human population. The battle was hard, but we—they've cleared the city, with heavy casualties. It is estimated that we lost more than three fourths of the population."

That was an insane number. Constantinople was a home to more than fifteen million people on both sides of the strait. The city-state had stood independent for centuries, a bridge between the east and the west, one side of the strait Christian and the other Muslim.

It was the cradle of history, religion, knowledge, and learning. How much was lost in that fight? How much would've been lost if the city had fallen as others did?

I wondered how many cities on Earth managed to survive like they had. Were there any? I knew that some of the oldest cities in Europe had covens of their own. If vampires actively fought, then it was possible that the situation was much better than I thought. Though there weren't that many vampires in the world. Shifters were more numerous, but they lived in compounds in the wild, on reservations.

"How is it, really?" I asked.

"The change has impacted us," Khalil said slowly. "We are facing the east now, and the Black Sea is no more. We are on the coast of a different body of water, an ocean, we think."

"Is the city moved to someplace else?" Daehyun asked.

Khalil shook his head. "We don't think so. The Balkans and Anatolia are still present, as far as our scouts could tell."

I wished that we had a way to see how the Earth looked now. But our satellites were gone, and the only one that knew was the Grand Spell. We would have to redraw all maps. It was going to be a nightmare.

Khalil's voice brought me out of my thoughts.

"I must ask." He was looking at Aurora. "Why were you not better prepared? I see that you brought no supplies with you."

Aurora's cheeks reddened. "Well, I didn't know what kind of a Challenge it was going to be! Like rifts could be just puzzles! And I . . . I wanted to make a good first impression on the others, so I was going through the town shops looking for something nice to wear and . . . and then it happened! Like boom! One moment I was putting on a dress, and in the next I was surrounded by gray mist. I didn't have the time to change or anything." She almost whispered the last part.

"How did you even survive till now?" It took me a moment to realize that it was me who had spoken.

Aurora's mouth opened, and she looked at me with the look of a puppy that was just kicked. "I'm good at things!"

"For all I know you have the Mask of a Cook," I said before thinking, then cursed myself. Something about the woman was pushing all my buttons.

"I am not a cook!" Aurora said with indignation. "Wait, not that there is anything wrong with cooks, or like, I do know how to cook, but I don't have the Mask of the Cook!"

Khalil interjected. "I believe that what Mari meant to say is that we are in a strange place probably surrounded by danger, and that she was worried about you taking care of yourself."

"Oh." Aurora's eyebrows raised, and then a smile grew on her face as she looked back at me. "You should've just said that! Of course I can take care of myself."

She shadowboxed the air in front of herself. "I survived the Underways. No dumb halo is gonna take me down."

"The Underways?" Daehyun asked.

"It's where I was sent as Exemplar, it's on Du'vir," Aurora answered.

"You met the dwarves?" I asked, intrigued, as we stepped into a clearing.

"A few, yes. There are not many of them in the Underways. It's like this big tunnel network that spans their entire continent. I spent most of my time in one of the abandoned sections. Only the Earth Wardens are allowed there."

I pulled out one of my daggers and offered it to her. "Here, you should have something to protect yourself with at least."

"Ah." She looked at the dagger. "I don't really know how to, uh, stabby-stab?"

I narrowed my eyes at her. "How do you then protect yourself?"

"Uh, well . . ."

I froze, the others doing the same. I heard something in the distance, something coming our way. I got close to the ground and pulled my backpack from my shoulders, dropping it to the ground. The others saw me and followed suit.

Then the ground shook, and a big roar filled the forest. I turned and saw something in the distance, charging at us with great speed, barreling through trees.

It broke into the clearing, and I saw what I could only describe as a giant plant beast, twice as tall as I was. Its bark was dark gray, almost black, and its head was a big mushroom looking cap, with no eyes but dozens of stalks growing out from beneath it. There was no mouth, but big cracks in the bark that released a loud noise that I had mistaken for a roar. It had limbs that ended up in a tangle of dozen root-like fingers.

It stomped in our direction, each step shaking the ground.

"Scatter!" Khalil yelled as he pulled his weapon and dashed to the side.

The twins did the same, while I grabbed Aurora, who was staring straight at the giant, and jumped back, flying through the air.

She stiffened in my hands, surprised by the suddenness of my movement, but quickly realized what I was doing. I dropped her at a safe distance, near the edge of the tree line and looked at her.

"Stay here," I said, not waiting for her to answer.

Then I ran back into the clearing. The giant smashed its tree trunk thick limb into the ground as it attempted to flatten the twins. They dashed to the side, their swords in their hands.

Jiyun dashed forward in a burst of speed with a skill that made her movement a blur. Her weapon was a lithe and long straight sword, with a ribbon attached at the pommel. She cut at the giant's leg, but barely dug at all into the bark. The giant turned, swiping its limb at her, and she dashed away.

Her brother attacked it from the other side. His weapon was the same type but slightly different. He stabbed his blade, managing to get halfway through the bark on the leg before his thrust was stopped. When he pulled it out, amber sap-like fluid flowed from the puncture.

The giant turned and raised both arms in the air then slammed them into the ground as Daehyun jumped out of the way.

The ground shook, and debris was sent everywhere, sending Daehyun stumbling.

Khalil attacked its back. His sword was long and thick, a standard European medieval weapon. As he hacked, his sword ignited with yellow light. It hit the giant's lower back and cut through the bark.

I watched them fight for a moment, seeing their strengths and weaknesses. Daehyun and Jiyun moved the same, utilizing the same style. They were quick, relying on that speed to step in, attack, then move out of the way before their foe could respond. I was pretty sure that both of them had skills that let them move with bursts of speed.

Khalil was a lot slower, but his skills packed a punch. I didn't know what that yellow light was, but it was cutting through the bark with ease.

They were struggling against it. It was too large, too strong for them. One solid hit, and they would probably end up with broken bones, at best. Though, as I watched I did think that they would triumph at the end. Their skills gave them a good advantage on it.

The giant beast was . . . weak. It was nothing compared to the beasts I faced on Ish Vimza. I hefted my serpent-tongue spear, and got ready. I'd seen enough of the others' capabilities to know that they could hold their own against the beast.

Before I jumped in, I felt the ground tremble, not in sync with the beast's movement. Worried that there might be another one, I turned around, and saw Aurora on her knees, her hands pressed against the earth.

Something made the grass ripple, a straight line blasting across the ground to reach the giant, and then the ground beneath its feet shook violently, a small quake. The ground waved, and the giant stumbled and started to fall.

Daehyun was caught in the quake, and he slipped. The giant was falling straight on top of him.

I moved, crossing the distance in a moment. I caught him and brought him out of the danger zone. As soon as the giant fell, Jiyun and Khalil jumped on it, stabbing and slicing with their swords at the mushroom cap on top of its body.

It didn't die that easy. Its limbs lashed out at them, forcing them off its body. The wounds did damage, more sap was leaking out of it, but it was a tree, there wasn't a critical organ that they could hit and kill it. I heard no heartbeat, no tendons, no bones, no muscles that moved—only the grinding and groaning of wood.

I dropped Daehyun down, and then just as the giant pushed itself up on its feet, I dashed close to it. I swung my sword in a large arc, cutting straight through one of its legs. My weapon sliced through it, splitting the trunk in half. The giant lost its balance and fell, and before it could do anything, my blade sliced again, this time chopping off an arm. Quickly, I cut it apart into smaller pieces, one swing at a time.

The others came to help, but it was clear that they didn't have the strength to cut through its body with the same ease I could.

I only stopped once the giant stopped moving.

Was this a trial, or just a random beast?

I didn't know how to judge the danger of this place. Was it made for the strength level of humans? Of vampires? An average? So many questions.

"Whew, look, we all got two hundred points," Aurora said from the side, pointing at the sky. "That was some tough work, but we did it, team! Congratulations on our first victory!"

One thousand points split among the five of us. From what the Grand Spell showed earlier, the points could go up to 100,000 for the trials. Did that mean that this was a just a beast? Was there a beast that would grant 100,000 points? How powerful would it be?

I pushed those thoughts away and looked at the young woman, taking her in for the first time. She didn't panic when the giant came. She used a skill and helped. It was more than I had expected of her, if I was being honest.

"You can shake the ground?" I asked.

She looked at me sheepishly. "Uh, yeah. The Earth Wardens taught me some of their ways. I have a . . . related Mask."

She didn't say the name of it, which was fine. She was an Exemplar. She understood that the name of a Mask was private information. She didn't need to say it.

"That's good," I said. "Though, next time try not to get your allies caught up in your skills."

She winced and glanced at Daehyun. "Sorry."

He looked a bit reserved and then walked over to me and bowed. "Thank you for helping me."

"It was nothing."

"You are very strong," Jiyun said.

"I'm a vampire," I said simply.

They said nothing at that.

"I guess"—Khalil looked around—"that we should keep going? Look for more things to do?" He raised his head and looked up at the sky. The board and the rankings. Numbers had started to go up.

"We should probably see about finding a place for a camp, a base of operations of sorts," I said. "Your supplies won't last for long, and we are going to need a water supply."

"You're right," Khalil said. "Let's do that."

* * *

We found a small clear stream. The others were a bit worried about drinking from it, but Khalil announced that he could make the water safe.

To prove it he filled a gourd from his pack and then put both hands on it. Yellow light blossomed in between his hands and surrounded the gourd. Once it was done, he took a swig.

"See, perfectly safe," he said with a smile.

"What kind of a skill was that?" Jiyun asked.

"It's my [Lesser Blessing of Purification]. It does various things, but one of them is cleansing."

I blinked. It would seem that his faith still remained strong. He had to have a Mask related to it somehow. I didn't even know how that worked. How would the Grand Spell even translate that to its power?

We found a spot nearby, next to a large boulder, which gave a good view of the surroundings, and we decided that would be our camp.

After that we set out to search for more beasts, rifts, or trials.

We spent the day searching our surroundings. We didn't run into another beast, nor did we run into any of the other summoned Challengers. They'd gone in different directions.

What we did find were two rifts. One was a simple puzzle, or rather obstacle rift, which was made trivial with me in the group. The goal was to reach the top of a tower that had various ledges on its surface with levers on the bottom that pushed out new ones while retracting others.

I just jumped, using two of the dozen ledges to boost myself up. The reward was gemstones and two torches. Nothing special at all. But it did spark a conversation about the gemstones and what others knew about them.

Of the five of us, only Aurora didn't know anything about them at all. But then again, she was all alone, while the others were with groups. Khalil said that there was an entire system set up for researching and discovering more about Masks in Constantinople, similar to what Max was doing at my camp.

The twins had something similar, too, at their family temple.

We found one more rift, a small one filled with dog-sized creatures that tried to swarm and overwhelm us. We dealt with them easily enough and got more basic gemstones as rewards, or F Grade Gemstones, as the twins called them.

Soon, I could see that they were started to get tired. This place didn't seem to have a day and night cycle, but I suggested we return to camp and rest for a bit.

"I'll take the first watch," I told them once we returned. I didn't really need to rest.

"I'll join you," Khalil said slowly. "For a while at least."

I hid my trepidation. It would seem like *the* conversation was going to happen after all.

Old and New Friends

We climbed on top of the boulder above our camp and took a seat on the cold stone. We sat next to each other in silence for what felt like forever, looking out at the forest and the world that curved up above us, but not at each other. I didn't know how to start. How did one even start something like this, after years of not speaking? How did one say, hey, I lied to you for years?

Thankfully, Khalil seemed to find the courage where I couldn't.

"You know, I tried to look for you, when you didn't return for the next semester. I called every Rojas family household I could find in the general area you gave me. I called the embassy even. I was even planning on taking a trip. You talked about Medellín, and I imagined I would be able to find you. It all seems so stupid now."

I winced. I was in the States with my real name, but most of the rest was fake. The history of who I was. The cartel made sure that I wouldn't be found, if anyone ever was to try in the first place. Apparently, someone did.

"How old are you?" It was his first question, and it was telling that he chose that to ask.

It put everything that had happened since we arrived in this place and met again into a different perspective. I listened to his heartbeat, to the blood moving through his veins, the subtle tensing of his muscles. The telltale signs of fear. He was afraid of me. I knew his belief about vampires. I had tried to show him good things, even back before I was turned, but it didn't seem to have been enough.

"Twenty-eight. It feels so much longer."

"You must think me a fool." He shook his head. "I know enough about vampires to know what your eyes mean. They are almost fully green, a sign of an Elder. That makes you at the very least a hundred years old. How did you do it? Contacts probably for the eyes, but everything else? Your skin was warm, you—"

"No," I interrupted him. "I'm not lying. I was turned after I returned home. My eyes . . . I think that the Mask is making them change faster. It happens as I gain Carvings."

He turned to face me. "Really?"

I met his look and nodded. "Really."

He turned away, and again the silence stretched.

"Was it your choice?" he asked finally.

I laughed, the first real laugh I had in a while. I saw him look at me, but I couldn't control myself. I laughed at the absurdity of the question. I saw that he was confused, perhaps even hurt. He thought that I was mocking him. I mocked no one but myself.

"I'm sorry," I said after I managed to contain myself. "I wasn't laughing at you. It's just that up until the Light came for me and I was picked as an Exemplar, I had made no real choice of my own in my entire life."

He looked at me, and I was reminded of Khalil who was my friend. Not this reserved person wearing armor. The scholar, the goof that I joked around with. And I made a decision.

Slowly, I told him my history, how I was sold as a child and everything that followed after.

When I was done, he wasn't looking at me. But then he reached over and took my hand with his own, grasping it gently, as if he was worried that I would break.

"I'm sorry that happened to you, Marianna. If I had known, if you'd told me—"

"It would've changed nothing."

"It would've changed everything, Mari," he said softly. "I could've helped you. I knew people—"

"People that could've opposed an Elder vampire? A cartel with means to reach across the world?"

"Mari," he started, "I, I was part of an organization too. Am still. I was in the States to learn, get an education. I'm a Knight Priest of the Order of the Dragon, of the Knights of Constantinople. We—"

I pulled my hand away from his, looking at him, and spoke in a whisper. "You kill vampires."

"No." He shook his head. "We protect humanity from those vampires that abuse their power."

I knew the stories, every vampire did. I grew up hearing from the other vampires. The Knights of Constantinople were their bogeymen. Villages roused to carry torches and pitchforks, led by knights in shining armor. That was who the Order of the Dragon was.

And now I was a vampire. Such a pair we were.

"Why did you stay?" I asked.

He blinked. "What do you mean?"

"When the others left, why did you stay here with me? You knew what I was the moment you saw me. Your people hate vampires, why did you stay?"

"Hate is a strong word." He looked away. "Some do, I have no doubt. Many find their way to the doorstep of St. George Church because of loss at the hands of vampires. I . . . I was an orphan. I was raised in it. I don't hate, but I understand the danger even a single vampire poses. I've seen it with my own two eyes. I've seen what the oldest of your kind can do, and the callous disregard of life they hold. One of your kind was an Exemplar on Elvaros. He was old, very old and powerful. Even with a low Investment Mask, he . . . he did terrible things. Killed so many. There are some of you that have to be stopped."

"And me?" I asked.

"I . . ." He paused, then took a deep breath. "I don't know. If you want to know why I stayed. Then that is the reason. To find out."

I sat alone for the rest of the *night* or rather until the humans were rested. I had a lot to think about. It seemed that both Khalil and I had secrets. What I now knew made so much sense. It put into perspective a lot of our time at the university together. As I'm sure my secrets put into perspective what he remembered.

But the truth was that neither of us was who we once were, or even who we pretended to be. I didn't know what to think of it, but I was glad that I had come here, that I had this chance.

We were separated by an entire world. We might never see each other again in this lifetime. At least this way I had some closure.

Except, that wasn't what I wanted. I had spent my life all alone, and I didn't want to be, not anymore. The people back at the army camp, the people here. I had a chance to make new connections, meaningful ones. Shadow had urged me to try, to not make the same mistake he had. To not end up like him, all alone on an isolated continent.

With that decision made, I waited for everyone to wake up, then jumped down to the camp.

"Hey everyone, I have something I'd like to share," I said. It was a new world, a chance to make new friends. They looked at me inquisitively. "Someone I'd like you to meet."

They exchanged looks, and I spoke.

"Saia, introduce yourself."

"Oh my gosh, you're soooo cute." Aurora had picked up Saia and was snuggling with her.

Honestly, I was surprised that she hadn't opened the girl's throat yet. I know that I was close to doing it myself. On the bright side, Saia was holding to her promise to me.

"Statement: This Unit is not *cute*, this Unit was designed to serve as a deadly asymmetrical warfare system."

Aurora just snuggled the dragon against her cheek.

"Input: I kill things."

"So cute," Aurora squealed.

"Query: Permission to assimilate biomass." Saia's blue eyes looked at me.

"Assimilate?" Aurora asked before I could answer. "Oh, like assimilate into a friends group? You want to be friends!"

"Feedback: That was not the intended meaning of the word I used."

"Don't worry," Aurora said. "We'll become best friends!"

"Your story is amazing," Jiyun said as Saia struggled to get out of the woman's grasp without harming her. "And to have found and took in such a spirit and gained its power is commendable."

I shifted. "I did what I had to survive. And I think that it's more like she took me in."

I'd given them the abridged story of my time in Ish Vimza. Nothing too in depth, of course, and nothing about Shadow yet. We still didn't know each other well at all. But we'd gotten through battle together, and this much felt right, at least. And on the bright side, by the end of my story I got one more Carving in my *Revelator* Ornament.

We spent the day looking for and completing rifts. Every rift that we finished closed after we were done with it. And slowly, we started gathering points. The board put Earth and Suul'dar at near even, but our group was falling behind most of the people on our list.

Obviously, smaller groups or individuals got more points. In theory, we should've been able to do things faster, but in practice we could only move as fast as the humans could.

I knew that if I was alone I could've done a lot more. But I didn't want to go it alone. I'd done that for far too long.

I sent Saia out to scout, which made finding rifts a bit easier. The ones that we cleared were mostly easy. Some were filled with beasts, others with puzzles or obstacles on the same level as the one we did previously. They might've been a bit more challenging to humans, but with me on the team, they were almost too easy. And the rewards were barely anything useful. A handful of gemstones, a gourd here, a dagger there. We were even forced to start leaving things behind, as we didn't have the room to carry it all.

On the bright side, having Saia's existence out in the open allowed her to assimilate mass from beasts we killed. She even got another centimeter or two in height too. I, sadly, didn't get another Carving yet, despite drinking blood from the beasts regularly.

The others though had a lot more luck, well, most of them.

"Another Carving," Daehyun said. It was his second in the five days we had been clearing rifts, bringing him up to First Investment; Seventh Carving.

"Congratulations, brother," his sister said with a smile.

She seemed very glad for her brother's fortune, even though she didn't have the same luck. She had gotten only one Carving, putting her on her First Investment; Sixth Carving.

Apparently they had slightly different Masks, both related to fighting with a sword, but the Investment gain had different ratios, it seemed. Her brother gained more from just fighting.

I knew how peculiar Mask Investment requirements could be.

"Ugh." Aurora kicked a stone with her foot, sending it flying off the edge of the small space island inside of the rift.

She, like me, had gotten no Carvings yet. Though, if these rifts gave Investment just by finishing them as those on Earth did, both of us were due for at least a Carving.

Even Khalil had gotten one.

"Don't worry," I said. "I'm sure you'll advance soon."

Aurora smiled at me. "Maybe if the rifts were a bit more dangerous, or you guys got into trouble a bit more . . ."

The ease of the rifts didn't help her at all, or me it seemed.

It was obvious that for her to gain Investment she had to use her skills in a particular way. Do something during the fight that she hadn't had the chance to. She'd been dropping hints, but hadn't come out and outright said it.

We gathered the almost worthless rewards and left the rift.

"That's the last one, right?" Khalil asked.

I nodded. "The last one in this area, at least."

"So, which direction should we go?" Aurora asked.

We had decided to designate the two sides of the halo that curved up to meet each other in the middle as north and south. It helped with orientation.

"Well." Jiyun turned her eyes and looked north. "The only thing of note is that mountain. Might be worth checking out."

I looked in the distance over the tree line. She was right that it was the only thing of any real note nearby. And with no real intel on anything, it was as good of a direction as any.

We decided to take a short rest before heading out.

* * *

"You don't need to stay with us, you know, *unnie*," Jiyun said as she came up and sat next to me. I was on watch, as always. It didn't make sense for any of them to do it when I didn't need to rest.

I tilted my head and looked at her. "What do you mean?"

"We are slowing you down."

I opened my mouth to deny it, but she interrupted me. "It's fine, we all know it. You are a vampire, much stronger and faster than us. You could've cleared these rifts in a day or two without us."

I closed my mouth, deciding not to say anything.

"I appreciate what you've been doing," Jiyun said, then bowed her head in my direction. "Letting us fight on our own."

"You didn't need any help," I said.

"Of course, but you could've ended the fights a lot sooner if you wanted. I see that you are letting us gain Investment, at a penalty to yourself. We've all come here to try to get stronger, to help our groups back home."

It wasn't much of a penalty, not really. My Investment didn't come from fighting, but from drinking blood. I got the blood either way. Though, yes, I did feel like I got more if I killed the source. Still, with such low-power beasts, it wasn't much of a loss.

"It didn't seem to help you," I commented.

She sighed. "My brother's Mask is more geared toward fighting with a sword. Mine is about mastery of it."

"That must be frustrating for you."

"It is, and it isn't. I love the sword. I've practiced with it since I was a child, same as Daehyun. Me being chosen as an Exemplar gave me a choice of my Mask, and my time on Asha Kai-ni had gotten me a good Mask evolution. Daehyun . . . he had unfortunately been granted a more generic Mask."

I could see how that could be a problem. The more generic Masks might be a bit weaker, but they also gained Investment easier.

"That's why I was wondering if you would be willing to do me a favor?" Jiyun asked.

"What kind of a favor?"

"I saw how you moved when you fought, when I could see you at all." She smiled. "I was wondering if you would be willing to spar with me, for a short while at least?" She raised her sword as she asked the question.

I blinked. I hadn't expected the question. Then I nodded. It would be a good opportunity for me to practice my own style against something other than beasts.

She smiled, and we stood, walking to a small clearing. She drew her blade and got into a stance as I was about to take my serpent-tongue spear out its sheath.

"Do you want me to use another weapon? A dagger or sword?" I wasn't as good with swords, or daggers even, but it wouldn't really matter.

"No." She shook her head. "Use whatever you prefer. What you are best at."

I shrugged and pulled my weapon out. Then I narrowed my eyes. I knew some things about the rules of how Investment was gained. The context mattered, yes, but also the intent, the power disparity. "Did you ever gain Carvings from sparring?" I asked.

"I have, yes," she said. "It is a good way to learn."

"Do you have a Student Ornament perchance?" I asked her.

She blinked, then nodded hesitantly. That made sense. It was a solid Ornament, according to Shadow, and most people on Earth would be able to get it, those that went through the educational system at least.

I didn't know what exactly her Mask was, but it had to do with the sword, that much was clear. I decided to give her a bit more than she asked for. She had stayed, had trusted me enough to work with me, despite me being a vampire and the others leaving. It was a small debt, but one I could repay.

I stabbed my weapon in the ground then started taking my clothes off. The vest then the shirt beneath. Jiyun was startled. I heard her make a small noise, and by the time I had taken my pants off, she had a full-blown blush on her face.

"What are you doing?" she whispered, looking over my shoulder toward camp.

"Don't worry, I'll know if anyone is heading this way," I said.

"That's not—why are you naked?" she asked.

Once I finished, I only had underwear on my bottom half. I only had the one sports bra, and I did not want to ruin it.

"I don't want to ruin my clothes or get them soaked in blood. I only have one spare set."

"Blood? I asked you to spar, not . . . whatever it is you think we are going to do!" Jiyun hissed.

"Just trust me, you'll thank me later. I think," I said. "Get ready." I closed my eyes and grabbed hold of my emotions as I pulled out my weapon and got into the defensive stance of the **Stalwart Mist's** first Kata: *In the Mist, Await.*

I bent my knees and got into a stable stance facing her, low to the ground with my elbows out and holding my spear pointing straight to the sky with both hands.

I waited with closed eyes and without moving a muscle. I didn't even breathe, no need to pretend that I need it that often.

I could hear Jiyun, her breath, her indecision. Finally, she realized that I wouldn't move, and she started stepping close.

Her footsteps were as loud as drums in the middle of the night. Her breath like a gale passing through a tunnel. Her clothes rustled against her, her muscles and bones strained.

She hesitated before throwing an experimental jab at my shoulder—and missing. I didn't move. The attack didn't touch me.

She retreated, then finally after what to me felt like an eternity, she stabbed forward. The moment her blade connected with my shoulder and pierced the outer layer of my skin, I moved. I twisted to the side, careful to match her speed as much as I could, then I opened my eyes and retaliated with a cut from above.

Her eyes widened, and she dashed to the side, my weapon cutting through the place her head was just a moment ago.

I saw understanding in her eyes. She would've died if I had moved any faster. There was nothing that she could do. I saw that familiar fear on her face, the knowledge of the difference between a vampire and a human.

A tiny drop of blood pooled at the pinprick wound that she had made. She had barely touched me, and my [Lesser Constitution] made my skin tougher. The wound closed up nearly instantly.

I looked at her. "Don't worry about hurting me, and use your skills."

She nodded hesitantly, and then seemed to compose herself. She got into a low stance, a more aggressive one. Her body turned sideways, her blade pointing at the ground. The corner of my mouth raised, and I closed my eyes again. She took two quick steps toward me at an angle, then used a skill. She dashed behind me in a quick burst of speed, then attacked my lower back with a piercing attack.

The attack itself was a skill too. It pierced my skin, deeper this time, before I reacted. I moved, cutting her blade out of my flesh toward my hips, opening up a shallow scratch as I retaliated.

The core of the **Stalwart Mist** was in retaliation. In waiting for the moment where the opponent was overextended and hitting them twice as hard.

I moved at the same speed I had before, but Jiyun had anticipated the attack this time. She was ready and made the mistake of raising her sword in an attempt to block.

My sword hit hers and sent her to the ground. The flat of her sword hit her the shoulder and made her drop to one knee. I didn't push through with my attack. Instead I stopped it when it was parallel to my waist.

I looked down on her, and saw her swallow.

I pulled my sword up and took a step back before returning to my previous position.

We continued fighting for a while. And the longer it went the more in tune with the Azure Moon Style I got. But I was also learning about my opponent's style. Seeing how she moved, how she utilized distance, and how her martial art dealt with an overwhelming opponent. I could feel my skill, [Practical Learning] working, making the process faster. I adjusted my movements based on what I learned.

Jiyun was moving at her top speed, using all of her skills, and she did manage to score a good hit a few times. It was just that it didn't matter in the end. My wounds healed, and she never managed to deal with my counterattack in a way that would allow her to survive for long after it.

Finally, I raised a hand and halted her as she prepared for another run at me.

"That should be enough," I said. Her breathing indicated that she had nearly exhausted herself.

"I . . ." She blinked for a moment. "Yes, you're right, I—oh, I got a Carving," she said excitedly.

"Congratulations," I told her, just as my own Carving came, along with a change.

Ornament of the Student (Physical, Weave, Esoteric)
No Investment; Tenth Carving
Ornament of the Student > Ornament of the Practical Student

Ornament of the Practical Student — First Investment; No Carving

My Ornament evolved, changed to better reflect what I had achieved. It made sense. I wondered how it would integrate into my Mask. I didn't know how to do that, though I knew that it could happen at any point, any Investment.

Jiyun beamed at me, then put her hands together and bowed over them. "Thank you for the lesson!"

"You helped me too," I said. It would seem that our debts were canceled. It was almost as if I could feel it in my soul.

She didn't push me as much as I had her, but I did get more familiar with my version of the Azure Moon Style. The opening form, at least.

"Now, you should head toward camp and stall for me," I said as I walked over to my clothes. I had dried blood marks all over me, though my wounds had healed already. I would need a few minutes to clean up. "Your brother is on the way, and I would really prefer if he didn't see me naked."

That made her straighten, then panic, and blush again. "Right, I'll make sure you have time!"

She bowed to me again, then ran off in the direction of camp.

I smiled. Things were looking good.

Trial of the Summit

It was two days until we reached anything of note. We'd cleared a few different rifts as we made our way through the forest heading toward the big mountain in the distance. Since all of my companions were so weak, we decided not to clear every rift in the area, but just to continue moving, hoping that we would find the higher difficulty ones along the way.

After clearing the third rift of the day, we decided to take a short break.

I sat on the ground, adding gemstones to each other and making different elements. I was trying to make some that would be useful for my current profiles.

I wanted to spec either [Sonic Screech] or my [Debilitating Wave] to be a bit more offensive. They were both good for stunning opponents, but not much beyond that. [Sonic Screech] could technically do damage, but it just wasn't strong enough yet. My current thoughts were to add something that would do more damage over time, like poison or radiation. Those two seemed like the best bets. The issue was that radiation took metal and fire, and I was saving metal for my [Lesser Constitution], to make a higher tier of it.

That left me with poison, which required water and darkness, and those I had and didn't need for anything else. The issue was that I was short, I almost had enough to make one tier-two poison gem.

I really didn't want to wait for too long. I stood up and walked over to Aurora. She was sitting nearby, her head turned up and her eyes looking at the sky.

She was whispering to herself, too low for anyone but me to hear. "Eighty-seven, eighty-eight, eighty-n—"

"Hey," I said.

"Oh, hi!" she said, turning to face me.

"I was wondering if you'd be willing to trade some gemstones?"

"Of course." She reached for the small bag she used, the reward from one of the rifts. It was simple, just a sack with rope around the rim to tighten it up. But it was more than she had before. She pulled out a pouch with her gemstones. "Which do you need?"

"Darkness, I'm five short," I said, and we traded some. I gave her five of my earth ones, as I didn't need them that much.

Once we finished our trade, she turned her head back to the sky.

"What's with the counting?" I asked her.

"Ah." She looked back at me, startled. Almost sheepishly, she answered in a whisper. "I'm, uh, counting the Challengers."

"May I ask why?"

She looked around, almost as if she was worried that someone might over-hear. "I think that some are missing."

I narrowed my eyes and looked up at the sky. "You mean people died."

She grimaced, then nodded.

"It was bound to happen." I sighed. It made sense, we'd fought easy rifts, well, easy for me and a group of five people. But if some had gone at it alone . . . I could see how even an easy rift could overwhelm someone.

"Yes, but that many?" She looked at me. "Everyone here was supposed to be strong. Like they've survived what happened, managed to get Carving. Just dying like that, barely days into the Challenge . . ."

I didn't have an answer for her.

"Let's just make sure that our names remain on the list."

I returned back to my previous spot and sat down, leaving Aurora to her counting. It pained me that people were dying, especially when we could've done this with more care, been safer. But people made their own choices. I couldn't take that away from them. Though, sometimes I wished that I could.

I upgraded my darkness and water to the second tier of gems, what Jiyun and Daehyun called E tier, then merged the two into a single E tier *poison* gem.

With that done I took my Mask out and pushed the gem in, slotting it into my [Debilitating Wave].

A while later, after we resumed our exploration getting near the base of the mountain, Aurora noticed something as we walked along the bank of a small river.

"Hey, can we go that way?" She pointed in a direction at an angle of where we were heading.

"Why?" Khalil asked, his eyes scanning our surroundings.

"I think that there is some kind of a structure over there, on that hill."

I looked where she was pointing, but I couldn't see anything from the trees in the way. It was fairly close though.

I glanced at Aurora, then back at the hill.

"Sure, one direction or another doesn't matter much."

Once we climbed the hill, we did indeed find a small structure. Something like a shrine made out of stone. It was obelisk-shaped with a pointed pyramid tip. There was an opening at the front, with something resembling an altar, and on it was a stone scepter growing out of the altar. I wondered how Aurora detected it, as did the others probably. Something to do with her Mask, obviously. She had to have some kind of a detection skill.

I quickly deduced that it didn't work on anything living. She hadn't noticed any of the beasts that we'd encountered along the way. The shrine was made out of stone, so . . . sensing stone? Possible.

"Oh, what is this?" Aurora approached the shrine and took a look. The rest of us followed.

There was a plaque on the altar, reminiscent of what I saw in my soul space.

> **Trial of the Summit—Gathering Point Three**
>
> Join in the Trial of the Summit! Touch the scepter to reserve a spot. Up to five individuals can register at a single Gathering Point.

"It's a trial!" Aurora said excitedly.

"And it looks like it can be taken as a team," Khalil added.

"It doesn't say anything about what the trial is about," I said. That was a bit . . . suspicious.

"It says that this is Gathering Point Three," Daehyun said. "Does that mean that more than one group can take it at the same time?"

"Should we take it?" Aurora asked, looking at the rest of us.

"We have been getting barely any points," Jiyun said, her eyes glancing at the score above us. We were behind the others.

"It is the first trial we've encountered," Khalil said. "It might be a good opportunity."

"It could be dangerous," I cautioned.

"It could," Khalil agreed. "But we also need to try something like it. We've all come here to try to get stronger. This is an opportunity to do so."

"We are agreed?" I looked around, and everyone seemed on board.

I stepped closer, intending to put my hand on the scepter when Aurora stopped me.

"Wait!" Aurora said, a look of horror on her face.

"What is it?" I asked as I bent my knees and looked around for threats.

"We don't have a team name yet!"

I turned my head, slowly, staring at her with daggers in my eyes.

"A team name?" Daehyun looked interested.

"I know." Aurora raised her hand, as if she was in a classroom. "What about

Team Sunny! You know, because you're a vampire and it's daylight, and Khalil's skills are yellow light, and—"

I turned around and put my hand on the scepter before she could convince the others to give us a stupid name like Team Sunny.

The words on the plaque shifted, changing.

Trial of the Summit—Gathering Point Three

Team Sunny spot reserved—1/5
Once four teams are gathered, the countdown to transport will commence.
You are free to continue with the Grand Challenge.

I looked at the plaque, then after what must've been at least ten minutes, I turned and glared at Aurora.

The Grand Spell was definitely fucking with me.

"Well, that didn't tell us much," Jiyun said after the others registered themselves.

"It told us that Aurora is forbidden from making sweeping statements about important things, like team names," I bit out.

She looked at me with a beaming smile, then pushed an errant lock of her red hair behind her ear. "What do you mean? It's a good name!"

I nearly growled.

After we were done, we looked around in confusion.

"I guess that we just, continue looking for rifts?" Daehyun asked.

"You don't think that we need to stay here?" Aurora asked.

"It would've said so, wouldn't it?" Daehyun looked at us, but we had no answer for him.

"It should be safe to go, right?" he added.

"I think so," Khalil added.

I narrowed my eyes. "This better not be a fighting trial with us against other teams."

Aurora's eyes widened. "Wait, you think that it could be like that?"

I glanced up at the scoreboard. "People are dying. This isn't a safe place. We are in competition against one another and another world."

Aurora swallowed, audibly. "Uh, you don't think that we'll have to kill anyone?"

"I hope not," I said. "For their sake. I have no intention of dying."

It was a day later, after we'd just dealt with a small pack of dog-like beasts in the forest, that the we all got a notification about the trial. It was pretty hard to miss, as it was burning in the air above us.

> **Trial of the Summit**
>
> All four teams registered! Countdown for transport: 60 minutes
> Get ready for transport, Challengers!

"An hour," I said.

"And four teams," Khalil said.

We exchanged a look. I feared that I was right, and that we were going to be in competition with another team.

Somehow, Khalil understood my thoughts. "We shouldn't go into this expecting violence," he said slowly.

"What we want doesn't matter. We joined the trial. We will play by its rules, the Grand Spell will allow nothing less."

Khalil didn't respond, but I could see that he didn't like that answer. It was one of our biggest differences. He was a believer that wished for peace. I grew up as basically a child soldier, serving a vampire criminal boss. We looked at the world through different lenses.

We got ready, our weapons pulled out, and our supplies neatly packed in our packs. I drank some of the blood I had stored and then waited.

When the timer hit zero, a bright light surrounded us, and a moment later we were someplace else.

Immediately, I looked around, on edge, looking for any threats. There were none. Instead we found ourself at the base of the mountain we had been heading for.

We were on a stone floor, and ahead of us was a gate set in the side of a tall cliff.

"Keep an eye out," I said as we approached the gate with the mountain looming ahead of us. It was a unique formation, an almost straight pillar, with a slightly wider base and narrower peak. Now that we were closer, I could see that there were levels carved into the side of the mountain, plateaus with stone structures on them.

There was a plaque at the entrance with instructions from the Grand Spell.

> **Trial of the Summit—Entrance Three**
>
> Goal of the Trial—Reach the summit, overcoming obstacles along the way.
> Be swift, for only one team may claim the reward.

Khalil sighed in relief. "It looks like it is a race."

So, not inherently a violent competition. Though I did not have faith in other people. At least we weren't obligated to fight.

There was a circular panel on the stone gate, and I approached it then put my hand against it. The gate slowly opened.

"We should hurry then," I said.

The five of us gathered and walked through. We were met with stairs leading up into the mountain. We climbed at a quick jog-like pace, well, quick for the humans. Once we reached the top, we entered into a small square area, illuminated by green crystals on the ceiling. Ahead of us was a massive, long, and somewhat narrow chasm, with an endless darkness beneath the edge.

"I guess that our task is to get across," Daehyun said.

"That's at least a hundred meters!" Aurora yelled. She was right, it was a very long chasm.

The next gate was on the other side, meaning that we definitely needed to get across.

"There is a lever on the other end," I said.

The others looked ahead, noticing it only once I pointed it out.

"Maybe we need to pull it somehow?" Aurora offered.

I looked around as they tried to figure out a way to cross. I doubted that they would. They didn't have the skills for it. I dropped my serpent-tongue spear and my backpack on the ground.

"We have rope," I heard Khalil say. "Marianna, you have some too, right? Marianna? What are you—Mari!"

I took off running next to the wall. Once I reached the edge I leapt forward at a slight angle toward the wall, then activated [Mist Step].

As mist I surged forward, keeping my momentum and speed until I reached the wall and re-formed. My feet hit the wall, and I started running across it, losing speed and altitude, but quickly resetting my cooldown.

I kicked off the wall, soaring across the chasm toward the other wall. I reached it and immediately kicked at an angle toward the other end, activating [Mist Step].

It took me across the chasm back to the original wall I started on, and as soon as I hit it, I re-formed, pulled a dagger from my waist and stabbed it into the wall. I'd lost most of my momentum by now, but I had crossed around 70% of the distance.

Holding on by my dagger, I got my feet under me and against the wall. I tried and cursed when I couldn't reset my cooldown by making steps along the wall while hanging by the dagger. I probably had to move at least somewhat from my position, and I was anchored somewhat.

Still, I had gotten close.

I tensed, bent my knees as far as I could, then pulled my dagger out of the wall and then pushed with my legs with all of my strength. I reached the other wall and twisted in the air, stabbing my dagger again.

I was close to the other side now, so again I repeated the same move and jumped all the way there.

I landed neatly on my feet and looked back to see Aurora jumping up and down with joy.

"Hell yeah!"

Daehyun and Jiyun looked impressed, and Khalil had his hand on his chest, looking relieved.

I smiled and walked over to the lever, pulling it.

A rumbling filled the chamber and a stone bridge started expanding from both sides, meeting in the middle.

The others crossed over, carrying my stuff.

"You could've warned us." Khalil gave me a long look.

"It's a race, isn't it? We should hurry." I turned to open the next gate.

Once we were through, we were again met with stairs, only this time they led left.

We climbed, accelerating our pace. We reached the next chamber, and were met with a strange room.

The only thing that we could see was a wall, with a single square mirror in the center. As we approached, I could see the rest of the room beyond the mirror.

As we got close, I realized that the mirror was nothing of the sort, but rather a strange field that reflected us but nothing else from the room behind us. The reflections were standing on the other side of the room. I was pretty sure of it, since it was different, and it had the next gate at the end.

"Well, this is interesting," Khalil said as he got closer and studied it. I stepped next to him and did the same. It was wide enough that all five of us could stand side by side and pass through.

The field looked like a thin layer of film, almost see through, but not quite. "We shouldn't touch—"

I was too late. Aurora screeched and fell on her behind.

I was next to her in a second, looking at her arm. "Show me," I said.

She shook her head. "I'm fine, I'm fine," she said as I grabbed her hand and looked it over. It was indeed looking fine.

"Why did you scream then?" I asked.

"I was just surprised, that's all. It felt like I was touching my own hand."

I frowned, then glanced at the reflections, then approached it myself. Slowly I raised my hand and put a palm on the surface. My reflection mirrored my movement, and the moment I touched it, I felt as if I was touching myself. It was a strange sensation.

I pulled my hand back, and narrowed my eyes at the reflection me. There was something weird going on here.

I pulled my hand back then punched at the barrier. I encountered my own fist, and felt the exact same amount of force which I used, canceling each other out.

"It would seem that it is a puzzle of some kind," Khalil said. "We are supposed to get by our reflections, I assume."

I didn't see any way we could. Anything we tried would be blocked by ourselves on the other side. I looked around the room, trying to see if there was another way through, but I saw nothing.

I tried a few different things, like going behind the corner, then jumping out at top speed. I even rammed it with [Mist Step] and only managed to bruise my shoulder.

Khalil tried to hit it with his sword, boosted by his blessing skill, and again it did nothing. His reflection just copied what he did.

Jiyun looked around the room, then spoke up. "Maybe we can get the reflections to disappear somehow."

"How would we do that?" Aurora asked.

"For there to be a reflection, there needs to be light, and the only light sources are those two crystals behind us."

I blinked and looked. She was right. This room had two small green crystals on the walls, put on top of the rods so that they looked like torches coming out of a wall.

"Oh, that's smart," Aurora said. "Can we cover them up somehow?"

"I have my extra set of clothes that might do the trick," I answered.

"Want to try it?" Khalil asked.

I took a shirt and pants out of my backpack and walked to the two crystals and wrapped them up. The light dimmed considerably, but it wasn't pitch-black. Some of it came through my clothes.

"Hey! I can push my hand through." I saw Aurora struggling against her reflection.

It seemed like the lack of light did weaken the reflections. I walked over as others struggled to push through. They were overpowering their reflections now, but it was still like they were fighting against themselves.

I reached the reflection and jumped through. My reflection was much weaker. I assumed that its strength scaled with light. The difference between me and it was much more pronounced.

Once I was on the other side, my reflection vanished. I saw the others struggling to enter, though I didn't see their reflections from this side.

I reached and pulled each of them through.

"Another victory for Team Sunny! On to the next challenge!" Aurora pumped her fist, and the rest of us groaned.

Still, we followed after our fearless leader, heading to the next gate.

Team Sunny vs.

The next three rooms were filled with beasts. The first had mushroom looking monsters, smaller versions of the big beast we fought in the forest, and much weaker. I let the others deal with it. Aurora shook the ground and toppled the large group of about a dozen, making sure to target the area at the back of the formation and away from the others. That left only a couple running toward us, so Daehyun, Jiyun, and Khalil cut them up while I looked from the back, watching in case I needed to interfere.

Aurora surprised me by also using a skill that allowed her to create a shaped stone spike at a distance, rising from the floor. It impaled one of the beasts on the ground, and once we cleared the room, I approached and saw that the skill had used the stone of the floor to shape the spike. There was an indent where the mass had been moved around to create the spike.

The next two beast rooms were filled with fewer beasts, but they were stronger. One had large beetle-type beasts, six of them, each the size of a pony. Their carapace was strong enough to be resistant to the human attacks, though Aurora's stone spike managed to skewer one with relative ease.

Jiyun found a weak spot on one of their heads and stabbed her sword deep.

Khalil was holding two off, his shield glowing with his blessing and taking their attacks head-on, while Daehyun tried to clobber them with his sword.

I interfered, catching one as it was flying through the air and then smashing it against the wall. Its carapace splintered, and gore exploded in all directions.

The second one was flying toward me when I sidestepped and swung my weapon, cutting its wings off and then stomping on its back when it fell to the ground.

By the time I was finished, Daehyun managed to crack one's carapace, then used a skill that made his overhead attack blur downward and cut through the beast.

Khalil jumped back from his beast, then raised his sword hand, and a circle of yellow light appeared above it, like a hammer. It fell on top of it and splattered it against the floor.

They hadn't been using many skills. At most each of them had shown one or two, though that didn't account for any passive ones that they might have. They should all have at least three by my counting.

The third room had a single beast, a lizard of some kind that reminded me of the weirzi, only wingless. We dealt with it by surrounding it and attacking from all sides until it died.

I, of course, took blood from every beast we killed.

We continued our climb, the stairs getting longer and steeper the farther we went. It had started to impact the others' stamina a bit. I could tell that they were getting tired.

The next room we climbed into was empty. Just a stone rectangular space with the next gate on the other side.

I frowned and looked around as we entered, the others taking a few steps ahead.

"Stop!" Aurora yelled suddenly, and everyone froze.

"What is it?" I said as I focused on my perceptions, but I detected nothing in the room.

"There something, just wait a moment, don't move," she said then walked forward a few steps. Then, she knelt and put a hand on the stone floor.

After a few seconds she raised her head and looked at the ceiling with a frown.

"You sense something?" Khalil asked.

"Some of these stone tiles are pressure plates," Aurora said.

I blinked. I hadn't noticed anything wrong about them.

"And," Aurora continued, "the ceiling has a gap down the middle. I mean the stone isn't connected in the same way the rest of the room is. And there are rocks on top of it."

"What do you mean by rocks?" Daehyun asked.

"I can only sense the stone, but there are gaps in between them. It could be earth, or just air. With the way the ceiling is configured and the pressure plates on the floor, I'm thinking that the ceiling opens up and drops them on us."

I looked up again. "Ah." That would make some sense. I wondered if I could survive being buried under a few tons of rocks, or however much they weighed.

"Okay!" Aurora clapped her hands and grinned at us. "Just follow, and step exactly where I do!"

She started walking, weaving across the floor, avoiding obstacles invisible to the rest of us. It took us a few minutes, but we finally crossed the entire room.

"Whew," Aurora said. "That could've been bad. Y'all glad you have me with you now, huh?"

We entered the gate and continued up the stairs, again.

I couldn't tell if we were making good time or not, but we were clearing rooms at a solid pace it seemed. Then as we reached the top of another set of stairs we stepped onto an open plateau. Wind howled around us, and I stepped over to the edge looking both down and up. We were very high up.

"We are close," I said. The plateau was fairly large, almost the size of a basketball field.

"There are two gates," Khalil commented, and he was right. One gate was directly across from us, on the other side of the plateau, the other was on the side of the cliff.

"I'm thinking that one." I pointed at the cliff. "Leads up."

"Is this just a choice, you think?" Aurora asked. "I'm not seeing any puzzles or beasts."

"Unless something is about to swoop down on us," Daehyun commented.

I turned my eyes to the sky, looking for threats. "Aurora, anything?" I asked.

"No, everything looks good," she responded.

With no sign of any threat or obstacles, we started walking toward the gate in the cliff. Once we reached it, we realized that the circular panel wasn't present, but there was a plaque next to the gate.

Two enter, one leaves.

"What the hells does that mean?" Aurora asked.

"A riddle of some kind?" Khalil suggested.

"Do you think it has something to do with the other door?" Daehyun asked.

"It's the only thing that makes sense," Khalil said. "Maybe we need to do something there before this one opens?"

Before we had the chance to head for the other gate, a loud grinding noise echoed, and the gate on the other side started to open.

Immediately, we got ready, dropped our backpacks and pulled out weapons and spread out, expecting trouble.

The doors swung open, and then four beings walked onto the plateau. Immediately I reached for the helmet tied to my waist and put it on my head.

They were tall, towering over us by at least a full head, probably standing somewhere around just shy of three meters in height, even as hunched as they were. They looked reptilian in nature, or perhaps bird-like, though I saw no clear resemblance to anything that I was familiar with. Their legs were powerfully built, with thick thighs, and their three toes ended in curved talons that were raised so not to touch the ground. They walked on digitigrade legs, and had long tails stretching behind them.

Their gray skin was covered in brown and yellowish scales, tiny in most parts like the torso and inner areas of their bodies, the inner thighs and the armpits. Larger, more plate-like scales covered their shoulders.

Their waists were thin, narrower than the average human, with a wide chest area above and two strongly built arms ending in three clawed digits.

Their necks were long and had short dewlaps from the point where the neck met the torso all the way up to the jaw, with tiny barbs sticking out the edges of it. Their heads were elongated with a flat snout. Two nostrils covered the top part of their snouts, while sharp teeth covered the bottom with no lips. The teeth ran all the way along the bottom of their heads to the end of their jaw near the back of their heads.

They had horn-like spikes growing out from the top-back part of their head straight behind them, parallel to the ground. The number of horns differed between them, but most had four, two on each side, with one of them having those four, with two smaller additional ones growing out of the bottom of the back part of their jaw.

Their eyes were set above their mouths, covered on top by a thick bone ridge, and set at an angle that would let them be both forward facing and able to look at a wider angle to the sides.

Their bodies were covered in paint—their torsos had swirls drawn across both sides of their chest with blue paint. Their thighs had yellow paint, lines drawn in elaborate waves that curled around their legs.

Each of them had paint over their eyes. Three of them had blue paint over their eyes and stretching in a line back to their horns, while one of them had red paint over the eyes and their snout.

They had fabrics wrapped around their bodies, though I would struggle to consider them clothes. Around their necks hung strands of rope, adorned with tiny coin-sized pieces of colored stone. They had something resembling a thin green sash wrapped around their thin waists, and one of them had something similar around their thigh. Around their long necks, two had bands of strings wrapped to make up a band, alternating red and blue. All four of them had fabric wrapped around their horns, not larger than the size of a wristband, with strings pulled from them and attached to another thin ring that was higher on the horn.

They all had piercings in different places. Some had rings in their horns. Others had a nose ring, or a bone pulled in between.

One had two rings in their dewlaps just beneath their jaw, with teeth hanging from them.

Each carried weapons that were long and thin, spear-like, or perhaps halberd-like, and wrapped in colorful fabrics with strange feathers hanging from near the top. The top of the weapons split, with two spur-like spikes curving downward, and a single continuing forward like a thin and long needle.

I couldn't tell what they were made out of, but they looked fragile. Half of them also carried shields, painted in red, and wrapped with fabric around the rim. It looked like wooden planks placed together.

They looked as if they came straight out of a tribal reptilian village. Which I guessed they probably had. They were no beasts. These were the Suul—there was no doubt in my mind.

Both of our groups froze for a moment, and then they walked onto the plateau fully and spread out to face us.

"Uh, guys?" Aurora whispered, taking a step back.

Khalil took a step forward, his weapon pointed at the ground. "Well met, strangers!" he called.

The four Suul tilted their heads, looked at each other, and then I heard one of them whisper too low for others to hear.

"*Terrans,*" one with a bone piercing through its nose said. "*Hashul, the faithless are after our reward.*"

"*Should pull their teeth quickly,*" another, this one with the piercings in its horns, added. "*We can't know if another group is ahead of us.*"

"Do you understand me?" Khalil called. *Oh, yes, they do,* I thought to myself. They just probably didn't care.

The one with the red paint on its snout responded. "*Kill the faithless.*"

"I wouldn't do that if I were you," I yelled as I stepped up to Khalil and glared at them from a distance, hefting my weapon on my shoulder.

They froze at that.

"What are you doing?" Khalil hissed at me.

"They are discussing killing us."

He blinked, then looked at the Suul.

"There is no need for violence," he said. "We were both caught in the machinations of the Grand Spell, the Great Mistake. There is no reason for us to be enemies."

The Suul with the red paint on his snout stepped forward. He appeared to be the leader. "Enemies? A faithless cannot be an enemy to the people of the grass, for you are not people at all."

Yeah, I could see how this was going to go already. Khalil though, bless his soul, wasn't about to give up.

"But we are, maybe not like you, but people still. Like the other races on Kirios. Is any of you an Exemplar perhaps? You must know what has happened to your world? And if not, we have answers we can share."

The Suul raised his head and straightened his back, now towering even more over us. "What use is there for answers given by the faithless? Only words of the

Plains hold any meaning. The great Voice of the Ancestors has spoken, and new lands have been granted to the Horde of the Plains. All we have to do is take it. It will be a glorious crusade."

The leader looked at the others, and then spoke to them. "Kill them."

"Wait!" Khalil yelled, but there was no use. These people were not like us, and they were not ready to learn, to find common ground.

Their decision was enough, a declaration of impending violence against us unprovoked, a debt incurred.

I reached for my gun and drew it before they could even start their charge. I aimed at the leader and pulled the trigger. Before my finger even twitched he moved, getting low and rushing forward at incredible speed.

My round missed, and I changed targets. The Suul next to him was slower, and as he leaned forward to charge, I fired. The first bullet hit him straight in the collar, punching through his skin and exploding flesh, light red, almost pink blood splattering everywhere. My second shot hit him straight in the throat, exploding out on the other side. He gurgled, blood flowing out of the wound and his mouth. My third round hit him in the side of the head, a grazing wound. He still went down, twitching on the floor, his hands over his throat. I turned to target another, but they were close now.

One of them reared its head, then flung it forward and spat something in my direction. I jumped to the side, evading, and then heard it splatter on the ground behind me, a hissing sound filling the air as it ate through the rock. *Acid?*

Khalil stepped forward to meet the leader, while Daehyun and Jiyun moved behind him to meet the others. Aurora was behind us, her hand on the ground. A spike exploded out of the ground targeting the one that had spat acid at me, but the Suul twisted out of the way. The ground shook, and it stumbled.

I holstered my gun as the leader met Khalil and stabbed his weapon forward. Khalil raised his shield, glowing with yellow light.

The Suul's weapon glowed green, and it pierced straight through Khalil's shields, the thin and long spike at the top pushing straight through and into Khalil's shoulder.

For a moment I froze, then the cross part of the Suul's weapon hit Khalil's shield with enough force to crack it and send Khalil flying backward.

They were strong, monstrously so, and they had weight and size behind them. I could hear it in the way they moved, in the way their hearts pumped blood, the heavy thuds of their footsteps. And they were quick. I would put them at the level of young shifters, not yet fully developed. Dangerous for humans.

The second one reached our lines, meeting Daehyun and Jiyun. They danced around it, evading its sweeping attacks that attempted to skewer them on the spur-spikes of its weapon.

I glanced back at Khalil, saw him getting back on his feet as he dropped his shield, blood flowing from a small puncture wound in his shoulder.

Seeing that he was all right, I stepped forward and intercepted the leader as he tried to attack Daehyun from behind.

My serpent-tongue spear sang through the air, a shrill sound following its passage. I wasn't holding back at all. My weapon was going to cut through anything it encountered.

The Suul leader blurred and turned to face me in a moment, its eyes widening as its shield was raised to protect its head. I could sense a skill at work, as it moved faster than it seemed capable of.

I struck it at an angle, cutting in the top edge and slashing through nearly all the way to the Suul's arm before my weapon was stopped.

We were both surprised by this, probably for different reasons. I was surprised that whatever material the shield was made out of managed to stop my attack, and the Suul was surprised that it did damage it at all.

As I tried to pull my weapon out, the Suul leader twisted, trying to wrench it out of my grip. Immediately it realized that I was much stronger than it was, so it changed tactics. It moved, standing up with its legs and using leverage and its greater height to its advantage.

I could've kept my grip on the weapon, but that would've sent me in an arc that would've taken me farther away from its body. Right now I was close, making the length of its main weapon ineffective.

I released my grip and pulled out my gun, firing from the hip as I raised it. The Suul recognized the danger and managed to twist out of the way of the first bullet. Then it leapt, clearing my height in a moment and sailing over my head. I ducked, raising my gun and continuing to fire. On my third shot, I nailed in it the thigh, blood spraying everywhere from the big caliber round.

Two more shots went wide, and as it landed, I aimed my last shot straight at its head.

Its arm lashed out, green light surrounding it. It had created distance with its leap, and now its spiked weapon swung. The spur-spike impaled my upper arm, beneath the plate of my armor, just as I fired, making me miss. It caught me on the cross and picked me off the ground.

I twisted in the air, grabbed the tip of the weapon with one hand, and put my legs around the lower part. The Suul moved forward, its jaw opening up as its throat bulged.

With my free hand and leverage of my legs around the haft, I twisted, breaking the weapon in half and losing my gun from the sudden jerk of my arm. It was much tougher than I had expected. The material felt like wood, but it was as strong as steel.

I dropped to the ground and ripped out the spur-spike out of my arm as the bulge in its throat depressed. A stream of acid flew in my direction, and I dropped the enemy weapon and leapt straight at it, using [Mist Step].

The acid passed through me, pain spreading through my body but with no damage. I re-formed in front of it, a blast of sound spreading around me. It winced, raising its head.

It was enough of an opportunity for me to draw my daggers and stab them. My left went for its throat, piercing the soft flesh and cutting out, my right then came around and slashed its stomach, cutting in deep, disemboweling it.

I stepped beneath its left arm as it tried to stab me with the sharp end of what remained of its weapon. Once I was behind its back, I stabbed with both daggers in quick succession, a half a dozen attacks across the length of its back. Then I kicked its leg out and dropped it to the floor on its back. As it fell, I rammed my dagger straight through its chest and left it there.

Without staying to see it die, I turned to the others.

Aurora was running, holding her dress up. I should've given her my spare clothes, I realized. A Suul was chasing her, a stone spike sticking through its lower chest, which didn't seem to be slowing it down too much. The other three were harrying the last of the Suul. Daehyun's thigh was soaked in blood, and Jiyun was dancing around the Suul while Khalil's sword glowed with bright yellow light and he held back looking for a moment to strike. There were wounds on all of them, but the Suul seemed to be losing.

"Glaive," I whispered to Saia. She had grown, accumulated more mass, was now large enough to cover both my forearms, enough to make larger weapons.

A weapon similar to the one I had in the jungle of Ish Vimza formed in my hand as I moved.

I jumped at the Suul chasing Aurora. The ground trembled ahead of me, and the Suul slowed, trying to keep its balance. The shaking didn't impede me too much.

My cooldown reset, and I used [Mist Step]. I reached the Suul and attacked, swiping my blade from below. The Suul reacted quickly, moving out of the way. I was still faster, and I scored a cut along the side of its thigh. I didn't stop my movement, but instead I spun and brought the other side of the glaive in a thrusting attack that speared it through the stomach. It growled, its neck bulging, and it opened its mouth, spraying acid straight at me.

[Swap Profile]
[Dodge]

My body wrenched itself to the side, violently, I could feel my bones and muscles burning from the effort. The acid sailed past me as I released my grip on the glaive and then stabbed with my hand formed into a spear.

My hard nails helped me punch into its body, picking the heavy Suul off its feet with my strength. I pulled my hand out then jumped over its tail as it tried to swipe at me. I grabbed its head and pulled myself onto its back. Then I opened my mouth.

[Sonic Screech] left my throat next to its head. The effect was immediate; blood started leaking out of the earhole in its head. And its eyes rolled back in its head. I opened my mouth and leaned down, biting its throat and drinking.

Memories hit me, the group of Suul clearing obstacles and killing beasts on their way up the mountain. The same as us. There wasn't any information to be learned. The memories were only the immediate past, and they only ever spoke about the matter at hand.

I was pulled back out of the trance and immediately looked back.

The last Suul had sent Daehyun flying, I saw him rolling to his feet near the edge of the plateau. Khalil had his Mask on his face; one half of it was golden, the other white. He raised his hand, and then a larger version of his smiting attack appeared. A large round and mostly transparent disk, just floating in the air above. He dropped his disk hammer down, and smashed into the Suul's head, breaking its horns and sending it to the ground.

Jiyun took advantage. She stepped in, and her weapon blurred, leaving a white crescent in the air where it passed. I blinked. That skill was very powerful, almost as fast as I was at my full speed.

The Suul blinked on the ground, and then its head rolled off its shoulders. We'd won, barely.

I walked over to Aurora, who had stumbled onto her butt, and I helped her up.

"Uh, thanks," she said slowly, her eyes wide.

"You did good," I said. And she had. She had held off one of them all by herself. It had taken three others to take down one of the Suul.

"I—I didn't think that they would just attack like that," she said.

It was unfortunate, both that we met in a trial and that their culture seemed incompatible with peaceful discussion. Though, I wasn't going to make the same mistake again. For now, I would treat this incident as an isolated one. I had killed people before by making assumptions.

"It's your first time fighting against something sentient?" I asked her. "A thinking being?"

She nodded. "I fought monsters in the Underways, but never anything that could . . . talk."

"They made the choice to attack. You only defended yourself."

She nodded, but I didn't know if she really understood. But I didn't worry, that would come in time.

I walked over and picked up my backpack, then headed to the others, and saw Jiyun kneeling next to Daehyun looking at his wounds while Khalil put a hand over them and used his blessing.

"That actually does something?" I asked. His Mask was gone, and I didn't ask about it.

He blinked and raised his head. He was bleeding as well. "It doesn't heal, if that's what you're asking," he said. "But it does help, a little. It'll prevent it from getting infected at least."

I nodded as I rummaged through my pack, pulling out the first aid kit that Max had prepared for me.

We bandaged our wounds. The worst ones were Khalil and Daehyun, who had both gotten stabbed. And Khalil probably had a fractured forearm.

It was . . . unfortunate. Their wounds would slow them down. They didn't heal as fast as I did. My wounds were already gone. But, we would have to make do.

Once we were finished, we looked over the corpses of the Suul. I drank their blood, still not getting a Carving, then I recovered my weapons and walked over to their gate to retrieve their sacks from where they had left them at the entrance. From the memories, I knew that they did that before every room, making sure that they entered without any extra encumbrance.

There wasn't much there, which surprised me. They had only limited food supplies, and nothing that would indicate that they had been clearing rifts. It was strange, but we didn't have time for answers. We headed to the gate and climbed the stairs.

We reached the summit, the encounter with Suul being our last obstacle. On top there was a chest, surrounded by four shrines, similar to the ones that we had used to register for the trial, though these ones were hollow, and two of them had rifts glowing inside of them. On top of a chest was a plaque.

Congratulations for finishing the Trial of the Summit!

50,000 points split across all team members.
You may leave the Trial through one of the available rifts.

The points were a welcome addition. It pushed all of us back into the upper third of our list. It also made me realize that I got points from the three Suul that I killed, since I was a lot ahead compared to the others. I didn't know how to feel about that, but it was a good dent toward Earth's overall points.

Khalil approached the chest, and the lock crumbled.

"Let's see what we got," he said and opened it.

Inside were several items. A small chest filled with tier F gemstones of various colors, as usual. Next was a shield, made out of proper metal, though it was simple and unadorned. Just gray with a brown leather strap.

Khalil took every item out and put it on the ground next to the chest. Next, he pulled out a sword in a scabbard. Pulling it out of its sheath revealed a pale blue blade. It was sharp looking, and at least appeared like it was of a greater quality than what we already had. It was simple, but elegant.

After that came long gambeson, a padded jacket that would come down to the upper thighs for someone of my height.

The last item was the most baffling: a simple wooden ring.

Khalil looked it over and frowned. "Any idea what this is?" he asked.

Saia's voice answered from my forearm. "Feedback: I am detecting a slight Source-Weave signature from the item."

I blinked, not expecting her words. That was very interesting.

"What does that mean?" Aurora asked.

"It means that it might be an infused item," I said. "Basically a magic item."

"Ohhh, what does it do?"

"That I don't know," I answered her.

"Should I put it on?" Khalil asked.

I shrugged. "I doubt that the Grand Spell would give us something that could kill us, though, you never know."

Khalil narrowed his eyes, then in one quick motion slid the ring over his finger. A tiny, barely perceivable ripple expanded out of the ring and over his skin.

"Whoa," he said.

"Everything good?" I asked, ready to reach over and rip the ring off his finger.

"Yes, I got a skill," he answered. "[Lesser Barkskin]."

"That's so cool!" Aurora said.

"We should decide who gets what," Khalil said as he pulled it off.

"I'm thinking that Aurora should get the gambeson," I said.

She blinked. "Why?"

"Because you have no protection, and it will cover you whole. It'll be like a dress on you." I smiled at her.

Jiyun nodded her head. "I agree."

They gave the jacket to Aurora and had her put it on. As predicted, it did look more like a dress on her, but it would offer her some protection at least.

"The sword should go to you." Khalil offered it to Jiyun.

She tried to refuse, but I interjected. "You're the best with the sword, you'll use it best."

She looked at us, then bowed, accepting the sword with a bow. That left the ring.

"One of you should take it," I told them. "I don't really need it."

"And I have my shield." He tapped his new shield, one recovered from the Suul. It was a bit larger than he was used to, but it was tough.

He offered the ring to Daehyun, who tried not to look too eager for it. "You sure?"

We all nodded, and he took the ring.

"Now, which one of those rifts leads to our exit?" I asked.

"What do you mean?" Aurora asked.

"I assume that the two exits that are active belong to the Suul and us."

I looked around, but there was a thick fog or perhaps clouds around the summit, so I couldn't orient us and pick the exit that was in the direction of our entrance. And we'd walked around the mountain and stairs too much for me to know what side of the mountain our entrance was on.

"It's a fifty-fifty," Daehyun shrugged. "And it's not like it matters. We'll just pick a new direction and start walking anyway."

He was right, it didn't really matter.

"How about the left one?" I asked.

The others shrugged. We decided to take a short break, allow our cooldowns to return and rest after the fight, then we walked to it and entered. We arrived at the shrine at the same time, appearing in front of it.

It was not the right choice.

Overwhelming

We landed in a clearing, surrounded by Suul. By my quick count there were sixteen of them around us. With the four they had killed inside, it was a very specific number, an exact number of how many Challengers there were in a single group. It would seem that these Suul decided to stick together.

They had made a camp around the trial shrine, probably waiting for their team to arrive, and instead they were met with us.

They noticed us immediately and sprang to their feet. They had a variety of weapons, though most were the same as what the Suul in the trial had. All were made out of the same wooden material, but I knew that it was deceptively strong.

I scanned them as I pulled my backpack off my shoulders slowly, and noticed something different among them. Most looked the same as the ones we faced, but two of them were unique. Taller by at least a meter, with gray skin and black scales. Their paint was a lot more elaborate, covering a greater portion of their bodies. Their clothes were colorful, and they even had what looked like simple robes that were sleeveless and fell down to the floor. Both of them had the same weapon, a thick rod as tall as they were, with a round ball attached at the top. Like a giant mace.

They were too different from the others. It made me think that they were likely a subspecies, the same as we had on Earth. Though I didn't know nearly enough about them to be able to tell. What was certain was that they would be stronger.

"Terrans," one of the big ones spoke, its voice deep and gravely, solemn. "The Ancestors have made their will known. Our riders have failed. May their haama ride the plains forever."

I stepped forward. "We don't need to resort to violence. Your team attacked us, without allowing us even a moment to speak and negotiate. Don't make the same mistake."

The second of the larger Suul walked up to the first one. "It appears you were right, Aakor, all Terrans think that words can save their lives. As if a field *skarnk* can demand anything of the sun above its head."

All? Had they met other groups before? They had to have.

The first one, Aakor, flared its nostrils. "A faithless will never understand. Nevertheless, Somer, we shall observe the rites."

Aakor stepped forward and looked at me. "Do you believe, Terrans? Do you know the will of the Ancestors?"

I blinked. We were getting more of a conversation now, but I didn't understand anything about what they were asking. The rest of the Suul watched us carefully, ready to attack at a moment's notice. They were several meters away, a little bit down the hill, but too close for comfort. We wouldn't be able to get away, not with their speed and strength. Not the others at least.

"Belief?" Khalil asked as he stepped up next to me. "We have belief, faith. Is that what your kind considers a people? Those who believe in something greater?"

"You have the belief?" The other one, Somer, looked surprised. "You hear the Voice of the Ancestors, whispering across the Way?"

The Way? Oh, this was something more than what I thought. The Way was a real thing. It was something related to the Source.

"There are many different religions, beliefs, among our people. We all choose what we believe in," Khalil explained, trying to defuse the situation. I could already see that it wouldn't work.

"Ah, so no true faith," Aakor said. "You are faithless, you hear no Voice. You shall be but a blade of grass for the Horde to trample as we take these lands, then all those beyond. Kill them."

I grabbed and pushed Khalil back, then yelled. "Run!"

They listened. All of the others turned and started running down the hill on the opposite side. I stayed where I was.

It was funny, I had been alone for so long, and then I met Shadow. I could've abandoned him when he got injured. I owed him nothing. And yet, even then I couldn't do it. It was not in me, to do something like that.

Yet, even when I was surrounded by other people, I felt alone. A vampire, standing apart from the rest. But that group of people, a team, I could see us becoming friends in the future. True friends, like what I had with Khalil before, a lifetime ago. No, better than that, because I didn't need to hide myself or my past.

They were good people. They had stayed when the rest left. I didn't owe them this, but I wanted to do it. I realized that this was who I was. I didn't run when it mattered, I didn't turn and leave.

It would incur a debt on their side, but I was sure that they would pay it gladly.

The Suul charged me, some trying to get around me and pursue the others. I activated my skill.

[Debilitating Wave]

A red wave tinged with green expanded out of me, hitting at least half a dozen of them, dropping them to their knees. I wished that I had reloaded my gun, but we didn't have the time in the trial, and I thought that we would be safe outside of it once we reached the summit. A stupid mistake. I rushed forward, my serpent-tongue spear flying through the air. I decapitated the closest stunned Suul, then jumped on to the next, stabbing him through the chest. The others did not like that at all.

One of the larger Suul, Aakor, reached me, its mace raised above its head. It pulsed with black energy then came down.

[Dodge] was the only thing that allowed me to get out of the way in time. It smashed into the ground, a pulse of black expanded and hit me, sending me flying through the air. I hit the ground and rolled, getting up to my feet immediately.

A regular Suul rushed me, stabbing with its halberd-like weapon. I dashed backward, but the Suul leaned forward extending the range more than I had expected. It pierced my hip, in the gap between my plates. I growled, then pulled myself off the spike as I dashed back.

More of them came at me. The ones that had recovered from my [Debilitating Wave] were wobbly on their feet, probably the poison element of the skill, if it had that much effect.

I screamed, using [Sonic Screech].

It made every Suul in front of me try to cover their ears, even the larger ones. I rushed forward and speared the Suul that followed after me straight through the throat. I cut out and spun, then cut at another one, opening up a large gash over its chest, but didn't kill it yet.

They were quick to recover, and as I went for the third one, the Suul had adjusted. They were starting to surround me. I could see the anger in their eyes, the disbelief that I had been able to kill them with such ease. If they had faced anyone from my world before, it had to have been humans. Even a shifter would've put up a fight.

The two big ones were together now. They rushed me, their maces coming for my head. I weaved in between them, using [Overburn Skill—Lesser Dash] to pass below their attacks and spin on my feet, cutting one's leg as I passed. Its scales were tougher, and I barely cut deep enough to do damage.

Behind them, a group of Suul came for me. Skills activated and attacks sped toward my body. I tried to avoid them, but two got me. They had insane reach.

One speared me straight through the chest, hitting armor. I felt it push and get stopped by my vest, but it still sent me stumbling back and off-balance from the force. The other took advantage and got me with its spur-spike in the thigh. That immobilized me for a moment, forcing me to twist and break the spur while it was still impaling me, doing more damage.

That short delay was enough that I didn't have enough time to avoid the next attack. The massive ball mace of the larger Suul, Somer, smashed into my side as I tried to evade. It was a glancing blow, but it still sent me flying, I felt my ribs fracture, not break fully, but the pain of it was agonizing.

I flew through the air and crashed against a tree. I shook my head, and raised my eyes as two Suul charged at me.

[Swap Profile]

I leapt forward using [Mist Step]. Mist flowed in between the two Suul, startling them. I landed next to one of the Suul that I had hit with [Debilitating Wave], who was on one knee, struggling. I stabbed straight through his chest, then dropped my weapon and grabbed him, opening his throat and drinking big gulps, pushing the memories away.

A surge of fear made me stop, and I dashed back, trusting my instinct. The mace came down, pulverizing the poor Suul, sending blood and gore everywhere along with my weapon.

As soon as I landed, I grabbed and pulled out the spike still in my body and felt the wounds heal. I was afraid. I saw at least ten more Suul around me. I'd lost count of how many I'd killed. My mind was a haze of battle lust.

The large Suul were as strong as me, and almost as fast. Too much for me to handle when they had this much of a numerical advantage.

"Glaive," I whispered. There was no room for chain and blade in the forest, not with this many opponents.

Saia flowed into a weapon, and the Suul paused. I closed my eyes, taking hold of my emotions, pulling them to the forefront.

I was afraid of many things. But what I feared the most was death. That I would die here without the chance to do all the things that I wanted to do. It was my choice to be here, in this Challenge. And it was my choice to stay and buy the others time to escape. I hadn't thought it through, but my idea had been to delay then catch up to the others. I didn't count on the large Suul being my equals.

I did not shy away from my fear—it was as natural of an emotion as anger was. It taught me many things. As my fear rose, as I let it fill my body, I settled into the first Kata of the **Stalwart Mist**: *In the Mist, Await.*

With closed eyes and open mind, I waited.

My senses sharpened. I heard the shuffle of feet, breaths coming in and out. The thunder of heartbeats—each of the Suul had two, thundering offbeat. I heard the sound of a liquid surging through narrow funnels, the stretching of skin—then the spit, the whistle through the air. I stepped to the side, avoiding the acid attack.

A Suul on my left attacked at the same moment, I heard his attack coming. It hit my vest, trying to punch through. I twisted, letting it rip the first layer of fabric as I pushed with my legs and jumped over its spear, straight toward its head.

My glaive sang through the air as I spun in the air and slashed through its head, straight down the middle. An imprint on the Way announced a skill, and I opened my eyes to see a blast of black coming for me, the size of my head. With [Mist Step] I dodged to the side, and two Suul cornered me when I re-formed. Their spurs came, and I let them touch me; the moment they hit my skin I twisted, turning stabs into scratches. My glaive retaliated, stronger, faster.

[Overburn Skill—Quick Strike]

Another Suul died.

Then the big one reached me, it moved at a speed rivaling my own, then exceeding it for a moment. Its mace smashed into my chest, sending me flying back through the air to smash against a tree, cracking the trunk in half. I fell, and the tree toppled over me. I rolled, getting out of the way as it fell.

I coughed, spitting out blood, both from my stomach and from the damage. My hair spilled over me as my helmet got loose and flew off somewhere after that strike.

My ribs were definitely broken now, but already I could feel them mending, I could hear the grinding as they were pushed back into place. The **thirst** didn't do that, but I knew that Saia was helping now, a nano swarm inside of me, using her [Repair] to help. I pushed myself to my feet and felt another attack entering my leg. With a burst of speed, I pulled it away kicking in the opposite direction faster than the attack was coming, then spun on one leg and lashed out with my glaive. I caught the Suul on the upper arm, making it fall back.

The larger Suul came at me. My vision was blurry, and I focused.

[Overburn Skill—Lesser Sonar]

I roared, and the world blossomed inside of my head. A map of it built in my mind's eye. My skill filled in the gaps of my senses. The second of the larger Suul was behind me, I ducked, then jumped to the side and rolled. They attacked in unison, and as I avoided one, the second one's mace came down on top of my leg, shattering my knee.

I cried out in pain as I hit the ground, then rolled away from them as they advanced. I pushed and got to my feet, my one foot, and leapt away. The other was completely unusable, even though it was already healing. The blood in my stomach was threatening to burn a hole inside of it.

The **thirst** was roaring with me. It craved blood, it wanted me to feed.

"Saia, help with the leg," I whispered. She knew what to do, even though I didn't explain, support in situations like this was her purpose.

Half of my glaive vanished as one part of her flowed to my knee and surrounded it, making a brace, one that moved on its own. The part left in my hand changed into a short sword.

The larger Suul's throat was bulging, preparing to spit acid again. I dashed forward with my good leg.

[Overburn Skill—Quick Step]

I blasted past it, too quick for its strike to catch, and hit a smaller Suul before it could react, my blade piercing its throat. I grabbed hold and climbed on top of it as it fell, my fangs sinking into its flesh. A gulp, two, then my fear spiked, and I moved, avoiding the attack that crushed the Suul's body to paste.

Healing accelerated, but it wasn't enough. I swallowed the blood still in my mouth, and finally it came.

Mask of the Blood Invoker — First Investment; Tenth Carving
[Blood Gout] skill gained.
Mask of the Blood Invoker > Mask of the Blood Reaver
Mask of the Blood Reaver — Second Investment; No Carving
|Potential Augmentation| trait — Combat type gained.
[Quick Swap Slot] skill gained.

Power flooded me. I felt stronger, faster. An attack hit my neck, and I pulled away, my reaction so fast that only a pinprick managed to pierce my skin. I dashed back, then leapt, my leg nearly giving out, but Saia held it for me. I landed on the ground and opened my eyes, looking at the Suul rushing toward me.

I could feel the new skills inside of me. I could activate both. I didn't know what they did, but I had a suspicion about one of them.

I smiled, and put my hand over my heart, then pulled my Mask. Perhaps I could survive this, perhaps I would have enough time before it drained me completely. I won or I died. Either way, I was taking a lot of them down with me.

I felt my trait take effect, my cooldowns shortened instantly, my attributes soared. A Suul came at me, and I danced away from its attack, then I stepped back into its thrust and grabbed the haft of its halberd. I pulled it to me then swung my weapon.

It raised its shield to try to block, but it didn't matter. I cut through it, its arm, its shoulder, half its chest, and parted its spine before my blade left near its hip. Its body fell back, hanging on by skin and flesh.

The large Suul surprised me. They pulled their Masks too, putting them over their heads. One's weapon was suddenly copied in his other hand, a spectral version of the mace, only made out of black energy.

The other Suul didn't have any visible effects, but I could tell that it too had gotten stronger.

The remaining Suul followed their lead, and I settled into my stance, waiting for their attacks. I shifted my stance, changing from *In the Mist, Await* to the second Kata: *Overwhelming Mist.*

With my left hand, I pulled out my dagger and raised my short sword with my right. I wasn't that good with these weapons, but I had little choice.

Cold seeped through me, and I prepared. The two big Suul came, one on each side. My Mask was on my face, cooldowns reduced.

[Swap Profile]
[Debilitating Wave]

My skill billowed out of me. They stumbled but didn't fall as the others had. I didn't move as they attacked, their coordination off from my skill.

The closer one swung his mace, and I braced and put my sword in the way. I blocked, the strike pushing me across the ground, my bones groaning. Then as the other Suul approached, and prepared to attack from the other side, I relaxed. I allowed the last vestiges of the first Suul's attack to get through, using it to build momentum.

I launched myself at the other one, leaping through the air. [Debilitating Wave] had made the Suul sluggish, at least compared to me. I stabbed with my sword, intent on piercing its head—it moved it out of the way, and I changed my stab to a slash.

My blade cut through its eye, blinding it. I twisted over its shoulder, then fell to the ground, my injured leg nearly giving out beneath me, but Saia held me up.

The Suul's tail lashed out and struck me in the stomach, sending me flying. I gritted my teeth, took advantage of the energy it had transferred to me. I angled myself through my flight, and smashed into a Suul, my blades piercing its chest.

I fell on top of it, in the middle of the group of Suul and the dead. The ground was soaked with blood—it was in the air, the scent of power, and the **thirst** was pounding inside of my mind. It was trying to lean on me, on my emotions, drive me into a rage, but I wasn't ever going to be controlled by my emotions again.

I was the one who used them, not the other way around.

I could feel my new skill, felt its call. I trusted my Mask. My mouth opened, the Mask dislodging and splitting to allow it, and then I used [Blood Gout].

All the blood around me suddenly moved, rushing in my direction, flying through the air like fast moving rivers. I saw the Suuls exclaim in surprise and horror as blood poured out of their wounds too, a trickle, but still it flowed to me, into my mouth, down my throat. Feeding me, giving me power.

The **thirst** was thrumming inside of me. I could feel its heat spreading through my entire body. My muscles spasmed, my bones groaned. I didn't know what was happening. My skill slipped my grasp, and the blood still in the air fell to the ground.

The Suul took advantage. A spur pierced my calf, then another my thigh. Something impaled me through the side, through the gap in my vest plates. I raised my head and twisted, avoiding a stab to my eye.

Whatever happened to me was fading, and only strength remained. I moved, ripping the Suul's weapons out of my body. The two large Suul reached me, moving fast, but not as fast as me. It didn't matter. I was surrounded. My Mask and whatever had happened to me had drained me. I could feel the fatigue of my body. Knew that I wouldn't be able to hold on for much longer.

With the last of my strength, I avoided their attacks, falling backward. Then my body gave out. A mace caught me in the side, glancing off my head. I fell, my back hitting a tree as exhaustion and pain fully took me. I slid down to sit on the ground. Half of my vision was red, blood filling my eye. I could barely see.

My Mask slipped from my face, falling down to my lap and vanishing. I was breathing deeply, my heart beating every few seconds, trying to push more blood through my veins.

One of the larger Suul approached, just a black shadow in my eyes. I struggled to raise my head to look it in the eyes. It was speaking.

"You've cost the Horde much, faithless," it said. "But even a young hunter knows that sometimes a riding party must pay the price to take down a great beast. Their lives were well spent."

It raised its mace, about to end my life.

Then its head was just gone.

A sonic boom followed. I felt it in my bones. Blood showered me as the Suul toppled. I saw movement, I saw death, flashes of black and blue. And then before I could even process what was happening, it was over.

A beat of wings approached me, and I struggled to raise my head, through blurry eyes I saw black feathered wings, and blue skin.

The last thing I saw was a pair of completely emerald eyes, staring down at me. Then my body gave out, and darkness took me.

Legacy

Consciousness came to me slowly, as if I was waking up for the first time. My body felt rested and new. As if I was reborn. I heard voices in the background, but I couldn't think clearly. The only thing that was on my mind was the whispering of the **thirst**. It was so strange, I couldn't quite put a finger on it. It was almost as if I could hear a real voice in it, and not just the imagination that my mind fabricated as a result of the thirst's presence.

I understood nothing that it said though, as if it spoke in a completely alien language. And yet, somehow, those whispers were comforting. Then, my mind caught up, and I remembered what had happened.

I jumped up to my feet, looking around ready to fight. Immediately, I froze.

I was in a small grove, surrounded by tall trees, with rocks and leaves covering the ground. On one of those rocks, just in front of me, was Saia. Across from her sat my sire, Akatsuki Jin.

"Statement: You were correct, she was waking up. Greetings, Mari, I am glad that you are well. My [Repair] has taken care of all of your damage, alongside your own considerably increased capabilities. I also need to report that our current synchronization rate has exceeded 50%. My power requirement has relatively lessened as I've come to understand your physiology better."

I blinked at her words, barely comprehending them. The only thoughts that occupied my mind were those about my sire. He was as regal as he always was in my memories, even though he was different.

His hair wasn't as impeccable. It hung loosely, resting on his shoulders, half obscuring his face. He wore a camo shirt, one that I recognized as my spare one. His pants were black and covered in dried blood. And yet, his posture was perfect, his back straight as he sat on his knees, in a seiza, with his hands on his thighs.

He only took a single breath from the moment I woke up, and I hadn't heard his heart beat yet. He was what humans always imagined vampires to be. In a word, cold, unmoving, emotionless statues that could kill you in an instant.

His eyes set him apart from all others, even vampires. I had grown up surrounded by vampires with eyes as blue as the clear sky. His and mine alone were different, like the seas. He had no pupil, only an iris that was the color of the deepest of emeralds.

"Saia-san has been telling me about your journey, your trials," he said, his voice low and level, barely audible to human ears, but not to mine. I would've called it a whisper, except this was how vampires usually talked amongst themselves. There was no need to speak words that could spread far when the tiniest of whispers could be heard. "You have acquired quite an interesting companion, well done."

I didn't say anything.

"Input: This Unit hasn't shared any information of crucial importance."

"I can confirm, she has not." He inclined his head in a barely perceivable motion.

"What are you doing here?" I asked, lowering my voice as low as his. I didn't even consciously do it. It just happened out of habit.

He turned his head slightly, so that he was facing me more fully. Then he gestured with a hand across from him. "Sit, we shall talk."

I glared at him. I wished that I could rage, that I could spit in his face, that I could ask so many questions. I could not. He terrified me. I had gotten so much stronger, and still I was nothing compared to him.

"Input: Your sire saved our lives," Saia added when I didn't move.

I had assumed as much. I didn't know about many things that could've done what I remembered happening there at the end.

"Why?" I found the courage to ask a single question. "You let them hang me. Why would you now save my life?"

A sigh escaped his lips, a tiny breath of air. His emerald eyes closed, and he inclined his head, leaned forward in a bow.

"I am sorry," he said, holding the bow.

I waited for him to add anything, to say anything more. But that was it. He had always been a man of a few words.

"Sorry," I whispered, I didn't use any honorifics when talking to him, as I would've in the past. He had lost the right to my respect. "For what? Saving me or letting them hang me?"

He pulled back, obviously realizing that he would get no acceptance from me. He met my eyes, then spoke.

"For what happened before. It was not in my power to change."

This time I snorted, then laughed. "Not in your power? You couldn't have told the Master not to hang me? He would've listened to you."

He shook his head. "No, he didn't," he said.

I paused. "He didn't?" I repeated. "You asked him?"

"Indeed I did. He refused." He gestured again. "Sit. There is much that you do not understand. And I am free of my obligations now. Pascual's decision to have you executed cleared all debts between us. That you were saved by a hand of fate is a fortunate outcome that I am greatly thankful for. Now, I may speak freely."

I frowned. He spoke about my possible death so lightly. Had I died, nothing would've changed for him. He would've still been free. A part of me wanted to be stubborn and stay on my feet, but I knew that would be childish. And I did want to hear his excuses, I wanted to know.

I walked over and sat down, mirroring his pose. Saia jumped over and landed in my lap. I looked at my sire, and waited for him to speak.

He didn't.

I waited some more, then finally lost my patience.

"Why did you save me now? How were you even near to help me in the first place?"

"I have been following you and your group since we arrived here."

My jaw twitched. "Why were you following us?"

"To make sure you haven't lost yourself in the blood madness."

I wanted to scream at him that he had lost his obligations to me when he let them hang me. But I also knew how dangerous vampires could be if they went mad, and many Fledglings did. I didn't understand him.

"Your eyes have changed," he said, changing the topic.

I grimaced, then decided to tell him my thoughts. He was the only vampire that I had met since I came back. I had to talk with someone about everything. "Yes, I think that my Mask is accelerating the vampire maturation cycle. It happened when I gained my First Investment."

"It is not because of that." He shook his head.

I narrowed my eyes. "What do you mean? That's the only thing that makes sense. I was still a Fledgling barely a month ago."

My sire looked at me, then spoke, changing the topic and not elaborating further on what he had just said. That was one of the most frustrating things about him. He spoke about things in his own time.

"I served Pascual de Andagoya because I owed him a life debt. I was oath-bound to obey him, to repay the service he has done to me."

I wished that talking to him was less frustrating. But he was older, the way his mind worked . . . Sometimes it was so hard to have a conversation without him avoiding it. He was so old and powerful that if he didn't want to talk about something he just changed subjects, didn't even acknowledge it. It was blunt, a contrast to his way of appearing to the world. I had so many questions, but I knew my sire well enough to know that he would tell the story in his own time. I could prod, but unless he wanted to answer, he wouldn't. I decided to keep quiet for now.

"He saved my life, and I had served him ever since. Almost five hundred years."

I blinked. That was how old Master Pascual de Andagoya was in the first place. That would mean . . .

"He was a young vampire, barely out of his Fledgling stage, back then. I've tried to guide him as best as I could, but he was, and still remains, hardheaded and arrogant," he said, his eyes calmly watching mine.

"Five hundred years," I said slowly, unable to keep quiet after all. "Is saving your life really worth that much?"

My sire inclined his head. "And more, much more. The weight of my debt was great because of how old I am."

That intrigued me, as I didn't know his age. No one in the cartel knew it. They knew that he was older than the Master, and powerful, but little more than that.

"In the recent years," my sire continued, before I could ask any more questions, "Pascual had started asking favors of me. Most of which I had refused. Until he offered me one that would have paid off my debt in full. He asked me to sire a Fledgling for him, and raise them to Adult."

"Me?" I pulled back, shocked.

"Yes." He inclined his head. "He had brought forth many candidates to me, and I refused them all. Until you. I did as he had asked, and turned you."

"Why would he want that?" I asked.

"There are many different reasons. They all boil down to the one that often moves Pascual to do things—power."

"I know that you are older than him, but that shouldn't matter," I said.

"The reason is the same as the one why you now have the eyes and power of an Elder vampire."

"What?" That couldn't have been true. My eyes had changed into those of someone that had just become an Adult vampire. Elder was impossible. It took vampires at least a hundred years after becoming an Adult to move into that stage.

"How much do you know about how vampires mature?" my sire asked me.

"I know that we mature with time, become stronger with age."

"That is true. All vampires get more powerful with age. However, the speed at which they grow and mature differs greatly depending on who a vampire was sired by."

I opened my mouth, then closed it and waited for him to continue.

"Most vampires think that age is the most important, that the older the vampire that sires another, the stronger the Fledgling. That is what Pascual believes. It is correct, but not in the way that most believe. The most important factor is the generation, how close a vampire is to the first of our kind, not age."

I blinked. "So I am growing faster because you are older and therefore closer to the original?"

My sire inclined his head. "Marianna, I am over forty thousand years old. I am the first born of my sire, the originator of our bloodline."

My mind exploded. So many thoughts rushed through my head that I couldn't even grasp one of them. He was over forty thousand years old? That seemed insane. That was before history, before . . . everything.

"It had been a long time since I had sired another," my sire continued. "More than thirty thousand years in fact. There are reasons for that. My children grow faster, but they also inherit a much greater thirst. They are just one removed from the original. It causes most of my Fledglings to go mad, to turn into monsters. My siblings were the same way. Out of hundreds that my sire turned, only a handful survived with their minds intact. Now only I remain of my siblings, the first generation that my sire had made. All the other vampires of our bloodline came from those far down the line, children of my and my siblings' children's children. As is the case for other bloodlines as well. There are only four of us from the early generations that are still around."

That was so much to take in, so much information. But it explained everything. How I was able to kill an Adult vampire, a shifter, and their human muscle that night when I was sentenced to death. Why my eyes changed so quickly. It wasn't abnormal at all.

"You were not sentenced to death for making a mistake, Marianna," my sire started, and all of my attention turned back to him. "You were sentenced to death because Pascual was afraid of you. He had asked for a vampire that would be strong, that he would be able to control, a weapon in his hand. When you killed an Adult and a shifter, he realized just how fast you were growing. He decided that you were too much of a risk for him to use. That you would match him in strength too soon. He decided that you were a threat."

My heart thumped inside of my chest. So many emotions rose inside of me, and I let them. My brow furrowed with anger, with . . . My hand reached up to the scar along my neck, a silver-made wound that would never fully heal.

"Why didn't you stop him?" I asked, my voice a low, barely audible whisper.

"Because I am old, Marianna. It is so hard for me to operate on the scale that you all do. It is why I do not involve myself in vampire politics." He looked at my scar, his face an unmoving mask. "And also because I made a mistake of giving my word to the wrong man, because fate had him in the right place at the right time to save my life."

"Is that how much I was worth to you? Less than your word?" I asked, my voice breaking halfway through. I was doomed to be disappointed by those who were supposed to care for me, it seemed.

He looked away, and for the first time since we started this conversation, I saw emotion on his face. It was the same one I had seen on his face when they sentenced me to death.

"Was I that much of a disappointment?"

He turned his head back instantly, then spoke. "No, Marianna, you misunderstand. I am not disappointed with you. It is in myself that I am disappointed. I have no defense, nothing to say that could make things right. I failed you. *Moushiwake gozaimasen.*"

I didn't know what to do with that. I needed time to think, away from him, to process everything that I had learned. Yet, there was so much more that I wanted to know.

"All that I can offer is the truth. Ask, and I shall answer."

I didn't even know where to start. "How fast will I mature?" I asked in the end. That was the most relevant question to my situation, to the world's situation.

"Very fast. It will depend on the quality of blood that you consume. But, it took me a decade to reach a level comparable with my sire back when I was turned." He closed his eyes. "A decade to reach full maturity, what now we call the Ancient vampire stage."

I blinked. An Ancient vampire was one that was fully matured. That was insane. It took thousands of years for vampires to reach that point.

"You are halfway through that," my sire said. "And at the rate you are going, you might reach it in around the same time."

I couldn't even comprehend that. Me, an Ancient vampire?

"The mature form is what my sire called Ascension. It is the truest form of our evolution, the separation of vampire and humankind. It is the thirst's change of us made manifest."

"Uh, is that something I need to worry about?" I asked. His words sounded somewhat ominous.

He inclined his head. "Yes, I shall show you what I mean."

He stood up and then removed his shirt. Then I heard bones cracking, and his skin started to change color.

Two limbs extended from behind his back, and then feathers grew out of them, black as the night. His skin turned light blue, and the tips of his fingers hardened. The last joint of every finger extended and turned into a spike-like bone extension. Not quite claws, more like rounded spikes.

"This is what a fully matured vampire of our bloodline looks like," my sire announced in a deep voice that reverberated, as if he was speaking at two different pitches at the same time. His fangs had grown longer too. His eyes glowed with emerald light. They were actually giving off light, not just reflecting it.

"I *did* see you with wings," I murmured. The memories of what happened to the Suul were hazy. I had thought that I had imagined it.

His wings were shaped like those of a falcon, narrow and long. They were beautiful. "You can shapeshift," I said slowly.

"This surprises you? Are you not already changed? Your body shifted when you were turned, altered by the thirst. The shifters can change their forms too, and they are an offshoot of our kind, an alteration from our experiments."

"Vampires created the shifters?" I asked, surprised.

"One of our kind experimented on animals, attempting to pass on the thirst to them. It was a success, and shifters were born from those humans bitten by the experiments."

The way he was talking about it, so casually, it reminded me of Khalil. How he thought that vampires were dangerous. I always knew that we were, but this was more than that.

"Can the other bloodlines change too?" I asked.

"Yes, though each bloodline is different. The Sky bloodline can separate their body into a swarm of small creatures, allowing them a great versatility, while the Desert's is more similar to ours. Though theirs looks far more brutal, with bat-like wings and monstrous features—their gift is strength. A mature Desert bloodline vampire physical power is considerable. Our gift is speed."

With a crack of bone, his wings pulled back, and he shifted back.

"That is amazing," I said finally. For a moment, I even forgot all the things that still stood between us. The pain of being hanged, the betrayal I still felt. Learning about my kind felt good in a way that I hadn't expected. But then again, I'd always been hungry for a place to belong, for a history, a family. Now I had it. Shadow had given me a family, a name. And now I knew that I was sired by the firstborn son of the original vampire of my bloodline.

It was a lot.

He put the shirt back on, and sat down again. "I am sorry for not preparing you before. For what happened. I thought that I had time. For me, a decade is a blink of an eye. It got away from me."

"I don't know if it makes much difference." My mood soured again. The truth still remained. He let them nearly kill me.

"I assumed it would be as such. In the end, only time can mend some wounds."

"Perhaps," I said, not committing to anything.

"I would ask you a favor, if you are willing?"

I tilted my head and waited.

"Would you tell me of what you learned as an Exemplar, what has happened to our world? I have known nothing until I arrived here."

He wasn't an Exemplar. It made sense. I didn't know what type of Mask he had, but the fact that he had advanced it so far, with his strength, it probably wasn't something that was combat related. I didn't know if that was a blessing or a curse. What I did know was that people like him were important if Earth was going to survive. They had the strength to hold off the most powerful of the other races.

"I—of course."

I started my story at the beginning.

The Future

I told my sire a lot. Explained what I knew about the Grand Spell, and even shared what I'd learned from the message left in the ruins. The origins of the Grand Spell and the threat that was out there. I had problems with my sire, but he was one of the most powerful beings on Earth, even more so than I had previously thought. If there was anyone that could do something, it was him. I finished my story by telling him what Shadow warned me about.

"Your friend's advice is correct," my sire said afterward. "The world is already fractured. If we want to be strong enough to resist their incursions, we will need to be as united as we can be. Sadly, the world is a lot larger now. We will never have a global, or continental, response. A small empire, a place that can take in our people, keep power, and hold them at bay, is the best course of action. A faction that can eventually grow to be on an equal footing with those already existing in this world."

"Could you do it?" I asked. Uniting people would be a lot easier for someone as strong as my sire.

He shook his head. "I have another task that I must fulfill, now that I am free of my obligation."

"What could possibly be more important? Are you still with the cartel?"

"No." He shook his head. "I left Pascual the moment the Light took you. I am at the coast, or at what I believe to be the northern coast of our continent."

I blinked in surprise. "How far did you go? Do you know how the Earth is arranged now? What the situation is where you are?"

"I know some. If you head directly north from Colombia you will reach a great new sea that separates the Americas and the African continent. The sea is long, but narrow, covering the entire western and northern coast of Africa, the Sahara, until it spills into the Mediterranean. If you continue along the coast of that sea, you will reach North America. If you continue farther you will reach

Europe, as it is now connected along the northern border of the North American continent directly by a great plain. Europe was rotated, and what was once East is now North. I have reached Ural and beyond it northern Asia. That is where I have found the coast, though a lot of Asia is missing. It has been moved somewhere else. The world has ended. There is death everywhere, and nature has reclaimed the cities in a matter of days what should have taken centuries. Animals have mutated and prey on everything. People are dead everywhere."

That was a lot of information, and I was glad for it. But to know that he had crossed so much in barely a month, and without any transportation vehicle . . . But then again, he could fly. And now that he didn't need to worry about the sun, it was probably easier.

"What are you doing there?" I asked.

"I am doing what I should have been doing for the last five hundred years: searching for my sire."

I opened my mouth, then closed it in shock. After a few seconds, I found my voice again. "He is still alive?" I asked. That had never even entered my mind as a possibility.

"She is," he said, making me blink once again. "I lost her five hundred years ago. If I hadn't made the oath to Pascual, I would have been searching for her immediately, but . . . I asked Pascual to release me, but he always refused, and I could not tell him the reason why I needed to go."

"How did you lose her?" I asked, wondering if he would answer.

He didn't speak for a long time, then he bowed his head and started speaking. "She sleeps often, for thousands of years, at times. She is much older than even I, and the drain of living makes her . . . lethargic at times. It is so with the other original, the one that still lives. I was transporting her. I often moved her with me when I changed lands I lived in. Our ship was ambushed by the Knights of Constantinople, off the coast of Japan."

Realization suddenly dawned inside of my mind. "Oh my God."

He bowed more deeply, not showing his eyes. "Our ship was sunk. I could not reach her, and her sarcophagus fell to the ocean floor. Waking up is a lengthy process for her. It takes her days to regain all of her senses. I do not know what happened, I only assume that she woke up beneath the ocean, that she panicked and lashed out."

I raised a hand, covering my mouth in horror.

"She had to have cracked the tectonic plate, caused the Ring of Fire to erupt. The volcanic eruptions and earthquakes were . . . it was Armageddon. Japan sunk. And I took on a new name, Akatsuki Jin. I adopted the culture that I was responsible for ending, making sure that it would never be fully lost, a penance."

"You are not Japanese?" I asked. I didn't know why that was the first thing I asked. I could hardly wrap my mind around everything that he had just said.

"There is nothing that I am. I predate all cultures on Earth today. If you want to be technical about it, it was my people's descendants that crossed the water and reached ancient Japan. But I have lived everywhere across the world. The Earth is my home."

"How did you come to South America?"

"The sun does not burn me as much as a newly born vampire, but it hurts me all the same, or at least it did. I tried to search for my sire, but the storms that followed the catastrophe interfered. I was weakened, flying across the ocean. I got turned around, lost. I was broken, barely alive when I washed up on the shores of South America. Pascual found me and saved my life."

I understood my sire a lot more now. He did not stay with Pascual just because of his word, of his debt. I could hear it in his voice. He felt the guilt of what had happened. It was all penance for him.

I did not know how to feel about that, the fact that even someone as ancient as him could feel things the rest of us did. I was not someone who could judge him, or even forgive. It did put into context a lot about him.

"You think that she is still alive," I asked.

He raised his and looked at me. "She is, I would know if she was not. Her kind does not die easily."

Well, there was a super vampire, a beyond Ancient one, walking around the Earth, and an alien god had invaded and basically changed everything about the reality as we knew it.

"Looking for her seems more important than this Challenge." He would lose five days for it, though he would spend thirty in here like the rest of us. Perhaps he thought it worth it to learn more? He wasn't an Exemplar. This would've been a good opportunity to find out what was happening to the world.

"You are the only reason I entered this Challenge. I am your sire. You are my responsibility. I had to make sure that you had not succumbed to your thirst. You do not yet know what it is."

I tilted my head inquisitively.

"Have you started hearing its voice yet?"

I blinked. "I . . . I heard something when I first woke up, but it's gone now."

He nodded. "Your thirst can sense me. It is silent because of my presence."

What he said had a lot of ramifications, and implied a lot of things. "You mean, the thirst is—"

"For the longest time, my sire believed that the thirst was sent by the gods, a gift. Now we know more, as the world has learned. It came from the stars. It is not life like we are, but it is life. Bacteria, or at least that is the closest analogy that we have for it. The more you mature, the louder its voice will become. It is not an enemy, though it does not understand us perfectly. You need to be careful with it. The thirst cares only about spreading, about feeding. But it can be a valuable asset, if you are in control of yourself."

"I guess that I will have to see," I told him.

"I have watched you these last few days. You are in control, but you did not learn how to suppress your emotions, did you?"

I shook my head. "On Ish Vimza I learned another way, to embrace them and use them instead of pushing them away." I told him what Shadow taught me, his school of being, the Heart of Azure and Scarlet.

"There is a reason why all vampires are taught to suppress. I have never encountered a vampire that didn't go mad without learning how to push the emotions away. But we have perhaps never fully tried. And what you've learned is an alien art. Perhaps it will work for you. We shall see. If you fail and lose your mind, I will be there to put you down, you have my promise."

I tried to suppress my grimace. He probably meant it as comforting, not a threat. But I could see that he meant it from a good place. In his world, that was the right thing to do. In my world now too.

He stood up. "I have done what I have come here to do, explained and passed on the knowledge that you are entitled to know as my child. It is time we part ways."

I stood as well. "What are you going to do?" I asked.

He looked up at the scoreboard, at the halo stretching above us. "I shall explore this Challenge, remind myself of who I used to be, regain skills I had allowed to rust."

"You could—" I stopped myself before inviting him to come with me. It was too soon. My feelings toward him were complicated, I could say it.

He looked at me, then his face softened for the first time as he gave me a smile. "We shall meet again. Survive this place, go back and build your empire. Make this new entire world and all these new races looking at us as easy prey learn who we are."

He took a step back, then bowed over his hands. I did the same.

"Oh," he added, then pulled at his shirt with two fingers. "May I borrow this shirt?"

I smiled.

"Statement: Your sire is a very interesting being."

"Yes," I answered her as I walked through the forest.

"Statement: Are you not satisfied with reuniting and getting answers to your questions?"

I grimaced. "It is too much, Saia, too much for me to think about right now. And . . . it doesn't change the fact that he watched them put a noose around my neck."

"Statement: In Ke Erzi society, one's word is paramount. To go against it is to kill a part of your soul."

"I'm not Ke Erzi."

"Statement: No, you are not."

I was angry, I realized. It always felt like the world was mocking me. Was it fate that I chose obligation and debts to be the crucial part of my school of being, my sacrifice for the Heart of Azure and Scarlet? Or was it just coincidence that my sire valued such things too. Was there more to the turning process than I thought?

The time before I was turned, when I was a human, was such a dream to me. Memories of my actions then were vague. I remembered it, but I wasn't that person anymore. But then again anyone would be changed by being turned.

It wasn't worth the effort of thinking about it. I didn't have the time, nor could I afford to get wrapped up in it. I had the Challenge to think about, and I had the Earth—Terra now, as the Grand Spell had named us. An entire camp of people, some that had tried to kill me. A pathetic attempt, to be sure, but still an attempt. I had wanted to do things differently, to instill in the urgency of what we had to do and what was coming, but perhaps a heavier hand was required. Maybe both my sire and Shadow were right. Perhaps a tyrant was who was needed now.

And then there were the Suul. They were just one of the new races, one that was supposed to be sympathetic. They were in the same boat as we were, yet they only looked for their own gain. I understood it, even though I was saddened by it. Still, if there was one positive from all of this it was that the efforts of Kirios factions would be split between our two worlds. Perhaps we had more of a chance than I thought.

I reached the area of the battle with the Suul. I could already hear the others. They had come back for me.

I walked in, making noise on purpose. Jiyun noticed me first and exclaimed. The others all turned and ran in my direction.

Aurora jumped and caught me in a hug.

"You're alive!" she yelled in my ear, nearly rupturing my eardrum.

"Was that ever in any doubt?" I asked with a smile as I untangled her and moved her away from my body. She pouted for a moment as I held her in the air, as if she was as light as a feather, then dropped her to her feet.

"Mari," Khalil said, his expression complicated. "I'm glad that you're safe."

I nodded. Then looked at the carnage left by my sire. Everything was covered with blood, gore, and body parts.

"You, uh, made quite a mess," Daehyun said.

I blinked at him. Of course, they thought that I had done it. I opened my mouth to tell them the truth, but Khalil interrupted me.

"Your eyes are different," he said.

I closed my mouth. My sire had mentioned that my eyes were now those of an Elder, fully emerald.

"I advanced my Mask." I didn't know why I didn't tell the truth. But one thing echoed inside of my mind, something that my sire had said. The ship carrying his sire, the originator of a vampire bloodline, had been ambushed by the Knights of Constantinople. Khalil's people.

"You've reached Second Investment! How is it? What skills did you get?" Aurora launched a barrage of questions at me, and I smiled.

I would have to go to my soul space, see what exactly my skills did, though I already knew one. There was a lot to do. We had a Challenge to survive with a hostile race and people from our own world that were isolated and out for themselves.

But the conversation with my sire had put more things in perspective. It had given me closure, as much of it as I could get. I looked forward to the future, and what awaited me.

Being on Earth, surrounded by humans, had brought out the old me. I so easily slipped into the person I used to be before I was chosen as an Exemplar. But I was not that person anymore. I was *The Star That Dances in Blood Beneath the Light of the Broken Moon*, and my way was to carve a road forward, regardless of what or who stood in my way.

The others didn't care about winning the Challenge for Earth, but I needed every advantage that I could get. Ever since the conversation with my sire, a real plan had formed inside of my head. He had mentioned a sea, stretching the length of the coast of the Americas, Africa, and then Europe. We were divided, but sea travel could connect us again. I finally had a way to do what I had planned on doing since I returned from Ish Vimza. Make an empire.

Epilogue
Elders

Hashal swam through the corridors of Aman Hall. Deep beneath the waves, off the coast of Okean, the capital of the Naga-shan Empire had stood for time immemorial to most. The ancient citadel was a beacon to all Naga-shan, announcing where their true heritage remained. No kingdom and no clan could replace the belonging that all Naga-shan felt in this place.

Other races might splinter off in their little factions, but Naga-shan never did. Perhaps individuals might join others, but the true heart of the empire remained. For they alone ruled the oceans, and had no need of the surface land.

Hashal entered a massive domed chamber at the heart of the city. And inside looked upon a giant form lying curled around itself. The eldest of their kind, so ancient that he had swam through the waters of the homeworld before the Great Mistake found them.

He swam through the water, climbing up until he was level with the Revered Naga-shan's head. A Naga-shan never stopped growing, for as long as they lived. And the Great One was old indeed.

"Greatness," Hashal spoke. His voice carried through the water like a song, echoing of the chamber's walls, amplifying it.

The Great One stirred. "HASHAL-ORI," the being spoke as it opened one great eye. His voice shook the chamber.

"The Exemplar was sent back to his world. We have equipped him with all that we could, only time will tell if our investment will pay off."

"IT WILL," the Great One said. "IT ALWAYS DOES. WE DO NOT NEED MUCH, NOT LIKE THE OTHERS ON KIRIOS. A SMALL STRETCH OF THE COAST IS ENOUGH. THEIR OCEANS ARE ALREADY OURS."

Hashal curled his tail and dropped on the platform next to the Great One's head. "The expedition is ready. We only need you to choose who is going to lead it. We can reach the barrier around the new world in a week's time."

"YOU WILL LEAD IT," the Great One spoke.

Hashal covered his eyes with his upper arms. "You honor me, Great One."

"HONOR WILL COME AFTER YOUR SUCCESS. PREPARE. WE DO NOT KNOW WHAT LIVES IN THEIR OCEANS, HIDDEN EVEN FROM THEIR SIGHT."

Hashal bowed. "By your leave, Great One."

He would prepare, and once the barrier fell, he would be ready to take the ocean floors of the new world. He knew that a similar expedition was being sent to the other new continent, and a single expedition was being prepared for when the portals opened.

The Naga-shan would grow. They would prosper with the arrival of the new worlds, as they always did.

Knight Mage Herim of Roughrock stood behind the chair of his monarch, the Storm King, and looked out at the others sitting at the table. Every king or queen of Elvaros was present, each accompanied by a single bodyguard. The summit was something that happened only in times of great need, such as another Grand Interval.

The Queen of the Forest Kingdom sat next to Herim's king, her flowing red hair and warm skin a great contrast to the dark gray skin of his monarch and people.

The King of the Kingdom of Blades sat next to the King of the Mountains, and the Queen of the Northern Coast next to them, on the other side of the table. The twin monarchs of the Kingdom of Glass completed the table. Each of them was as different as the people of Elvaros were. As their land had shaped them.

"Three portals is what each continent gets," Salla El Ohku, the King of the Mountains, said, his pale eyes looking over the others. "We must decide how to split the expeditions among our kingdoms."

"New land must be conquered," Alura El Amet, the Queen of the Forest Kingdom, said. "My rangers are the best suited for that task."

"As if my blademasters cannot do the same," Leor of Hansi, the King of the Kingdom of Blades, said, the only one among them who had earned his position.

"You bicker, and argue," Herim's king spoke up, Jaun El Annur's voice carrying across the room. "We know what awaits on that continent. You need to send our best, our strongest. Otherwise, death is all that we shall gain."

The other kings and queens tried to hide their looks, but it was obvious. Jaun El Annur was young, the weakest of them all. The Storm Kingdom had once been grand, with knights capable of great deeds, but the age of their peak had long since passed. Other monarchs were far older than he was. They were certain in their power.

Ama El Leu, the Queen of the Northern Coast, answered him. "We appreciate what you've brought to us, and we mourn with you for the deaths of your people. But we've spoken with our own Exemplars, and we've learned a lot. It is not our belief that the danger is as high as you say."

Before Herim's king could respond, the twin monarchs answered in a singular voice. "Sending even one high Invested individual reduces the amount of people we can send. The stronger someone is, the more of the portal's resources they take. The expeditions must be properly gathered. People of the third or lower Investment are all that can go if we want to send a sufficient number of them."

It was true. The portals had only so much energy, and the higher Invested an individual was, the more of that energy they took up. A single individual of the Sixth Investment might cost them as much as a third of what the portal could transport. Herim grimaced behind his visor. He knew that his king wanted to speak more, but he did not have the standing among the others to do much. He could not change their minds.

They did not understand; they didn't see what that vampire did. They did not feel the air surge at the beat of its wings, the monstrous features and teeth that drained blood out of a person in an instant.

They wouldn't heed their warning, Herim realized. He did not look forward to the moment when they understood exactly what they faced. All Herim and his king could do was prepare their kingdom and their people, and hope that it was enough.

The mist gathered deeply around a small shack at the base of a massive mountain. So thick that one couldn't even see two steps ahead. It was almost complete darkness, as the Old Tree stretched far above and blocked the sun. Only the light grass illuminated the world this far below the tree's shadow.

Inside of the small shack, a being sat in a chair and painted with a brush upon a canvas. The image depicted was detailed, incredibly so, a clan of Oni-yi, every member perfectly captured, going about their day. And above them a mountain, a rockslide dropping down to bury them.

With an elegant and final stroke, the painting was done, and the being smiled wickedly. A hand touched the painting, and across the continent a mountain started to shake, and the people that had scorned her, living beneath the mountain, looked up in alarm and—

The woman in front of the painting pulled her hand away and turned. Something had disturbed her home, something unexpected. She stood and walked across the room to a small wooden plate, empty for centuries, where now a piece of wrapped paper sat.

She was surprised, and for a long few minutes just stared at the paper, thinking. Finally, she reached over and picked it up. The thread tying it was dark blue, with a ribbon attached made in patterns that she knew by heart.

She pulled the thread out and the opened the letter. Slowly, she read, savoring it, dreading what it would say. And by the end, she felt her old and shriveled heart warm.

It had been thousands of years since she had last heard from her son. She had feared his hate, that he cursed her and abandoned all that she taught him. And yet, here his words were, in front of her to see. Her son had not forgotten, he had not abandoned the ways that she had taught him.

She looked back down at the letter with a smile, her tails waving gently behind her, and read the last part again.

I have met an Exemplar of another world. She has saved my life on Ish Vimza, and I hers. I have decided to adopt her in our family as my younger sibling. I have thus named her The Star That Dances in Blood Beneath the Light of the Broken Moon.

She is young, but I see the spark of greatness in her. She has a great ordeal ahead of her, as her world integrates into Kirios, and I have armed her as best as I know how.

I hope that you will accept my decision and honor the right that you have given me.

Your Son, the Shadow That Quells Empires Stands Grinning and Triumphant Beneath the Light of the Broken Moon

The woman, *The Cruel Mist That Lurks in the Deep Shadows of Old Tree Beneath the Light of the Broken Moon,* the oldest living Kitsu-oi in the world, smiled. Her son had not forgotten.

And she had a new member added to her family.

A new world. There would be portals. Perhaps she could steal one. It should be enough for someone like her to pass through, and if not, she could add power to it herself. She looked forward to meeting her new daughter.

"Are you sure that I did that?" Shadow asked, looking at the now empty wooden plate.

"I don't know," his companion said. "All I know is that she came."

Shadow looked out at the ocean and the light of the two moons reflected in it.

He hoped that he had done the right thing.

About the Author

Ivan Kal is the author of Vae Victis, an apocalypse LitRPG series originally released on Royal Road. He has been writing for over a decade and, in addition to producing his web serial, has published more than thirty books on Amazon. His other interests include martial arts, computers, and gaming. Visit his website at www.ivan-kal.com.